In the summer of '44,
across the ocean, there
was a brutal war
that killed.
In Crowley Flats,
there was a smaller war...
Something more horrible,
more terrifying than
the mind could imagine...

THE BLOODING

YOU ARE ABOUT TO SHARE
THE GRIPPING AGONY
OF A TOWN UNDER SIEGE...
TO EXPERIENCE THE
NAKED FEAR OF CHARACTERS
YOU CARE ENOUGH
ABOUT TO BE DEEPLY
FRIGHTENED FOR...

THE
BLOODING

WILLIAM DARRID

Based Upon a Story by
Linda Gottlieb & William Darrid

BANTAM BOOKS · LONDON
TORONTO · NEW YORK

THE BLOODING
A Bantam Book / April 1979

ISBN 0-553-12004-2

Published simultaneously in the United States and Canada

PRINTED IN THE UNITED STATES OF AMERICA

FOR
Diana

The author is pleased to acknowledge that this story was suggested by an idea from Linda Gottlieb ... and enriched by the author's editor, Peter Gethers.

PART ONE

1

August sun slanted down on the coyote. He was tired. He had run through the Colorado night, a swift shadow against the moon, searching for prey. Now, in the mountain noon, his belly still empty, he moved slowly down the eastern slope of the Sangre de Cristo range. He glided through the wild columbine. His small, delicate paws failed to bruise the blue petals. His narrow face quivered in anticipation as he followed the tiny movements of a harvest mouse feeding on the tips of grass.

He sprang.

The harvest mouse died, sweet grass still in its mouth.

His jaws stained with blood, the coyote stepped lightly through the aspen grove. He stopped. His long nose twitched. He smelled water and turned toward it, moving swiftly through the brush.

The mountain stream raced over rock and clean white gravel, its waters banging boulder sides and spraying into the air like a foam of dead dandelion. The coyote drank quickly. But his eyes were not on the water. Across the stream, a dirt road, pockmarked with weed, led from the farther bank deep into the woods. The coyote was puzzled. He had seen roads before but, always, there had been the scent of men. And if there were men in the woods, there would be traps. There would be poison. There would be death.

He sniffed cautiously. He recognized the tang of wet moss. The rich humus rot. The spice of yellow pine. And, from somewhere in the distance, the wind carried the musk of carrion. It was a pleasing fragrance. His eyes still on the abandoned road, he leaped onto a small rock in midcurrent and from there to another rock and then a third. He reached the other side of the stream and scrambled up the bank. He sat, his tail sweeping slowly back and forth, back and forth, like some feathery pendulum ticking time away. He was curious. He started up the mysterious road.

The dark bending pine shadowed the woodland. The coyote moved straight up the center of the road, where the pines thinned into aspen and birch. The shadows on the road disappeared. The coyote stepped into sunlight. In front of him, silent in the heat, was a dead town.

A dozen scattered buildings peeled in the sunlight. Their wooden clapboards were rainstained and splintered. Iron shutters, unhinged by rust, rested in the dust under broken windows. The wooden walls of a shallow sluice box were pitted with time and no longer held the dream of gold. A boardwalk which had once echoed under leather heels stretched in shredded fragments alongside a ruined hotel. Near it was a splintered wagon wheel, its only remaining spoke pointed eastward back to the prairie land, back to its buckboard birth, to where the frontier dream began.

Panting from the heat, the coyote scratched the dust, and turned over an amber hairpin. He listened to the sound of wind and to the dying buzz of locusts. Something moved and caught his eye and he looked up. Behind a shattered window pane in the ancient hotel a scrap of lace, caught on a nail, shifted slightly in the wind, a Victorian skeleton, unboned, moving from shadow to sunlight and back into shadow. The coyote shifted his gaze. There was no longer a door opening in to the hotel. There was only space and, behind the space, an invitation to the cool and quiet darkness. He stepped forward.

The room was shadow and decay. Once, perhaps a hundred years ago, the piney boards had reverberated to the clang and clatter of searching men and to the waltz of whores. Now it lacked resonance. The wind had whipped it clean of memory. And because the smell of men had long since vanished, the room held no terror for the coyote. Slowly, he circled the room, instinctively seeking a defendable location. He settled into a corner. He stretched and rested his muzzle on his front paws and then closed his eyes. His tongue flicked once as he freed the last of the matted mouse fur from his jaws. He slept.

High above the coyote a horseshoe bat clung by its claws to a crevice in the ceiling. The bat emitted an undetectable, high-pitched sound and then waited for its echo which would deliver instantly exact information about the size and shape and distance of any object encountered. It revealed the coyote.

The bat plunged silently through the gloom of ghosts and sank its needle teeth into the coyote's neck.

The bat was rabid.

2

He reached for his wife and his fingers closed on air. It awakened him. It always did. For twelve years, since the day Sarah died, Ben Custer's first moment of morning had been empty. He lay in the gray dawn light trying to hold onto the dream. Trying to reach remembered flesh. His calloused hand slid along the cool sheet toward the other side of the bed, searching for a woman's imprint on the linen.

He found nothing.

He opened his eyes and squinted across the room at the picture on the wall. Thumbtacked to the pine planks was a cheap print of Grant Wood's "Dinner for Threshers." Ben studied the painted figure of a woman standing by a stove. Her black dress covered by a white apron, she was about to ladle soup into a bowl. Dark hair haloed her heart-shaped face and accentuated her vulnerability.

Looking at her now, Ben remembered last Christmas.

He had awakened to a soft tapping sound. When he opened his eyes he saw his twelve-year-old son Charlie lightly hammering the tacks into the wall as he hung the picture. The boy, his breath frosty in the room's cold morning air, turned to his father.

"I studied the photographs some," he said. "She looks like Ma."

Oh, Christ, Ben thought, how would you know? He was not a man who wished to be reminded of what he'd lost. Nor, he thought as he looked at Charlie, how he'd lost her.

"Yeah," he said. "I guess."

The figure of the woman in the picture arrested Ben's attention. It was her attitude. Her simple action at the stove had been suspended by the painter. She was waiting for something. Ben squinted hard at the picture.

What, he wondered, are you waiting for?

She looked just like Sarah.

Avoiding the boy's eyes, Ben looked outside. An ice storm covered the prairie and its cold crystal weight cracked loose a limb from the walnut tree. Later in the day, Ben cut the limb into long dark strips, fashioning them into a frame for the print. When the house was midnight quiet, when he thought both boys were asleep, the frame in one hand and a chipped coffee cup half filled with bourbon in the other, he examined the leaning woman in the picture. He felt an ache but was unable to decide whether he grieved for the woman or for himself. He lifted the frame and then, from behind him, heard Charlie's soft voice.

"Don't."

"What?" Ben turned and saw the boy standing in the doorway, his eyes dark and somber, his bare toes gripping hard to the cold floorboards. The boy pointed to the frame in Ben's hand.

"Don't put anything around her, Pa. She couldn't rightly hear then."

"Hear? Hear what?" Ben felt the sharp impatience rising in him. As usual, the turning of Charlie's mind confused him.

"See," the boy said, his eyes now on the leaning figure of the painted woman, "she's listening for sumthin'. I don't know what, but it's sumthin'. Could be, you put that frame up, you fence her in, she's never gonna hear it. She's never gonna hear it at all."

"Damn it, Charlie," Ben began, but when he saw

the darkness in the boy's eyes, he turned away. It wasn't until he heard the boy's bare feet slip back into the hallway that Ben broke the frame in half. The next morning, he threw it away and whittled the remainder of the walnut into a stock for his Winchester.

He was not a wasteful man.

And now, on this September dawn, Christmas long gone, he studied the unframed figure of the woman in the print. The woman who leaned and listened.

So like Sarah. So exactly like Sarah.

He was not a man who catalogued his griefs, and so it puzzled him that the sight of the painted woman could roil up such dull anguish.

He swung his legs out from underneath the blankets, expecting to feel the familiar comfort of Sarah's hooked rug under his bare feet. But his flesh touched paper. He looked down. Last night's newspaper was on the floor. He must have let it slip from his fingers when he went to sleep.

His eyes dropped to where the paper had been neatly creased.

American casualties in the Seventh Army commanded by General Hodges ...

Ben kicked the newspaper under the bed.

He looked out the open window, and because he was a prairie man, he examined the sky. He saw the beginning of light and shadow play along the building cumulus. Good. No rain. He shrugged. Only a fool gave credence to a Kansas sky. He knew that at this moment other men stood in front of their open windows looking at the sky and hoping for a steady sun. Shortly, these same men would walk into their fields and lift earth to their lips. They would taste the soil. They would crumble it in their fingers. They would measure it. They would decide whether this day was the day to plant their winter wheat.

A sound startled him. It was the squeal of a pig. Puzzled, his gaze shifted toward the barn. The first thing he saw was the faded sign. Dr. Custer D.V.H.

Doctor of Veterinary Medicine. In his mind's eye he saw behind the sign. His clinic. His laboratory. Animal pens. Sterile instruments. Operating table. He frowned. He remembered no pig. The squeal was harsher this time, and it came from some high place.

Ben looked up. The yellow-headed blackbird mocked him again as he fluttered his wings in the hickory tree and cried like a wounded pig.

"Son of a bitch," Ben said.

He left the room and crossed the hall and eased open the door behind which his sons slept. He moved quietly, not wanting to awaken his older boy, Pete. The boy's uniform was neatly folded on a chair. The single stripe of a private first class was freshly sewn under the patch of an airborne division. A badge of expert marksman was exactly positioned under the wings of a paratrooper. Everything neat. Everything in order. Everything secured.

Except, Ben thought, except the boy's life.

Ben studied his son. He had Sarah's dark hair and slender features and, even in sleep, his face held the same humor. Like Sarah's, it was a face which looked at the world with delight and with a constant surprise at the savories each day offered. Glancing again at the marksman's medal, Ben remembered the day he had taken Pete to the Cheyenne Bottoms, the place of wild bursting geese and fluttering ducks. Together, they had crouched in the high grass and ignored the November wind as it swept in from the north and burned their skins raw. He had marveled at how still the boy was as he waited for the first flight to wing in over the blind. And suddenly the birds came. Wood ducks and mallards and Canadian geese riding the horizon. Father and son had held their fire until the birds glided into the true distance of their guns. Then, and Ben almost held his breath remembering the swiftness of it, Pete had raised his blue-barreled birthday gun, had arced the barrels high overhead, had sighted into the sunless sky and had squeezed off both barrels killing two mallards on the rise. The birds had died side by side.

Side by side. The swift precision of that November kill had given grace to the act. But Ben knew there would be no grace in the mud and mutilation made by the men of Europe, and the sky would mirror blood. Side by side. Who would die by the side of his son?

He leaned over the boy's bed. For just an instant, Ben's fingers touched the curve of Pete's cheek and then he turned and left the room.

Not once had he looked across the room at the other bed. The bed where Charlie slept. And so he had failed to see the flutter of the young boy's eyelids as he feigned sleeep. When the door closed behind his father, there was no longer need for pretense. Charlie opened his eyes and looked across the room toward Pete. He was startled to see that Pete was staring back at him. Slowly, Pete winked and he withdrew one hand from under the covers and tapped his cheek where Ben's fingers had rested.

"Now, see, Charlie," Pete grinned, "if I'd a let on I was awake, if Pa'd known I'd felt him, why he'd of bust into fuss and flutter. Old Pa, he is not one to be caught playin' hen to his chicks, no sir."

Pete wished that his brother would smile or nod or make some acknowledgment that he understood. Damn, Pete thought, this is my last leave 'fore I ship out and then what the hell's Charlie gonna do? Who's gonna run interference 'tween him and Pa? He thought about the skirmish tactics he'd learned at the training camp, how sometimes it was best not to meet the enemy head on but just sort of ease around his flanks and come up on him gentle like and even as these thoughts drifted through his mind he disliked the analogy because it hinted at the fact that his father and his younger brother were enemies and Pete thought that he couldn't hardly stand that idea because Pa and Charlie were the two people he loved best in the world.

Although he was only eighteen, Pete understood the problem. He'd come to grips with it one day when he'd watched a quarterhorse race on one of the dirt tracks in Kansas. Their muscles bunched and quivering in anticipation of the race, the horses had stood together at the starting gate and when the bell had sounded they leaped forward in unison. A chestnut bay, blinders on its eyes, had plunged straight down the center of the track but another horse, a pretty little pinto, had balked, faltered, and veered away from the track and galloped into the bordering field where, despite the pleading of its rider, it had stood firmly and munched off the yellow heads of dandelion. They'd both been splendid animals but, like Ben and Charlie, they sure as hell ran in different directions.

"Shit," Pete said to himself and then, remembering how soon he would be leaving the world of soft beds, hunkered down under the blankets and pulled one of them over his head. But he left a slit open so that if he wanted to he could still observe the young boy across the room.

Charlie looked up at the two mallards which were mounted on a wall plaque over his brother's bed. Their blue wing patches shimmered as if they were gathering strength for a final flight. They were iridescent. How could Pete have pulled those triggers? It would be like shattering the heart of a rainbow.

Charlie wondered what it felt like to die. He tried not to think about it because it frightened him terribly but, as always, he was unable to suppress his imagination. He could hear the thump of his pulse diminish and then grow dull and his breathing became swift and shallow and difficult to maintain. He felt the skeletal shape of himself separate from its soft, fleshy covering and he lay trembling as he waited for some giant hand to pull the bones from his body and, uncaring, toss them into a lime-kiln where they would burn whitely into dust. But no giant hand descended in front of his eyes. Instead, he remembered the vision of his father's fingers touching Pete's cheek and Charlie wondered if he, too, would ever feel the lightness of that hand.

He did not think so. Not after what he'd done to his mother.

"Hey," Pete said.

The sound of Pete's voice surprised Charlie and it gave him inordinate pleasure because now he knew he was not, after all, dead. He would not have to journey to that silent place where his mother waited.

"Hey," Pete said again. "It's just that I'm going away. That's all it was. It's just that Pa figures I'm going away. You know, Charlie?"

Charlie's gaze shifted from the flight-frozen mallards to his mother.

"Sure," Charlie said. "Oh, sure."

3

Outside, on the small planked porch, Ben drank his coffee and looked again at the sky. In the distance, he could hear the sound of a tractor. Lorraine Tower was plowing her fields, checking the growth of weeds after the last heavy rain, preparing the warm earth for the seeding of wheat. The low rumble of the tractor was clear as it drifted across the fields. There was a comfort to the sound. It gave focus to the pleasing paradox of nature. The rich green of summer was turning into rust. A city man might think it was a time of dying but Ben knew better. It was a time of planting and renewal and faith in the greening of land.

It had not always been so.

Thirteen years ago, Ben Custer, a loose-limbed rawhide man in his early thirties, Doctor of Veterinary Medicine, had watched wheat turn dry under the hot Kansas sun. The golden grain blackened and covered the sky as it was wind-whipped to the west. Ben had watched the prairie spiral into dust and cloak his neighbors in despair as they stood silently in their fields staring, vacant-eyed, at the sky, waiting for a miracle to wash Kansas clean.

There had been no miracle. There had been no escape from the awful dust. It tore the skin off a man's face, lacerated his eyeballs, made his gums bleed, blew into the farmhouse and sifted into corners and cracks. Every plate and saucer and cup was so layered with the fine grit that a man couldn't eat without spitting, and the black phlegm that was hawked up finally turned bloody.

And all across the Kansas land great herds of cattle fell to their knees and died in that ever-descending dust.

It had not been a time of splendor on the prairie.

Except, Ben thought now as he sipped his coffee and listened to the distant tractor, *except*. We stood together in the goddamned wind and we dug irrigation ditches and farm ponds. And, although there were some who, slack-jawed with weariness, had piled their ownings into trucks and tin lizzies, and others who had tied bedding to wheelbarrows and set out on the long walk to California, most of the prairie people had accepted the risk of failure. Together, they had fought the wind and the dust until the green grass grew once again. Wheat sprouted. Cattle ranged. Windmills turned and pumped. The land was no longer hostile to horses or dogs or men.

There had been pride in the community's stand against crisis.

Shivering a little from the dawn's chill, Ben raised his cup and drained the last of the chickory-bitter coffee. The taste reminded him of the long, long days of crisis through which they all lived now. The war was in its fourth year. It seemed to Ben that this little prairie village of Crowley Flats had been forever saving tin cans and rendering fat and dimming their lights and lining up, with a minimum of complaint, to receive rationed gas and cigarettes and coffee and meat and butter. The men had lost their trouser cuffs, the women their frills, but they had been too busy buying bonds, rolling bandages and giving blood to care. The elderly learned about first aid and the young planted victory gardens and, together, they shared a sense of danger. There was even, Ben speculated, a kind of exhilaration to these past bloody years. A man knew what had to be done and, in the doing of it, found himself.

But Ben sensed that a subtle change had come over the community. These prairie people, once secure in their traditional values of right and wrong, had been edged away from innocence. There were too many gold stars in too many windows to believe in the perfectibility of men. Morality had tilted out of focus as men and women discovered imperfection. The resiliency with which they had faced the dust bowl and the depression and at first the war was no longer as apparent. The constant news of death and destruction had begun to erode community spirit. Sacrifices were greeted with grumbles rather than cheers. The sense of sharing danger was no longer exhilarating. Ben could not help but wonder what would happen if this little town of Crowley Flats were suddenly threatened by some real and tangible peril. He worried about it.

Well, he thought, it is just one more reality to the days of our lives. One more risk.

The sound of Lorraine's tractor changed. The engine was idling. Ben listened carefully. There was a tiny skip to the rhythm of the engine. The sparks needed adjustment. They needed, Ben thought, the hands of a man, but he knew that Lorraine's husband, Tom, would never again touch metal. He had died in July during the savage hedgerow fighting as the Americans slogged toward Saint-Lo. His hands were still now as he lay in his piney box waiting for the long ride home.

Now the tractor pulsed with an even beat and stroke. There was no longer the infinitesimal pause of a skipping spark. Lorraine had made the adjustment. Oh yes, Ben thought, she was good at adjustments. She was a prairie woman and so she had adjusted to the death of her husband as if to the change of seasons, with no public grief. But Ben wondered in what room she had wept.

And he tried not to think about the cellar.

After the death of Sarah, Ben Custer unconsciously and with no determined path to follow, withdrew from emotional commitments. Slowly, gradually, he built a barrier around himself through which no pain could burrow. He sealed himself off from future grief.

The long-ago memory of Lorraine's warm skin now made Ben uneasy. The remembrance of sensual excitement didn't disturb him. He accepted that as a fine and splendid thing, a simple and clean and natural joining of flesh. What troubled him was not the physicality of that one time in the cellar but the implication behind it. The recognition of need. It was a vague feeling and Ben did not wish to give it credence.

He turned back toward the house. Out of the corner of his eye he saw a light flash. He looked down the road.

Through the border of shade trees, he saw a battered Chevrolet pickup truck bouncing over road ruts as it headed west, its headlights glowing in the dawn. The lights annoyed Ben. The eastern gleam of sun was spreading low over Kansas. There was no need for artificial light. It was waste.

Ben was not surprised. The truck belonged to Caleb Dodd. The truck swerved suddenly and then, just as quickly, resumed its straight path along the ribbon of dust. Laughter from the truck floated on the air. Ben swore softly. He understood the quick maneuver. Caleb had rushed his wheels at a prairie dog.

Ben let the screen door slam behind him and he moved quickly into the kitchen. He turned up the fire under the coffee pot and prayed, with a conscious lack of hope, that the taste of chickory would boil away. He pulled a small sack of Bull Durham out of his pocket along with a slim pack of rolling papers and began to build the first cigarette of the day. Shreds of tobacco spilled out of the paper. He licked the gummed side. He twisted one end closed. Carefully, he placed the cigarette in his mouth. He thumb-flicked a wooden match and held the flame to the pinched end of paper. The cigarette flared and crumbled apart. Ben spat it out.

Jesus, he thought, why did they send Lucky Strikes to war.

And he tried not to think about the cellar.

The revolving concave disks of the plow cut into the hard soil. Seated on the tractor, Lorraine Tower shifted down into a lower gear and turned to look back at the fresh furrows behind her and admire the straightness of the rows. The smell of newly turned fields drifted toward her in the following breeze. It was the incense of approaching autumn and she savored it. She turned forward again and sighted on the cottonwood clump at the far end of the field, using it as a target so that the furrows she left behind would be true. In the spring the rising lines of wheat would have no bend in them.

She let the tractor idle and she stepped down onto the field. She leaned down and scooped up a handful of newly turned earth. She held it to her lips, her tongue flicking at it lightly, and then she crumpled the earth with her fingers, letting it drop back into the furrow. There was good moisture in the soil. If a sudden rain didn't drench the earth or if a blazing sun didn't turn it into iron or if the warm air masses moving up from the Gulf of Mexico didn't clash with the air currents drifting in from the Pacific and subject the land to the whim of hail, the fields would shortly be ready to receive the seeds of this year's winter wheat.

If. It was the operative word of the prairie farmer. And maybe, Lorraine thought, it is the operative word of my life. *If* there were no war, Tom would still be alive and plowing these fields. *If* there were no war, Dippsy would still have a father. She raised one hand to shade her eyes against the morning blaze and peered toward the far end of the field. Her son, small even for ten years old, was racing in and out of the

cottonwoods ·which Tom had planted as a barrier
against the wind.

Oh lord, she thought, this prairie is sweet land but
it needs men walking on it. Like a house, it needs the
clump of a man's boots.

Her thoughts were interrupted when she saw a
sudden flash of white at the far end of the field. A
dog burst out of the cottonwoods and sped toward
Dippsy. He was a huge white German shepherd who
rippled with muscle and spring. He'd been a puppy
seven years ago when Tom had brought him home as
a gift for his son. When Dippsy first held him, first
felt the warm, loving tongue lick his fingers, the boy
had said ain't he a Jim Dandy though and in that moment gave the shepherd his name. From the beginning,
Dippsy and Jim Dandy had been inseparable and
Lorraine no longer knew who followed whom; knew
only that boy and dog were constant companions who
shared a secret language. It was a language of gesture.
Dandy leaped, begged, rolled over, played dead,
reared to his hind legs, jumped through hoops, fetched,
carried, and generally cavorted with tail-thumping
glee with just a hint of communication from Dippsy.
A wink. A nod. A lift of a shoulder. A beckoning finger.
It seemed to Lorraine that over the years Jim Dandy
had learned to anticipate Dippsy's desires and the
dog was often able to inaugurate actions even before
the boy shrugged his message. At night, boy and dog,
both comfortably weary from the day, slept together.
Lorraine did nothing to discourage this. Ever since
Tom's departure, Dippsy was consoled by being able
to reach out in his sleep and touch the warm and loving body next to him.

She wondered if her days of reaching were over.

She had lived close to the earth all her life and she
was part of its sensuality. She was a thirty-five-year-
old woman, strong-boned, whose wind-coppered skin
still tingled in the sun. She touched her breast lightly,
remembering the weight of flesh on flesh, the move-

ment of thigh on thigh. Suddenly, she blinked. The picture in her mind blurred, turned fuzzy at the edges, fragmented; the remembered figure of her husband split and became two men. She saw Tom. And she saw Ben Custer. She saw Ben holding the hand of a girl as they raced from a harvest field under a tornado sky, the violent funnel rising and falling and twisting toward them. The image sharpened now and Lorraine leaned against the tractor because her legs trembled and her body was filled with longing as she remembered how she and Ben had heard the ripping of wood and seen the rise and sail of roof as they reached the cellar. Deafened by the freight-train roar of storm, their skins flaming from hail, they tumbled onto a bed of burlap where their bodies arched in mutual appetite, their tongues flicked, their fingers searched, they bewitched each other's flesh.

It had been their first and final touching. Not long after that cellar day, Ben had returned to the river boats on the Big Muddy, and during his long absence, Lorraine met and married Tom Tower. When Ben finally came back to Kansas, a certified Doctor of Veterinary Medicine, Lorraine had not been surprised that he was accompanied by a new wife. Lorraine was a realist. She did not labor under the illusion that one man and one woman were destined to share each other's life. A pragmatist, she accepted the practical consequences of her actions and the actions of others. Because she lacked guile and had no patience with pretense, she offered herself fully, flesh and spirit, to the man she chose, asking only that her giving be returned. It had been. Her life with Tom had been rewarded with quiet pleasure and if, occasionally, perhaps glancing unexpectedly at Ben on a night-shaded porch as the four young people shared a summer's moon, her heart clenched with the memory of that swift ecstasy in the cellar, she would deliberately pluck an ice cube from her frosted glass of tea and crunch down hard on it until it cracked and splintered in her mouth, its iciness numbing her tongue and lips and finally the memory itself. It was, however, at moments like that that she would think:

What if?

Lorraine shook her head and, with a sudden awkward motion, swung back onto the seat of the tractor. She slapped it into a higher gear and the tractor rumbled forward toward the cottonwoods.

"Mama?"

Lorraine looked down. Dippsy and Jim Dandy were trotting alongside of the tractor, the boy shouting to her above the clank of engine. She shifted to neutral and let the boy climb up beside her. Dippsy had only half turned toward Dandy when the dog sprang, easily clearing the high rear wheels of the tractor, and landed on the towing bar behind the seat, his huge white muzzle firmly between Lorraine and Dippsy, his eyes cocked lovingly toward the boy. Lorraine scratched the dog's ears and then turned toward her son whose face was all freckles and missing teeth and curiosity and, oh lord, the deep brown eyes of Tom. Impulsively, she scissored the tip of his nose with her fingers.

"I do believe I'll have some of this for dinner. Ummm ummm, won't it taste good."

"Mama?" The boy's voice was sober and he was rejecting the game.

"Uh huh."

"When they send Papa back . . . will he be . . . alone?"

"No, Dips," she answered quietly, "there'll be soldiers with him. Well, at least one or maybe two. They wouldn't let your papa travel alone."

" 'Cause they like him?"

"Yeah," she said, her heart hurting for his sweet innocence, "yeah, 'cause they liked him." With one hand, she slipped the tractor into gear and pulled out the throttle and then whipped the wheel over hard. The other hand, trembling slightly, rested on Dippsy's knee. She looked straight at the boy, momentarily letting him see her own wounds, knowing that it would be fraudulent to share their love for Tom without giving credence to his death. Dippsy did not avert his eyes from his mother's pain.

"Goddamnittohell," the little boy whispered.

"Yeah," she said, "yeah."

Jim Dandy swung his huge head around and rested it on Lorraine's hand and softly licked her fingers, and Lorraine made herself think of crunching ice cubes between her teeth so that she would not weep as she began to plow a furrow into the field which no longer vibrated under the clump of a man's boot.

A young doe, her sides heaving from exhaustion, her velvety muzzle glistening with sweat, stood in a gathering of yellow pine. She had become separated from the herd and now, after her long run down from the high places of the Sangre de Cristo range, her hooves were bleeding and she was famished. Her eyes were dull as she stared at a mountain stream. A dam linked the banks of the stream. It was made of sticks and logs and its upper surface was reinforced with stones and mud. A birch limb, one end freshly slashed by teeth, lay across the top. A beaver hunched next to it. He was ripping strips of bark from it and then gnawing at the strips.

The doe's nostrils quivered at the scent of bark. One hoof silently pawed the ground. She stepped out of the trees. Instantly, the beaver's small head shot up and his black scaly tail slapped against the water below and then he dived deep toward the comfort of his lodge. The doe took another step toward the dam, her starved body shivering at the sight of fresh bark. She stumbled and her legs buckled beneath her. Her head rested on the ground, leaves filling her mouth.

She was in this supplicating posture when the rabid coyote's jaws closed on her jugular.

The coyote clawed open the doe and sank his jaws into the animal's belly and sucked on the hot blood. His teeth tore out great chunks of flesh, snapping them into his throat and down deep inside him. When he was sated, he lay down next to the doe and wiped his muzzle in the leaves, cleaning it of the doe's bristling hair and the shreds of intestines which clung to his jaws.

And then he vomited the bristle and the blood of the doe. His body shook in violent spasms. He lurched to his feet and began to race in frantic, aimless circles through the wooded mountainside and all the time he ran, his jaws snapped viciously at his own flesh as if he were trying to rip out some awful animal which was clawing inside him.

He was howling as he sped easterly. Toward the Kansas side of the mountain.

4

"They catch us jackin' deer, it'll be our ass."

"Damn meat rationin' what it is, a man could loose all the red outa his blood. You want that, Emmett?"

"Nope."

"Then lock yer jaw."

"Yessiree, sir, I'm gonna lock my jaw. I'm gonna zip my lip so's we don't loose no ship."

"Keerist, you're beginnin' to sound like all them posters you paint."

"Well, way I see it, a man's gotta take his work serious. It don't get under your skin, you're just an amateur. And I am one pure and purty professional."

"Shit." Caleb spat tobacco juice out of the truck window and shifted down into a lower gear. They had crossed the Apishape River hours ago and left the high prairie behind them. Now the truck climbed steadily up the narrow fire roads cut into the eastern slopes of the Sangre de Cristo range. He glanced once at Emmett Flack who was slumped in the seat next to him. Emmett was singing softly to himself. Caleb looked away and pretended he wasn't listening. Music gave him a case of prickly. He didn't trust no growed man who sang. A man oughta fart, fuck and forget. There weren't nuthin' else that give shimmer.

"I got spurs that jingle jangle jingle. I got . . ."

"Shit," Caleb repeated.

Emmett stopped singing.

Emmett was a cautious man and he was glad that the gray light of dusk was fading into night. There was little chance that he and Caleb would be caught. Beads of saliva formed at the corner of his mouth. He could taste the venison. Caleb was an ornery son of a bitch but he had been right. They had spotted a scattered herd of pronghorn antelope grazing on the high plateau sagebrush and Emmett had wanted to give chase. Caleb had called him a damn fool.

"Ain't no broken-spring Chevy made can catch them buggers," he'd said, "an' 'sides, we gonna kill, we gonna kill sumpin'll fill our bellies. We gonna get us a big-point buck."

Caleb stopped the truck when the moon was high in the sky. He and Emmett covered it with pine boughs and aspen branches. They removed their camping gear and hefted their rifles and tested the lantern light which would soon stab into a deer's eyes and transfix the animal into a frozen panic. They moved into the deep woods toward the salt lick. Caleb chuckled, thinking about the salt. He'd stolen it the night old F.D.R. was gabbin' by the fireside. Tellin' more lies. Fillin' God-fearin' folk with pap an' puss. Old Franklin, he was surely some kind of silver-tongued sapsucker. Caleb knew what was really goin' on. He knew that them German bastards wuz slaughterin' our boys on the glory road. And he knew what to do about it but nobody would listen. Gas. That was the answer. Poison gas. Come in low with them buzzin' planes and spray the whole goddamn kit and kaboodle of 'em. Fuckin' krauts!

He never thought about what a shift of wind might do.

Caleb chuckled again thinking about stealing the salt lick. One evening, while delivering feed for Morgan Crowley's Herefords, he saw the lick hanging from a post. He knew that Morgan would be sittin' ramrod straight in front of the radio as he listened to ole Franklin. Well, maybe not quite straight. Maybe leaning a little, one hand resting on his wife Lottie's shoulder. Pleasured at getting something for nothing, Caleb cut the slab loose, stuffed it under his shirt, purred his pickup down the road, returned to town, poured a cup of Chet Beam's potato grain and farted in his sofa faster'n hot pee smoked the snow. Goddamn. The following morning, Caleb traded Virgil Foster a quart of the potato liquor for a tank full of rationed gas and drove into the Colorado mountains. He had shuffled, fat-thighed and moon-faced, through the heavy stands of pine and aspen until he saw deer droppings. Using a thin strand of baling wire, he had bound the thick slab of salt against the trunk of an aspen. He knew that deer fed on the tree's leaves. He knew that they would return nightly to lick the salt.

Yes, sir. They would be waiting for him. He was impatient to see blood stain the lichen and moss.

"Look at her! By Jesus, jes look at her!" Emmett's voice was an excited whisper. He was lying on his belly, his head crooked awkwardly under a low-hanging bough, the pine needles almost piercing his lips. But he was as still as a long-lost arrowhead. The light from the lantern in his hand cut a yellow path through the woods and, in its beam, the two men saw the aspen and the salt lick and the deer.

Silently, Caleb slid the barrel of his rifle over a higher branch of the pine and, just as silently, thanked Chet Beam for the weapon. That sumbitch could lay his hands on anything and there was always a price for it. Caleb had paid gladly. The rifle was a self-loading clip-fed gas-operated semi-automatic .30-caliber Garand. Used by our glory boys to shoot the nuts off Nazis. Caleb wished Cora Zink were here to watch him. By Jesus, this'ld put a tremble to her tits. There was a rush of heat to his groin as his finger curled across the trigger. He knew he couldn't miss. Not with what he'd done to the Garand. He'd filed down the seer and made it into a fully automatic weapon which could belch nine bullets faster'n a snake could spit. He squeezed the trigger.

The eye of the buck exploded and his brain ran red.

Caleb and Emmett, Indian-wrapped in blankets against the Colorado chill, slept on the ground, curled back to back, opposing question marks of flesh and bone. They were dreamless and without guilt. They had washed their minds clean of the killing just as they had washed their hands of the deer's gore. A tin bucket of fresh water rested in the low embers of the campfire. The water would be hot for their coffee in the morning.

The buck, its belly ripped open and gut-cleaned, hung head down, suspended by hemp thrown over a pine limb. The carcass swayed in the midnight gust of mountain wind. The crimson glow from the campfire threw the shadow of the deer across the woods. The deer twisted and turned slightly in its hangman's noose and its corresponding shadow seemed to slide secretly behind the boughs. There were small sounds in the night, sharpened because of the high dry air. There was the creak of rope and the sough of the wind and the snap of embers and the adenoidal rush of air from the two sleeping men.

There was another sound. A clicking. Like bone on rock. Like the claws of an animal scraping across stone.

The men did not hear it.

Eyes narrowed and blinking, the rabid coyote inched forward on his belly. He moved slowly, his body trembling in unfamiliar pain, his jaws snapping at small stones and twigs in his path. Thick, sticky yellow saliva flecked his muzzle. His teeth and tongue and gums were covered with it. It ran down his throat and it choked him. A harsh, rasping sound came from his throat. His muscles bunched and he rose.

Like death slanting in the shadows, he stalked the two hunters.

The campfire glowed down into hot red marbles. There was a whisper of night winds. And there was the clicking of animal claws. The coyote's eyes, bold and dangerous, gleamed in the firelight as he inched out of the heavy pines and toward the campsite. The wind ruffled the surface of the bucket water. The animal froze. Bubbles of saliva slid along his jaws. His body shook violently. His throat burned with thirst but he was terrified of the water. Glistening in the scarlet shine of firelight, the water's surface wind-slapped the bucket sides. It was alive. It was an enemy.

The coyote exploded out of the shadows. His hurtling body slammed into the bed of hot embers as he charged the water bucket. Crimson coals splashed over the sleeping men and the awful raging cry of a rabid animal shattered the silence of the night. Emmett screamed at the dark fury of his nightmare and then opened his eyes and saw it was no dream. He tried to lurch to his feet but his blanket twisted around his legs and he stumbled to his knees. Desperately, he reached for a weapon but he found only the lantern. His thumb snapped against the switch.

The coyote wheeled toward the bright pain of lantern path and lunged. His teeth raked Emmett's hand. Emmett cried out and dropped the lantern. And then a gun barrel whipped across the body of the coyote and the animal tumbled again into the burning embers. Caleb was on his feet. He yanked the Garand to his shoulder and fired but there was no clip in the rifle and the hammer fell on an empty chamber. The coyote leaped. His jaws closed on the rifle barrel. Caleb swung the rifle as hard as he could but the animal would not shake loose. The coyote's teeth ground into the cold steel and blood and foam sprayed over the rifle.

Emmett, shaking loose from his blanket, scrambled up and swept the lantern from the ground. He lifted it high into the black air and whopped it down on the twisting animal. He heard the sharp crack of glass

on bone. The coyote's jaws opened and Caleb yanked
the rifle free and turned it in his hands. He grasped
the barrel and swung the heavy stock down at the
animal. But he met only shadow and air. The coyote
had whirled on Emmett and animal and man became
a rolling mass of fur and flesh, a cacophony of slashing
teeth and cries of pain. Again, Caleb whipped his
rifle through the air and this time he felt the heavy
stock bury itself into the belly of the coyote. The
coyote spun to his feet and raced toward the safety of
the dark woods, leaving behind him only a harsh sand-
paper cry of rage.

Sucking in great gasps of air, hardly able to breath,
their clothes ripped and burned, the two men sank to
the ground. Emmett shuddered. Desperately, he
pulled air into his lungs and then his voice was a
choked whisper.

"Sumbitch . . . was . . . crazy."

"Oncet . . . oncet," Caleb panted, "I seen a dog.
Hoot-owl crazy he wuz. He wuz . . . rabies bit."

Emmett's eyes opened wide with fright as he stared
into the woods where the coyote had escaped. Slowly,
he lifted his hand. He looked at the leathery skin and
at the cracked knuckles and at the bleeding slash
across his palm. His fingers began to tremble.

"We gotta burn it out, boy," said Caleb, "we gotta
burn that fucker out." And he lifted a slender stick
from the campfire. One end of the stick was white
with heat. Emmett said nothing. He thought he had
detected a small sense of pleasure in Caleb's tone but
when he looked at the moon-faced man he couldn't
see his eyes. Smoke from the fire drifted across Caleb's
face, a vapored veil hiding secrets of the soul.
Strangely, Emmett was glad. He didn't want to see
Caleb's eyes. The burning stick in his hand was
enough.

Emmett held out his hand.

The midnight mountains were scented with moss

and pine. There was a sweet incense to the air. And then another odor which gave lie to the innocence of moon. It came from the silent searing of flesh.

The human wail of anguish was not unlike the cry of the coyote as he ran east toward the prairie.

5

Sweat pouring down his face, the auctioneer whipped the Wichita buyers into higher and higher bids with his machine-gun voice. Dust swirled around the men as they flicked, nodded, whistled and grunted their bids. Some of the buyers stood alongside of the cattle pen. Others perched on the rails. A few circled the pen as they studied Morgan Crowley's beef cattle and listened to the auctioneer's singsonging sale. Out of the corner of their eyes, they watched each other. They waited to see who would falter as the price was driven up, and when they sensed the hesitation, the space between whistle and buy, they signaled. Their individual, idiosyncratic gestures were open secrets to the auctioneer. Not once did he fail to see them. He understood that if he had, Morgan would cut his balls off and feed them to the eagles.

Morgan, a thick, hard-muscled man in his fifties, stood on the bed of his ranch truck, one hand lightly on his wife Lottie's shoulder. He didn't know which gave him more pleasure, what he saw or what he felt. He squinted at the horizon and knew that his range stretched far beyond it. His eyes shifted to the cattle pen. The white-faced Herefords pawed the dust and rubbed their red-rust flanks against the planking of the fenced enclosure, and their huge heads lifted as they brayed the mournful anticipation of their future in the final feed lots of Wichita and Topeka and Kansas

City. The steers were a splendid sight in the sun, and the land, sea-rolling and furrowed to the east, soon to be sown by Morgan's neighbors into a checkerboard of wheat, was equally splendid.

Morgan had parked his truck in such a position that he could easily survey his spread. He took pleasure in the fresh paint on the outbuildings which housed tractors and reapers and cultivators, and he particularly liked an old sod house which he had converted to a storage shed for rolls of barbed wire and new plowshares and squares of salt licks and gunnysacks of seed. He didn't allow his eyes to linger too long on the sod house because the sight of it reminded him that the generations of Crowleys was coming to an end. His grandfather had cut the sod from this same land, had plastered it together with mud and stone, had fought Indians from behind its small windows. His father had been born within its walls. Over the years, the Crowley ranch expanded. Land was acquired, turned over, fenced in. Wheat was planted in the eastern section and cattle ran on the western lots. Barns rose, sheds were hammered together, and the sod house was vacated in favor of a sprawling ranch house. But in Morgan's mind, the sod house was a landmark of continuity. It represented that which had been hewn from the prairie. It was a symbol of the taming of the land and it embodied the history of Crowley men. The history which now, at long last, had been discontinued.

Lieutenant Roger Crowley, United States Marine Corps, only son of Morgan, great-grandson of a prairie sod-buster, was two years dead, his body rotting under the jungle growth of Guadalcanal.

Morgan lifted his eyes from the sod house and gazed out at the far reaches of his grazing land and when he saw the dotted silhouettes of windmills he suddenly did not care whether the blades were turning in the wind or were still.

And he was filled with a quick loathing of all men whose sons still lived.

Morgan felt Lottie stir. He looked down. She sat in her wheelchair, quiet and gaunt, and never without pain. Morgan's fingers slid softly across his wife's thin shoulder. He speculated on why she had stirred. Crippled for so long by rheumatoid arthritis, Lottie had perfected stillness. The raw and constant ache of socket and joint had forced Lottie to retreat from motion. She lived distant from action. It was why she liked auction day. She could sit in her wheelchair, which Morgan placed carefully in the center of the ranch wagonbed, first locking the wheels so that there could be no shift or sway, and, cooled comfortably by the prairie wind, she could without effort soak herself in spectacle. She could, on these special days, listen to the bringle-brangle and smell the bittersweet dung and pretend she was alive. Again, Morgan felt the tiny movement of her flesh under his fingers and he was glad. It meant she was about to ask him something. It meant she was in need of something and her needs gave definition to his day. It was that feeling, the feeling of being able to help her, that held more splendor for him than did all the greening land of Kansas.

He tilted his head toward her.

"You want something, Lottie? There's something you want?"

"No, ain't nothing. Only . . ."

"Only what? Just tell is all."

"Just . . . only." Ignoring the thousand teeth of pain which bit into her body, she reached up slowly and touched his hand. She had seen his eyes on the land and she knew that he was thinking of Roger and she wanted to tell him that they would have to make do with what they had. But she felt that would bring him more pain and so she remained silent.

Morgan sighed.

"Sold!" The auctioneer's voice whiplashed the air

and a hard-bellied buyer from Wichita hollered in triumph.

"Hoooeee!" Morgan yelled. "We got top dollar, Lottie. We got us top damn dollar!"

Her voice was soft and distant as a swallow's flight. "Just . . . only," she said, "just . . . only."

"Gonna get them cattle sweet and sassy on the grass by the creek," Morgan continued, "and then we'll ship 'em out. Lottie-honey, in two, three weeks you and me, we're gonna sashay up Wichita way and I'm gonna wrap you in a yard of yellow ribbon. By damn, you'll be my sweet canary!"

Morgan's eyes swept back to the horizon, toward the grazing land by the creek, toward the distant herd of prime which at this moment he could neither see nor hear. Even if they had been closer he would not have heard them paw the ground or bray the air because he was deafened by the echo of Lottie's voice.

Just . . . only. Oh, sweet Jesus, what did she mean?

Morgan's creek slanted from northwest to southeast across this grassland. It was a narrow creek looping off of the Cimarron. There was little rock resistance in the land so the creek ran as straight and true as a map-drawn meridian. Its waters flowed fresh and cool between flaring banks. Clusters of purple Blazing Star sprinkled the edges of the creek bank. The purple petals were fading into lavender, preparing for death in the September sun. Here and there flowers had been flattened into the damp creek banks. They looked like pale violet memories pressed between the leaves of a gentlewoman's book. But no yearning yesterday-finger had touched them. They had been crushed under the hooves of cattle.

The grazing land looked like a warped table, its surface swelling and dipping and rising again into small hills and hidden gullies. Occasional shade trees thrust up from the bluestem grass and their perpendicular lines bisected the sky severely even as their shadows softened the land. Barbed-wire fences sealed in the roving herds and casually caught the blowing tumble-weed. The sigh of wind was everywhere.

The cattle bunched along the western bank. Some munched on the grass which grew almost to the edge of the creek. Others lay in the shade of a peach-leaved willow. A few formed an almost perfect circle, their huge shaggy heads bowed toward the earth, their patient eyes contemplating nothing. The rest of the large herd were scattered, with no design, farther back from the creek as they tail-switched on the prairie.

A single steer backed out of the animal circle and turned toward the creek. He was thirsty. Slowly, he moved toward the water. The great weight of his body allowed him not to slip on the muddy banks. He moved hock high into the water and lowered his head.

The coyote sprang.

He hurtled out of the brush and, in a foam-flecked fury, sank his teeth into the neck of the steer. The steer bawled in fright. His great head whipped around as he slashed at the coyote whose jaws were tearing at the steer's flesh. A horn ripped the coyote's flank and the animal dropped. For just a moment, the coyote was caught in the tumbling current of the creek but then his head broke water and he scrambled to the bank. He raced away from the bawling steer and ran, blood dripping from his flank, through the startled and terrified herd who scattered swiftly before him and whose huge bodies slammed into the wire fences where their hides were lacerated by deadly barbs.

Only the mockingbird winging high overhead heard the far-away cry of Morgan Crowley's auctioneer.

"Sold!"

That evening, long after the sky had turned red with the end of day, Lorraine and Dippsy sat together in the farmhouse kitchen and listened to the news of war. Jim Dandy lay between them. Mostly he was still but whenever he heard Dippsy shift in his chair or when he heard Lorraine cluck softly at the grievous reports, he would twitch an ear toward the sound or his tail would thump twice against the wooden floor and then, abstractedly, either Lorraine or Dippsy would reach down and rub him softly along the belly until they heard a sweet rumble from his throat and could see one of his rear legs quiver with pleasure.

The news bulletins were brief and bitter.

Lt. Gen. George S. Patton's armor and infantry forced the Moselle below Metz today, gaining a bloody foothold on the river's east bank. In fighting of rising fury, however, American forces farther down the Moselle in the Pont-Mousson area were thrown back across the river after they had put a force on the east bank. The fighting there was heavy and losses were of considerable proportions as the Germans held the dominating hills.

The German radio declared today that a British bridgehead pushed across the Albert canal toward the Netherlands had been liquidated.

Suddenly, Jim Dandy growled and, under her hand, Lorraine could feel the muscles ripple along his back. She cocked her head and listened to the noise of a Kansas night. She heard the soft hoot of a barn owl and the rustle of raven wings and the tiny tomtom beat of cicadas. These were all familiar sounds and gave her no cause for alarm. Dandy rose and stretched and shook himself and padded to the door. He growled again and lowered his head and sniffed at the crack under the kitchen door.

"See what, Dips," she said, her concentration still on the radio reports of beachheads and bombs and the death of young men.

"Full moon, I betcha," Dippsy said as he crossed the kitchen and opened the door. "Ole Jim, he hates the moon."

And he is not alone, thought Lorraine.

Dippsy patted the dog and let him out into the night, closing the door behind him. The boy sat on the

floor in front of his mother and rested his head against
her knees and both the woman and the boy drew
solace from the contact. Dippsy found it difficult to
visualize the geographics of battleground droned
forth by the newscaster and so he shut his eyes and
let his mind wander to the games of tomorrow which
he and Charlie Custer would devise. Because the older
boy never lorded his two superior years over him,
Dippsy had elected Charlie to be his best friend. Of
course, there were other reasons; Charlie was special.
He never called Dippsy a kid and, when they played
together, Charlie always let Dippsy have the first turn
at what they were doing. It didn't make any difference
what they were doing. It could be Red Rover, Red
Rover come over or mumblety-peg or king of the hill
or trading baseball cards from bubblegum or battle-
ships in the creek or making Jim Dandy fetch or just
any old thing. And Charlie had a way of looking at
things and making Dippsy see them. The two boys
could be walking through a field, just sauntering like,
not knowing where they were going and not caring
either and maybe they'd come across some big old ant
dragging the wing of a cricket behind him and Charlie
would stop dead in his tracks and say c'mon Dippsy
we gotta help that bugger and he'd find a stick and
pull it through the ground, making a sort of special
road for the ant to more easily reach his hill; or maybe
Charlie would wake up Dippsy early in the morning,
even before the stars were down, by throwing pebbles
at his window and tell the boy to get up and get moving, and, with Jim Dandy trotting at their heels, they'd
take the long, long hike to the abandoned quarry.

The stone quarry, long since worked out, was on
the edge of a prairie woman's wheat land. Her name
was Willie Mae. Many years ago, during a season
when grasshoppers had darkened the sun, Willie Mae's
father had purchased the small quarry from the railroad and sold the stone to the town of Crowley Flats
so that the new tin-lizzie roads could be graveled. The

quarry was rutted out now and half filled with water. Its unplumbed depths were surrounded on three sides by a high plateau of bluestem grass but one rock wall remained jutting over the prairie.

For a time, the older boys of the town had used the quarry as a swimming hole, challenging each other as they swan-dived from the rock ledges to the water below. But one day a boy had failed to rise from the dark, unsunned waters and it had been assumed that the boy's plunge had driven him deep into a hidden crevice of rock where his head or a leg or an arm had been caught, vise-like, and where his lungs had filled and finally burst. His body had never surfaced and the grieving town had called the quarry a devil's glen and ordered its sons away.

But Charlie Custer saw no devils at the quarry. He saw the ghosts of Indian chiefs.

The boys and Jim Dandy would arrive at the quarry just as the rising sun painted the walls and Charlie would point out the different shapes and figures on those walls, which seemed to move under the shifting light. He'd make Dippsy see that those shapes were people, Indian chiefs, Charlie'd say, who got caught by the night and frozen into stone. Under the flash of morning sun, they came to life because their bones were warmed again and the red glare from the eastern sky was the blood boiling back into their bodies; the prairie wind which sang within the stones was really the Pawnee breathing again.

Those Indians, Charlie'd say, they just hate to be dead. See, he'd tell Dippsy, it doesn't make any difference if you're an Indian or a hog or whatever, being dead's all the same.

It's just silence, he'd say.

It's just nothing.

You can't smell anything.

You can't see anything.

You can't taste anything.

You can't touch anything.

It's like the world is missing, he'd say.

But just about the point where Dippsy'd start worrying about the world being gone, why, Charlie'd jump up and cry out that it was time to swallow the wind and he'd race down the hill away from the quarry, away from the Indians born fresh by the sun, and toward the distant fields below and where, once more, he might rescue another ant.

Yeah, Dippsy thought, Charlie could sure point out things. And, with his head still resting against his mother's knee, he fell asleep and dreamed of the days ahead when he and Charlie and Jim Dandy would be warmed by the sun forever.

Jim Dandy sped across the newly furrowed field until he reached the cottonwood clump. There, he stopped quickly. He stared at a thicket of bramble. His nose quivered. The hackles rose along his muscled shoulders. His lips pulled back as he bared his teeth. Slowly, he stepped toward the thicket.

He rushed the bramble.

There was a terrible snap and snarl of jaws. The bramble bush quivered violently; a single black crow flapped and cawed but did not leave its branch high overhead in the cottonwood tree. Then the night was quiet. Even the wind had stopped. The crow was motionless in his tree. And then the bush, its tiny thorns blood-wet and rigid, yielded to the weight of a passing animal. Jim Dandy emerged from the tangle, panting heavily. He sat down at the edge of the field. Finally he turned his head and in the darkness watched the rabid coyote burrow deep within the cottonwood, twitch convulsively and then stiffen into death.

Dandy's huge white head lowered and he began to lick the blood from the coyote's bite on his rear left leg. It was a small slash almost hidden by the dog's thickly matted white hair, the kind of wound that could have been made by a sharp thorn or a strand of barbed wire. It would soon be covered by a scab, the natural incrustation that signified the beginning of a healing process and the scab, in turn, would flake off; the only thing left on the dog's rear left leg would be a tiny scar obscured by his glossy white coat. In just a matter of days the wound would be camouflaged. Concealed from the citizens of Crowley Flats.

There is a double horror to rabies. The ease with which it can be communicated, and its final agony.

Rabies can be transmitted in the simplest of ways. The body secretions of the carrier contain the virus. His saliva, semen, tears and urine are all infective agents. Should any of these secretions be introduced into the skin of a warm-blooded animal, that animal will carry the malignancy.

Man is a warm-blooded animal.

Although the rabies virus can penetrate the body through healthy but sensitive mucous membranes, the greatest danger is that the carrier's virulent cells will come into contact with skin which is already lacerated to some degree. An open blister, a cold sore, a hangnail, a small cut, the slightest abrasion are all invitations to death.

The incubation period of the disease fluctuates and is generally contingent on the site of the virus introduction. The virus proliferates in the area of the wound and then begins its deadly surge through the nerves until it claims the brain; therefore, the site initially infected will determine the length of time it takes before the final symptoms of the disease become apparent. Any infection commencing around the extremities of hand or foot will take longer to culminate at the brain than an initial infection of the head or neck or face.

The preliminary symptoms of the disease do not startle the victim. He may be afflicted with a general weariness, headaches and indefinable pains, a lack of appetite. But as the virus proceeds in its inexorable climb to the brain, the symptoms become more severe. The area of the wound may alternate between itching and numbness and the victim is subject to sudden apprehension and nightmares. He becomes restless and depressed. But these conditions, too, can be tolerated.

It is when the virus finally attacks the nerve centers that the terror begins.

The flesh of the victim quivers incessantly and is bathed in sweat. His muscles spasm and contort. He cannot stop tearing and yellow saliva oozes from his mouth and his whole body jerks and writhes uncontrollably as he is locked into the horror of his own pain. The sight of water, a sudden noise or a flash of bright light can trigger him into a violent fit and he is constantly terrified of drowning in his own saliva and so he spits and hacks and spews in order to rid himself of any liquid which he is sure will choke him to death. It is this which causes the frothing at the mouth. The muscular contortions of the victim's throat produce a strange and awful barking sound and finally a howling as harsh and wild as a wolf.

Death by rabies is a long and awful agony.

From the edge of the field, Jim Dandy could see the welcoming lights of the farmhouse. A sudden gust of night wind carried the sound of laughter from a woman and a boy. The dog shook himself and, in a moment, he was racing across the field toward the hands which would so lovingly caress him.

Perhaps, in the days to come, Lorraine would not cut herself on a paring knife. Perhaps Dippsy and Charlie, playing their war games, would not skin their knees. Perhaps Ben Custer would not graze himself on any of the sharp instruments of his profession. Perhaps the wheat farmers and ranch hands and tradesmen of Crowley Flats would not, in the normal pursuit of their hard and manual labor, open a blister or chafe their flesh.

Perhaps no one of these prairie people would reach a hand toward Jim Dandy.

Perhaps.

6

A golden spike was driven into steel at Promontory Point, Utah, on May 10 in the year 1869. It did more than sledge together east and west. It united the long Missouri with the western ocean and changed the landscape of the prairie.

Buffalo gave way to cattle and high grass to wheat. A traveler no longer saw bones of the Pawnee or Kiowa; the guns of the Dalton boys were silenced. The Union Pacific and the Central Pacific and the Southern Pacific and the Atchinson, Topeka and Santa Fe sowed their steel, planted their towns, harvested their rebates, and left behind them a thousand miles of spur track, most of which died in the tumble-weed.

Crowley Flats was a spur town. In the swollen yesterday years it had served as an engine-switching station. A single standard gauge track, exactly four feet and eight and one half inches wide, ran along the edge of town. A faded clapboard depot stood next to the rails and gave a tired welcome to the one morning train which passed from the west and the one afternoon train which passed from the east. On the rare occasion when either train stopped it was, these days, to pick up a young man and carry him to war.

A spur track, its rails rusted from disuse, angled off from the main rails and ran through a bed of weeds before it entered an abandoned roundhouse. Once, the roundhouse had reverberated to the clang and grind of giant locomotives as they were serviced by their crews and then slowly wheeled around on the massive turntable and pointed back toward their return. Now, the circular, worn wooden building sagged from its own rotted weight and was empty of echo. Its great glass panes were missing, victims of the onslaught of time and weather and the stones from small boys' slingshots.

But today it would once more become a home for steel.

Last winter, the citizens of Crowley Flats had learned from Morgan that an ancient locomotive stood frozen and forlorn in a field of ice as she waited to be towed to a final graveyard. Morgan had proposed that the town buy the locomotive and turn her into scrap for armament. The idea had fired the town's collective imagination. As Morgan secretly had wished, it provided a war-weary people with fresh purpose. The townspeople saved pennies and nickels and dimes. Wives patched their mens' jeans instead of buying new ones. Farmers gave up sleep to plow more fields. Kids sacrificed their allowances. The people pulled together and today the dream would become reality and harden into steel.

The locomotive was on its way.

In preparation for a ceremonial celebration, the men and women and children of Crowley Flats had erected a wooden platform stage outside of the roundhouse and decorated it with red, white and blue bunting. The prairie people had been promised a special presentation by the town's young children and the long rows of benches surrounding the stage were quickly filling up with early arrivals. At this moment, their attention was riveted to the distant parade which slowly weaved down Main Street toward the depot. They listened to the stirring patriotic songs being played by the Elementary School Band.

"Praise the Lord and pass the ammunition.
All aboard, we ain't a' goin' fishin'!"

Shoulder to shoulder, citizens of Crowley Flats lined the narrow main street of their small, rural town and as they sang in joyous unison, their eyes mirrored the passing parade. The high noon sun flashed against the gold of trombones and tubas and cymbals. The drumbeat pounded like a high-pressured pulse. The boys and girls of the band sashayed sweetly down the street. The children were dressed in scarlet tunics and shiny black belts and each head, bobbing to the butterfly beat and boom of parade, was covered by a plumed cap, the feathers waving glory to the sky.

Oh, it was truly a struttin' time!

Main Street was a narrow, pitted asphalt ribbon bordered on either side by the dull rectangles of old store fronts and the occasional spear of telephone poles. Above most of the doorways leading into the stores were painted signs, unimaginative and uniform in their black block lettering, which identified the goods or services offered within. There was very little seductive advertising because the people of this Kansas town knew what they wanted and when they wanted it and where they would get it. Items of necessity, sickles, skeins of wool, toothpaste, pliers, bib overalls, were haphazardly displayed in window fronts. There was little attempt to please the potential purchaser's eye because there was no need to. Commerce between shop owner and rancher was conducted on the basis of day-to-day urgencies. There was a hardware store and a two-chair barbershop and a small furniture store whose owner's sign also made clear that he was a licensed embalmer and funeral director. There was a United States post office near the drugstore and two gas stations, one of which had been closed for over a year because of the shortage of supply, and a motion-picture theater faced in faded brick, and a grain store and a diner and a Western Union office and a general store which sold tins of molasses and penny candy

and, when fortune smiled, meat and sugar and tobacco. Like its citizens, Crowley Flats was unadorned
with either frill or fancy.

The men and women who watched the parade,
whose feet stomped to the rhythm of the band, whose
voices rose high in song, were dressed in their Sunday
best and their faces shone as if they had made a public covenant with joy. They were simple, hard-working
people. Their lives, their failures, their hopes, were
etched in their weather-burned faces. They were
united by an unsentimental faith in their God and in
their country and they were unashamedly stirred by
the passing of the flag.

Side by side, middle-aged and elderly men and
women and little boys and girls removed their hats,
placed hands over hearts, and prayed silently for the
young men who had gone to war. Listening to the
thrilling thump of drum, each spectator could not help
but feel a twinge of guilt about the safe ground on
which he walked. All recognized that a huge shadow
had fallen across a distant land and that under that
shadow was a killing ground where death waited
around every corner as men hunted men while they,
the prairie people, stood in the sun.

Their inner visions were inaccurate. They, too, stood
on the killing ground.

Jim Dandy led the parade.

The huge white dog trotted proudly in front of
trombones and tubas and not a man or woman or
child noticed the small scar on his lower left leg; nor
did they know that the deadly rabies virus was moving
relentlessly through his nervous system and that at
any random moment those who felt the dog's loving
tongue flick across their broken skin had better make
their peace with God.

The crashing band pumped and pomped its way
past the movie theater whose unlighted neon adver-
tised Abbott and Costello in *Buck Privates*. The band

passed the town's one grocery store with its woeful window signs. *One pound sugar per customer . . . No cigarettes . . . Butter next week . . . Hoarders are on the same level as spies.* Across the street, in the Western Union office, a man watched the band pass on. He was an elderly, wizened wisp of a man who wore a black bowler hat and a stiff celluloid collar and worry in his eyes. He was Sam Hanks, and as he listened to the soft clatter of teletype keys he prayed the message would not begin . . . *We regret to inform you.*

He smiled as he watched Jim Dandy weave in and out of the snaring legs of children.

At the gas station, further down the street, Virgil Foster watched the approaching parade as he filled the tank of a shiny new convertible. Sitting behind the wheel of the convertible was Chet Beam, a thirty-year-old hustler in an ice cream suit. Virgil, his gum snapping in good humor, knocked sharply on the car door and shouted over the noise of the bam-bam band.

"Knock knock!"

"Damn, Virgil," Chet muttered, "ain't you run outa them yet?"

"C'mon, Chet. Knock knock!"

Jim Dandy pirouetted out of the passing parade and pranced toward the gas station. Again, Virgil knuckle-rapped the car door and Chet resigned himself to the old man's dull humor.

"Who's there?" Chet asked.

"Alby."

"Alby who?"

"Alby glad when you're dead you rascal you!" Virgil's face cracked in glee and his skinny features looked like an unsolvable jigsaw puzzle. Chet thrust a handful of counterfeit A coupons into the old man's hand, turned the ignition key, revved the engine and pulled away, his voice weary with disgust.

"That's a real knee-slapper, Virgil, a real knee-slapper." There was no point in riling the old man. He might look too closely at the phony print on the gas coupons.

Jim Dandy leaped up at Virgil, his tail beating the wind in affectionate gesture. Playfully, the old man wrestled with the dog and scratched him vigorously along the belly. Virgil talked to the dog as if he were an old friend waiting for a tire to be changed.

"You're real perky today, ain't you, son? Well, you got a right. By gum, we all got the right. This is surely some huff 'n' puff day. Let's you an' me skeedaddle down to that ole roundhouse an' get us a lookin' place. C'mon, son, let's move it out." Gently, the man tweaked the dog's ear and then turned on his heel and started toward the street. The dog followed him and, together, they hooked up with the rear of the passing parade. Walking behind the scarlet-tuniced children, Virgil felt his pulse quicken. His rheumy eyes teared a little and he didn't give a damn who saw it. His normally shuffled gait changed and one foot snapped in front of the other as he counted a secret cadence. *Left right left right left right.* A man don't forget, he thought to himself, a man don't ever forget. And for a moment, somewhere in the dim recess of memory, Virgil Foster was marching again with Teddy. He was a boy drumming up San Juan Hill, charging toward the fame and the fire. *Left right left right left right.* Virgil Foster felt so tall he feared his head would pierce the sky. Not breaking stride, he reached down and squeezed Jim Dandy.

"Damn," he said, "hot damn."

Caleb grinned as he watched Virgil marching down the street. He nudged Emmett who was standing on his ladder.

"Ain't he jus' piss-proud though?"

The two men were outside Caleb's feed and grain store. The tail end of the parade was disappearing down the street and moving toward the roundhouse at the far end of town. Emmett turned on his ladder and, wiping his hands on a waste rag to scrub off the paint, stared after Virgil. He was aware of how straight the man's back was and he was suddenly irritated at Caleb's mocking tone.

"Ain't no need to fun him, Caleb. Virgil's a good man."

"Was, Emmett, was. That ole rooster ain't got no crow left in him, no crow a'tall."

Emmett didn't answer. He didn't want to provoke Caleb into an argument because he knew that would only increase his headache. He'd had the goldarn thing for a few days now and couldn't get rid of it. It made him weary and took away his appetite and he was glad that he had some poster-painting assignments which would take him out of town because he didn't think he could tolerate much more of Caleb's yammering. Or anyone else's either.

Hitler Smiles When You Waste Miles. The bold black letters were perfect. The width of Emmett's stroke never varied and the letters' edges and ends were sharp and clear. The letters had no rounded corners and therefore stood in pleasing juxtaposition to the signature below them. *B. F. Goodrich.* Emmett had used a cursive script to inscribe the name. The flow and form of his paint was a graceful tribute to the poster's sponsor. For a moment Emmett admired his own work and then climbed down from his ladder. He shoved the ladder into the bed of his truck and then placed paint cans and paraphernalia next to it. He wiped his hands again and then folded the rag neatly and put it, too, in the truck. When he turned back to Caleb, he wasn't aware that again he was scratching the small scar on his hand. He leaned close to Caleb and spoke in a conspiratorial whisper.

"Where at you got it hid?"

"She's cut up and packaged somethin' pretty in the ice chest back of the store."

"You save my half of that venison for when I come back, you hear?"

"Where you headin' this time?"

"Paintin' my way east, Caleb. Wherever there's glad tidin's to paint, that's where I'll be." Emmett climbed behind the wheel of his truck and waved a heavy paintbrush in a triumphant flourish. "I'll see ya."

He peered up at the poster he'd just finished. And he took pride in it. But he sure wished the itch on his hand would go away.

"I'll see ya," said Caleb, and started back into the store. He heard Emmett's truck pull out and he turned to wave once more. But his hand froze in mid-air as something else caught his vision. Across the way, at the far end of the street, the door of the town's diner opened and a man and a woman walked out. Still in the air, Caleb's hand curled into a fist. Caleb hawked up phlegm and spat into the tire-rutted dust in front of his store. He ground the spit under his heel and he could feel the hard muscles tighten under his belly-fat. In his mind, he substituted the man and woman for the spit under his heel and his boot pounded the dust. He felt better. He moved into the store, letting the door slam behind him.

"Fuckin' Krauts," he said to the unseen rats in the store.

Ernst and Sophie Jurgen stood on the steps leading up to their diner. Ernst carried a pail of scraps but at this moment it was just an ignored weight in his hand. He concentrated on the dust rising behind the disappearing parade. He didn't look at his wife when he spoke and his voice was low and tight.

"We were late, Sophie. We should not have been late."

"We are not late, Ernst. Not yet has the train arrived." Her voice was calm and deliberate and she patted Ernst gently on his cheek. He ignored her touch.

"We must do as the others do. If there is a parade, we watch. If there is a flag, we salute. If there is a drum, we march. It is an important thing to do as the others do. Do not forget this."

"*Das kann ich nicht tun!*"

"English, Sophie, please speak English!"

Sophie studied her husband. A muscle twitched nervously under his eye. She sighed. She had seen the tic before. She would never forget the first time. Ernst's face had glistened with sweat and his skin had turned a dark and ugly red from the nearby glow of the fire. On a street in Berlin, they had gripped hands as they watched the Reichstag burn. Sophie looked down at her hand. *Mein Gott*, what a baker's fingers can do. She was still surprised that the bones had not cracked. Later, on that fearful night, they had made swift plans. Sophie closed her eyes and listened to the distant beat of drum and blare of horn and the raised voices of Crowley Flats. *Coming in on a wing and a prayer*. She wondered if the bakery in Berlin still stood and she found she didn't care. This was her home now. Hers and Ernst's. It had been for eleven years. It would be forever. She wished Ernst understood that.

"*Kommen Sie . . . kommen Sie*, my darlings."

Sophie opened her eyes. Ernst had left the steps and stood by the garbage bins which were tucked neatly behind wooden lattice work. He had poured the bone scraps into two cracked bowls and now he whistled softly and then spoke again.

"*Kommen Sie*, my darlings."

Sophie smiled to herself. The only time Ernst allowed himself to use his native language was when he called the dogs. Perhaps he felt that animals would not challenge his loyalty. She waited before going back into the diner. She liked to watch the affectionate arrival of Ernst's darlings. Every morning, with the precision of a Dresden clock, Ernst's whistle summoned the town's strays.

The far away whistle of a train was clear in the morning's dry air. "It comes soon," Sophie said, "soon."

"*Ja, ja,*" murmured Ernst as he hugged a mongrel to his chest and tried to wipe clean the corner of his mind which still held the picture of Caleb Dodd grinding spit under his heel. He petted the mongrel in his arms and then leaned down and placed the dog in front of one of the bowls of scrap meat. In the dog's eagerness to get at the food, he nipped one of Ernst's fingers. The German didn't mind. He just sucked at the scratch and started up the stairs into the diner. He paused when he saw dust churning at the far end of Main Street where the parade had already passed. For an instant he thought the wind was blowing tumbleweed, but then saw the streak of white headed his way and he knew immediately that Jim Dandy had swerved away from the parade and was racing back to investigate the bowls of scrap which were placed every morning under the stairs of the diner.

Ernst nodded to himself and was pleased. Although he had severe doubts about the aura of friendliness displayed by the men and women in this American town, he felt he could rely on the allegiance of animals. As Jim Dandy skidded to a stop in front of a bowl of scraps, Ernst allowed himself a small smile and then stepped inside the diner.

He was still sucking at the scratch on his finger.

The youthful elementary-school band lined up below the bunting-decorated stage and banged out another chorus of "Coming in on a Wing and a Prayer." The townspeople surged around the roundhouse, chatting together, peering down the tracks in expectancy, tasting the tang of triumph in the coming celebration. The laughter and the talk and the music was a sweet cacophony on the Kansas air.

"Hot damn, it's a Yankee Doodle day, citizen!" Chet Beam shouted above the crowd as he elbowed his way toward Emmett's parked truck. After leaving Caleb, Emmett had started toward the highway which would lead him eastward, but the sugar-sweet sound of song had seduced him. He sat on the hood of his truck, his tobacco-chewing jaws moving to the rhythm of the band. Chet swung up onto the running board of the truck and bent close to Emmett.

"Yes, sir, a real Yankee Doodle day."

"Makes a man sweat with glory," said Emmett.

"Brings on a thirst to the righteous, don't it?"

"It does that."

They understood each other. Their eyes never moved from the festivities in front of them. Their hands were lightning quick in the exchange. Chet slipped a pint of potato from under his white linen jacket and palmed it to Emmett. The older man thrust a handful of crumpled dollars into Chet's pocket. Chet winked, leaped off the running board and started back into the crowd, his eyes searching for parched lips and dry throats.

Emmett spat his chaw onto the ground. Behind a flap of his denim jacket, he unscrewed the cap of the pint bottle. He bowed his head, a suddenly humble man in prayer, and when his face was hidden by the collar of his jacket, he lifted the bottle toward his lips. And stopped. A strange look crossed his face as he stared at the liquor sloshing in the bottle. Now what the hell, he thought, this here is fine mash. I'll just take me a little bite of it and put the bubble back into my blood. But he didn't. His throat constricted at the thought. He didn't feel like swallowing anything. Anything at all. The idea filled him with quick anxiety. Slowly, he tipped the bottle and Chet Beam's saucy snakebite splendor spilled to the ground. Mesmerized by the pool of potato mash soaking into the dust, Emmett scratched at the scar on his hand.

And his jaws began to move. Just a little. It was as if he were snapping at air. Like an animal.

He slid off the hood of his truck and scrambled up behind the wheel. He didn't look behind him and he didn't hear the band as he drove off toward the east to paint glory on the land.

Emmett swerved once as he avoided the great white dog running freely through the crowd.

Ben Custer's foot stomped down hard and Pete thought maybe the accelerator pedal would go right through the floorboards. The pickup sped away from the barn and the wheels slid dangerously over the slippery, hard-packed ground. Ben double-clutched and shifted down into a lower gear and the heavy-treaded tires bit solidly. Ben spun the wheel over hard and the truck bounced over the ruts leading to the field and then raced across the furrowed land spraying stones and dust behind it. Ben yanked the Bull Durham sack out of his jacket and, driving with only one hand, tried to roll a cigarette. Shreds of tobacco cascaded onto the seat and the floorboards and into Ben's lap, and the wind whipped the single thin sheet of rolling paper out the window. Pete grabbed hold of the rifle rack behind him, trying to retain his balance as the truck lurched and swayed. He averted his head and hoped to God that Pa didn't see the grin.

"Damn fool," Ben said, "that's what I am!"

"Right, Pa."

"Plain hog-dumb, chicken-crawed damn fool."

"Right, Pa."

"Wasting gas on a thing like this. Jesus, it puckers the mind."

"Charlie doesn't mean any harm, Pa. It's just he . . . he forgets."

"Knew a man once . . . forgot to screw his belly button in . . . nice feller . . . 'til his ass fell off!"

The truck sailed over a ditch.

The special presentation had begun. On the wooden stage set up by the roundhouse, a dozen little boys and girls performed their special pageant. It was a song and dance festival celebrating victory gardens and the children were all dressed in vegetable costumes. They represented the cabbages and tomatoes and celery and radishes of the gardens in Crowley Flats. The chorus was a conglomerate blaze of reds and yellows and bright, bright greens and on the head of each performer was a cap of roots. The line they formed on stage was as straight as a hoe but its unity was interrupted by a single space. Between the third and fourth boy (who was a radish named Dippsy) was a hole. It lacked produce from the mythical garden. It lacked a carrot.

The carrot stood forlornly on the edge of the crowd. The carrot was Charlie Custer. His body was a ridge and bulge of dull orange. He looked as if he had only recently pushed up out of the damp earth. But his cap was missing. He was an outcast with no roots. His eyes searched the fringes of spectators and he tried not to listen to the wonderful song of vegetables. Then he saw the truck skid off the road and over the spur track and past the depot and the looming water tower and slam to a stop by the wide, gaping door of the roundhouse. Momentarily shedding the costume of carrot, Charlie slipped on the mask of the Lone Ranger and, slapping his thigh with an imaginary rawhide, galloped toward his father. *Hi ho, Silver, away!*

Ben thrust the cap of carrot roots into Charlie's hand.

"Here."

"Gee, Pa, I . . ."

Charlie saw the impatient look in his father's eyes and so he didn't bother to finish what he figured would be an unacceptable explanation for his forgetfulness. He wheeled around and ran through the crowd and leaped up onto the stage and shoved his way into the empty space as he slammed the cap onto his head and grabbed Dippsy by the hand and then, beaming, joined the others in a chorus of the vegetable song.

Ben just shook his head.

"Forget his head if it wasn't screwed onto his shoulders," he said to Pete.

"Well, you know Charlie," Pete said.

"Yeah," Ben answered quietly, "I know Charlie."

A quick darkness swept across Pete's face as he heard his father's tone. He spoke carefully.

"Sometimes, Pa, sometimes you quick-mouth Charlie. You don't really listen to him."

"Maybe." Ben's tone was noncommittal.

But Pete didn't want to let it go. He had not been able to forget Charlie's face that morning two weeks ago when Ben, thinking it was his own secret, had leaned over him, Pete, and so gently touched his face.

"You remember that blacksmith you used to tell me about when I was just knee-high to a grasshopper?" Pete asked his father.

"No."

"Yeah, you do. The one Ma used to like to hear about. That blacksmith, he was one of those fancy 'knew a man once . . . nice feller' stories that tickle your fancy. You know, the kind you sorta drift in to when you want to sound like a wise old owl."

Pete saw the tiny smile play around his father's lips and so he felt he could lean just a little bit more without pushing Ben into any tightness.

"Go on," the boy continued, "go on, owl, hoot me a little about that Mr. Blacksmith."

"Well," Ben said, "hell, boy, you know so much, don't see much need to go into it."

"But you will, right?"

Ben looked at his elder son and he saw the devilment in the boy's face and he thought, oh lord, he is so young. He does not know that he might return from the fighting dim-eyed, with a mutilated mind, or that he might not return at all. Faintly aware of the thin, high voices of the vegetable chorus on stage accompanied by the crashing chords of the band, suddenly Ben wanted to reach out and hold his son and tell him that it would be all right, that he, Ben, would understand if the boy wanted to run, just run and get the hell off the face of the earth until he found some place dark and safe in which to hide. But Ben didn't reach out and he didn't say anything like that because he knew there is never any place to hide, nor is there a place to run, nor a land without risk.

And so he talked of the blacksmith.

"Knew a man once," he said, "nice feller. A blacksmith. Used to put a horseshoe on his anvil and whomp it with a hammer. And he'd listen to it ring. He said if a man had a hundred different horseshoes, you could bet on a hundred different rings. But he allowed as how he admired each and every one of those shoes 'cause they were all steel and each of 'em had a sound that stayed in a man's head. And men, the blacksmith said, why they're like those horseshoes. Each of 'em has his own ring. All you have to do, the blacksmith said, is ..."

"Listen," Pete said quietly. "All you have to do is listen."

Pete's gaze was steady as he looked at his father and then the boy turned and stared at the little wooden stage on which the vegetable chorus was pantomiming the growth of seeds in the sun. The individual boys and girls were kneeling, with heads bowed, as if they were vegetables in a row waiting to sprout and then, one by one, to the flourish of schoolband trumpets, a head of lettuce or a radish or a stalk of celery would unfold slowly and then gain strength and speed and pop out and up from the imaginary furrow in which he was planted.

A carrot shot out of the ground.

It was Charlie Custer.

"Pa," Pete said, "all you have to do is listen."

"Charles Remington Custer," Ben said. "Your mother chose that name, Pete. She said it had a ring to it. But she never heard it because she died too soon."

Ben paused a moment and when he spoke again his voice was so low that Pete had to lean forward to catch the words.

"Maybe I will, too," Ben said. "Die too soon."

"Damn it, Pa," Pete pleaded, "give him a chance. Give him a . . ."

"There's no steel to him, Pete. There's just no steel to him."

Before Pete could reply, he heard a sharp shout from Lorraine Towers.

"Dandy!"

Pete and Ben turned toward the cry and saw that Jim Dandy was now racing toward the stage. He dashed up to the line of folding chairs which were arranged below the stage and on which sat the boys and girls of the band. The muscular tail of the white dog whipped the air and it slapped hard against one of the young trombone players. The children in the band doubled over with laughter, then jumped up from their seats and tried to grab the dog. But Dandy plunged through them, knocking some to their knees, and in one great surge, leaped onto the stage. The crowd was whooping and hollering and having a grand time watching the frantic efforts of the vegetable-children to restrain the dog as he ran in circles around the stage. The dog reached Dippsy, reared up on his hind legs and thrust his front paws over the boy's shoulders. Barking happily, the dog shoved his great head close to Dippsy's face and tried to lick him, but Dippsy collapsed into giggles and his arms were wrapped around his own head as he rolled on the floor of the stage and tried to avoid the rushing weight of the playful dog. Charlie was laughing as hard as Dippsy but he dived at his friend Dandy and caught hold of the dog's rear legs. As the dog and both boys tumbled around together under the legs of the other children, Lorraine sprinted up to them, seized Dandy's collar and wrenched him loose. She pulled him across the stage, down the steps, and through the hooting spectators. Scarlet-faced, she reached the edge of the crowd where she knelt by Dandy and soothed him with her quiet voice and stroked him along his back and under his belly.

And down his legs.

Ben's eyes were on the stage where Charlie and Dippsy were dusting themselves off to the applause of the crowd. Charlie, responding to the shouts of spectator approval, raised his hands high and clenched his fists, a victorious fighter circling the stage, bowing and preening and acknowledging the applause.

Ben felt the muscles twitch in his jaws. The boy was making a clown of himself, responding to an undeserved ovation. He was about to turn to Pete and point this out when the school band struck up a Sousa march and, under the jangle of horn and drum, Ben thought the hell with it, that's all, just to hell with it.

"Those soldier pants sure do hug true."

Pete spun around. Cora Zink's face was only inches away and her body curved insolently toward him. Pete grinned, a flush rising like flame to his face.

"Hey, Cora! Where you been?"

"What do you care?"

"Been home for a time but I haven't seen hide nor hair of you."

"Yeah, well, I been busy."

"Doin' what?"

"Things."

"What things?"

"Could be I'll tell you, could be I won't," Cora said and shifted a bit until her breast pressed against Pete's arm. The boy took a small step back as he glanced at Ben.

"Pa, you remember Cora."

"Morning, Dr. Custer."

"Morning, Cora." Ben kept his face straight. "Thought you were back east working in defense. St. Louis or Chicago, wasn't it?"

"Detroit." Cora's face squinched with distaste.

"Couldn't rightly face it anymore, the factories being so dirty and all. Would you believe it, that old sky was so yellow with smoke a body'd choke to death. Why, I couldn't catch one real night of sleep. Just lay in my bed, my eyes burning so I thought sure as sugar I'd go blind, and I figured my going blind wasn't going to help any of our sweet fighting boys so I just picked up stakes and came back to where I'm needed and where I do believe I am wanted and I'm going to drive the school bus and, my, my, listen to me run off at the mouth. I swear I haven't been so riled up since that night by the windmill when the boys . . ."

She stopped. Her glance flicked at Pete. His eyes were round with surprise and his mouth was open as if he had just exhaled a burst of air after being jabbed hard in the belly. Shoot, she thought, that little ole boy thinks I'm gonna 'fess up to his daddy. Why, he like to tremble himself right into the dust. She thought of what else had trembled under the windmill and she lowered her eyes modestly. She looked back at Ben and dipped a tiny little curtsy, her skirts as neat as a nun.

"It is truly fine to be home, Dr. Custer, and you better believe it."

Ben heard his son breathe again.

"I do, Cora, I do truly believe it," Ben said, his voice deacon-serious.

A great shout went up from the spectators around the stage and the school band blared into "Yankee Doodle Dandy" and Ben and Pete and Cora were rescued from further revelation. They turned toward the sound of music and saw Morgan shouldering his way through the crowd. The bulk and bone of the man moved lightly and the citizens of Crowley Flats were on their feet stomping and whistling and singing their approval and the words of the grand old American song were altered to fit the head honcho of the prairie. I'm a Yankee Doodle Dandy became *he's* a Yankee Doodle Dandy. Morgan leaped onto the stage and the little carrots and radishes and cauliflowers lined up behind him. As Morgan held up his hands to silence the enthusiastic spectators, Dippsy broke from the chorus line. The boy grabbed a standing microphone from the edge of the stage and placed it in front of Morgan and then scurried back to the other vegetables. The din and dip of voices died. In the silence, Morgan pulled a jackknife from his pocket and in one swift swipe severed the cord of the microphone. His voice shattered the sunlight.

"That damn thing's for a whisperin' man . . . and Morgan Crowley don't whisper!"

A thin, reedy voice piped up from the rear of the crowd:

"Go get 'em, Morgan!" A few of the spectators tittered. The voice had come from Sheriff George Carter. His shrill approbation of Morgan Crowley was a constancy to be counted on by all of Crowley Flats. Carter was Morgan's man. When Morgan said "frog," George Carter jumped. As Virgil Foster put it, "George, why he's long lost his clank. 'Course, you listen real careful like and mebbe you can still hear his balls tinkle just a little-bitty. You know, sumpin' like a Judas goat."

But the sound of mockery died in the air when Morgan stared hard at the townspeople and then continued in his booming voice.

"I ain't here to soft-mouth you. I'm here to speak the truth. Our boys are havin' a bad time of it. We're in one helluva fight. But we ain't never been licked . . . an' we ain't never gonna be licked!" The crowd was silent as the American flag fluttered behind Morgan's head. "We stand here waitin' for an old train engine this here town's bought so's we could rip her into scrap and send her to the factories where they'll pound her into bullets and guns and tanks. It's our part of the war effort and we're gonna do it! Most every one of us got someone fightin' an' they ain't comin' home till it's done."

Ben's eyes were on Pete but the boy was looking

straight ahead and he was listening attentively to Morgan's words. Even Cora seemed to have leaned out of her voluptuousness, and she looked strangely vulnerable in her scuffed saddle shoes and baggy sweater and single blonde pigtail secured with a shoelace.

"Some of us ain't never comin' back an' so we all gotta help." Morgan's voice was a sword of patriotism. "We gotta stick together. We're gonna cut that old engine apart and build us a hallelujah hill of steel!" Morgan sledged the words home. "Now I want you to take each other by the hand and pledge with me . . . come on now . . . take your neighbor's hand . . . come on!"

Ben saw Lorraine. She was very still. As still as the dog at her feet. Lorraine's eyes were closed. And then, as if she could feel his gaze, as if some silver spider-thread joined them shoulder to shoulder, she turned slowly and opened her eyes. She looked at Ben. Her eyes were as grave and solemn as an icon's and there was no smile on her face as she took three small steps toward him and then reached out her hand. Awkwardly, his fingers touched hers.

Hand holding hand, their arms formed an arch. Slowly, Jim Dandy rose from the ground and walked under that arch and stood between Ben and Lorraine, his bulk filling the space between them, his flanks touching their legs. The dog's rear left leg tingled strangely and so he inched forward until it touched Ben's boot. The leg twitched a little against the leather.

But Ben didn't feel it. He was too aware of the hand within his. He saw Lorraine's eyes sweep over the people who were joining hands.

"Like square dancin'," she said.

"A bit."

"Need a fiddler, is all."

"I guess."

He wondered how she kept her fingers so soft what with all the plowing.

"Been a time," she said. And then she looked straight at him. "Been a long time."

He didn't answer.

Risk, he thought.

As friend touched friend and neighbor moved to neighbor, they all heard the chug of wheel and whistle of steam and a great cheer went up when the train rounded the bend of track. It was a short and strange train. There were no passenger cars. There was no caboose. There was only a forward-pulling locomotive and its burden. It was the burden which carried distinction. It was an ancient American-type 4-4-0 locomotive. Years ago, it had been a thing of magnificence. Now, it was a mass of metal rust and rot. Its smoke box and boiler and outside cylinders and cowcatcher and vast oil headlamps and diamond-shaped spark-arresting chimneys and connecting rods were all caked with dried oil and flecks of orange rust. A tired, tarnished brass lamp was mounted on the top.

"I want us to pledge that ole roundhouse will be fairly swole with steel!"

Morgan, his face shiny with sweat and excitement, leaped onto the cowcatcher as the 4-4-0 was backed up into the roundhouse.

Men and women and children crowded around her sides and the ones who were not singing were laughing and the ones who were not laughing were cheering and behind the steam and soot there were tears. Morgan grabbed an acetylene torch which had been hooked up for the occasion and climbed the boiler's iron ladder to the top of the engine. He lit the torch. Sparks spurted and then grew into a steady flame. A little boy cheek-puffed his tuba and there was the staccato rat-a-tat-tat of a drum and the high hum of horns. The flame from Morgan's torch burned into the bell bracket and a piece of history fell to the floor.

The crowd roared.

And moving in and out of the cheering crowd, his body brushing against legs, his moist muzzle searching out and exploring a dozen friendly outstretched hands, his jaws open just a little bit so that he could suck in air to cool the burning in his throat, was a great white dog named Dandy.

When the sparks from Morgan's acetylene torch streamed into flame, the dog stopped moving. He stood motionless. He stared at the flame. He winced at its brightness, his eyes clicking open and shut convulsively. His jaws opened a little wider and a soft rasping sound came from his throat but in the roundhouse din of celebration the throaty sound was too low for anyone to hear.

Morgan, hoisted onto the shoulders of his neighbors, hung the locomotive's bronze bell high on a rafter and as the citizens of Crowley Flats once more joined hands and sang hallelujah to the land, a speck of saliva oozed from Jim Dandy's jaws. It was slightly yellow and sticky and it took a long time to drop from his mouth to the floor of the roundhouse where, under the shuffling shoes of spectators, it was ground into the dirt.

Slowly, Jim Dandy backed away from the thunderous blast of celebration and eased out of the roundhouse. He lay down, hoping the weeds would cool his body and put out the fire which he felt burning in his belly.

There is, in the course of rabies, a period when the victim does not show the furious symptoms of the disease but he is, nevertheless, contagious. Jim Dandy entered that period.

It is called the quiet phase.

7

The potholes on the rural road were filled with moonglow. Their surfaces shimmered as if they were white buckets being carried by witches to a coven. The pickup weaved expertly around the holes as Ben and Pete listened to a voice coming from the truck's radio.

". . . the first Marine division advanced approximately one third of a mile Saturday on Peleliu, six miles northeast, against stubborn Japanese resistance. The enemy used artillery and mortars in considerable numbers against American positions . . ."

Ben's face tightened as he thought about the imminent departure of his son.

". . . Spearheads of the first U.S. Army held on grimly to their positions twenty to twenty-five miles from the Rhine city of Cologne, turning back waves of hoarsely screaming Germans making shoulder-to-shoulder psychological attacks . . ."

Ben snapped off the radio. He rubbed his eyes. He was tired. There were just too damn many hogs and horses and heiffers for one veterinarian in this part of the prairie. His mind was filled with the litany of disease. Pink-eye and foot rot and wooden tongue and sunburned udders and black-leg and hardware sickness and lumpy-jaw and damned if he hadn't forgotten to order more caustic potash so he could burn off the horns on Lorraine's calf.

"Watch it!" Pete's voice snapped.

Just in time, Ben saw the black-tailed jackrabbit in the shine of his headlights. He twisted the wheel over hard and the long-legged animal jumped over the pans of moonglow into the safety of shadows. Ben eased the wheel back and the truck skidded away from the deep road ditch. He wondered if he would ever feel young again. He wanted a cigarette but he wasn't up to another battle with the goddamn sack of Durham.

"Helluva way for you to spend your last two days," he growled at Pete, "pulling a calf from a cow's belly."

Pete was amused at his father's gruff tone. He knew that Ben was not likely to adorn his son's coming departure with sentimental words or gestures. He recognized that because Ben was a man who hoarded his privacy, he felt that all men would do well to do the same. Verbalizing grief or love did not change the circumstances which gave rise to the emotion. At least that is how my father sees it, thought Pete. No, Pete mused to himself, it's even more than that. My father thinks that asking a man to reveal his feelings is an intrusion.

Although Pete was accurate about his father, he was too young to carry the logic one step further. He did not comprehend that his father's reluctance to give word to a man's disquiet was based on a fact from which even Ben shied. That fact, if pointed out to Ben, would have astonished him. It was, simply, this. Ben Custer was afraid to take the ultimate risk; the risk of sharing another's life. He had done it with Sarah and her departure had caused infinite grief.

He had no wish for further wounds.

Pete looked out the truck window and saw that they were approaching Morgan's grazing land. In just a little while they would arrive at the barn where he and Ben would have to pull a calf.

"Better'n watching haircuts," Pete said.

"Now that never crossed my mind," said Ben.

"No?"

"No."

"What, then?"

"I was thinking of a little filly with a pigtail all blonde and shiny and roped up with shoelace."

"You're a dirty old man."

"Hope so."

"Count on it."

"Sure you want to ride with me?"

"Don't want to but I'm afraid to let you out of sight."

"That's why you're coming, huh?"

"You don't think I look forward to working all night with a dirty old man, do you?"

"Be a fool if you did."

"Be a fool, all right."

Ben didn't succeed in hiding a small smile as he glanced at Pete and then, quickly, glanced away. Looking through the windshield window, he saw the distant lights of Morgan's ranch and he thought of the animal waiting for him and he began to whistle softly.

Many miles from the farm and the barn and the birthing cow, there was another animal on Morgan's grazing land. A steer. The steer was in agony. His great shaggy head twisted around as he tried to bite at the deep, raw scar on his neck. His horns slashed the midnight air and his hooves drove wildly into the wet creek bank. His raging bellow frightened the rest of the herd and the animals backed away. One of the Herefords scraped his flank against the barbed wire and a quick line of blood etched his side. He moved away from the fence and lay down under the umbrella branches of the willow. The bed of dead flowers was still damp from the urine of the neck-wounded steer and the urine moistened the wire scratch on the other animal and then seeped into the narrow and bloody laceration.

A single overhead bulb burned down on the birthing cow.

"Jesus, Morgan, you're lucky that cow's alive."

She was lying on a bed of straw in her stall and her low bawl penetrated the barn. As Ben slipped a pair of white coveralls over his clothes, Pete opened the medicine bag and removed rubber gloves and a cold-pack with presterilized instruments and hemostats. He kept his back to his father and Morgan, not wishing to get involved in the tight anger between the two men. He knew his father was right but Morgan's subtle squirm of self-justification embarrassed Pete.

Watching the efficiency with which Pete helped his father, Morgan could not help but think of his own son and he knew that the anger in him had more to do with the death of Roger than with the bawling cow in the stall, but he couldn't restrain himself. He stared at Ben as he changed into the clean uniform and his voice was full of heat.

"This ain't no masquerade party, Ben. You don't need no fancy dress. Just pull that damn calf out."

"I warned you about a prolapsed uterus."

Morgan's hand slammed against the stall. "Tell that to the bull."

"I told you. That should have been enough."

"No need to get your balls in an uproar."

"Pity the bull didn't know that."

"Damn if you don't rub a man's skin raw. You're always jumpin' to conclusions, Ben."

"I face facts, Morgan. That's my job."

"Your shit stinks same as mine, *doctor*, best you remember it." Morgan bulled his way out of the barn and the door rattled behind him. The naked bulb quivered and Ben's shadow slid back and forth across the stallboards, a dark, elusive ghost hunched over a cow's pain. Ben's hands were gentle as he stroked the cow's swollen belly. He looked up at Pete.

"I'm going to need . . ."

"I know." Pete moved away from the wash sink where he had scrubbed his hands and gave Ben a syringe filled with anesthesia. "This'll calm her down some."

Ben smiled. Oh, Peter, he thought, you're just like your mama. You forget nothing. And he remembered how he'd taught Pete to use a needle when the boy was only eight years old. Ben had placed an orange on his laboratory table and given Pete a hypodermic. It's just like the skin of an animal, he'd instructed the boy, you plunge that needle quick and hard and there won't be any pain. And, oh Christ, Pete had stabbed that orange faster'n spit fries on a griddle.

"You want to do it, Pete?"

"Uh huh."

"You shoot her just . . ."

"Above the tail head. Gosh almighty, Pa, I'm not snake-brained, you know."

"Yeah. I know." Ben watched his son administer the anesthesia and he felt a pride and a warmth in the boy's steady hands. Well then, tell him, he thought. Tell your son what good hands he's got and tell him where they belong and tell him what they're for. To pull catfish out of the wide Missouri. To touch a girl's skin lightly and with love. To slide over the walnut spokes of a riverboat wheel. To wrap around a sweat-smooth stick of ash when the count's three and two and the bases are loaded in the bottom of the ninth and whack the horsehide into the blue, blue sky. And tell your son that tomorrow or the day after that or the day after that day when his hands are covered with blood from a belly cold-steel stuck, tell him that there will be time to wash the stain away; that his hands will not tingle forever with the killing. But Ben said none of these things. He said only:

"By God, you slipped her the old oskafagus."

Pete looked up quickly, his grin crooked with delight. "Hey, yeah! The old oskafagus. Boy, wasn't that a time though!"

"You really remember? For true?"

"Well, hell yes, I remember. You 'spect a man can wipe the Georgia Peach out of his mind?"

The Georgia Peach. Ty Cobb. The flash of his spikes as he dove knee high into second was silver-clear in Ben's mind. He'd taken Sarah and young Pete to St. Louis. My river town, Sarah had called it. It was where they had met during the early years when Ben worked the river boats and squirreled his dollars toward the veterinary college. It had been one of the good times. Ben loved the Big Muddy. He liked the reflection of lights in the water which haloed his own image and he liked the shiny brass of rudder controls and the thick hemp lines and even the brooms and mops which hung so neatly in their locker waiting for the tide. Finest of all was the infinite peace as his ship rode at her mooring near a bridge which would open to her whistle in the mornings. Pete had been only five years old when Ben had taken him and Sarah back to her river town to see the great Georgia Peach play out his time. Although Cobb was part of the visiting Philly team, the stadium had rocked with the roars of the crowd each time the old man had come to bat. He was one of a kind.

But, sweet Jesus, Ben thought, the shriek and scream of spectator had not been loud enough. Not nearly loud enough. Because he'd heard the sound. The dim and distant dying sound. It had been like a wind in the rigging. It had been Sarah. There had been a sudden stab of pain and a thin sigh had parted her lips. A sigh of such length that Ben had thought there would be no end to it. And, really, there had been no end to it because Ben heard it now and knew he would hear it forever. It had been the beginning of her dying. The doctor had warned against bearing a second child but Sarah had smiled and thanked him and, with soft assurance, had made light of danger. Through the rip and tear of membrane she had remained silent, her hair damp and dark on the rustling sheet, her head tilted slightly as she listened for what she wanted. The infant cry of birth.

"Charles Remington Custer," she had said, "it has a ring to it."

Three days later she died.

Ben stretched the rubber gloves tight over his fingers and then kneeled down next to Pete and the quiet, pregnant cow.

"Okay," he said, "I'm going inside now and turn that critter around."

The farmhouse bedroom was small and unfrilled and pale under the moonshaft. Lorraine's hands gripped the edge of the sheet which was pulled up tight under her chin. She had tried everything. Counting backwards from one hundred. Reciting, slowly, one by one, all the names of the children she could remember from her days in school. Mentally sketching the shape and size of leaves in the box elders near the barn. Methodically ordering her limbs and joints and various parts of her body to relax. And still she couldn't sleep. She wished God had a monstrous mouth and that he would open it and suck the moon out of the sky. The goddamn moon. She realized that she should turn off the bedside radio. The tune was an unwanted ally of the moon. They conspired together. "I Don't Want to Walk Without You." The woman singing had a low, throaty voice and she was unashamedly squeezing sentimentality out of the song. Her voice pushed and pulled at the lyrics, caressed and fondled and stroked the words. Lorraine removed the pillow from under her head and placed it alongside of her. She turned on her side and moved one leg over the pillow and then, angry at her own foolishness she yanked it from under her and heaved it onto the floor. It lay in the path of moonlight, soft and shapeless and mocking the memory of a lover's head. Lorraine closed her eyes.

Click click click.

Lorraine's eyes flew open. What was that? She lay very still. Listening. Had she heard a door open? Was it the night cicadas? She held her breath so that the sound of her own breathing would not interfere with her listening. All she heard was the radio. She switched it off. The room was silent. She lay back on the rumpled sheets. She closed her eyes. She pulled a light blanket over her head so she could shut off any sounds which might keep her awake. She took a long, deep breath and exhaled as slowly as possible through her mouth. She felt the tenseness in her muscles begin to ease.

Click click click click.

She threw the blanket off and swung her legs out of the bed. She curled her toes against the cold floor. *Click click.* As she rose from the bed, she slipped on a cotton robe and moved to the window. Outside, the box elders speared the sky. They did not sway in the windless night.

Click.

Lorraine whirled around. The sound was coming from inside the house. But where? She saw no movement inside the bedroom. She crossed the room and opened the door. *Click click click click click.* The sound was louder. Steady. Persistent. It came from down the hall. No moonlight penetrated the interior of the house and she had to squint against the darkness. Slowly, she moved down the hall. She placed one hand against the wall to help guide herself. She extended her other hand in front of her to ward off any unseen objects, things Dippsy might have left after a day of play, things over which she might trip.

Suddenly, she gasped.

She felt a quick sting on the fingers of her hand which slid along the wall. She pulled her hand away and held the fingers close to her face, trying to see what had caused the sting. *Click click click.* She heard it again. And know she knew it was coming from inside Dippsy's room. Her eyes narrowed and adjusted against the darkness and she could see a tiny band of wetness along the fingers of her hand. She knew it was blood. She took a step closer to the wall and saw that a small section of wall paper had become unglued and was curling free. The paper was a pattern of roses and the edge which had become unglued was sharp and jagged. For one wild and illogical night moment she thought maybe the roses were real and her flesh had been penetrated by thorns.

Click. Click. Click. Click. Click. Click.

The sound was louder. Steady. Relentless.

Lorraine edged up to Dippsy's room and her hand curled around the doorknob. Holding her breath, she pushed open the door.

Like the ghost of a white wolf, Jim Dandy drifted back and forth across the room, his short, sharp paw nails clicking against the pine floor. The white dog moved in a restless agitation from the open window to the bed where Dippsy slept and then back to the window.

Lorraine breathed a sigh of relief. There was, after all, nothing dangerous in the house.

She watched the dog standing at the window, his muzzle resting on the sill. He is like me, she thought, impatient with the night. And she thought how strange but consistent it was that an animal takes on the characteristics of those with whom he lives. She knew that she had been edgy recently and restless and without much appetite, and so too had Dandy. She had been fidgety and, she acknowledged, with some reason. Sam Hanks had delivered a telegram from the Army telling her that soon she could expect the delivery of a coffin, a coffin which held what was left of Tom Tower. Details to follow. Oh, Christ, she thought, it is all so neat and orderly and finished, finished forever. And without wanting to, she thought of what was not finished. She thought of Ben Custer's hand in hers as they listened to the clang of the train's bronze bell.

The cut on her fingers stung. She searched the pockets of her robe and withdrew a handkerchief and wrapped her hand in it and then moved to the bed and looked down at Dippsy. He slept, as always, absolutely motionless, his head buried under a pillow. Gently, she lifted the pillow and placed the boy's head on it. He stirred and mumbled something incoherent and as Lorraine watched him burrow deeper into his sheets, she stroked his head.

Behind her, the dog turned.

Dandy's eyes gleamed as he watched the movement of Lorraine's bandaged hand. The handkerchief around her fingers was wrapped loosely and one end of it hung down. As the hand moved back and forth, the loose cloth seemed to twitch and sway. The dog's eyes followed it. He began to blink rapidly and he was fearful that the cloth would move faster and faster and perhaps coil into a snake and strike at him and he was confused. The ribbon of heat which coiled inside of him and which he felt was crawling through his belly and into his throat where something awful was pulling it tighter and tighter, that ribbon of heat, his instinct warned him, was the same as the strip of white cloth which snaked toward him. He knew he would have to attack it.

His shoulder muscles bunched. His ears flattened on his skull. His lips pulled back. Although only slightly tinged with yellow saliva, his fangs still glistened. He took a step forward.

Click.

Lorraine turned.

"Dandy," she said softly, "Dandy."

And as she moved toward him in the night-cold room, she slipped her cut fingers into the side pocket of her robe. The handkerchief disappeared. The dog whimpered and then sat back on his haunches. Lorraine pulled a rocking chair to the window. It was a small chair, painted white and made for a child. A scarlet rooster was stenciled across the horizontal back support. Lorraine eased into the chair, silently admitting to herself a vain pride in her own trimness.

She stared out the window at the moonlit prairie. Jim Dandy whimpered again and then rested his great head in Lorraine's lap. Gently, with her unwounded hand, she stroked his ears, her eyes never moving from the September sky.

"It's the moon, Dandy," she said, "it's the goddamn moon."

The dog's rear left leg twitched once again and then was still. Finally the only sound in the room was Dippsy's soft breathing and the creak of a rocker.

And the very soft whimpering of a rabid dog.

Dawn brought the moan of doves and the soft bleat of a newborn calf. Pete carried the medical supplies out of Morgan's barn and walked leisurely to the pickup truck. He put the supplies in the truck and then sat down on the running board. He stretched. He yawned. He felt fine. The calf was a beauty. A real beauty with the long, wobbly legs of birth and an almost perfect white-star marking on her forehead. He guessed maybe the prettiest blue he'd ever seen was the gossamer sack in which she'd been born. Pete smiled, thinking of how gently Ben had toweled her off, and he knew that even now Ben was having a hard time taking his hands from her as he placed the calf on the straw bed next to her mother so she could suck. Pete looked at the early gray horizon. Damn, he bet this land was wider than the sea. Well, he sure God was going to find out, and quick. And of a sudden, his belly constricted in an unexpected pinch of fear as he thought of traveling toward the killing ground. Sitting here, listening to the soothe of mourning doves and cooled by the Kansas wind, it was hard to imagine what he knew was coming. He was not fooled by the flimflam of film. Hollywood heroes never died. Like all the other barrack boys, he had cheered the celluloid celebrations of flesh wounds and shoul-

der stabs and nicks and scratches; and, like all the
other barrack boys, he had sensed the lie. He knew
that where he was going he would taste the blood and
that it would be like rust rising in his throat. He wondered if he would come back.

"You okay?" Ben was looking at him carefully.

Pete hadn't heard or seen his father come out. He
glanced up and then gestured toward the barn. "She's
a cute little bugger, isn't she?"

"She's a cow," answered Ben noncommittally.

Pete grinned. Hogs'ld go to heaven before Ben revealed his heart. Pete remembered one eavesdropping
night when he had listened to Ben and Sam Hanks
as they shared a bottle of bourbon on the kitchen table.
They had been talking about his mother, Sarah, and
Sam, more than a little drunk, had said he reckoned
that without her Ben would have to make peace with
a tiny hole in every hour. And, as clear and clean as
ice, Pete had heard his father's short reply.

"You live. You die. You get through the in-between."

Now, perched on the running board of the pickup
and smiling up at his father, Pete hoped that Ben's
"in-between" had been filled with fair promise. Suddenly, his mind turned like a clock and ticked out a
name.

Charlie.

What fair promise was in store for Charlie? Pete
wished he knew the answer. He thought what a sweet
little son of a bitch Charlie was but how vulnerable,
so empty of confidence, so filled with hesitation. Pete
knew that given an event in which to plunge or
ponder, Charlie would cloak himself in the image of
heroes, narrow his eyes like Alan Ladd, hunch his
shoulders like John Wayne, hitch his belt like Jimmy
Cagney, tighten his mouth like Bogie and then, at the
last minute, weave some fine and foolish fabrication to
give lie to action. And each time that Charlie backed
away from deeds, Pete knew that he would see a flash
of anger or a swift disappointment from his father.

There's no steel in him, Ben had said, no steel at all.

Maybe, Pete thought, maybe, and he wondered if steel was what made a man. He guessed he'd soon find out.

"You okay?" Ben asked again.

"Oh, yeah," Pete said, shaking the reverie away and rising from the truck's running board. "I mean I will be if you ever come to your senses, old man."

"Like what?"

"Like feeding the troops. I got an ape roar in my belly."

"Think you got strength enough to climb back into that truck?"

"Don't know. Power's plumb gone from my bones."

"Could you maybe lift a fork?"

"Depends on what's on it."

"Uh huh. Wasn't thinking of anything special. Just one of those flakey things filled with red and the steam burstin' out. Nothing special, you understand."

"Couldn't be Sophie's raspberry strudel?"

"Could be."

The thought of the hot delicacy made Pete grin. He leaped to his feet, threw his father a snappy salute and scrambled back into the truck.

"C'mon, Cap'n, let's shag ass!"

Lottie heard the sound of truck tires spinning over rough gravel and she rolled her wheelchair close to the window of the bedroom in the ranch house. There was a spume of dust rising behind the truck but it wasn't thick enough to obliterate Lottie's view of Ben and Pete. Sitting side by side on the front seat, they were laughing. Lottie wished she could hear them. It would be a nice way to start the day. Instead, she heard Morgan's footsteps behind her and then felt his huge hand on her shoulder. The lightness of his touch always surprised her and she yearned to bend her head so that her cheek could feel his caring fingers. But she was afraid to bend. She was certain that her neck would snap like a twig of hazel.

"Sure in hell, he's gonna burn up them tires," Morgan said. Lottie could hear the sharp irritation in his voice. "Damn lot he cares," Morgan continued, "him a fancy doctor an' all, why, he can just requisition whatever he goddamn wants."

"Now, Morgan," Lottie said.

"An' that boy of his. Time he was jumpin' outa airplanes 'stead of squattin' in some barn. He's a soldier boy, let him soldier like the rest of 'em. Like . . ."

He stopped because he could not bring himself to mention Roger's name. He breathed deeply to inhale the fragrance of Lottie's lavender.

"It's peeling. The sun got at it and it's peeling," Lottie said.

"What? What's peeling?"

"You know." Lottie's voice was thin and impatient. "Him."

Morgan's eyes followed the path of Lottie's gaze. She was looking at the window, at the bright gold paper star pasted to the pane. One point of the star curled away from the glass.

And Morgan knew, in the hollow chamber of his heart, that Lottie, too, had been thinking of the scattered sinews of her son.

It was the time of day Ernst liked the best. Dawn had dissipated and the slowly rising sun yellowed the eastern horizon. Soon the dew would dry on the grassland and the whistle of the eastbound train would fill the diner with its sound of sweet loneliness and each man sitting at the counter or in the booths would pause, knife lifted in air, cup not quite to mouth, and tilt his head toward the sound, silently sharing the mysteries of a stranger's travel. The whistle spoke of long farewells and in this war land each man recognized the sound as his own. And, finally, when the whistle had died over the prairie, Ernst knew that each man would lift his eyes to the map.

Ernst had pasted the huge map of Europe to the

wall on the day war was declared. It was stained now from more than three years of rising bacon grease and buttered thumbprints and the dirty steam of dishes, but none of the men who regularly took their morning coffee in the diner had ever suggested to Ernst that he replace the map with a new one. This one map belonged to all of them. Tiny thumbtack holes circled and crossed and slashed diagonally across the paper terrain. These holes marked the victories and the defeats, the attacks and retreats, the position and progress, of fighting men. Along these pinpricked paths lay the future, or the denial of future, of the sons and brothers, husbands and lovers of Crowley Flats. After each night and morning newscast, Ernst would shuffle and switch his thumbtacks, methodically outlining the exact locations of Allied and enemy forces. *Ja,* Ernst thought to himself, without this old German, who in town would know of the safety or danger about to be encountered by those most cherished? It was when Ernst walked his fingers across the face of Europe that he felt most accepted by the prairie men. It was during those few minutes each morning and each night that he believed they forgot his Germanness. He was afraid to tell Sophie how fast those moments passed because he knew that she would accuse him of being too sensitive. Now, looking down the length of the counter at the men who sat quietly drinking their coffee, he waited eagerly for the sound of the eastbound whistle. He waited eagerly for the men to look once more at the map. At Ernst Jurgen's map.

At the far end of the counter, sitting apart from the others, Chet Beam wet the tip of his finger and turned a page of the newspaper and then carefully wiped the newsprint ink from his finger before he lifted a slice of buttered toast.

"What's doin' with Superman, Chet?" asked Pete.

"He's still flyin' around, citizen, savin' the world."

Caleb lifted his saucer where he'd slopped coffee and slurped from it and then snorted. "Any feller wears a cape like that, he gotta have somethin' wrong with his sex organ."

Chet ignored him as he chomped on his toast and studied the paper. An item caught his eye and he spoke casually, his words edging out around the chunks of toast.

"Says here they had a rabies problem over to the state line. Kid foolin' round in one of them caves an' a bat bit him." He glanced over at Ben, who sat next to his son. "What happens with a thing like that, Doc?"

"You're dead," Ben said. "You are very, very dead."

In a booth, sitting across from Virgil, Caleb turned sharply. His elbow cracked against an edge of the table but he didn't feel the pain. He looked at Ben. Then he looked away and leaned across the table. He spoke softly to Virgil.

"You hear anything from Emmett? Know where he's at?"

"Nope." Virgil grinned. "You know Emmett. He just pops up like toast . . . whenever he's ready."

Caleb stared down at his plate. He let his fork trail through the soft, running yellow of a fried egg. He lifted his fork a little and the wet threads of yolk dangled from the tines. Caleb was surprised at how much they looked like the stringy intestines of the buck he and Emmett had gutted. He twisted the runny yolk around and around his fork, watching little beads of wet yellow drop onto the table, secretly pleased that he was making a mess for the goddamn German to clean up. He put down the fork and leaned back against the booth's cracked leather seat and scratched dried egg from the stubble of his beard. He sucked a piece of bread loose from his gums and then, working hard to sound casual, he spoke.

"I hear tell you can burn out rabies. Ain't that so, Ben?"

Sitting at the counter with his back to Caleb, Ben shook his head and smiled. "An old wives' tale, Caleb. Only way's the Pasteur treatment. Twenty shots in the belly. But a man's got to get them right away. Any time passes, he doesn't have a chance."

Caleb stared at his cold coffee. He was very silent.

"You ever seen rabies, Pa?" Pete asked.

"Uh huh. An old man I knew. Cut himself stringing wire. Didn't know his dog was a carrier and when the animal licked his hand, saliva got into the cut."

Virgil clucked to himself like a tired rooster. "You sayin' a man could drop over from dog spit?"

"Hell," Ben said, "he'd wish to God he could just drop over."

Caleb wished his knee would stop trembling. He hunched down lower in the booth so no one could see it. He thought of Emmett painting his way East and he thought of how he'd held the burning stick of wood to the painter's hand. Well, shit, he said to himself, stop gettin' yourself all riled up. Emmett, he's a growed man. If'n he'd felt somethin' wrong in his flesh, he woulda spoke up. 'Sides, he'd been with Emmett and he, Caleb, hadn't seen no itch nor no scratch to the man. Lessen it was 'tween his legs and a man's always got a itch there. But when Caleb spoke, there was a tremor to his voice.

"I hear tell they howl like a wolf."

For the first time, Ben turned on his counter stool and looked at Caleb and he spoke very quietly.

"They got a right, Caleb. It's a lousy way to die."

Looking out the window, Ernst saw Sam Hanks leave the Western Union office. He had a piece of paper in his hand and he was studying it carefully. Ernst prayed that it was not one of those sonsabitching wires. There had been too many wires, too many gold stars, too many returned coffins. And each time it happened, Ernst dreaded the corners of the street for he knew that when he rounded one he would stare into some citizen's black, burning eye of hatred. Now, he watched Sam, and prayed away the corners of the town.

The little man shoved the paper into his black

bowler and then placed the hat on his head. He mounted his bike which leaned against the wall of the office and started to pedal up the street. He was moving toward the diner.

Please God, Ernst almost said aloud, *let me hear the eastbound whistle*.

The long narrow mirror behind the counter reflected the interior entrance of the diner and when the door opened every man in the diner lifted his eyes to the mirror. They saw Sam's black bowler hat and it was enough to make all of them stiffen. Not one of them wished to know what was underneath that hat, what message of doom was tucked neatly into the band.

Sam walked in and softly closed the door behind him. He hoped the click did not disturb the men. He wanted no sound to remind them of the pull of a trigger. Slowly, he removed his black bowler and his eyes, the saddest eyes in Kansas, swept over the men.

"Ain't got no wire," he said, "just come for coffee."

The slow release of a collective sigh was a gentle sound in the diner as Sam slid into one of the booths. He removed a strip of yellow teletype paper from the bowler and smoothed it out on the table in front of him. He nodded to the German.

"Ernst, you'd best juggle some of them tacks. News service just come in, says the Panzers are closin' in from the south. They're cuttin' our boys to ribbons."

All eyes watched Ernst hurry to the wall. Quickly, with the discipline of a general deploying his troops, he began to move his little tacks around the map.

"*Ja*," Ernst said, "*ja*, you see here? This is Arnhem. This is where we must outflank the Siegfried line."

"Radio last night said old Monty, why, he wants to cut Holland smack in two," Virgil said. Then he shook his head solemnly. "But that old boy 'pears not to done his homework."

Caleb snorted. "What the hell you 'spect from a goddamn Limey what wears a beret?"

Ernst's eyes clouded with worry. He didn't want

these men to dwell on the bad news. He spoke hurriedly. "It's a matter of the weather, that's all. You'll see. It will clear *und* then, then we can drop our troops *und* we strangle these damn Germans."

Caleb's voice was flat and cold.

"You don't know diddly shit, Ernst."

Pete started to turn on his stool but the pressure from Ben's hand restrained him and Ben's voice was very quiet.

"You got a quick mouth, Caleb."

Before Caleb could respond, the door between the counter room and kitchen swung open and Sophie pushed through. The men knew she must have heard their voices but her face was placid and she ignored Caleb as she placed a pastry tray in front of Ben.

"Raspberry strudel," she said, "fresh baked."

"How come you got sugar, *fraulein?*" Caleb spat out the words so quickly that spittle hung from his lips. He didn't bother to wipe it away.

Ernst felt the little muscle under his eye begin to twitch. "You think maybe we hoard the sugar, *ja? Nein nein nein,* we save all the coupons, we . . ."

"That is enough, Ernst!" Sophie spoke sharply.

"I asked you a question," said Caleb, "*fraulein.*"

Ben kept his eyes on his plate as he spoke. "This is one helluva fine strudel. I would surely like to eat it in peace."

Caleb twisted sharply on his seat and glared at Ben. "You some kind of a Kraut lover?"

Sophie's voice was a whip. "*Das Schwein einen sehr . . . !*"

"By goddamn," Caleb roared as he leaped out of his booth, "you Heinies oughta go back where you come from. An' if'n you need a shove, I'm jus' the feller can do it!"

Ben wiped pastry crumbs from his lips and slowly swung around on his stool. His voice was dangerously quiet.

"You looking for exercise, Caleb?"

No one moved. The only sound in the diner was the crinkle of paper as Chet lowered his news journal. A scarlet flush rose in Caleb's face and he took one step toward Ben and then stopped and his right hand moved to his belt and curled around the bone handle of a sheathed knife which every one in the diner knew was razor edged from an Arkansas stone and which, it was rumored, Caleb had used for more purpose than splitting gunny sacks of grain. But when he looked into Ben's eyes, Caleb let his hand fall away from the knife.

The silence was broken by a low chuckle. It was Sophie.

"Like my strudel, *Herr* Dodd," she said, "*ja*, your face is a raspberry like my strudel."

Caleb stared at her with such hatred that for a moment it looked as if he might pull his knife but he didn't. He whipped a cap from his pocket, slapped it on his head, turned away from Ben and clumped to the door of the diner.

"Krauts," he muttered, "friggin' Krauts!"

The door slammed behind him. And in the awkward silence of Caleb's departure, Ernst finally heard the whistle of the eastbound train.

Too late, he thought, *it comes too late.*

Charlie was late. He knew Dippsy was waiting for him in the wheat fields and that the young boy would even at this moment be digging the foxhole they had planned. They had scouted the area carefully and chosen a secret piece of ground which lay on a slight rise under bordering trees. It was a perfect place to observe the enemy and plan their attack. He hoped Mrs. Tower would not be too frightened when he and Dippsy fixed their bayonets and charged. He knew if he traveled along the road he would reach the fields faster than if he continued across the alfalfa pasture. But the war would have to wait. Charlie had another mission. He was in search of a butterfly. Each sum-

mer, before the alfalfa was leveled into stubble,
Charlie roamed the rows of grain chasing winged
beauty. He loved the smooth, slender bodies of the
butterflies and the way their vertical wings quivered
in the sunlight when they were at rest and the delicate black and yellow and blue and green patterns on
their gossamer scales. He had learned to identify the
swallowtails and monarchs and peacocks and tortoise-
shells. But his favorite was the alfalfa butterfly. Each
spring hundreds of them flickered over the field, a sea
of orange flutter, dipping, rising, trembling toward
the grain. During those days Charlie thought maybe
God had chipped off slivers of the sun and floated them
toward the prairie. He knew the butterflies were a
danger to the crop and so he never told anyone when
he saw them. He elected himself as protector and because of this he would examine the field in autumn
hoping that perhaps one small wing would quiver into
sight. He purposely ignored the irreversible cycle of
pupa and larvae, refused to give credence to the summer sun which burned life out of the eggs, shut his
eyes to the predatoriness of birds and, in general,
prayed against the plunder of nature. Each autumn's
failure to uncover a single flying chip of gold had not
killed the dream. Charlie continued the search.

Something glittered in the stubble and Charlie
skidded to a stop. Holding his breath, he leaned down.
But there were no wings to touch. Half buried in the
field was the rusted, broken blade of a scythe. Charlie
pulled it from the ground. He hefted it in his hand. He
whipped a red bandana from his pocket and wrapped
it around the blunt end of the blade to serve as a
handle. He tucked the blade into his belt and when
his eyes narrowed against the horizon he released the
dream of butterflies. He stood stiff and straight and
his hand rose in a rigid salute. His voice was crisp
and filled with courage as he addressed his imaginary
commanding general who was, in point of fact, an
alfalfa stalk, deaf and dumb in the summer heat.

"Cap'n Charlie Custer. Volunteering, sir!"

He listened carefully to the orders of the alfalfa general. He nodded once, never questioning the command. His hand snapped down, completing his salute. He did a perfect about-face and started to march across the short spikes of grain. And then he paused and turned back. He took three precise steps toward his general and his voice was unwaveringly brave.

"One request, sir. If I don't make it, tell . . . tell Pa . . . that I only did what any man would do!"

And, the rusted blade swinging in his fist, Charlie charged headlong across the field, swinging left and right, cutting the dead stalks in two and shouting over the prairie.

"Die . . . die . . . you Nazi dogs!"

Charlie was sweating and out of breath when he approached the Tower wheat fields but he didn't stop running until he reached the bordering line of trees which had been planted against the constant threat of wind erosion. He hid the rusted blade in the hollow of a tree trunk and then, a silent Kiowa scout, slipped through the woods. As he reached the edge of camouflage, he closed his eyes. He thought of what Dippsy had told him and he wondered if it was the truth. The boy had said that a cadre of United States Cavalry guards would deliver a special work force to help some of the local farmers to plant their wheat. The work force would be comprised of German prisoners of war. The prisoners were from the enclosure at Fort Riley and they were battle-hardened veterans from Rommel's defeated Afrikan Korps.

Charlie opened his eyes and looked toward the fields. A handful of men were clustered around a truck. They were all dressed in faded blue army fatigues, and stenciled on the back of each of their jackets were three bold black letters: POW. The bed of the truck was filled with large burlap sacks of seed and two of the prisoners were pulling them toward the open tailgate. A short, heavy-set prisoner standing on the ground at the rear of the truck flashed a baling hook and caught each sack at its roped neck and yanked it out of the truck. A fourth prisoner slashed loose the binding and then tilted the sack into the long seedbox of a grain drill. Charlie was riveted to that fourth prisoner. He had a lean, tough body with a hard, flat-eyed face. Charlie could see that his close-cropped blond hair was shot with gray and that a thin scar slanted down his cheek, its tissue as wrinkled and red as a fishing worm. The prisoner was whistling softly to himself and each time his short-hooked knife slit through the burlap he would break off the whistle and wink at the dark prisoner who had delivered the sack of seed. The thick-set man would grunt and grin in response but neither of the men broke the rhythm of their work. Whistle slash wink grunt and grin. Looking at them, Charlie remembered when he had witnessed a hog slaughter and he had a terrible feeling that the sack of seed would begin to bleed at any moment. He forced his eyes away and toward the grain drill.

The drill was attached to a tractor on which Lorraine sat. Although the engine was still idling, Lorraine's hands rested on the throttle. It was as if she were impatient to ram into gear and let the tractor surge forward. She was twisted around in her seat looking at the men who worked behind her. Charlie wondered if she was looking for the man who killed her husband. But then he realized that she wasn't looking directly at the men. She was examining the grain drill itself. Lightly, she leaped off the tractor and walked behind it to the drill. Charlie was fascinated at how easily she ignored the prisoners of war as she bent to examine the machine. Behind her, Scarface and the heavy man glanced at each other. Scarface moved forward.

Charlie wanted to shout out, to warn her, to tell her to run but sound was frozen in his throat.

Then she turned. She looked up at the scarfaced

man. He stopped moving forward. Silently, the German and Lorraine stared at each other. Even in his hiding place some distance away, Charlie could feel the string of tension between them. The German was smiling slightly but Lorraine's face was unlike any face Charlie had ever seen. It was distorted with loathing. It was as if two tiny animals raced inside her head and were clawing to get out through her eyes. Without turning her head from the German, she lifted a wrench from the ground near the drill and then, with her other hand, she made a gentle plea. Her fingers curled in the air, flexing and unflexing as if she were pulling the strings of a puppet. She was beckoning the German toward her. She was *willing* Scarface forward. But the German didn't move. He looked at the wrench in her hand and then he, too, saw the animals behind her eyes and his smile disappeared. He took one small step backward and then turned and retreated to the truck and when he slashed open the next sack of seed he was no longer whistling.

For a moment, Lorraine's fingers were a frozen curl of flesh painted on the air. She stared at them as if examining some stranger's hand and then a tremor ran through her body. Charlie thought she looked like an aspen leaf caught in an unexpected gust of mountain wind. Slowly, her eyes lowered and she hunched over the rear of the grain drill. She slipped the wrench over a nut on the axle, tightened it and then poked the handle of the wrench through a seed tube which was suspended over a sharp-toothed disk which would soon cut a shallow furrow for the planting. Kneeling, she moved along the length of the drill, poking her wrench through the series of tubes, making sure that the seeds would drop free and true on her next run across the field. When she reached the end of the row of tubes she paused for a moment. She put down the wrench. Then, slowly, with great deliberation, she ran her open hand across the sharp teeth of the last cutting disk. When she pulled her hand away, Charlie could see the scratch of blood across her palm and when Lorraine lowered her head, put her lips to the thin wound and sucked at the blood, Charlie was sure she was smiling.

Two young men in the uniforms of the United States Cavalry started across the field toward her. They were carrying rifles and Charlie knew they were part of the armed cadre guarding the German prisoners. Lorraine rose from behind the grain drill and climbed back onto the seat of the tractor. She glanced back once to see that the hopper was fully loaded with seed and then threw the tractor into gear and the machine lumbered forward. When Lorraine raised her hand into the air, the glinting sunlight colored the thin streak of blood on her palm into an orange rust and when she waved at the two young guards Charlie thought he might, after all, be watching the final flutter of an alfalfa butterfly.

Quietly, Charlie slipped deeper into the tree line and circled the field until he found Dippsy. The young boy was hip high in the hole he had dug. He had encircled the hole with strands of barbed wire against which he'd placed old bales of hay. A broken B.B. gun rested against a dirt wall of the foxhole, and next to the butt of the rifle were three potatoes. Charlie knew immediately that they were really hand grenades. Boy, he thought, that kid's really dug in.

But Charlie had been a keen observer of brave men; men like Robert Taylor in *Bataan* and Robert Mitchum in *Gung Ho*, and he realized how vital it was to be protected against a surprise attack and so he decided to test the freckle-faced kid in the prairie foxhole. He reconnoitered the wooded area in which he hid. A small, lower branch of a tree was rotted halfway through. Charlie crawled to it, using his elbows and knees and heels to slither belly-low on the ground. Quietly, he snapped the branch loose and then reversed his direction as he stole toward Dippsy. When he reached the strawbale perimeter of the foxhole he leaped to his feet, threw the broken branch to his shoulder and fired down into the foxhole.

"Pow! Pow! Pow!"

Dippsy jumped to his feet, his hand clawing at a potato, and a fierce snarl on his face. His arm reared back and he hurled the potato at Charlie. The potato caught Charlie in the middle of his chest and the brown skin split open and the mealy white contents splattered over Charlie's shirt. Even as he threw his branch rifle into the air and staggered, mortally wounded, Charlie thought, *Wow, the grenade was cooked*, and then he clutched his chest and spun in wild circles and fell across the barbed wire. It was a graceful fall, one which he and Dippsy had labeled a spindrop. Which was more difficult than what the boys called a bellybend-and-groan. That was performed in a slow-motion twist and was reserved for non-experts. Charlie was an expert. He did his spindrop perfectly, knowing that the younger boy's eyes would be judging him. Then he added a lurch-and-gurgle which was a subtle combination of body-jerk and throat-rattle. It was the last desperate thrust toward the enemy by an heroic but dying soldier.

He did not feel the barb tear through his denim pants and scrape his skin.

Dippsy waited patiently at the bottom of the fox-hole. He hefted another potato in one hand. If Charlie moved a muscle, he would have to powder him with a second grenade. Boy, he thought, Charlie sure could do a swell lurch-and-gurgle. He looked real dead. Dippsy studied his friend and, without being aware of it, started to remove the peel from the potato in his hand. He took a bite of the coarse interior meal. He wished he had some salt. He was munching on the grenade when he noticed the streak of blood on Charlie's leg. Quickly, the battle forgotten, he dropped the potato and scrambled up the bank of the foxhole and over the straw bales so that he could kneel by Charlie's side.

"You okay, Charlie?"

"Geez," said Charlie as he opened one exasperated eye, "Cap'n! You okay, Cap'n!"

"Yes, sir. Cap'n!"

"I'm goin' fast . . . better send for the sergeant," gasped Charlie.

Obediently, Dippsy spun around and raised two fingers to his lips. His whistle shrilled through the treeline and across the adjacent wheat fields. It pierced the rumble of the tractor engine and the whoosh of disks rotating through the soil and it rose above the grunt and groan of the German prisoners as they sweated seed sacks and it startled the young cavalry guards who turned quickly toward the woods and all who shared that single second of sound thought of the fleeting freedom of an eagle's scream. But there was nothing in the sky.

And on the ground, only one thing moved. Jim Dandy. The massive white dog sped to the whistle. He raced across the fresh furrows, slipping swiftly past the cutting teeth of the drill as he heard Lorraine's sharp cry of warning. One of the young guards crouched and spread his arms wide, hoping perhaps to be granted one quick touch of Dandy's luxuriant coat so that he might remember a sudden softness during the coming days of blood and pain. But the dog swerved around him and plunged deep into the woods.

"Goddammittohell," said Dippsy, "he's comin', Cap'n, he's comin'!"

Charlie started to giggle. Dippsy's swearing always made him laugh. And it came pouring out at the goldarndest times. Like when they had agreed not to pee all day long and then at the end of that day, they had met under the moon in the alfalfa field, each with an empty mason jar and each peed in his jar having previously agreed that whichever boy filled his jar first could have his pick of the other's bubblegum baseball-card collection. With a great sigh of relief Charlie had let fly and had heard Dippsy's stream splat into the glass jar which had at one time held plum jam or pickled beets. And out of the shadows of the moon had come Dippsy's cry of wonder.

"Jesus H. Christ, Charlie," he'd shouted, "I'm pissin' on fireflies!"

And so he had. Later, Dippsy admitted that he had been in such an all-fired rush to get to the field and relieve himself that he hadn't checked which mason jar he'd pulled from the bottom of his closet. It wasn't until he'd removed it from the paper bag in the dark alfalfa field and, at the same time, pulled his pecker from his pants, that he'd seen the wink of tiny lights and by that time he was flowing faster'n the Missouri tumbles south to the Delta.

Jim Dandy burst out of the woods and hurdled the barrier of hay bales, his tail thumping the air with affection. Dippsy grabbed him and roughhoused him over to Charlie who, in a weak and dying gesture, saluted the dog.

"It's all yours, Sarge," Charlie cried, "it's all yours!" And the boy flopped over into his final agony.

It was a superb performance.

Charlie Custer's acts of pretense were always superb. Heroic. Larger than life. And exquisitely in control. He was not a potluck kid. He did not welcome hazards. He did not trust to the chapter of accidents. It was not by chance that, in the war games which he and Dippsy played, Charlie constantly elected to enact the role of fallen martyr. With the unconscious hope that he might be able to stave off his own mortality, he chose to suffer a series of false deaths. It was as if he thought that on his Judgment Day he would be entitled to speak firmly to God and tell Him that he, Charlie, had died so often there was really no need to repeat the experience. But Charlie was unequivocally cautious in his portrayals of little deaths. He never put himself into real jeopardy. He did not wish to be betrayed by his own dramaturgy and, unexpectedly, find himself plunging toward that awful endless, silent place which he feared so much. That place, Charlie thought, where the mother he had never known stood listening forever for a sound which would never come.

Charlie closed his eyes and let his head drop low onto his chest as he draped himself a little more comfortably across the barbed wire. He could smell the bits of baked potato that still clung to his shirt but he made believe it was the fragrance of cordite. It wasn't easy.

But Charlie was an expert.

Jim Dandy leaped at him.

The dog's lunge was so swift it took Charlie by surprise and he was unable to keep his balance as he curved in heroic posture over the wire. He slipped off the fencing and rolled onto the straw-scattered ground and Dandy pounced again and the shepherd's head drove into Charlie's chest. Charlie heard the dog's jaws snap and it startled him because it was just a game that was being played but then he saw Dandy's tongue flick out and scrape across his chest and he realized that the dog was after the bits of cooked potato which still clung to Charlie's shirt. The thought of Dandy chewing on *grenades* tickled Charlie and he reached up and grabbed a handful of the dog's thick white mane. He pulled Dandy's head down close to his own and tried to whisper into the dog's ear about how he'd be blown apart if he swallowed one of Dippsy's handmade and very lethal weapons but the dog twisted away from him and buried his muzzle into Charlie's neck and tried to lick him. Because the dog's ears were flapping so close to Charlie's nose, the boy began to sneeze so hard that he had to wrench himself out from under Dandy and then try to get his breath as he lay belly down on the ground.

Charlie was still on the ground, listening to Dippsy laugh so hard that he was fit to be tied, and spitting out dog hairs, and gasping for breath in between sneezes when Dandy rushed him again. The boy saw the charge and curled himself into a ball as he anticipated the weight rushing toward him. The dog slammed into him, and because Charlie was an old friend, began nipping playfully at the boy's shoulders and back, his tongue fluttering close to the boy's bare hands which were crossed behind him. But Charlie flopped over onto his back and quickly scissored the dog between his legs. Dandy couldn't move forward but his huge head stabbed downward at Charlie's legs.

The leg which was scratched from the wire barb. The leg which was bleeding just a little.

The dog's jaws were inches from the open cut. His tongue, moist with death, flicked forward.

"Pow!"

Charlie heard Dippsy's yell and a split second later heard the thump of a potato grenade as it smacked into Dandy's flanks. The dog leaped away, the mealy grains of potato splattered all over him.

"I got him, Cap'n!" Dippsy was dancing with excitement. "I got the Nazi son of a bitch!"

When Dandy backed away, licking potato from his white coat, Charles Remington Custer, Don Quixote of the prairie, once again lay safely on the ground laughing at the memory of piss-drowned fireflies and never dreaming that soon he would be tilting at terror.

8

It was the mask of a devil. Crimson-skinned and
sharp-horned. Pete's voice was muffled as he spoke
through the thin, twisted slot that represented the
devil's mouth.

"Save it for me, okay?"

"Yeah," answered Charlie.

Pete slipped the mask off his face and tossed it toward the corner of the room where it landed on the
minutiae of his life. The room was a mess. Open
drawers tilted out of a bureau, their contents scattered
and scrunched. The closet door was wide open and
propped against it was a splintered hockey stick. The
corner next to the closet was piled high with broken
fishing tackle, discarded dungarees, dog-eared school
texts, torn photographs from *Field and Stream*, one
dirty sneaker with only half a sole, a spikeless spinning
top, and crowning the past paraphernalia of Pete's
life was the red devil mask which leered empty-eyed
at the ceiling.

Sitting cross-legged and very quiet on his bed,
Charlie watched his brother and understood, with a
sad reluctance, that the older boy was trying to make
light of his coming farewell. Pete motioned toward
the mask.

"Next year, we'll scare the bejesus out of old Virgil."

"Yeah," said Charlie.

Pete glanced quickly at Charlie and then turned

toward the closet and started to rummage through
boyhood junk. He kept his back to Charlie because
suddenly his eyes were smarting and he didn't want
Charlie to see that.

"Pete?"

"Uh huh."

"You think you'll . . . you'll be back next Halloween?"

His back still to Charlie, Pete almost snapped in
two the slender band baton he'd found on the floor
of the closet. He waited a moment before he backed
out of the closet and turned to face the young boy.

"*Next* Halloween!" He grinned at Charlie. "Why,
shoot, boy, I'll more'n likely be back *this* Halloween. I
don't figure on spending more'n a couple weeks cleaning up the mess they got over there. I mean to stop
the whole damn war and let Adolf himself come
crawlin' for mercy."

"Yeah," said Charlie.

Damn, Pete thought, if he'd just smile once, if the
kid would just smile. He kneed back into the closet
and found his old first-baseman's mitt and, after crawling back out, threw it on the bed next to Charlie.

"Think you can handle that?"

"Guess so."

"You gotta oil the pocket. Rub it in good. I mean,
I come back to any cracked leather, I'm gonna skin
you alive."

Charlie smiled. "You and what army?"

"Tough guy, huh?"

Charlie snarled his best Bogart. "Drop the gun,
Louie!"

Pete shook his head in admiration. "Damn, Charlie,
how'd you learn to do that?"

"I don't know. Saw all his movies, I guess."

"Do some more," Pete said, and he felt good that
the boy had regained his perk.

"There was this time in *Sahara*," Charlie's voice had
a bubble in it now, "and Bogie grabbed a machine

gun and he . . . he . . ." The boy stopped, a sudden stricken look on his face.

"What? He did what?"

"Nuthin'," said Charlie.

"C'mon, what did he do?"

Charlie looked away from his brother. He looked down at the bed and saw the first-baseman's mitt and he picked it up and slid his hand into it and then spoke very quietly.

"He got killed."

Pete thought he'd never heard such an awful silence as this room held. He rose from his knees and sat down on the bed next to Charlie. He wanted to touch his brother but he had a terrible feeling that if he did Charlie would loose control and maybe even burst into tears and he, Pete, didn't think he could handle that. At least not tonight. Not on his last night home when he was trying so hard to be nonchalant about the dangers he would soon discover; not tonight when he was trying to fill himself with steel and, in so doing, give pleasure to his father whom he might never see again.

"That was a dumb movie, Charlie," Pete said, "that's all. A real dumb movie."

"Sure," said Charlie. And he began to pound his fist into the pocket of the baseball mitt.

Downstairs in the kitchen which was under the boys' room, Ben licked white frosting from his fingers. He'd saved sugar against this day. He'd baked an angel food cake which was Pete's favorite, *and Sarah's*, and he'd traded this month's meat coupons for a thick sirloin and he'd raided Charlie's victory garden for the last of the ruby lettuce and he had hot rolls in the oven already split and dripping with real butter and he was determined to make of these things a feast to remember.

Ben crossed to the oven and removed the hot but-

tered rolls before they could flake black. He placed
them on the table. He was about to call the boys but
then decided that perhaps they had better be given
a quiet moment to themselves. Christ knew when the
next one would be. If there was to be a next one. He
switched on the table radio and dialed until he heard
the voice of a newscaster. He moved to a wall cup-
board and took out his bottle of bourbon and the
cracked coffee cup he always used. He poured two
fingers of the whiskey but when he heard the words of
the newscaster, he tipped the bottle again and added
another half inch. He leaned against a kitchen counter
and listened to the news.

It was bad. The Allied gliders soaring through the
skies of Europe on their way to Arnhem had been deci-
mated and there were rumors that the Germans had
captured Montgomery's battle plan which revealed
the strategy of Operation Market-Garden. If this were
so, the Germans would launch a swift and deadly
counter-attack. One could, said the dry and precise
radio voice, contemplate heavy casualties.

Ben heard a low, dull thumping overhead and he
looked up as he continued to sip his whiskey and
listen to the radio.

The British Second Army, the announcer droned on,
was dug in on the banks of the Meuse-Escaut Canal
and were preparing a drive north where they would
relieve the stricken First Airborne.

The thumping sound above Ben was muffled but
persistent and it distracted him. What the hell were
they doing up there? He drained the remainder of his
whiskey, put the cup in the sink, and walked out of
the kitchen. He was annoyed that he would miss the
further statistics of the current battle.

When he reached the landing at the top of the stairs
all irritation fled. The door to the boys' room was
ajar. Ben could see his sons. They sat, side by side, on
Charlie's bed. The younger boy still wore the baseball
mitt on his left hand. His right hand was curled into

a fist and he thudded it deep into the pocket of the
soft leather. And then Pete did the same. His right
hand, balled tightly together, thumped into the pocket.
Neither boy looked at each other as they took turns in
a measured cadence of slapping leather. And Ben
could hear their quiet voices.

"... And she used to take a carrot, you know," Pete
was saying, "and she'd carve little cars out of it."

They were talking about Sarah.

"You're kiddin'," said Charlie.

"Honest. It's how she'd get me to eat it. Boy, I hate
carrots."

"Me too."

"She'd say, 'Okey-dokey' ... that was one of her
favorite sayings ...'Okey-doakey, Peter, now bite off
a wheel.' Boy, I musta eaten a thousand carrot wheels."

There was a long silence before Ben heard Charlie's
small, wistful voice. "She musta been neat."

"Yeah," said Pete, "she was neat."

Slowly, Ben backed down the stairs.

Charlie's body tensed. He heard the creaking of
the stairway. He held his breath and listened but
when he realized that the sound of steps was receding,
was moving away toward the kitchen, he became less
rigid. But he cocked his head a little so that he would
be able to hear any further approach of his father's.
He hoped that Ben had not heard him talking about
his mother. Charlie knew he didn't have that right.

He had, after all, killed her.

That false idea was central to Charlie's cowardice
and it was what made him feel like a stranger in the
world. He knew of no others who had committed such
an act and he dreaded the penalty which he was sure
he would face one day. He knew the nature of that
penalty. He would die and go to that awful place of
silence where his mother waited, leaning and listening
for his arrival, and as he stood trembling in front of
her she would slowly lift her arm and point her finger
and Charlie would finally hear what he knew was true.

"You, Charlie Remington Custer," she would say,
"it was you!"

The accusation haunted Charlie and the specter of
the ultimate confrontation with his mother was a
source of terror. He had visualized it many times. He
believed that *the silent place* was inhabited by all who
had died. Not just men and women and children, but
all things. Animals and fish and insects and birds. And
in his fertile imagination he had seen that anything
which had once walked or fluttered, crawled or given
wing, finally hung like frozen smoke in the silent
place, each form waiting to return to its own hard
shape and feel the beat of its pulse. And in Charlie's
mind these people, these animals, these forms and
shapes had all been informed of his infamy. He
dreaded the thought of facing them, and he was
stricken with the notion that all who entered that
place would be privy to the abomination of his crime.
This supposition drove him to alter that which was
impossible. He tried to stave off his death of all things
and in so doing prevent the further ghostly broadcast
of his guilt.

Most of all, he avoided any jeopardy which could
lead him toward that silent place.

And he avoided his father's eyes.

Silently suffering an inappropriate guilt, Charlie
doubted the possibility of his father's approval and so,
self-protectively, pretended to no longer seek it. Unconsciously, he behaved in a way which disallowed
approbation from his father. He was forgetful and
careless and sought sanctuary in dream rather than
deed and in this way denied any opportunity of
fatherly sanction. In such a manner, he eliminated the
challenge, for if there were no occasion for endorse-
ment, nor could there be a decisive denial.

Punishing himself needlessly, Charlie Custer had
become an alien to his father and in so doing had denied himself redemption.

It wasn't until he heard his father's footsteps return safely to the kitchen that Charlie turned to Pete.

"You wanna know somethin'?" Charlie asked Pete.

"What?"

"I'd a eaten 'em."

"Eaten what?"

"The carrots."

"Well, sure, if she cut 'em into cars."

"Even if she didn't."

"Maybe."

Charlie didn't answer. He just pounded the baseball into the oiled pocket of the mitt and thought how wonderful it would be to sit in the kitchen on some cold winter's night, with the frost on the windows, and your mother at the stove, *like in the picture*, and he saw her turn to him, a plate of carrots in her hand.

"Will you, Charlie?" she asked, "will you eat just one?"

"All of 'em. I'll eat all of 'em. That's what I'll do."

"Oh, Charlie!"

And maybe, Charlie thought, maybe she would have reached out and touched him.

Well. Just maybe.

"German panzers have attacked and sealed off the Allied forces in what one reporter has called 'a pocket of death.' There's little hope that . . ."

Ben snapped off the radio. Seated around the kitchen table, none of the Custers looked at each other. Both Pete and Ben reached for the rolls. Their hands collided. Each withdrew as if seared by flame. Their voices held the courtesy of strangers.

"Sorry," Ben said.

"Go ahead," Pete said.

"Let me heat 'em up for you."

"No, they're great. Really."

Silence. The clink of knife and fork. Outside, an owl hooted. No one looked up.

"There's this movie comin'," started Charlie at the same time that Pete tried to fumble through the silence. "Did you hear the new one about Little Audrey?"

"One at a time," Ben said.

Pete waved his fork at Charlie. "Go ahead."

"No, you."

And Ben wondered how many departures were panaceaed by politeness.

"What movie's coming?" Pete asked.

"*The Phantom Lady*." Charlie's eyes gleamed as he thought about it. "It's supposed to be real scary. A guy uses a knife to . . ."

"You can live without it," said Ben.

"Aw, c'mon, Pa, all the kids are goin'."

"All but one."

"Gee whiz. I never . . ."

Ben turned to Pete. "Little Audrey?"

"Well, Little Audrey's brother broke out of jail, see, and so the warden put bloodhounds on his trail but Little Audrey laughed and laughed 'cause she knew that . . ."

"Her brother was anemic!" Charlie shouted quickly. "That's an old one."

"Damn it, Charlie," began Ben, "can't you ever . . ."

"I guess this is about the best steak I ever had in my life," Pete interrupted. Not tonight, he thought, please not tonight. Let's keep it easy and smooth.

And the silence stretched intolerably.

"Seared the juices in," Ben said finally.

Pete nodded with hyperbolic enthusiasm. "It's real rare."

"Not too rare?"

"No. No. Just right."

"Good."

Each Custer searched for further words and found none. The piercing jangle of the telephone bell shattered the tension. Ben leaped up before the others and crossed the room to where the telephone hung on the wall. Grateful for the diversion, both boys listened to their father.

"Custer here. Yeah, Morgan. Uh huh . . . uh huh. When'd your man find her? . . . I couldn't say without looking . . . Well, it's Pete's last night and . . . She was what? . . . Uh huh . . . Yeah, that's hard to figure. Okay, I'll check it out."

Pete saw the puzzlement in his father's face as Ben returned the phone to its hook.

"Mr. Crowley got trouble?" the boy asked.

"Sounds like." Ben removed a mackinaw from a wall peg and shrugged into it. "One of his men spotted a steer down at the creek. Got a bad bite on its neck."

"Why didn't he bring him in?"

"Tried, but the damn fool cow run himself into the brush. Funny, Morgan said he was bucking like a bronc."

"You going after him?"

"Somebody's got to. Somebody's . . ."

Charlie looked up. He'd placed an empty glass at the far end of the table and leveraged the handle of one spoon under the bowl of another one. He was preparing to flip the second spoon into the glass when he heard his father pause and when he looked up to see why, he noticed that Ben's face was drawn tight and there was a sudden weariness in his eyes.

"Somebody's always got to go," Ben said.

Charlie's eyes moved back and forth between his father and brother. They were staring at each other as if each was trying to memorize the other's features.

"Seems like there's not much choice," Pete said quietly.

"Seems like," Ben nodded.

"You want help?"

"Now when'd I ever need help with a damn cow?"

"Best you be careful, Pa."

Ben nodded again and when he spoke Charlie thought he'd never heard such a tired voice.

"You, too," Ben said. And then he touched Pete lightly on the neck.

Charlie looked away. His hand rose and fell and slapped against the spoon. The second spoon somer-saulted up and then splashed down but it did not fall into the empty glass. End over end, it tumbled into the angel food cake. Thick, sugared icing splattered over the table.

In the long silence that followed, Charlie was sure that he could actually feel heat from the anger which radiated from his father, but the boy did not look up. He waited for Ben's rebuke but all he heard was his father's whisper.

"Oh, shit."

"It's just a cake," Charlie said defiantly. "It's just an old cake."

There was no answer from his father. There was just the sound of receding footsteps. The boys heard the door slam behind Ben as he left the house and they remained still and quiet at the kitchen table. Charlie's finger traced a thin path through the white frosting. He lifted his finger and stared at the crown of icing and then licked off the sweetness. When he spoke to Pete, his voice was very quiet and he kept his eyes downcast.

"You know that honeysuckle down by the barn?"

"Uh huh."

"I got this thing I do to it."

"Yeah?"

"Uh huh. I milk it."

"You what?"

"Honest. I milk it. Those yellow flowers, they're loaded with juice and I squeeze it out, you know? And I been saving it in a jar and I'm gonna sell it."

"Ah, Charlie," Pete smiled at him. "You're crazy. Just a little, but crazy."

"Nope. I'm not crazy, Pete. See, that juice is awful sweet and I'm gonna sell it to people who want to feed hummingbirds. I mean they can put it in their feeders and all like that. I'll probably make a lot of money."

And, finally, Charlie looked up from the table and right into Pete's eyes.

"And when I do, Pete," he said, "I'll buy you another cake, okay?"

It was a long time before Pete could answer, and when he did his voice was strangely gruff.

"C'mon, kid," he said, "let's eat."

Together, the brothers ripped off pieces of the demolished angel food cake and began to eat. Soon, each young face was decorated with a mustache of white icing, and as they looked at each other both boys began to laugh and Pete thought, he's going to be all right, yes sir, Charlie's gonna be all right.

And Charlie, his mouth filled with sweetness, thought of the unframed print hanging on his father's wall and he wondered if the leaning woman could hear the sound of their laughter.

He wondered if that was what she was waiting for.

9

Sieg heil, sieg heil, right in the Fuhrer's face . . .
Spike Jones' fast-driving musical spoof almost shook
the jukebox into a life of its own. Cora Zink thought
she'd just about die if she had to listen to that record
one more time. She glanced up from the connecting
rod she was trying to cut in two with a hacksaw and
looked at the spinning platter in the jukebox. Well,
thank the good lord a'mighty, the record was about to
drop and right soon she'd be able to hear the real good
ones. The ones that brought tears to her eyes and
made jelly of her knees. The ones that made her go all
over tremble. She giggled to herself thinking about
where she liked to tremble best.

The dissonance of brass screamed to an end and
Spike Jones dropped from the holding lever. Cora
waited expectantly. A new record snapped into position. *Saturday night is the loneliest night of the week,*
'Cause that's the night that my baby and I used to
dance cheek to cheek . . .

Cora looked around the roundhouse. Shoot, she
thought, there's not a body here she'd do cheek to
cheek with. Much less the other thing. Ol' Virg, why
he probably still had a couple good ones left but she
bet he'd be snappin' his gum all the while. And Caleb
had heft but it was turnin' to soft, and she sure in
shoot didn't want to belly to belly with no fat man,
his sweat runnin' between. She caught sight of Sam

Hanks in the corner. Slowly, methodically, he was pulverizing a valve gear with a five-pound sledge. My goodness, Cora mused, he doesn't put halt to rhythm one little bit. She watched the sledge rise and fall, rise and fall, and her nipples began to harden. Whew, she told herself, girl you are in a bad way. Why, that old man would thump his way to heaven and never once remove his big black hat. But she kept staring at him. She thought maybe he would be one who would talk soft and sweet while they did it, and she knew that she had the pounding pelvic power to shake loose that old hat and maybe even take the sadness out of his eyes.

The sledge rose and fell, rose and fell, and Cora prayed that the drum of her pulse would remain silent. She noticed a wooden two-by-four sawhorse near her and she remembered how, when she was younger, she used to wheedle the local farmers into letting her ride their horses and she remembered just how it felt to grip the muscled animals between her legs and how she would spur the animals into a canter so that she could slip back and forth on the saddle, hitching herself close to the pommel in order to feel that hard horn drive against her.

She wished the young men were home from war.

She wished she had a horse to ride.

She decided to mount the sawhorse. She rose from her knees and dragged the long iron connecting rod behind. She rested the bar against the sawhorse. Slowly, casually, she straddled the sawhorse. She leaned forward and studied the iron bar whose one end rested on the floor and whose other end slanted against the sawhorse. She pretended she was figuring the most efficient way to cut through the steel rod. Her body bent forward and with her hacksaw she began to rip through the iron bar. The wooden crossbar of the sawhorse was between her legs and her body slid back and forth along the wood as she cut through the iron bar in front of her. She started to saw faster

and faster and her body slid to and fro in a quick,
hard rhythm and she began to feel a delicious heat
from the sawhorse's wooden crossbar which she
gripped tightly between her legs and, with no diffi-
culty at all, she pictured the tough young body of a
soldier boy beneath her and she believed, oh yes, she
believed that he was thrusting into her but even as
she told herself the truth of his flesh she, being a practical girl, prayed to God that she would come before
her thighs filled with splinters.

She did.

On the other side of the roundhouse, the cacophony
of wrecking tools almost drowned out the melody of
the jukebox. Men, women, and children were wielding
hacksaws, crowbars, sledges, and acetylene torches.
High above them, hanging from the rafters, was the
old tarnished brass bell of the locomotive. It was silent
now but every once in a while one of the citizens of
Crowley Flats who was working below would glance
up at it, and a passing stranger might wonder why
such an obvious grin of excitement would pass across
that man or woman's face. The stranger would not
know that the people of this small prairie town had
an agreement among themselves. That bell would not
jingle, tinkle or tintinnabulate until an ancient engine
had been pushed, pulled and pounded apart and a
dozen mounds of scrap steel lay waiting for collection.
But on that day, that great collecting day, a hundred
hands would rock that brass and glory would rise
from the Kansas land.

Caleb Dodd inserted the tip of his crowbar between
the steel plates of the locomotive's cab. He had already
pried loose the plates and he knew when he next hung
his weight from the bar the plates would tear apart.
He rested a moment, waiting to savor the sound of
ripped metal, and he tried to picture what these strips
of steel would look like when they were melted and
running hot and bubbly into bullet molds and he con-

centrated his inner vision so that he could imagine what those bullets would do to German flesh. By Jesus, if it were up to him, he'd order each and every bullet to be made with a soft nose so that on impact it would burst like a melon and send its murderous seed to all points of the body's compass. The thought sent a rush of heat through him and he swallowed against the dust in his throat. He looked around for the water bucket. He saw Virgil kneeling by the bucket, the tin dipper raised to his mouth. Caleb laid down the crowbar and stepped carefully through the mound of twisted, cut steel on which the locomotive rested.

When Caleb was only a foot from the bucket, Virgil raised the now empty dipper and clicked it sharply against the side of the bucket. It rang with a thin tin sound but it seemed to please Virgil as he grinned up at Caleb.

"Go on," said Virgil.

Caleb stared at him. "Go on . . . what?"

"You know."

"I don't know."

"I just knocked."

"What the hell you talkin' about?"

"When I banged the dipper. That was a knock."

"Jesus, you startin' that again?"

"Knock knock," said Virgil.

"Shit."

"Now, Caleb, it ain't gonna hurt you none. Knock knock."

"Gimme the dipper."

"Gimme knock knock first."

"Shit. Knock knock."

"Who's there?" Caleb was disgusted.

"Argo."

"Argo who?"

"Argo fuck yourself!"

For a moment Caleb thought about kicking Virgil. Instead, he kicked the pail and water sloshed out and drenched Virgil's pants, but the thin old man didn't

give a tinker's damn 'cause, by God, he'd suckered ol'
Caleb. Caleb was so damn mad he turned right away
from the pail of water, ignored his thirst, and started
back toward the locomotive cab. He was suddenly
irritated by the din of clanging steel and jukebox
song and when he picked up his crowbar he decided
to jam it home and tear the cab's steel plates apart in
one hard thrust and then get the hell out of the roundhouse and maybe look for Chet Beam and get himself
a pint of potato dew. He hoisted the heavy iron bar
and started his stab when, from the corner of his eye,
he glimpsed Cora Zink. He lowered the crowbar and
turned a little so that he could see her better.

She was motionless. Straddling the wooden sawhorse, her scuffed saddle shoes touching the floor on
either side of it, she was leaning so far forward that
her body was parallel to the crossbar and her head
was resting on it. Her long and fine blonde hair cascaded across her face and hid her features. Both hands
hung limply by her sides. On the floor next to the sawhorse was a freshly severed connecting rod, its cut
ends winking silver through the rust. Near it was a
hacksaw.

By Jesus, Caleb muttered to himself, she's plumb
tuckered out. Ain't right that a little kewpie like that
gotta sweat and strain over steel. Sweet little thing
like that oughta be plumped with powder and fuss,
oughta be stroked smooth and sashayed through silk.
He looked down at her limp hands. Why, hell, didn't
nobody think to give her no gloves neither? Caleb
swore. Put a callous on flesh like that, a man might as
well pluck a rose and keep the thorn. It was unnatural,
that's what it was. Young or old, a woman's place
warn't with hacksaw and hammer. Lady hadda know
two things. How to bake and how to fuck, with the
heat comin' outa both ovens with sweet distribution.
Damn world was tipped upside down with nothing in
its right place. Little girls rippin' their sweet flesh on
steel while their daddies got their asses shot off and

the friggin' Krauts hid sugar and drank real coffee.
Friggin' Krauts, they're all the same. Oughta line 'em
all up an' . . . !

A familiar and comforting fury rose through Caleb's
body and his knuckles were white around the crowbar.
Although he was still staring at Cora, he no longer
saw her. There was a glaze across his eyes and another
picture shimmered in front of him. He saw Sophie
Jurgen laughing at him. Once more Caleb lifted his
crowbar and he jammed it between the steel plates of
the cab and anger swelled his shoulders and arms.
He took one long, deep breath, held it tightly inside
him, then let it rush out of him in an explosive grunt
as he put all his weight into a jerk of the crowbar. The
steel plates tore apart. With one swift strike of the
bar, Caleb smashed them loose from the cab and they
tumbled clanging to the roundhouse floor. Breathing
hard now, excited by what he was going to do, Caleb
turned and let his eyes shift across the roundhouse.
No one was watching him. Slowly, he eased out of the
tangle of scrap and backed out of the roundhouse
door.

The moon was flat and white, like a paper plate
pasted to the sky. Or, Caleb thought, like a target
lacking only a black bullseye. Like many heavy men,
Caleb was light on his feet. He moved quickly through
the weeds outside the roundhouse. The nearby wooden
and rickety water tower threw a shadow across his
path and the ground underneath the shadow was
moist from the constant dripping of the tower. Caleb
could feel the earth squish as he ran across the shadow,
and as each shoe rose out of the dampness the sound
reminded him of a bass popping to a bug.

He didn't hear the whine of a dog.

Jim Dandy lay in the square of darkness underneath the raised tank of the tower. He squirmed un-
easily in the dark weeds and watched the incessant
drip of water. His jaws were open slightly and he was
panting. The dog was puzzled. He was aware of a

strange heat in his body and an unfamiliar, constrict-
ing rawness in his throat. He was thirsty and his eyes
never left the falling drops of water as they formed
a shallow pool on the ground. But he didn't drink. He
was frightened. He looked at the dark water and
thought how cool it would feel on his tongue but he
was imprisoned in his own hesitation. Each time he
bunched his legs underneath him to edge toward the
water, his body faltered. It was as if his muscles were
part of some vague anarchy. A single drop of water
plunked into the pool and Dandy winced at the tiny
sound and was afraid that the pool of water would
take some moving form and slide across the grass and
crawl into his mouth and choke him. He whined.

Across the debrised ground a door opened in the
roundhouse and the sudden flash of interior light hurt
Dandy's eyes. Quickly, he closed them. He opened
them again when he heard the man. He watched
Caleb slip through the wet weeds and turn onto the
gravel path which led to the main street of Crowley
Flats. Dandy thought of the comfort he would feel
from the touch of a man's hand.

He rose and followed Caleb.

Main Street was dark except for one light at the
end of the street. Caleb moved toward that light. It
came from the diner. In his mind, Caleb was a com-
mando advancing through the dark and silent hedgerows of France. Taking advantage of the wind-drifting
clouds, Caleb waited until one of them shadowed the
moon and then slipped furtively from doorway to
doorway, his eyes darting from left to right, checking
that no one saw his progress toward battle.

Ernst was alone in the diner. It was too late for
customers. He was glad of the solitude. Of the silence.
He was even pleased that Sophie was at the roundhouse helping to tear apart that old locomotive. The
townspeople would see her hard at work and they
would know for certain that the Jurgens' allegiance

was steadfast to America. Ernst looked at his map.
Black tacks outlined the dreaded Nazi forces. A ring
of them surrounded Arnhem. Red, white and blue
tacks pinpointed the positions within the black circle
of the British 1st Airborne and the United States 82nd
and 101st Airborne. South of the closing German circle
a line of white tacks arrowed up from the banks of
the Meuse-Escaut Canal. It was the British Second
Army racing toward rescue. But Ernst knew they were
outflanked by the enemy and they were stalled below
the south bank of the Rhine. Montgomery's plan to
make an end run around the Siegfried line had failed.
The intricate logistics of supply had been disrupted
by God. For that's how Ernst thought of the sky. Was
it not His walking ground? Why? Why would He
cover it in cloud? The Allied planes could not penetrate such sky cover and so good men would perish.
Ernst sighed. He crossed the diner and opened the
door and looked at the sky. He shook his head bitterly.
Here, he thought, here over the Kansas prairie, there
was light. Here, where it was not needed, nor sought,
was there light for vengeance.

He left the door open so that the sweet night air
could freshen the diner and, when he turned to look
back at his map, he failed to see a shadow move out
of its recess.

Crouching low, Caleb scurried out of a doorway
across from the diner. His eyes were glued to the
lighted window and to the man behind it. He looked
up. A cloud drifted across one edge of the moon.
Shortly, it would cover it and the glow would be gone
from the sky. Caleb slipped into a nearby alley. He
searched the ground. He found what he wanted. The
rock was large and round and smooth and it fit neatly
into Caleb's hand. Obsessed with his own image now,
Caleb put his teeth to one end of the rock and then
snapped his head back, pretending to jerk loose the
pin of a grenade.

Once again, Ernst was studying his map. His back was to the lighted window.

The cloud covered the moon.

Caleb raced across the street, his arm raised in a graceful curve. He lobbed the grenade. The rock crashed through the window, shattering the glass, and struck Ernst. It split open the back of his head and as Ernst fell from view behind the broken window Caleb sprinted down the street and was lost in the shadows of the night.

Ernst lay on the floor behind the counter. He was numb with pain. Blood ran down his face from the open wound on the back of his head. He had been holding armies in his hand when he fell and now the tiny tacks scattered underneath him and in front of him like thin colored paths radiating from a distorted compass. He tried to rise but he lacked the strength to lift himself. He wanted to reach the open door. He wanted to feel the cool air on his face. He wanted to believe he would breath again. He started to inch across the floor, pulling himself forward with his fingers, and as he wormed his way over and across his tiny armies, his flesh was pierced by the tacks and pinpricks of blood laced his fingers. He was almost at the end of the counter when, through his dimmed and cobwebbed eyes, he saw a blur of white slip through the door. Ernst stopped moving. He lifted his head a little and shook it, trying to clear his vision but the slight movement caused pain to flame behind his eyes and, for the first time since the rock had struck him, he moaned. The white blur moved toward him. It was Jim Dandy.

"*Kommen Sie,*" he whispered. "*Kommen Sie . . .* my darling."

Slowly, Jim Dandy trotted toward the prone figure of his friend. The great white head lowered and then the German felt the warm, affectionate tongue of the dog as the animal licked his face and his neck and his head and then flickered into the gaping wound.

As rabid saliva entered the bloodstream of Ernst Jurgen, he thought how wonderful it was that God had had the wisdom to carry comforting creatures on the Ark.

PART TWO

10

Ben was driving the cattle truck. It was a six by six with four-wheel drive and a wooden tailgate which, when lowered, allowed a large animal to climb up onto the truck bed. A heavy, coiled lariat lay on the seat next to him. He glanced out of the window and up toward the sky. He hoped the wind would grow stronger and push the clouds swiftly to the west, leaving the moon uneclipsed. He would need all possible light to find the injured steer. He wondered if maybe he should have hitched a horse trailer to the truck so that he could ride the steer down. He shook his head. No. He'd need the truck to transport the animal back to his barn where he could do an examination. Bucking like a bronc, Morgan had said, and run off into the brush. Strange. What had spooked that steer? Well, he'd know soon enough.

Wheat fields stretched across the land on either side of the road. He slowed down a little, knowing that he would soon pass Lorraine's farmhouse. He looked at the land he was passing and even in the shadow-sprinkled light he could see the progress of planting. He could smell the freshly turned soil where it had fallen back into the long furrows after the grain drill had passed over them. It was a good smell. A clean smell. Like Lorraine, he thought. She never hid behind perfume. She smelled of wind and sun and rain.

And once she smelled of smoke.

It was the day they had burned the barberry plants. Lorraine's father had packed his old Ford and gone to California. He had looked at his land of dust and diseased wheat and he had told his wife and daughter that it was time to search westward for something better. When he found it, he would send for them and they would leave Kansas to the crows. That late summer, Ben had returned from the Big Muddy, returned from the river boats, to help his own father during the short spell he had had before starting once again on the study of veterinary medicine. Lorraine had ridden her horse to his home and said it straight and simple. I need help, Ben, she'd said. I need help real bad. And she had leaned from the saddle and reached down her hand so that he might take it and leap up behind her on the old draft horse she rode. Together, they had ridden to the fields.

And she had needed help. The small, strangled plants in her fields were covered with a parasitic fungus. They were sick with rust, the grain shriveled and worthless. Goddamned wind, Ben had thought. It not only blows the land away, it sweeps the deadly spores from leaf to leaf. Come the autumn, the fields would be nothing but stubble and stalk and all turned black.

Mounted, one in front of the other, on the old horse, they had looked at the sad land.

"It's too late," Ben had said, "it's just too late."

She'd stiffened and her voice had whipped at him. "Goddamn you, we can burn off the bush. We can set the land on fire!"

He'd put his hands on her shoulders to calm her but when his fingers had felt the flesh under her shirt he had suddenly lost the thought of her as just a neighbor girl and he knew he would set fire to the land exactly as she wished.

They knew what they had to do. They rode slowly around the fields and marked all the barberry plants. These were the host plants whose leaves were plas-

tered with small cups filled with the deadly rust spores
which were so easily windblown. They mulched each
plant with dry twigs and newspaper shreds and then
soaked that with gasoline and they set fire to the land.
Red and yellow flame raced around the perimeter of
the fields and Lorraine had said the land looked just
like a hoop of fire through which a trained circus dog
might leap and then they talked excitedly about the
circuses they had seen as children, about the tumbling
acrobats and the slapshoe clowns and the cannon-shot
man, and the heat in their eyes came from more than
the flaming fields and they were laughing as the first
of the hail drove down on them and the black tunnel
appeared in the sky.

In the root cellar, lust had interrupted their laughter.

Afterwards, lying naked and unashamed on the burlap sacks, one of Lorraine's legs lying lightly across
his, her head resting on his chest, Ben's fingers gently
tracing the curve of her face, he had told her about
the girl he'd met in the river town. He had not revealed his attachment to Sarah out of any sense of
guilt or shame but, rather, because the thing that had
happened between him and Lorraine had been so open
and full that he did not want to taint the act with
duplicity. Lorraine had remained very still as she
listened but once he had felt the muscles in her face
move against his chest and he had been surprised because he knew she had smiled. When he had had
nothing left to say she had lifted herself from his body
and kneeled beside him. Her voice had been as un-
troubled as her eyes.

"You don't owe me anything, Ben," she'd said, "not
anything."

"Well," he'd said, wondering just a little.

"Pleasure," she'd continued. "It's not like some animal you can trap and put in a cage and visit when
you want. It just comes unexpected like, of a sudden,
and when it does, why it's like a nice surprise."

She'd paused then and when she went on, Ben remembered the hint of wickedness he'd seen in her eyes.

"And surprises, Ben," she'd smiled, "you don't forget 'em. No, you just don't forget."

And, of course, she'd been right.

Ben saw the single light burning unstairs in her farmhouse. He braked to a stop. That was Lorraine's bedroom. It had been her parents'. Her father had found work in California and sent for them but, by then, Lorraine had met Tom Tower and, together, they had decided to bring the land back to life. When her mother left for the west, Lorraine and Tom had married and in a few years the wheat grew taller than a boy named Dippsy.

Ben stared at the lighted window and hoped that Lorraine was not thinking of Tom in his coffin. He hoped she was finding some sweet solace from the light of the moon.

He released the brake and drove on.

He reached the gate to Morgan's grazing land. He climbed out of the truck, opened the gate, drove through, returned to relatch the gate, climbed back behind the wheel and started across the land. He drove slowly, the headlights of the truck picking up scattered cattle as he searched for the injured steer. The hired hand had said he'd seen the steer near the creek and so Ben headed in that direction. He drove with one hand, the other hand unconsciously fiddling with the coiled lariat on the seat.

He heard the running water before he saw the creek. He stopped the truck and turned off the engine. He switched off the lights and started out of the truck but when he saw that the wind had not driven the sky clean of clouds he knew that there would be spasmodic interruption of the moonlight and so he switched the headlights back on. He began walking toward the creek.

Most of the herd was bunched together. The cattle brayed softly as Ben moved through them. He talked quietly to them, calming them with small sounds. He

was a shadowy figure as he moved in and out of the
headlight beams from the truck behind him. He was
close to the creek bank when he stopped. He kneeled
on the damp earth. His fingers moved over a large
patch of ground. The earth was pulverized. It looked
as if it had been ripped and scarred by an animal's
hooves. Ben was examining it closely when he heard
the rasping bellow of the steer.

He spun around. He was almost blinded by the flare
of headlights but he saw what was coming through
the light. Haloed in the yellow beams, the steer
charged Ben. His head was lowered and his horns
flashed wickedly. Earth spurted up under his pounding hooves and he was bellowing with rage. Still
crouched over the torn patch of land, Ben knew he had
no time to run. A ton of fury rushed at him, hooking
with his horns. Ben saw the gaping neck wound and
then dived away from the charge. The animal was
moving too quickly to change his direction but one
flank slammed against Ben's hip and sent him sprawling down the damp banks of the creek. He was rolling
down the bank when the steer veered toward him
again, trying to reach him with horn or hoof. Ben
splashed into the water, his hands clawing at air. He
went under the fast-flowing creek and his rolling momentum carried him deep and scraped him against
the gravel bed and then he bobbed up, his head
breaking through the water, and he sucked in air. He
had one quick glimpse of the wild steer before he
went under again. The animal had not entered the
creek. He stood at the edge of the water, snorting and
pawing the ground.

Ben lowered his legs and found that his feet touched
the bed of the creek but his boots could find no purchase on the slippery stones. He lifted his legs and let
himself float with the drift of the current, knowing
that it would carry him around the bend of the willow
stand. The willow branches swept low over the water,
and when he floated under them he reached up and

clutched a limb. For a moment, he hung there letting
the current curve around his body while he regained
his strength. Then he pulled himself higher out of the
water and, hand over hand, worked his way down
the length of the limb toward the trunk of the tree.
When he felt his boots sucking into the mud, he knew
he had reached the bank and he lunged high toward
the level ground. He fell across the dry yellow leaves
and crawled under the umbrella boughs of the willow.
And he listened for the sound of rushing hooves. He
felt a moment of panic when he heard a dry, choking
sound but then realized that it was he who was making
the sound as he gulped night air into his lungs. He lay
quietly until his breathing returned to normal. His
hip felt as if it had been hammered on an anvil. He explored it gingerly with his fingertips. His pants had
been torn open where the flank of the steer had caught
him and he could feel the lacerated skin. His whole
body was drenched but he knew the wetness on his hip
was blood. He flexed his leg, drew it slowly across the
ground. Pain stabbed through him but it was dull and
with no knife edge to it and he knew the bone was
bruised but not broken.

   He had to find the steer. He inched his way across
the ground and when he came to the drip-line perimeter of the willow limbs, he parted the tender
leaves carefully and peered upstream. The steer was
motionless as he stood on the edge of the bank staring
at the running current. His shaggy head twitched once
as if he were going to stab the water but then he regained his stillness. His body was slanted away from
Ben but Ben could see the animal's neck. The wind
had risen and cleared the moon and under the white
light Ben saw that the animal's hide had been ripped
and mutilated around the neck wound and that the
dark slash was festering.

   Christ, Ben thought, what did that? It sure in hell
was no barbed-wire scratch. A wire cut would leave
a clean incision, like a knife, not this awful punctured

gash. For just an instant, a picture of Pete's baseball mitt flashed in front of Ben. Why? What made him think of that? He saw the graceful curve of leather and the deep oiled pocket and the rawhide stitching around the rim of the glove. He saw the curve of holes where they had been punctured with an awl and he thought how once Pete had joked that the mitt looked as if some animal had gnawed his way through the leather. Some animal. Through the web of leaves, Ben studied the steer. What animal's teeth had ripped with such fury? Was a wild dog pack roaming the prairie? He didn't think so. There would have been reports. A coyote. It had to be a coyote. But why attack almost two thousand pounds of steer? The land was dotted with lambs and pigs and poultry, the natural prey of a coyote's rampage. What had driven such a small and wily predator to violate his own instincts of survival? As Ben watched, the steer suddenly bellowed again and he shook his head terribly as if trying to rid himself of the wound and his front hooves pounded the already scarred earth and he snorted at the running water below him. What kind of bite inflicted such a trauma and turned the animal toward fierce aggression?

And then, with an awful cold certainty, Ben knew. *Rabies.*

And, although he was alone on the land, he spoke aloud.

"Oh, Jesus," he said, "oh, Jesus."

He backed his way out of the tree's protection and, crouching low to the ground, he sped silently toward his truck. He jumped behind the wheel, glancing quickly at the coiled lariat on the seat, slammed into gear and drove toward the creek.

The steer wheeled away from the blinding stab of headlights and bolted. The animal fled across the grazing land, zigzagging in convoluted patterns as Ben pursued him in the moonlight. The engine roaring under him, Ben whipped the truck back and forth,

using the headlights to blind and confuse the animal.
He maneuvered the truck as if it were a well-trained
cowhorse. He knew Morgan's land well and forced
the fleeing steer toward the northwest corner of the
pasture where heavy barbed wire boundaried the
land. When the steer stumbled once and went to his
knees, Ben knew the race was over. The steer regained
his feet and, flanks heaving with exhaustion, lumbered
away from the blinding lights but Ben gunned the
engine in short spurts and continued to drive the animal ahead until, finally, the steer was trapped between
the flaring sides of wire and the lights which burned
into his wild eyes.

On foot now, Ben twirled the lariat high over his
head and the twist and turn of rope sounded as if it
had set the air on fire. Ben threw. Swiftly, the rope
uncoiled, sizzling in the moonlight, and its widening
loop plummeted over the head of the steer. Driving
his heel into the ground, Ben yanked back on the rope.
The noose grabbed tightly. The steer bucked and
pulled against the pressure of the rope and the noose
only tightened more. Holding firm to his end of the
lariat, Ben worked his way to the rear of the truck
and threw two half hitches around the trailer hook
and then two more. The steer was secured.

Ben collapsed against the tailgate, doubled over
with fatigue. When the wave of nausea swept over
him and he vomited, he knew it was not caused by
the muscular battle with the steer but by the fear of
his own suspicions.

Rabies!

Lottie looked at the two men who faced each other
across the room. The anger between them was palpa-
ble and cold. Dressed in her thin nightrobe, sitting
stiffly in the wheelchair, she shivered. But it was not
from the cold. She was chilled by apprehension.

"You're no ranch hand, Ben," Morgan spat out,

"you're a goddamn needle pusher. I'm tellin' you, you spooked that cow!"

"That cow was bitten, Morgan. My guess is a coyote . . . a rabid coyote."

"You're just guessin'! You ain't sure of that."

"Not till I get the head to the lab. They'll examine the cow's brain. Until then . . . I'll have to quarantine your herd."

Lottie heard the ugly sound in Morgan's throat and for a moment she thought he might strangle. She spoke quickly. "Ain't you movin' kind of fast, Ben?"

"I hope to God it's fast enough, Lottie. Your herd drinks from that creek. They rub against the wire you've strung, open up their hides. They mill around, rub up against each other. Any saliva or urine from that steer gets into a cut or sore or scratch and it can carry through the whole damn bunch."

"You're a vet, for chrissakes," Morgan shouted, "you can cure 'em!"

Ben snapped back. "You don't cure rabid animals. You slaughter them."

"Why, you son of a bitch, I sold those cattle. I got a delivery date on 'em. I aim to take 'em to Kansas City . . . every goddamn one of 'em. Now get off my land!"

Lottie saw Morgan's hands clutch into fists. They looked like hard hammers of flesh and she knew they were capable of pounding a man into the floor. She couldn't stand the thought of that because then how could she continue to accept the light flight of his fingers across her pain. Straining against the familiar agony of her own flesh, she lifted her hands to the wheels of her chair and turned toward Ben. Her voice was a gentle plea.

"You'd best go, Ben."

Ben looked down at the floor. A puddle of creek water and sweat had formed at his feet and was soaking into Lottie's handhooked rug. It was a handsome rug, hooked in warm earth colors, and patterned with old Kiowa calendar symbols, and in the exact center of the rug Lottie had outlined the stone image which the Kiowa had worshipped. *The taimay.* The dripping creek water had darkened the taimay, had blurred its strong lines, and the strange thought occurred to Ben that, by standing on this spot, he had caused the disappearance of an Indian god. He remembered that many years ago American soldiers had killed all the horses of the Kiowa and that slaughter had delivered the tribe into bondage.

Lottie's voice floated through his fatigue.

"Makes no never mind," she said, "that stone. It'll come back dry. It always does."

Ben looked at her and wondered how she always seemed to know what was in a man's mind. He envied Morgan. He stepped away from the wet Indian god and walked toward the door. He opened it and he spoke softly, his back still to Morgan.

"I'll stop you, Morgan. Believe it."

He stepped out of the room, closing the door behind him, and when he heard the tiny click of the latch it was like the fall of a firing pin on an empty chamber. He was certain that the next rifle he held in his hands would be loaded.

11

Ben walked away from Morgan, from the woman in the wheelchair, and from the Indian god drowning in the rug.

When he drove home, he was conscious that the steer, hobbled in the back of the truck, was silent. And he was conscious that every time he shifted gears his torn pants scraped against the flesh on his hip.

He was glad when he saw the dark silhouette of the windmill which identified the swimming pond close to his land. His foot pressed against the accelerator and the truck picked up speed, but not before he had heard the sound of laughter from the weed-tree grove. He glanced into the rear-view mirror and saw a small light bobbing through the grove and then the road in front of him curved away and he saw only darkness and he heard only the humming of his wheels.

Lying on his back in the rear of Chet Beam's convertible, Pete thought that he heard the grind of shifting gears somewhere on the road. He couldn't be sure because Cora Zink's tongue was in his ear. She was lying on top of him, her heavy thighs weighted on his loins. He couldn't figure out how that had happened. He'd been on top. Couldn't of been more than a twinkle ago. He tried to reconstruct events. He blinked. Pink fuzz filled his eyes and he moved his head so that he would not be blinded by Cora's angora sweater. He moved his fingers and realized that he had a handful of mounds. Well, I'll be sumbitch, he thought, I've grabbed some ass. And then he remembered.

After Ben left in response to Morgan's telephone summons, he, Pete, had sat with Charlie in the kitchen for a long long time. Together, they had demolished the angel food cake, figuring that to do so would please their father. When they were belly-bursting full, they washed the dishes, dried them, put them away, dusted the table, swept crumbs from the floor, removed two mason jars from under the kitchen sink, raced each other to the alfalfa field (Pete being careful not to patronize the younger boy by letting him win) and dived after fireflies. Which had been hard to do because of course there were no fireflies. The season was gone. They had both known that but had pretended otherwise. Each had taken turns shouting to the other that by gum there goes the little bugger with his blinking light and, thrusting their mason jars through the air, they had dived head first toward what they knew was not there. Together, their bodies had thudded to the field and, jars and fireflies forgotten, they had wrestled across the spikey stalks.

It had been a way to touch each other.

Later, body frazzled and breathless, Charlie had collapsed into bed. He was asleep instantly, a smile on his face, Pete's baseball mitt on his hand.

In the silent house, Pete had pressed his uniform. It had been something to do. Besides, he liked to wet his finger and flick spit beads onto the hot plate of the iron and listen to them sizzle. But as he hot-creased his trousers into knife-edge, he had wondered why neatness was demanded as a prelude to death. He had been admonishing himself to stop thinking that way when he had heard the horn.

He walked outside, making sure that the door didn't bang shut behind him and awaken Charlie. Chet's convertible had rolled up to within inches of the porch.

He sat behind the wheel, his face flushed Santa-Claus red, his ice-cream suit as always unwrinkled, waving a pint of mash. Sprawled on the back seat, her saddle shoes pigeon-toed out the window, her skirt slid high on her thigh, Cora smiled at Pete and her voice coiled like hot molasses.

"We come to farewell you, honey," she'd said.

Chet winked. "Billy Lee Thompson and his Susan Anne an' some other hijinkin' citizens are settin' down to the windmill. You know, watchin' the blades go by." And he'd winked again.

Chet and Cora were drunk. An hour later Pete was, too. And now he lay on his back holding ass in his hands.

Although, like the convertible, the other cars had been pulled deep into the grove of weed trees, Pete could see their vague outlines in the moonlight and he heard Susan Anne's high, thin giggle. Then he saw a light moving toward him and he squirmed out from under Cora just as Chet leaned into the car, his flashlight sweeping the front floor boards for something.

"Jus' gettin' a little potato dew, citizen," Chet said, "go back to work." He pulled a handful of pint bottles out of the car and started back into the grove.

"Wait a minute . . . wait a min . . . wai' a min . . ." Pete hooked a weak finger in the air as he tried to call Chet back. "Gotta water the troops, ol' buddy." He fumbled for a bottle and Chet slapped one into his hand.

"That'll be five bucks, citizen."

Cora shot straight up. "He's a hero, for chrissakes, he's goin' to war!"

"Tomorrow," Chet said, "he's goin' to war tomorrow. Tonight he's jus' another hog at the trough. Here, I'll throw in some leg paint." Chet snapped open the glove compartment of the car and removed a small bottle of leg paint and threw it into the rear seat of the car. Pete was trying to pull dollar bills from his trouser pocket but his hand kept slipping down his leg.

"Sheeeeeeet," he said, "I can't find the hole."

"I'll help you, honey," Cora said kindly.

"I'll jus' bet you will," Chet smirked.

Cora stuffed her hand into Pete's pocket and yanked out some crumpled bills and threw them at Chet.

Cora hooked her legs over the front seat and when Pete raised the bottle to his lips he saw that she was without panties. He didn't remember removing them but he looked around and didn't see anyone else in the car so he figured he must have. The night wind was cold on his neck and he was suddenly filled with concern.

"You best cover up, miss," he said, "it'd be a helluva place to take cold."

Cora started to giggle. "Sure be one for Ripley's, wouldn't it?"

"What?"

"You know," she said, "if I sneezed down there."

They were both laughing so hard that when he pulled the stopper from the bottle, he spilled the leg paint.

"Hey," Cora said, "steady, soldier. I want me some leg seams. Paint 'em real straight now!"

"How high you want 'em?"

"Jus' as high as you can reach."

"Hallelujah, I'm walkin' toward the Glory Road!"

"You foolin' with me?"

"It's sure God what I had in mind." And his mouth covered hers.

Ben hitched the lariat trailing from the steer onto a winch and cranked the exhausted animal, stumbling and sliding, down the sloping tailgate of the truck. The wildness was gone from the steer's eyes. His muscles twitched and spasmed and his forelocks buckled under him twice before Ben was able to get him into the shed behind the barn.

Working carefully, avoiding any contact with horn or hoof, being particularly cautious to sidestep the slobbering jaws of the animal, Ben roped him to iron stakes. The steer's body was now in constant tremor and convulsion and his eyes were gelatinous orbs of pain. Ben knew what he had to do but his mind and muscles rebelled against the act. He was too tired. He had to sleep first.

He left the shed and entered the sterile room in the barn which served as his clinic. He scrubbed his hands and face with carbolic soap and then painted the lacerated skin on his hip with a stinging disinfectant. He stripped off his torn, wet clothes and threw them into a corner along with the boots he had removed. He would burn them in the morning. If he were right, if the steer did have rabies, he would have to make dead certain that any contaminated articles were destroyed. He put on clean white coveralls and a pair of old sneakers and turned out the light. He turned toward the door and then was arrested by the shine of an object. A thin shaft of moonlight pierced the window. It fell across a tray of instruments which rested on the operating table. Propped against the tray was a surgical saw, its cutting teeth silvery in the light.

I will pick it up soon enough, Ben thought, and then walked out of the clinic.

When he reached the landing at the top of the stairs, he eased open the door to the boys' room. He wanted to look at Pete while he slept, while innocence was still on his face. Ben knew how soon that face would change. But the boy was not sleeping. He was not in the room. The blankets on his bed were undisturbed, pulled drum-tight as the army had taught. Ben looked at the other bed. Charlie was dreaming. His eyelids fluttered over secret pictures. One arm lay outside the blankets and, on his hand, Charlie wore the baseball mitt.

In the stillness of the room, Ben studied the young boy. Through what world was he racing in his dreams? From what was he running? Strange, Ben thought, strange that when I think of this boy, I always think of the space around him. It is as if Charlie is constantly suspended, floating, drifting, moving untouched through the air. And always moving away, away from stone or substance. He is as elusive as the spindrift of the sea.

Charlie stirred. His head tilted slightly as if he were listening to a secret.

Quickly, Ben closed the door.

He walked toward the witness tree. He hoped he would find Pete there. It was the place where, for one hundred years, men had sought solitude and solace. At least Ben thought of it as such a place. The Burr oak stood at the far end of the alfalfa field. Over one hundred years old, its massive, gnarled branches witched over the prairie like the limbs of druids. Not a single tree stood near it. It reared in splendid isolation. No one knew who had planted it or if its original seed had been borne by the wind. No one cared. It was enough that it was there. It gave credence to the past. It gave truth to the future.

It marked a corner of Custer land. Beyond it, to the north and to the east, stretched the Tower wheat fields. As his canvas shoes slid silently over stubble and stalk, Ben remembered that long-ago day with his grandfather. He had been a little boy when, hand in hand, they had walked to the tree. He had sat among the acorns and listened to the old man. His grandfather had read the deed to the land and the boy had never forgotten the words.

Let this oak bear witness that so long as the rivers shall run and so long as the fruit of this tree shall lay on the earth, for that long shall this land be yours.

And then the old man had told the boy that the oak was a favorite of Thor's, the god of the people, who was as fearless as thunder. His grandfather had told Ben that Thor's magical hammer had been made from oak; the hammer which, after being thrown by Thor, would always return to the hand of that god. The tree was a symbol of strength, the old man had continued, and any man sitting underneath its boughs would be cleansed of fear.

On the night Sarah died, Ben had sat under the tree. Later, he had taken Peter to the oak and told him of Thor.

Ben smelled whiskey and vomit under the witness tree. Pete lay on a bed of acorns, his eyes closed. Quietly, Ben parted the boughs and sat down next to his son.

"I'm not asleep," the boy said. "I wish I was."

Ben picked up two small acorns and juggled them in his fingers and said nothing.

"Damn," Pete said, opening his eyes and looking directly at his father, "damn damn damn. I'm scared."

"I know," Ben said, "me too."

"Not you," Pete said, "not ever you."

"You're wrong, Peter." And Ben told him about the steer. When Ben was finished, Pete lifted himself onto his elbow.

"What about the herd?" he asked.

"I'll have them quarantined."

"If you're right . . . if it is rabies?"

"I'll slaughter them."

"Jesus."

Ben spoke very slowly, needing his son to understand their common future.

"Killing stinks, Pete. Killing anything. A cow or coyote . . . or a man. It all stinks. But you live with it. You never forget it. But you live with it. Will you remember that?"

After a while, Pete nodded.

"I wish there was something I could do," he said.

"There is," Ben said.

"What?"

"Come back."

Neither boy nor man moved and the clicking of the acorns in Ben's fingers and the sough of the prairie wind were the only sounds in the night.

12

They clustered around the old and rusted oil drum and watched the smoke spiral toward the sky. The smoke was acrid and as white as the dawn. Ben had soaked his jacket and pants and boots in gasoline and stuffed them deep into the incinerator and then thrown a lighted match onto the dripping mass. The clothes had exploded with a soft whomp and flames had leaped out of the drum.

Their flickering light threw a soft glow across the faces of Ben's sons. Pete and Charlie stood side by side at the burning. Pete was wearing his dress uniform and his stuffed duffel bag lay on the ground by his feet. He was ready to go. His marksmanship medal shone with a newly rubbed brilliance and the creases of his trousers were stiletto sharp. There was not a fleck of dust on his boots. Ben looked through the rising smoke toward Charlie. The boy was terribly still, his head cocked away from the fire, his eyes on some distant point of the horizon. He's listening again, thought Ben, and then he knew why.

He heard the far-away whistle of the train.

"I guess," said Pete, "I guess it's time."

"I guess," said Ben.

None of them said a word on the drive to the depot.

Steam hissed from the engine. The elderly engineer thrust his arm out of the locomotive cab. An ancient pocket watch was in his hand. He moved the face of

the watch out of the path of steam and studied the
dial and then, with his other hand, pulled down hard
on the whistle chain. The whistle was shrill in the
morning air. The iron wheels began to rumble as the
train edged forward.

Quickly, Pete crouched down next to Charlie.

"Listen," he said, "you take care of yourself, you
little sumbitch, you hear?"

In a quick and awkward gesture, Pete's arms
wrapped around Charlie and he hugged the boy but
Charlie couldn't answer because the tears were starting. There was another sharp blast from the locomotive and Pete wheeled toward it.

"All right, goddamn it!"

He turned to face his father. "Pa . . . I just . . . oh,
shit . . . I just want you to know . . . oh, Jesus . . ."

The whistle blast was louder now and the wheels
churned and clanked against the rails and as the train
picked up speed a cloud of steam ballooned over the
depot. Pete ran and swung himself up the steps of the
train and he was hanging by one hand as he sped
away from Crowley Flats, his face lost in thick white
vapor as he shouted to his father.

"I love you!"

And then he was gone.

Ben closed his eyes, unable to speak.

All the way home Charlie tried to think of something to say to his father. Sitting next to him in the
pickup, he sneaked glances at Ben but nothing came
to mind. Like a phantom, Pete rode between them.
Charlie felt as if he were rubbing shoulders with a
ghost. He scrunched hard against the door of the truck
and tried to remain as still as possible so that he would
not disturb his father. He closed his eyes but opened
them quickly because the picture of Pete's face swallowed by steam floated before him. He looked out the
window. Stirred by the vacuum wind of the truck,
dry goldenrod quivered in the roadside ditch. The

stalks looked like the weave of striking snakes. He thought of the hognose snake he and Pete had found. They had been hiking down a summer road when they heard the hiss. Coiled in the dust, the western hognose had frightened Charlie. He had leaped back, away from the danger, but Pete had picked up a stick and prodded the snake and had told Charlie that if he watched carefully he would see something sure God funny. Pete had waved the stick close to the nose of the snake and the hognose had hissed one more time and then rolled over and played dead. It was, Pete had said, how the hognose protected itself. It was a game they played.

Charlie wondered if, in the game Pete was about to play, he could just roll over and play dead.

He was thinking about this when the truck rolled to a stop outside the barn. Without a word, Ben got out of the truck and started toward the shed. Staying a few feet behind, Charlie followed. They had parked alongside of Charlie's victory garden. Most of it had gone to seed now but it was still greened by lettuce. At the far end of the garden was a scarecrow. Charlie had dressed it to resemble Adolf Hitler. There was even a face mask with a toothbrush mustache and its cottonball head wore a paper bag which had been cut into the shape of a German helmet, water-painted dark green. Charlie had angled the broom-handle arm into a Nazi salute. It was a fearful jest which had rid the garden of crows. Charlie looked at it for a moment and then called to Ben.

"Pa?"

Ben kept on walking toward the shed. "I got something to do, Charlie. It best be done alone."

"The thing is," Charlie shouted, "can't nuthin' hurt Pete."

Ben turned. "That so?"

"That's so, Pa, I swear!" Charlie saw that he had his father's attention now and he wanted to hold onto it, to feel it wash over him like rain. He ran into the

garden and up to the scarecrow and tweaked it by its
clothespin nose. "See . . . I put a . . . a magic curse
on old Adolf here and before you know it . . . why, all
those Nazi fellas'll be wavin' a white flag so hard . . . .
their arms'll likely drop off. Ol' Pete . . . he'll capture
the whole kit and kaboodle of 'em . . . and come home
a general . . . and there'll be this great big parade
an' . . ."

"Charlie."

Charlie didn't know if his father was asking him a
question or just saying his name but there was something in Ben's tone that made Charlie stop talking
and, slowly, he let his hand slip from the scarecrow's
nose. He watched as Ben walked into the garden and
then crouched down and ran his fingers across the
heads of lettuce.

"Charlie?" Ben asked, "you think this lettuce grows
'cause of magic?"

"Course not."

"Then what makes it grow?"

"You know," Charlie said, weighing his words carefully, "water . . . and sun . . . and . . . things."

"Not . . . things . . . Charlie. Cow shit. You get your
hands knuckle-deep in cow shit and one day you have
a garden. But all the magic in the world'll just give
you an acre of weeds. And that's how it is."

Ben stood up and turned away from the scarecrow
and from his son and walked out of the garden and
into the shed. He walked like an old man. Charlie sat
down at the straw feet of the scarecrow. He picked
up a handful of dirt. He let it dribble out between his
fingers.

"Cow shit," he said.

Then he heard the rifle shot and he ran.

13

"Ain't no point gettin' rump-raw," the woman said and she slid a calico cushion between herself and the hard wooden bench in the Grange Hall.

Lorraine laughed. She liked Willie Mae. Everybody liked Willie Mae. She was a big, raw-boned woman in her fifties who always spoke her mind true and quick. Her hands were callous-thick and big as a man's. She could scythe a mowing faster than most men and she took a perverse delight in challenging any who didn't believe it. It had been a long time since anyone in Crowley Flats had dared to risk his reputation by matching his curved blade, swing for swing, against Willie Mae in the fields. Lorraine was glad that Willie Mae was her partner this morning in the Grange.

Because of the absence of men, farming women like Lorraine and Willie Mae were locked to their land by chores. But during these war years, there was a common need among the prairie women to contribute something extra to a community effort. They had talked among themselves and, without ever articulating it in words, had sidled up to the fact of their own loneliness. Willie Mae had suggested the solution.

"What we need is sharin' time," she'd said. "And it got to have purpose. Land's too wide to hang clothesline to natter over one to other but we ain't no different from sisters in the city. We got to have us a woman time, a sharin' time. But it got to have reason to it."

A town's lady had suggested a sewing bee but no one had agreed on what to sew. A rancher woman'd thought putting up preserves together might be a good thing. Plum jelly and raspberries and spiced apples. Her round, impatient eyes rolling toward the Grange ceiling, Willie Mae had asked where in tarnation they were going to get the sugar.

The women had gathered on a Sunday. They had had a tacit understanding that, after silently listening to the sermon, they would leave the church (to which most had shared rides on their tractors, carefully clutching gingham and lace away from oil spill) and congregate in the Grange. Acknowledged as their leader, Willie Mae had sat at the head of a long wooden table. The other women had been seated on the equally hard flanking benches. In the quiet that ensued after Willie Mae's dismissal of preserves, she had looked down the length of the table and listened to the cricket clicking of knitting needles. She was the only woman without wool. She had thought of her husband, a Seabee on Saipan, a man without need of sweater or scarf. But, she had thought, there are other things he might one day need.

"Bandages," she'd said, "we'll roll bandages."

Because of the constant care of crops and chickens and hogs, none of the farm women could devote full time to their shared activity. Two by two, they took turns. In pairs, they ripped open the large cardboard containers, removed pounds of gauze, cut it into varying lengths and widths, and rolled these strips tightly into neat white cylinders, pretending to ignore the fact that one day the porous cloth might soak up the blood of a brother.

"Thought you was rollin' next week," muttered Willie Mae, her snipping scissors almost hidden in her huge hands. Lorraine cocked her head toward the words and measured the sound. Sometimes, it was difficult to understand Willie Mae. She was forever chewing on the end of a wooden kitchen match and her words were like splinters spit from her lips.

"Yeah," answered Lorraine, "was to be next week but Morgan, he promised the drill to George Carter. What with sheriffing and all, that man's way behind in seed."

"Ain't fair." This time Willie Mae spat real splinters.

"Now, Willie Mae, he's kin to Morgan. You can't blame him."

"Ain't fair we don't got us our own drill, that's what I'm sayin'."

Lorraine sighed. She knew how Willie Mae hated to be beholden to anyone. "It works out," she said, "one way or t'other, it works out."

The arrangement between Morgan Crowley and the wheat farmers was a way of life in Crowley Flats. Only Willie Mae questioned it and that, Lorraine mused, was because of her orneriness of spirit. Morgan, with his huge beef spread, was the only man rich enough to own the massive machinery needed to sow and harvest the fields. He did not charge a fee for the loan of his drills and combines. He gave freely of them, insisting only that each farmer had fair turn. Although most of the farmers avoided mention of it, they recognized that Morgan's gesture did not come as much from a generosity of spirit as it did from a useful reciprocation.

Each year, a prairie farmer sensed the urgency of autumn. It was the time of sowing. Lorraine always thought of it as the days of Turkey Red. That was the name of the winter wheat originally sowed on the prairie. She did what others did during Turkey Red. She watched the skies. She tasted soil. She cursed the wind. And knowing that the weather would allow her only a few special weeks in which to sow, she made her judgment and called Morgan for his drill. If the wheat was not furrowed to the land in time, the spring fields would be barren.

Morgan never failed to deliver his grain drills. He realized the symbiosis of cattle and crop. By late autumn, row after row of tender shoots sprouted into green stalk. This was the fearful time for the farmers of winter wheat. It was essential to hold back the growth of grain so that the young stalks would not blossom too early and be killed by the coming winter. They needed to impede growth so that the wheat would not ripen until spring. Morgan insured their success. He opened the gates of his grazing land and the Hereford herds walked over the new wheat and nibbled the danger away. And the steers retained their fat for market day. This profitable arrangement was the underpinning legs of the town's economic table. It provided a cash flow for Virgil's gas station and Caleb's feed and grain store and Beetle-browed Bessie's picture show house and Ernst's diner and the barber shop and the grocery store and, as Morgan was wont to point out, the etceteras of the prairie.

Everybody in Crowley Flats was happy.

Clipping and rolling, the two women worked in a companionable silence. Neither of them gave much weight to gossip. They were content to share each other's presence in the lonely early hours. Lorraine ran out of gauze and started across the Grange toward the stack of cardboard boxes.

"You taste that new coffee down to the store?" asked Willie Mae. "I swear it's pure chicory."

"Uh huh."

"I swan, somedays I think this war'll never end."

"It'll end."

"I guess."

"You feelin' fit for song?"

"Whatever."

Lorraine hunkered down by the old Emerson console radio in the corner and turned it on. An announcer's adenoidal voice droned out the price of commodities and monotonized about soybean futures. Lorraine fiddled with the dials until song floated out.

I got spurs that jingle jangle jingle.

"Whatever happened to the good ones?" asked Willie Mae. "You know, 'Missouri Waltz' and the like? I just can't stand me these new-fangled bouncy things. They ain't fit for dance."

Lorraine didn't bother to answer. It wasn't required. A fresh carton of gauze in her hands, she stood at the window and looked down the street. In the distance, she could see the diner and its shattered window. Ernst was plastering tape across the window to hold the broken pieces in place. On the back of his bald head was a neat white bandage.

"You see the Jurgen place?" Lorraine asked Willie Mae.

"Ummm. Window's busted somethin' fierce."

"How come?"

"Don't know. Sam Hanks, he said Ernst had hisself an accident."

"I can see that. Serious?"

"Don't guess so. Sam, he said they're servin' like always."

Lorraine saw Ernst walk away from the window and lean down. He picked up two bowls of scrap meat and placed them by the latticed garbage bins and then began to clap his hands in a continual beat. He was too far away for Lorraine to hear the sound of his hands but she knew he was calling his strays. It was only a moment before a small, fur-matted mongrel slipped around the corner of the diner and nosed his way to the bowls. Ernst patted him and then turned back to the diner. He opened the door but paused before he went in. He leaned against the door jamb, his chin lowered to his chest as if his head were too much weight to carry and he wiped his face with one hand.

He is a kind man who sweats too much, Lorraine thought, as the door, soundless in the distance, slapped shut behind him. And then she spoke aloud.

"Well, damn me."

"What?" asked Willie Mae.

"Dandy. Ol' Jim Dandy's got himself a bone."

"Where's he at?"

"Down to the diner."

"Fair piece from home, ain't he?"

"Looks like. Damn him, anyway, he's . . ."

"You swear too much, girl."

". . . rovin' to hell and gone these days. You'd think he had a case of the willies."

"Misses Tom, I 'spect."

After a long silence, Lorraine answered.

"I 'spect."

. . . Could have gone, but what for. It's so different without you. Don't get around much anymore. The unctuous baritone seemed to oil itself out of the Emerson. She stooped and turned the radio to another channel. When she rose, she looked out the window again. The little mongrel had backed away from his bowl and was eying the beef bone which rested in the dust between Dandy's two front paws. The mongrel moved toward it. Jim Dandy whirled, his muzzle tight in snarl, and leaped at the animal. The cur spun around and raced toward the garbage bins and then panic-squeezed behind the lattice work. His fangs still bared, Dandy moved back to his bone. He lifted it in his jaws and trotted toward the street and then began to run, picking up speed until he was only a white blur hidden by dust, disappearing into the prairie.

"Damn him," said Lorraine.

She heard Willie Mae chuckle but when Lorraine returned to the table to rejoin the other woman she saw that Willie Mae had not been laughing at her. Willie Mae sat, scissors frozen in her fingers, staring at the radio, her eyes wide with wonder. A woman's voice, jellied with evangelical fervor, came out of the box.

". . . And Commander Gene Tunney must be commended for his article, 'The Bright Shield Of Continence,'" the woman on the radio preached, "in which he argues against the idea that sexual indulgence is physically necessary. Tunney says that any boxer knows continence keeps a man at his peak. Any man above the emotional level of a tomcat must realize that the professional's embrace is not only a menace to health but a shameful desecration of ideal love."

Slowly, Willie Mae's frizzled gray head swung toward Lorraine and her voice was filled with awe.

"Well now, don't that beat all."

Willie Mae wondered if there was a sprinkle of harlots on such a tiny place as Saipan. At this moment, unbloodied bandages looped through her fingers, she asked the Lord to forgive her, but she didn't give a tinker's damn if her man fornicated up one side of a palm tree and down the other just so long as, please, please Lord, he came home to his fields.

As the woman's unctuous voice on the radio continued to lament the sins of the flesh, Lorraine couldn't help but wonder if that woman had ever been married.

Or had ever lain in a root cellar and been surprised with pleasure.

Charles Remington Custer sat under a prairie windmill. He was unaware that, only a short time ago, the gentle creak of blades had smothered the sounds of incidental lust. The light wooden arms rotated slowly as the rudder fan of the windmill faced the wheel into the wind.

The windmill was on the far edge of the Tower wheat fields. Years ago, it had been a central element of irrigation as it pumped water from an underground spring. More sophisticated artesian wells had been driven into the land and their gallon-per-minute rate of flow had antiquated the windmill. Tom Tower had back-hoed the land under the mill and built himself a farm pond which, in emergency, served as a source of fire protection or, in the not unexpected sporadic droughts, as an addendum irrigational supply. After Dippsy was born, Tom had laid drainage pipes in the

pond and circled it with rocks and had even trucked
in sand at great expense. That winter of Dippsy's first
year, Tom had waited until the pond froze over, and
when the ice was safely thick he had driven his six-
by-six truck onto it and dumped the sand. The ice
melted in the spring thaw and the sand floated down.
The bottom was, as Tom told Lorraine, as soft as a
baby's ass. And then, gently, he'd pinched his son. The
sweet trickle of stream water kept the pond fresh and,
soon, it became a favorite swimming hole for boys on
the prairie. Those same boys devised a game to measure their courage. They would challenge each other
to see who dared dive from the highest point of the
windmill. They hung an old scout knife just under
the turning blades. Any boy who plunged to the
pool from that height had earned the right to carve
his initials into the rotting wood of the mill.

Charlie Custer's initials were missing.

The sun flashed against the rusted blade of the jackknife and seemed to give movement to the steel.
Charlie hated the sight of it. The fact that he had
never felt the heft of that knife shamed him. Charlie
tried to wrap the quiet around him like a cloak. Even
the sound of his own breathing disturbed him and so
he held his breath and commanded his muscles to be
still. He closed his eyes so that he could not see the
jackknife which reminded him of his own cowardice,
and then he slid into the dark cave of his self, searching for the zero of his soul.

Nothing worked. He still heard the awful echo of a
rifle shot.

In his mind's eye, he watched a strange parade of
pictures. He saw his father, no longer a figure of flesh
and bone, but, rather, a garden scarecrow, a thing of
tatters and straw, of broom handles and marble eyes.
This black and tattered apparition had a fearsome
mouth. The lips were rubber and oozed across twin
cheeks of cotton as if they were melting under the

glare of some terrible and artificial light. And between those melting lips was a rotted row of teeth, intricately carved from the busted husks of corn. The mouth was open as if to speak but, try as he might, Charlie could hear no words. The apparition did not move with grace. It shuddered fitfully over the heads of lettuce. It jerked its way forward as if it were a hanged man struggling against his noose. But its progress never faltered. It twitched across the sky. It moved toward the shed. As the apparition flapped convulsively across the garden, the lettuce heads beneath it shriveled and turned into dry black balls as if scorched by some furnace heat spewing from the scarecrow's empty legs. The apparition reached the shed. It burned itself through the door and, when it turned to face him, Charlie could see that the scarecrow's cloth limbs were smoking. And then it happened. The thing that dropped stones of fear into Charlie's heart. The awful mouth curved even wider across its cotton cheeks and its corncob grin was oily in the light. It spoke.

"Now," the scarecrow said. "Now." And it lifted one straw finger toward Charlie.

Charlie opened his eyes. *Now.* What was *now?* Charlie tried to puzzle out the sound of the word. Was it a command? A question? An accusation? Was it all these things? What had the scarecrow wanted him to do? What was he telling him? He looked up again at the jackknife high above him and in some curious way saw a curve of connection between it and the scarecrow. He didn't understand why but he was certain it was so. The linkage, he felt, was fear. His eyes measured the distance between the pond water and the top of the windmill. It seemed an awful height. He was unable to accept the challenge.

He had been skillful in avoiding it. He had invented excuses. He'd slipped off a greasy hog, see, he'd say, and hurt his shoulder but tomorrow, oh yeah, tomorrow he'd rightly play Geronimo and dive through the sky. But when the tomorrows sneaked up at him, why he'd been quick to point out that he sure had the granddaddy of all fevers and his pa would lick him if got himself pond-wet, or he'd just squint his eyes in contempt, something like Randolph Scott looking down the barrel of a rustler's Colt forty-five, and spit around his chaw of grass and mutter what a dumb idea it was anyway.

But after each lie there would always be one boy who would say yeah, oh yeah, Charlie, yeah, and turn away without trying to hide the grin on his face.

Except Dippsy, of course. Ol' Dips, he maybe was just a little kid but he knew the worth of things. He'd listen to Charlie's lies and he'd just look at him with those dark, somber eyes and he'd climb down from the mill where he, too, had carved his initials and he'd speak in that high, grave way.

"Fuck 'em," he'd say, "just fuck 'em, Charlie."

Yeah, old Dips, he knew.

Suddenly, Charlie wanted to cry. He was afraid that Dippsy *really* knew. Knew of the terror of death with which Charlie lived. Knew that Charlie made up lies to hide his cowardice. At that moment Charlie hated himself for not being able to accept the everyday dangers of a boy's life. He wanted to shout out, to tell anyone and everyone, that he would dive from the windmill or ride a wild calf or do any dumb damn thing if only . . . if only . . . *if only there were no last and silent place*.

Now, the scarecrow said.

"What?" Charlie shouted aloud. "What?"

But there was no answer and the scarecrow's finger still pointed. Charlie thought it looked like a pale rifle. But what rifle? The gun that Pete would soon pick up? *Oh, please, please, let him roll over like the hognose snake and play dead*. Or the rifle his father held against the steer in the shed?

Charlie knew he should not have run. He heard the

whistle of a mockingbird but he didn't look for the
flutter of wing. He was too busy concentrating on one
word. Reality. Or, as his father so often clipped it out,
r-e-a-l-i-t-y. Ben would not just say the word. He
would announce it.

R-E-A-L-I-T-Y.

The mockingbird whistled again. Charlie whistled
back at it but the bird refused to imitate him and
flew off.

Fuck'em, Charlie, said Dippsy.

And when Charlie rose to return to the shed, he *was*
crying. He started up the slope of the pond bank.

Jim Dandy moved out of the weeds.

The dog looked at Charlie. He saw the boy's face
was wet. He heard the stifled sobs. Dandy's tail
weaved back and forth, welcoming Charlie to comfort.
He moved toward the boy. Charlie sank to his knees
and held his arms out and the dog came to him. The
boy clutched the animal to him, circled the heavy
chest with his arms, and buried his head in the soft,
white coat.

Jim Dandy and Charlie sat together under the windmill for a long, long time. The dog whimpered only
once. That was when Charlie edged closer to the
pond and pulled the dog with him. The dog squirmed
suddenly and tried to slip out of Charlie's embrace,
tried to pull back from the water, and so Charlie
stopped moving and sat very still except for his hands
which moved gently over the great white body, avoiding only the animal's rear left leg which seemed to
quiver and spasm at even the slightest pressure of
Charlie's fingers.

Perched at a high angle above the pond, Charlie
stared into the water. He saw the shimmered reflection
of himself and of Dandy and he wondered why the
dog's jaws kept opening and closing, silently, like a
trout, as if he were consumed by some mysterious
thirst.

He doesn't have the eyes of a scarecrow, Charlie thought, and he told himself: There is no risk here.

A brain smashed by a killing hammer or exploded into bloody slivers by a rifle cartridge is not suitable to microscopic scrutiny.

And so Ben Custer shot the steer through the heart. Then he cut off the head.

As he worked in his laboratory, Ben kept glancing at the wall clock. He knew he didn't have much time. He would have to deliver the head to the lab in Wichita before three o'clock in the afternoon if the tests were to be done today. He had called the Department of Public Health and told Doug Root about his suspicions. Dr. Root was not a man to waste words.

"For chrissake's, Ben," he'd barked, "chop it off, ice it up, and bring it in. Now!"

Ben would do just that.

His rubber gloves slippery with blood, he wrapped the steer's head in absorbent cotton. He placed the head in a tin bucket. Using metal shears, he cut a circle out of a galvanized tin sheet. He placed the circle on top of the bucket. He tapped all around the edge of the tin circle with a peen hammer, bending it down to fit snugly against the sides of the bucket. He was acutely conscious of how lightly he tapped. He didn't want to shake the bucket or tip it or even move it one goddammed inch. He wanted no spill or splash of blood. Any secretion from the steer's head would have to be contained. The rabid virus was as dangerous as a sputter fuse on dynamite.

He nailed the lid to the bucket. He went into the barn and found a large, water-tight tub and brought it back into the laboratory. He slipped the tin bucket into the center of the tub. He removed his rubber gloves and tossed them into a waste barrel. He would burn them later. He carried a steel washbasin to the ice chest, opened the chest, picked up a pick and started chipping at a large block of ice. He filled the

basin with small chunks of ice and then returned to
the water-tight tub which held the tin bucket inside
of which was the bloody steer head. He drew on
another pair of rubber gloves. He snapped them once,
making sure they were tight against his fingers and his
wrists. He scooped ice from the basin. He hand-poured
chunks into the tub, packing them tightly around the
circumference of the tin bucket. The ice rose in layers
until, finally, not an inch of tin showed. There was
only a hill of glistening ice. He sheared off another
circle from the sheet of galvanized tin. He bent the
edges with his peen hammer. He fit it onto the water-
tight tub. He nailed it. He stripped off his gloves and
threw them into the waste barrel. He removed the
white coveralls he wore and his socks and his under-
wear and his shoes and he threw them all into the
barrel. Naked, he stepped into the laboratory shower
and let the water scald him.

The gas pedal pressed to the floor, Ben sped down
the road toward Wichita, the rabid steer head by his
side.

Dr. Douglas Root, chief of the Public Health Department in Wichita, was a gray man. Gray hair and
gray eyes and gray skin. It wasn't his fault. He didn't
find much time for the sun. His gray lab jacket looked
as if it were part of his skin. Crinkled and dry and
worn too long. The only thing about him that had
luster were his eyes. They snapped with the excitement of continuous search. Doug Root handled a
microscope the way many men touched their lovers.
Tenderly and with the hope of surprise.

Peering through the eyepiece of the scope, he saw a
blur of black lines. It was a honeycomb of horror. It
was the rabies virus.

"Ugly little bastards," he said to Ben Custer who was
standing next to him. "They killed that steer."

He stepped out of the way so that Ben might see.
Ben pressed his cheek against the scope and stared

through the glass at the slide. Tiny micro-organisms wiggled their poisonous antennae.

"What about the bite?" he asked.

"Coyote, all right. Dead by now, I 'spect."

Slowly, Ben moved away from the microscope. He crossed to a window and separated two slats of a venetian blind and looked down into the street. Darkness had fallen and there were only a few men and women walking the street. He heard a distant sound of laughter and then it grew louder and, arm in arm, a sailor and a woman stepped around the corner. Their laughter had a raucous edge to it and he could see by the way they moved that both were drunk. They stopped suddenly and their arms circled each other and they pressed close together. It was an act more of balance than of passion. Clinging to the sailor, the woman lifted first one and then the other leg and removed her shoes which had long, spikey heels. She presented the shoes to the sailor who promptly tossed them into the gutter, an act which the woman applauded as if he had performed some extraordinary feat of magic. She took him by the hand and led him to a telephone booth which was situated on the street corner. She pushed open the door and the booth's light was activated and bathed the two in bright light. Together, they crowded into the booth. The sailor hunched himself onto the seat. Hiking up her skirt, the woman straddled him. But their carnal instincts were frustrated by the glare under which they sat. They both squinted at the light and then looked back at each other. The sailor's head drooped down to the woman's shoulder and Ben saw that his body was shaking but he couldn't tell if the sailor was laughing or crying. Suddenly, the woman jerked away and squeezed out of the booth and began running down the street. Quickly, the sailor followed and when the door of the telephone booth shut behind him, the light went out. Christ, Ben thought, these are not days of pleasure.

"Doug," he said, "I'm going to have to slaughter that herd."

"Uh huh. And then set a torch to 'em." So matter-of-fact.

"Morgan's gonna shit."

"He's gonna hold still, that's what he's gonna do. You can get a court order that'll let you get on with it."

"He'll try to get an injunction."

"Won't work."

There was a silence between the men as Ben pictured what he would have to do to slaughter all those steers.

"Messy goddamn job," he said.

"You'd best get George Carter and his deputy. That'll give you two guns for starters."

"Hell, Morgan's got George in his pocket. He picks up a gun against Morgan, he'll wind up with no badge and he knows it. Doug, I'm gonna need help."

"That's a fact."

"What about your department?"

"There's a war on, Ben. We're overloaded. Trailer camps spillin' their sewerage . . . damn bobby-soxers runnin' around all clapped up . . . bad meat bein' bootlegged . . ."

"Something for everyone, huh?"

"A prize in every package."

"Every one a winner."

"Nobody loses."

"Yeah."

The two men smiled at each other. They knew there wasn't anything else to say. Ben didn't want to leave. He wanted to sit there in the cool, dark lab and talk about riverboats. Or anything. Anything at all. Except what the land would look like soaked in blood.

Doug shook a cigarette loose from a store-bought package. Ben took it gratefully. Doug sat on the edge of his desk, one foot swinging lazily back and forth, as he watched the spiral of his smoke.

"Funny," he said, "funny how things slant, how they tip upside down to where a man can't get hold of it. I was over to Hobson City last week. There's a little café there. Best damn waffles north of New Orleans. Run by an old couple name of Robinson. Well, I finished what I had to do and so I run over to get me some of those waffles. But when I looked through the windows, I could see plain enough that there wasn't an empty damn seat. I mean to say each and every stool and bench and booth had an ass on it. Now, those waffles being so sweet, a man couldn't hardly be surprised, don't'cha know? But what I saw surely lifted my skin an inch or two. Each one of those asses perched so perky on the stools or the benches or in the booths belonged to a German prisoner of war. The stenciled letters on the backs of their uniforms were just as clear as sin. Now, understand me, I don't begrudge any man eatin' at those waffles, their being so damn sweet an' all, but whilst I was lookin' in, here comes this soldier, this United States soldier, his heels clickety clackin' down the street an' hot waffles an' maple syrup written on his face, an' he swings open the door to this café, his face ready to bust with the sweet smells of it, an' lickety split, old Mrs. Robinson comes runnin' up to him an' says 'No! No,' she says, 'this ain't a place of welcome!' The boy didn't say a word. He just looked around an' then turned on his heel and left. I am pleased to say that when he walked up the street, his shoulders were stiff with proudness."

Doug ground the butt of his cigarette into a number-ten can and then finished the story.

"He was black, don't'cha know? The soldier was black."

The store-bought cigarette tasted dry and bitter. Ben put it out. He flicked some ashes from his pants and then stood up.

"When I was a young man working on the river, there were times I raised some hell."

"I heard."

"How'd you like to join me an' kick some ass?"

"Ah, Ben."

"No time?"

"No time."

"Well . . . I'll see ya."

"Yeah . . . I'll see ya."

Walking down the street toward his truck, Ben felt the tension which had been building in him. He walked quickly, his shoulders hunched forward, his legs snapping out the steps, his arms swinging in tight arcs. He walked faster, trying to create a wind in his face, a wind which might wash through him and blow away the bleak pictures in his mind. He saw Pete's face swallowed in the locomotive's steam; he saw the sailor leaning drunkenly against his woman; he saw the black man being turned away from sharing the waffle-pleasure of German prisoners; he saw the severed head of a steer.

And he saw the rifle which would soon smoke in his hands. He could smell the coming drift of gunpowder and he felt drained by the anticipation of the slaughter.

Driving home, he kept the truck windows open and the night wind was cool and fresh as it blew against his face and helped keep him awake.

He wished he were in a tub of steaming water where he could soak the tiredness away and where he could lazily reach out and pick up the cup of bourbon he would have rested on the floor. He would drain the cup and when the fire hit his belly, why, he would just sink back into that steaming water, letting it ride up and over his neck, and he would close his eyes and maybe sleep the night away.

The thought of warm water reminded him of the swimming pond he would pass on his way back. The swimming pond and the windmill. The night was mostly gone now and the wind was steady and soft and the sky cloudless. There was no shadow on the moon and in the clear white light Ben could see for miles across the plate of the prairie.

When he reached the windmill, he braked to a stop. He watched the blades turn idly in the moving air and he thought how fresh and clean the water would be in the swimming hole below, how the water would still be sun-warmed from the day, how pleasant it would be to float alone under the sound of creaking blades.

Softly, he laughed out loud. He remembered a night so long ago. It had been one of those steaming prairie nights in June. No, no, it was July. July fourth. Of course. Lorraine and Tom Tower had asked him and Sarah for dinner and fireworks. Lorraine had made a picnic but she wouldn't let them eat until the dark fell and when it did she had led them behind the barn to a patch of soft clover and made them sit down on the grass and close their eyes. When she allowed them to open their eyes they had all sucked in their breaths because she had ringed the patch of clover with sparkler sticks stuck in the ground and she had lighted them and the tiny circle of the world in which they sat had looked on fire.

Afterwards, Tom had set the rockets off and they had all oohed and ahed at the swirling patterns which burst in the sky. They consumed quarts of iced tea but nothing could rid them of the sultriness of summer, and so Lorraine had given each his own burning sparkler and led them across the fields to the windmill and swimming pond and she had turned to them, her eyes brighter than the sparklers and a damn sight more wicked, and said no point in a body burnin' up. Fully clothed she had raced down the bank and plunged into the dark waters of the pond. When she surfaced, the sparkler was still in her hand, although dark and unfired, and her thin dress had been plastered to the curves of her body. She was wet and wild and beautiful.

Ben climbed out of his truck and made his way through the thick brush and weeds which surrounded the windmill and which led to the pond. He stripped off his clothes and hung them from a bush. He walked down the bank to the edge of the water. He leaned down and scooped up a handful of the sand which Tom Tower had dumped so many years before. He rubbed the sand along his arms and shoulders and over his chest. He liked the hard, gritty feel of it. Then he took a deep breath and dived into the water. It was colder than he had anticipated; it tingled his skin and he swam underwater until he had reached the far end of the pond. He decided to try to make it back still underwater and even when he felt his lungs were going to burst he stayed down. His fingers touched the soft edge of bank from where he'd dived and he kicked hard and somersaulted beneath the surface of the pond and started back across it. A fish brushed against his leg but the water was too dark for Ben to see if it was a bass or just a small minnow. His lungs were burning now and he felt his rhythm faltering as he pulled himself through the water. He arched his back and thrust his head up, and when his face broke through the pond surface he opened his mouth and pulled in a great gasp of air. He let himself sink back down as he blew the air out and he watched the explosion of tiny little bubbles above his head.

He felt wonderful.

Surfacing again, treading water, he waited for his breathing to return to normal.

There was a scratching sound.

And then a clicking.

He scanned the dark edge of the pond in front of him but he could see nothing unusual.

Click click click click.

Still treading water, Ben turned and looked across the pond. He saw nothing but a tangle of weeds. Using a breast stroke, keeping his head above water, he swam slowly across the pond to the sandy bank. When his toes kicked against the pond bottom he stood up and started up the bank and then heard it again.

Click.

It came from above him. He looked up.

"Well, damn me!" he said, and quickly retreated back into the water.

Lorraine laughed.

She was seated on the small platform at the top of the windmill, her legs dangling over the side. Her hair hung wetly around her face and she was wrapped in a huge towel. Squinting up at her in the moonlight, Ben was quite sure there was nothing under the towel. The rusted jackknife was in her hand. She grinned down at him.

"Evenin', Doctor."

"What the hell you doing up there?"

"Hard to sleep on a night like this." She glanced at the moon.

"Damn it," Ben said. Just standing still like this, his legs were getting chilled in the water.

"Thought I'd bedazzle my boy some."

"What?"

"Uh huh," she said. She held up the jackknife and then shifted a little on the platform and started to scrape the blade into a board of the windmill. It clicked against the wood and Ben realized what the sound was he'd heard. "See," she continued, "already carved the L and I'm about done with the T. Next time Dips climbs up here, why, he'll likely pop a gusset."

She turned a little more and her face slanted away from Ben as she dug deeper into the wood where she was going to leave her initials. Ben stood there watching her. He reached down into the water and kneaded the calf muscle in one leg.

"Listen," he said.

"Uh huh." She didn't bother to turn and look at him.

"Left my clothes on the bush," Ben said.

"Uh huh." The blade scraped hard at the wood.

"I'm gonna get dressed."

"That's nice."

"What I mean is . . ."

"I know what you mean."

"Oh."

But he stayed where he was. Perched high on the mill, her skin pale and luminous, Lorraine looked almost like a ghost floating in the moonlight.

Ben felt his toes beginning to cramp.

"Well," he said, "I'll get dressed."

"That's what you said." Splinters flaked out of the wood where she was carving.

Damn, Ben thought, she's making me feel like a goddamn schoolboy who's been caught skinny-dipping. He was annoyed at how casually she'd treated his nakedness. It didn't seem natural that a woman could be so offhand about a man bare-ass in the moonlight. But even as he thought that he knew it was a lie. Lorraine Tower had no need for disguise, nor would she accept it in others.

As he moved out of the water and over to the bush where he'd left his clothes, Ben couldn't help but tighten the muscles in his belly. Just in case, he thought, just in case she happens to turn. But she didn't. His back to her, he dried himself on his shirt and as he put his clothes on he was conscious of the jackknife clicking against the wood and of the sound of her whistling softly to herself. They were soft and peaceful and companionable sounds and, hardly aware of it, he, too, began to whistle her tune. He heard her chuckle and, fully dressed now, he turned and looked up.

"Tin ear, that's what you got, Ben," she said. "Always did and always will."

She placed the jackknife on the platform. She had finished her carving. She stood up and stepped toward the top rung of the ladder. Ben marveled at how leanly muscled her legs were. His throat was dry and he thought maybe he'd better not watch her come down that ladder. But he didn't turn away. Her hands gripped the top of her towel and then she pulled it loose and let it float down to the ground.

She smiled at him.

She was dressed in an old pair of dungarees which were cut off at the thigh, and a gingham shirt with no sleeves. She had tied the tails of the shirt around her, the knot resting just below her breast. The clothes were damp.

"Wind's cold up here," she said. "Towel was a comfort."

She took the ladder two rungs at a time. She sat on the bottom rung and toweled her hair dry.

"Listen," Ben said, "you always swim with your clothes on?"

"Nope." Her voice was muffled under the towel. "Only when the fancy takes hold."

She removed the towel from her head and draped it over her bare knees. She was shivering.

"You're cold," Ben said.

"Little."

"Coffee'd be good."

"Uh huh."

She sat on the bottom rung of the ladder and he stood in front of her and they looked at each other and the moon was very white and the silence seemed to go on forever.

"You remember," Ben said, "you remember that night when ..."

"Yes," she said.

"I mean that night when ..."

"Yes," she said.

"All those sparklers. All those damn sparklers." Ben paused. "Jesus, we sure had a time."

"We did."

"Well," he said, "the good things, they don't last too long."

"Don't they, Ben?"

"Not so's a man could see."

"Maybe," she said, and her voice held a fine edge, "maybe you ought to wrap 'em up."

"What?"

"The good things. Maybe you ought to wrap them up, tie 'em in a little package and put 'em in the storehouse. That'd be good, wouldn't it, Ben?"

She was on her feet now.

"I mean a man'd just have to open the door and pull 'em out whenever he got the notion. Like some kid with his goddamn toys. Why, just think of it, Ben. You could just sit in that storeroom and play all day long with the good things, all the things you saved, all the yesterdays you tied in a ribbon!"

She was moving now. Her barefeet stamped over the damp earth as she brushed past him, her shoulder knocking hard against his. And she was waist high in the weeds before she finally turned to look at him again.

"Wouldn't that be swell, Ben? Wouldn't that be goddamn swell?" She wheeled around and before he could even think of answering, she had disappeared, the weeds closing like a curtain behind her back.

Standing there under the sky where the stars were dying, Ben was very still as he heard the echo of her words.

. . . all the yesterdays you tied in a ribbon.

She had been as abrasive as the sand which he'd rubbed against his skin. Slowly, he leaned down and scooped up a handful of that sand and he began to scrub it along the skin of one arm. His hand moved faster and faster and the tiny particles of grit bit into him, lacerated him, rubbed him raw and finally broke the skin.

14

Ben sipped his bourbon from the cracked cup and listened to the dead voice of his grandfather.

"Well, sir, we are east of the Purgatoire and west of the Cheyenne Bottoms and south of Smoky Hill and north of the Cimarron and cut in two by that great one hundred meridian and we rove Herefords and plant Turkey Red over the dead Pawnee. And that, sir, is where Crowley Flats was born and where, sure God, she'll die."

The old man's geographical precision had always pleased Ben. It pinned down the land with a stroke as short and sweet as that which drove the golden spike into the railroad link.

It's where we were born and, sure God, where we'll die.

Mr. H. V. Kaltenborn said otherwise. His clipped and seemingly artificially pumped-up voice sputtered from the radio and he was just as precise as Ben's grandfather as he related the sad facts of Allied casualties.

Ben turned off the radio. He crossed the kitchen and poured another inch of bourbon. He set the cup down on the sink counter. He pulled the pack of Bull Durham from his pocket, together with his rolling papers. He held a paper between the first two fingers of his left hand. He indented it with his thumb. With his teeth, he pulled open the sack of tobacco which he held in his right hand. He poured tobacco into the cigarette paper. He closed the sack again with his teeth, pulling softly on the small string which bound the sack tight. He shoved the sack back into his pocket. Slowly, using the fingers of both hands, he rolled a cigarette. He was determined that this time he would not spill any tobacco. When he had formed the delicate paper into a long, white cylinder, although not perfect, he raised it to his lips and licked the one gummed edge and pressed it tightly. He twisted one end of the cigarette and slipped the other end into his mouth. He held the cigarette gently between his lips, wanting to keep its dry fragility intact. He struck a kitchen match against the sole of his boot and raised it to the twisted end of the cigarette. The paper flared and he sucked in hard, already tasting tobacco bite, but the cigarette end in his mouth matted thickly against the wetness of his tongue and the far burning end shredded against the flame. He spit the mess into the kitchen sink and washed it down the drain.

"Shit," he said.

Steam from the simmering kettle on the stove had fogged the window. He turned off the burner and then wiped the window with his hand. He stared out. It was the time between dusk and dark. There was a gray sheen over the land. The line between earth and sky was indistinct, as though a child had finger-smudged his crayon drawing. The evening lacked clarity.

But not for long, Ben thought. Soon this evening will be in focus. A hard line will be drawn and on either side of that line will stand the men and women who will offer obeisance to Morgan or join me in slaughter.

It had taken the better part of a week to work out the legalities and logistics of the slaughter. Ben had been right. Morgan had tried to get an injunction against the court order. It had been nothing but a delaying tactic. After Doug Root testified about his findings, the court had acted promptly. Reluctantly,

Sheriff George Carter and his deputy had joined Ben in building a huge fence which circled the cattle near the creek. Not one of the steers would ever reach the feeding lots of Wichita.

Ben drained the cup of bourbon. He looked around the kitchen. He hoped he might see some unfinished chores. He didn't. It was time to go. They would be waiting. But he didn't move. He stood there in the kitchen, leaning against the sink, staring into the empty cracked cup, listening to the silence. But when he heard the distant chug of a truck on the far road and knew where that truck was going, knew that confrontation was close, he opened the faucet on the kitchen tap and let water drip slowly into the cup. When the cup was filled, when it overflowed, he would go. He would give himself that much time.

By the time water had filled the bottom of the cup and then risen and covered the thin brown jagged crack in the cup, he had decided what caliber of guns he would use. As the water trembled at the rim of the cup and then spilled into the sink, he had decided that he would have to take Charlie to the killing. He knew there might be no one else.

It was time to find out.

He turned off the faucet and walked out of the kitchen. He stood at the bottom of the stairs.

"Charlie," he called.

There was no answer.

He took the stairs two at a time. He was in a hurry now. He opened the door to the boys' room. No, he thought, not the boys'. Charlie's room now. Only Charlie. But the boy wasn't there. The window was open and a sound came through it. Ben crossed the room and looked out.

Charlie stood some fifty feet from the side of the barn. He faced it. He wore Pete's first-baseman's mitt on his left hand. In his right hand, he held a red rubber ball. On his head was a long-visored baseball cap. He dug the ball into the mitt and let it rest there. He licked the fingers of his pitching hand. He tugged the visor of his cap. He squinted hard at the barn and then shook his head. He waited a moment and then shook his head again. Ben realized that the boy was shaking off some signal he had received from an imaginary catcher. The boy leaned forward, his eyes narrowed in concentration. Almost imperceptibly, he nodded. Ben wondered whether the catcher had called for a curve or the high, hard fast ball. Charlie straightened up. His hands rose to his chest. His head swiveled to the left. Of course, Ben silently approved, he's checking the runner on first. Charlie reared back, his left leg rising high for balance and later thrust. His right arm started the pitching motion and then, suddenly, Charlie whirled for one more look at the runner at first.

"Balk!" Ben yelled.

Charlie spun around and stared up at the window. "Two men on. First and second," he said.

"Who's up?"

"Stan the Man."

"He's tough."

"So's Hubbel."

"Carl Hubbel?"

"Yeah."

"Where's ol' Carl Hubbel?"

"Here," Charlie shouted up, thumping himself on his own chest. "Here's old Carl Hubbel."

"What's the count?"

"Two an' two."

"If I were you, I'd call the game on account of darkness."

"Yeah. Well."

For a moment, Charlie seemed to ponder this and Ben wished he hadn't said what he'd said. Damn fool, he thought to himself. Even here, in this mythical game, he should not have proposed a way out. It was

a path Charlie walked too often. Ben thought of the
last few weeks. School had been postponed so that
the boys and girls of Crowley Flats could help with
the planting. Those that didn't work in the fields had
formed a childish regiment called the Tin-Can Colo-
nels and they roamed the area for cans and scraps of
metal and piled them into a collection center outside
the Grange. But not Charlie. He chased butterflies
over the alfalfa.

"I don't know," Ben shook his head in mock concern,
"that Musial, he can bang one out."

"Nah, I'm gonna pitch him low and inside."

Ben found himself leaning far out the window, waiting to see what Charlie would do, hoping he would
take a chance and deliver the fast ball to dangerous
Stan Musial, chest high and maybe with a little spit
on it. The boy's jaws worked up and down as he pretended to chew tobacco. He tugged at his cap again.
He studied the batter in front of the barn. He checked
first base. He spit into the dust. And then, determina-
tion swelling his shoulders, he started his windup. He
was, after all, going to pitch to Musial. As his arm
swung back to hurl the ball, Ben called down to him.

"Dust him off, then curve him. That's what Pete
would do!"

Charlie froze. Slowly, his arm dropped to his side
and he let the red rubber ball dribble out of his fingers.
It bounced once and then rolled through the dust and
came to rest in front of the barn where Stan Musial
no longer stood. Casually, with no real meaning to the
gesture, Charlie threw his glove after it and then, just
as casually, sailed his cap after the glove. The imple-
ments of his trade discarded, Charlie made a shuffled
beeline to the pickup truck. He opened the door and
climbed in. He shut the door and leaned against it,
moving as far away as possible from the driver's seat.
He stared straight ahead. Not once had he turned to
look at his father.

Ben turned from the window, already anticipating the angry lift of voices.

"You ain't got the right, Custer!" Morgan's face was as scarlet as newly butchered beef. He wheeled toward the sheriff. "Goddamn it, George, you'd better set him straight. Now!"

The citizens of Crowley Flats were crowded into the Grange. Furious at the court order, Morgan had summoned the town to hear his grievance. Most of them had come running. Now they stood, sat, hunched, crouched and sprawled inside the hall. They faced Ben Custer. He leaned against a table which had been placed in the front of the hall and looked at the spectators. He searched for a sympathetic face. There were not many. Caleb's eyes were so black and small as he listened to Morgan that they looked as if a housewife had folded raisins into her rising dough. Next to him on the bench was Virgil, snapping and popping his gum in an excited rhythm. Behind the two men sat Ernst and Sophie. Ben studied them. He felt he could count on Sophie to support him but he wasn't sure about Ernst.

The German was distracted. Drops of sweat ran down into his collar but he did nothing about wiping them off. The nervous tic in his cheek had returned and each time the tiny muscle twitched, Ernst blinked and his head moved from side to side as if he were trying to shake something loose.

No, Ben thought, he could not count on Ernst. His behavior puzzled Ben. Ben thought of when Willie Mae had called him. She had been worried about her breeding bull. Ben had driven to her farm and examined the bull. The animal had lumpy jaw. The ray fungus had attacked the tissues of the animal's jaw, had swelled hard around the salivary gland and the bones of the jaw. Ben had cut open the growth and washed out the pus and swabbed the cavity with tincture of iodine. He had left Willie Mae and driven to the diner for coffee. He had seen the broken window, had seen the wide tapes holding the shreds together. But when he had asked Ernst about it, the German had shrugged as if it were of little matter and had said that he had been careless and had slipped in a puddle of mopping water and had crashed into the window himself. Ben had looked at the window again and he had seen that tiny splinters of glass still lay under the booth near the window. Inside. If Ernst had struck the window himself, the splinters should have been outside. Ben had started to ask about this but when he saw the dull resentment in Ernst's eyes, he had decided to question no further.

Now, as he looked at Ernst in the Grange, Ben thought how even the resentment had gone from the German's face. There was just emptiness and sweat.

Ben's eyes swung across the crowd. Willie Mae sat in the center row of benches. She was surrounded by other women of the prairie. It was as if they all hoped her strength would drain into them if some hard decision had to be faced. Her face was impassive. Not even the wooden match in her mouth moved. Further back, in one of the end rows, were Lorraine and Dippsy, and lying in the aisle at Dippsy's feet was Jim Dandy. Ben glanced down at the dog. A leash had been snapped onto his collar. The other end was gripped in Dippsy's hand. Dippsy had told Charlie that old Jim Dandy had been restless and taken to roving at night. Well, Dandy, Ben said silently to the dog, don't take it personal, the roaming days end for all of us. He smiled to himself as he looked at the dog. Dandy's muzzle was flat to the floor and his front paws were crossed over his jaws. Ben thought the dog looked as if he were trying to hide a grin, trying to cover up the delights he had discovered in the night's sweet rovings. Ben looked away and saw that Lorraine's eyes were on him.

Yeah, he thought, *the night's sweet rovings.* Then he heard Morgan's voice again.

"I got twenty . . . thirty thousand dollars in that beef. Son of a bitch wants to slaughter 'em 'cause one lousy steer got bit. Goddamn it, George, you got the badge, you tell it to him true."

Sheriff George Carter squirmed. He rose from the front row where he was seated and he twisted his immaculate broad-brimmed Stetson in his non-immaculate hands and he faced Morgan who seemed to be all of a shine in his bright light of anger.

"Well, now, Morgan," he said, "ain't no need to get riled up. I mean there ain't no rush to this here thing. Ain't that right, Ben?" When Ben didn't answer, George Carter hawked up some phlegm and looked for a place he could rid himself of it. He didn't see a cuspidor or even a number-ten can so he swallowed hard and turned to Ben. "The thing is, Ben, the law's tricky. You gotta read it careful like."

Ben pulled the court order from his pocket. "This is black and white and idiot simple. I've got the authority and I intend to use it."

Willie Mae stood up.

"Ben," she said, and Ben knew she was going to ask a careful question because she removed the match from her mouth, "meanin' no disrespect, but this here's ranchin' country. Town depends on it. How'd we know you're gonna stop after killin' Morgan's cattle?"

Before Ben could answer, Chet Beam's voice rang out.

"She's right, citizen. We gotta talk dollars and cents!"

Ben wondered if maybe he'd better count to ten before he answered the son of a bitch but then figured he didn't have the time. When he spoke, his voice was held in, cool and impersonal, as if he were explaining the arithmetic tables to an elementary-school class.

"More'n likely, the coyote that bit that steer is dead now. Once an animal turns savage, he's in the last stages. He's only got a handful of days left to him."

Ernst blinked rapidly. He was frightened at what he saw. He stared at Ben and watched the words spill out of Ben's mouth and each word took the same shape. The shape of a black-winged fly. And the flies droned toward him. They entered his eyes, blinding him, their wings scratching as the flies struggled through his iris and drove deep inside his head where they whirled in furious circles.

"As far as we know," Ben continued, "Morgan's cattle are the only ones that show signs of rabies. When we've killed that herd, we'll have cut out the danger of an epidemic."

Caleb was on his feet, shouting.

"What the hell do you mean, Ben? When *we've* killed that herd?"

A low murmuring spread through the Grange and Ben knew the fuse had been lighted. He saw an old man step away from the wall against which he had been leaning. The man was Richie Grover. His eyes were pale, as if the sun had burned the color out of them. The crowd grew silent when they saw him move forward. They knew him as a man who shied away from speech, who juggled words nervously, as if they were coals from a branding-iron fire. He removed his sweat-stained straw hat. It was a preliminary gesture toward the formality of statement. He cleared his throat and nodded gravely at the sheriff.

"George," he said, "what in hell's goin' on?"

George Carter was uneasy as he looked at the faces in the Grange. They stared at him. They waited for him. He wished he didn't have such a big belly, wished he looked more like them movie law-and-order fellers. He hitched up his pants. He sucked in his gut. He hooked a thumb in his gun belt, pushing the holstered

.45 Colt forward as if he wanted to remind the citizens of Crowley Flats just who they were dealing with. With tremendous effort, he avoided Morgan's eyes.

"Well now," he said, "the best me an' my deppity can do is to pen them cattle up. I mean to say, that is the very best we can do. Hell's bells, they's jus' the two of us to cover all this here territory an' . . . well . . . we got us pressin' business other side of the county. Yes, sir, pressin' business. So . . . so what Ben's lookin' for is . . . uh . . . what he's lookin' for is . . . uh . . ."

"Guns," said Ben. "I'm looking for guns."

This time there was no murmuring. The Grange exploded into an angry sea of sound. Voices buzzed, dipped, swelled, rumbled and ricocheted off the plain pine boards, and Morgan's fury rose above the sound.

"Ain't nobody gonna raise a goddamn finger less you wanna stop plantin'!"

The chorus of voices died. The quiet reminded Ben of the suspended silence of a church. Only, he thought, only Morgan Crowley is no minister of God.

It is possible that Morgan thought otherwise as he addressed his congregation. His words stabbed like icicles.

"Richie, you got what? 'Bout six, seven days left to put in your wheat? Too late to sow after that, ain't it?"

The old man's pale eyes seemed to fade to white as he nodded once.

"You gonna do it by hand?" asked Morgan. " 'Cause that's what you and Walter and John and Marcie and Luther and all the rest of you better figure. Any one of you take a gun to my cattle, you'd best step outa that line waitin' for my grain drills, my tractors, my combines. And if my meanin' ain't clear, you just speak your piece."

His eyes swept over the Grange. The possibility of ruin was painted on the faces staring at him. Ben shifted a little against the table and started to speak,

not knowing whether he would be able to move
Crowley Flats toward action but knowing that he had
to give sound to this awful silence.

"You people know about fire on the prairie. It guts
out the land. Whatever doesn't turn black in the
flame . . . rabbits . . . sheep . . . men . . . dies 'cause
the air's sucked out of the sky. Well, I'll tell you something. Next to rabies . . . a prairie fire's pure picnic."

For a moment, Ben wondered if he had spoken
silently to himself, if he had planned the words but
not given lip to them. His words might just as well
have been autumn leaves dropping dry and soundless
into a woods where no one walked.

Morgan smiled. He turned to Ben. He spoke softly.

"I do believe this meetin's over," he said and he
walked out of the Grange.

The legs of a bench squeaked against the pine floor
as Caleb Dodd rose and followed Morgan. The room
seemed suddenly filled with squeaks and shufflings
and whispers and the secret slide of boots. Willie Mae
stood and softly spat wooden splinters from her mouth.
She started down an aisle of the Grange toward Ben
but stopped quickly as if she treasured the distance
between them.

"Ben," she said, "if he come home . . ."

And Ben knew Willie Mae was talking about her
husband.

". . . if he do come home an' he was to see no crop,
I don't think I could hardly stand it."

Ben shifted his eyes away from her, not wanting to
see the sudden slackness to her mouth. It was as if
without the wooden match Willie Mae had lost her
strength. Ben saw that the only ones still not moving
in the Grange were Lorraine and Dippsy and old Jim
Dandy. Lorraine was watching him. In the isolation
of her own stillness, she seemed surprised. Her head
was cocked slightly as if she were listening to a question and her mouth opened partly as if she were

forming the answer, had not formed it yet but was searching for it and, to her own surprise, not finding it.

"Knew a man in Oklahoma," Ben said, and was startled by his own voice.

The flat whisper of footsteps died as men and women turned. As he looked at them, Ben thought of the children's game of statues. Rich Grover was in the doorway. He had just placed his hat onto his head and his hand was curled around the straw brim. He had turned at Ben's words but he didn't remove his hand. It was as if the rules of the game dictated an arrest to action. Idly, Ben noticed that a townswoman must have been opening her purse when he spoke. Now, it hung loosely in her hand, its sides unclasped, its lumped contents open to scrutiny. Ernst must just have stood. His back was still curved in the effort of his rise.

"Nice feller," Ben continued. As he spoke, he decided to roll a cigarette, not caring a damn if all the tobacco matted or shredded or spilled. "Jabez Dowell. Had the sweetest grassland I ever saw. Ran a thousand head of cattle. Then he got hit with the drought, just like the rest of us. No rain, sun frying the land, wind blowing it away. But Jabez, he was a brave and wise man. 'Hell,' he said, 'trouble come, a man just turns his back.' And that's what he did. The wind blew from the north, Jabez faced south. Wind swept in from the east, Jabez put his face to the west. Pretty soon, he was making circles clear around the compass. He knew if a man just kept turning in the right direction, he wouldn't have to watch his farm blow away. 'Course it was too late. The land turned to dust. The cattle burned up. But Jabez, he was a happy man. He walked through all that dust and dug up cow skulls and he used 'em for flower pots. He swore there was nothing prettier than a bright red rose poking up through a cow's eye. Well, hell, you people are just as wise and brave as Jabez Dowell. You just keep turning in the wind and then one day, one day . . ."

Ben took a drag from his cigarette and was very pleased that this time his hand-rolled was firm and dry.

". . . one day," he continued, "Crowley Flats'll be the biggest goddamn rose garden in the world."

He sucked in deep and held the smoke in his lungs for a long time and then slowly blew a series of perfect tiny rings which floated across the stunned silence in the Grange. Then he ground the cigarette under his heel and walked out of the hall.

It wasn't until he approached his truck that he remembered his son. Charlie had refused to enter the Grange. Obediently, he had driven to town with Ben but when his father had explained the nature of the meeting, had told him that he was seeking men for the slaughter, the boy had stiffened into bleak silence. And in that silence, father and son had driven the country roads. They had not looked at each other until the truck pulled up to the Grange and then Ben had turned to the boy.

"Well?" he'd asked.

The boy hadn't answered, nor had he moved. He had just stared at the floorboards of the truck. Ben had climbed out of the truck, his movements slow and deliberate because he was afraid of the anger building up inside him, and after he'd reached the Grange door, he'd turned back for a moment and he'd managed to keep his voice even and low.

"Charlie," he'd said, "you can come with me or you can stay there. Doesn't make much difference because no matter where you go, you can't hide. Not ever, Charlie, not ever."

Now, returning to the truck and seeing his son sitting exactly where he'd left him, and still smarting from the sight of men and women buckling before Morgan's threat, Ben's voice snapped.

"You and me," he said, "we'll do the killing."

"Ol' Pete," Charlie whispered to the floorboards,

"he'll dust off the cows for you. Sure, ol' Pete, he'll do it."

Suddenly, Ben felt bewildered.

"Damn it," he said, "Pete isn't here."

It was then that Charlie finally looked at him.

"Ain't he, Pa?" he asked softly, "ain't he?"

15

He had painted his way southeast over the Flint Hills to Coffeyville. Now, swinging in his scaffold seat, he could see the Verdigris River and the Oklahoma border. He wished he'd had a perch like this when he was just a little bitty tyke so that he could have witnessed the gun flare outside the bank when the Dalton boys stormed the town. By Jesus, that would have been a sight. He looked down, trying to imagine it. But what he saw made him wince. The setting sun flashed red against the side-view mirror of his truck. It looked flat and round like a burning nickel and it seemed to spin upward into his eyes, searing the corneas first and then flaming inside his head. He turned away, hoping to put out the fire. It didn't help. The heat continued. It spread from inside his head down to his throat and he tried to swallow it away. But he couldn't swallow. The muscles of his throat constricted and refused passage to the thick saliva on his tongue. He spat. There was no force behind the action and the saliva coated his lips and then dribbled into yellow tinged paths which clung to the stubble of his whiskers. He raised his hand to wipe his beard clean and stared at the thing in his hand. He couldn't remember what it was. It looked like a cluster of leeches in a summer pond. Their thin black bodies squirmed under a red wetness. He did not understand that the wind was riffling through his paint brush. He looked up in front of him. CAMELS ARE FIRST WITH MEN IN THE SERVICE. He scratched the hand that held the paint brush and he tried to hold on to the fractured memory of a deer in the Sangre de Cristo mountains but the deer leaped out of his head and he saw it bound high into the sky, its belly gut-ripped and bleeding. He raised his hand and the paint brush began to make its own scarlet trail. CAMELS ARE FIRST WITH MEN IN THE SERVICE disappeared under a crisscross of crimson. A tremor shook his shoulder, coursed down his arm, penetrated his fingers. He opened his hand. The brush fell to the ground. He followed it with his eyes and, once again, saw the hot nickel flash of sun. This time he welcomed it. He wanted to burn up within it. He wanted to be consumed. He untied the scaffold rope and, protected by habit, rode the board down. He staggered under the weight of his paint cans, the wire handles cutting into his numbed flesh. For a moment, he balanced precariously on the running board, then slipped behind the wheel. He drove westward toward Crowley Flats, westward where he hoped he could walk into the fire of the sun. And where, perhaps, he would remember his name.

It was Emmett Flack.

"I need three, four hundred rounds of thirty ought six." Ben made an effort to keep his tone casual.

The men in the feed store looked at each other, then shifted their eyes toward Caleb. He stood behind his counter, his heavy hands spread flat on the wood, his face impassive.

"Ain't got 'em," he said.

"Right behind you, Caleb," Ben said, and pointed to the well-stocked shelves behind the counter.

Some of the men who watched shifted their weight a bit and a boot crunched against spilled seed.

Caleb sucked on his teeth. He took a long time exploring his mouth with one calloused finger. He looked as if he were searching for something precious, and while he worked that finger around his gums and across his palate, his eyes never left Ben's. Finally, he removed his finger and rubbed it roughly across his shirt as if he were punishing it for its lack of discovery. His head swiveled toward the shelves behind him and he glanced at the boxes of ammunition and then turned back to Ben.

"What, them?" he asked. "Oh, I couldn't sell them. I mean to say, I gotta save them for emergency time. Suppose them Krauts come floatin' down in the sky and do bad to us?"

One of Morgan's ranch hands tittered. Slowly, Ben turned to him. Whatever the ranch hand saw in Ben's face made the laughter die in his mouth. The ranch hand looked away quickly and was consumed with a sudden interest in the faded printing on a burlap sack.

Ben walked out of the store.

When he moved down Main Street, Ben thought he'd never seen the backs of so many heads, nor heard such a scurry of feet. As he passed the citizens of Crowley Flats, he began to count the number of corners around which they disappeared, the number of alleys which gave refuge to their shadows, the number of ways a man or woman could incline his or her head away from him. The arithmetic disgusted him.

Silently, he cursed Morgan Crowley.

He saw Sam Hanks beckon to him through the window of the Western Union office. He went in.

Sam leaned back in his swivel chair, his black bowler tipped low over his eyes. He rocked back and forth for a moment as if he were pumping himself up for talk. Ben listened to the creak of the chair's old springs but said nothing. The rhythm of the rocking increased until Sam's small feet which didn't quite touch the floor were fairly flying up and down. Ben worried that the little man would snap out of the chair like a stone from a slingshot. But he didn't. At the peak of the chair's motion, Sam suddenly slapped his shoes against the floor and stopped rocking.

"There's some hold," he said, "that had Cleopatra's nose been a mite shorter, the world'd be a different place."

Ben said nothing.

"You understand such a thing?" Sam asked.

"No."

"Me, neither. The way I see it, the world is what it is. Good an' bad. Night an' day. Sweet an' sour. Looks to me like this morning you're suckin' on the sour."

"Looks like."

"People, Ben, why, they're mostly decent till you put scare to 'em. They don't none of 'em look to win no medals."

"Sam, you're a good man but I don't have time to cracker-barrel this morning."

"I know. I know." Sam revolved his chair around and stared at the yellow sheets of ticker tape in his machine. He looked up at Ben who stood across the office. "Ben, from where you stand, can you make out the words?"

"Some."

"I gotta squint. Ain't that a holler? Here I am, the number-one reader of life and death, and I gotta squint." Then he turned back to Ben and he said it very simply.

"But I could see a cow was I asked to. Yes, sir, I could see a cow."

Ben looked at Sam's tiny bowed legs and his celluloid collar and his hard black bowler and his rheumy eyes which were the saddest in Kansas and the image of this little old man being trampled under the hooves of cattle made his belly constrict. Like a busted doll, he thought, he'd look just like a busted doll. He spoke quietly, making certain to preserve Sam Hank's dignity.

"I appreciate that, Sam, but who'd mind the store?"

"Don't much like what I'm sellin' these days."

"But you do it."

"Yeah," Sam said, his voice older than Rome, "yeah, I do it."

"Been a long time since we bit some bourbon together, Sam. Could be you'd like to drop by some night."

"I'd like that."

"Make it soon."

"I'll do it." The teletype machine began to clack and Sam swung around to read the message. The clatter of the keys almost drowned his voice. "Soon," he said.

Sure, Ben thought, *everything will be soon.*

When he left the Western Union office, Ben no longer bothered to compute turned heads or shadowed alleys. He crossed the street to the gas station. Virgil was jacking an old tire from its battered rim. It popped loose and Virgil rolled the tire across the oil-stained and dusty ground of his station. With a gesture worthy of a cavalier dismissing his steed, he flipped the tire onto a pile of discards which he hoped to sell one day as retreads. He saw Ben pass the gas pumps and was about to speak to him but Ben went directly into the small supply office. Virgil followed.

Virgil started talking before he was through the door.

"Y'unnerstan', I'd go with you, Ben, but Morgan, him an' the others'll go clear to the state line for gas if'n I help. It ain't they scare me none, it's jus' my profit ain't much more'n spit now an' . . ."

He stopped talking as quickly as he had started. He looked at Ben and he didn't know what to do. Ben's back was to him. He had opened the glass cabinets on the wall and was removing box after box of ammunition. He was stuffing his pockets with every kind of cartridge he could find. Thirty-thirties and thirty-ought-sixes and seven-millimeters and point-two-seventies and three-ought-eights and even some wildcat homemades. Sweet Jesus, Virgil thought, the man's a walkin' arsenal. Virgil thought about Morgan and then, not sure why, but accepting the logic of it, he remembered the stories he'd read about the early days when Indians would strip the skin off a man and hang him up to dry like rawhide under the prairie sun.

"What I'm sayin', Ben," he started, "what I'm tryin' to tell you . . ."

"Don't," Ben said. He held a cardboard box of twelve-gauge shotgun slugs in his hand and was looking at it in a peculiar way. Virgil knew for certain that Ben was thinking about the size of the hole such a slug would blow through an animal. Ben put the box back on a shelf in the glass cabinet. He moved out from behind the displays of motor oil and fan belts and windshield wipers and key rings and good-luck miniature rabbit tails and passed Virgil, who jumped back swiftly as if afraid that the ammunition in Ben's pockets would explode on contact.

It wasn't until Ben was halfway down the street, a figure made lumpy by the pocket bulge of bullets, that Virgil realized he'd never mentioned payment for the shells.

Well, then, he said to himself, old Morgan gets his dander up, I'll jus' tell him true. Ben Custer, he took 'em, he jus' up an' took 'em without so much as a wham-bam an' thank-you-ma'am. Virgil nodded to himself with righteous self-justification. He went back into the supply office. He looked at the open cabinets. The shelves were dotted with patches of clean glass where the ammunition boxes had rested. The squares were neatly outlined by rectangles of dust. Virgil thought that the single remaining container of twelve-gauge shotgun slugs looked awfully lonely.

"But not near so lonely as you gonna be, Ben," he muttered, "no, sir, not by half."

Charlie watched the botfly circle the head of the Appaloosa. The insect lighted on the horse's muzzle and then crawled across his nose and up into the fore-

lock. The Appaloosa twitched his ears and the botfly
rose into the air and buzzed away. Charlie watched
its flight. He knew what the insect wanted to do. His
father had taught him that. The botfly was seeking a
warm, safe haven in the horse's hair where it could
deposit its sticky, abrasive film onto which the botfly
would attach its eggs. In the natural course of events,
the substance would irritate the horse and he would
turn his head and try to lick it away. The larvae would
enter the horse's mouth and would be carried down
into the stomach where, also in the natural course of
events, the process of parasitic damage would begin,
interrupted only by the larvae's need to pupate and
drop free with the horse's feces. This cycle fascinated
Charlie. And it repulsed him. He did not think it fair
or just that such a fine animal as the Appaloosa should
be subject to a torment the result of which could only
lead to the incessant breeding of botflies. When his
father had explained that this was the natural order
of things, that it was only a tiny detail in an unsolvable
scheme, Charlie had decided that there might come
a day when, if granted the opportunity, he might not
vote for God.

The botfly landed on a dark oval spot near the
horse's loins. Reluctantly, Charlie admired it. The insect had sought its own camouflage. Its wing tips were
invisible in the black patch of hairs. But the Appaloosa disdainfully switched his tail and brushed the
fly away.

Charlie wondered, if he flew into some dark place of
welcome would his father find him as easily as the
horse found the fly. He looked around and saw no
place to hide. He stood outside the barn and stared
at the horses. The Appaloosa was Ben's. Next to it was
Charlie's black and white Pinto. Both light horses
were fine cow ponies. Both were saddled. Hanging
from their saddles were saddlebags and rifle scabbards. The flaps of the saddlebags were open and

Charlie could see the ammunition glinting in the sunlight. The scabbards were empty. Now.

Charlie heard his father's footsteps and he knew what Ben was carrying.

"You keep the butt of this Winchester tight against you, you won't even feel the recoil," Ben said.

Ben slipped the lever-actioned, thirty-thirty-chambered model ninety-four low-velocity lightweight center-fire Buffalo-historied Winchester into the scabbard hanging from the Pinto's saddle. In his other hand, he held a Savage ninety-nine. He rammed it into the scabbard on the Appaloosa. The second scabbard on the other flank of the horse was empty and Ben started back toward the barn for another weapon.

"Guns'll get hot," he said as he passed Charlie. "We'll have to switch off, let 'em cool."

Charlie said nothing. He remembered that even the botfly could not hide. He heard the whisper of pneumatic tires in the dust and he turned. Lorraine Tower was seated on her tractor and she had geared the machine into neutral and let it roll down the slight slope leading from the alfalfa field to the barnyard. Her eyes were on Charlie. Ben heard the tractor, too, and he stopped at the door of the barn to watch Lorraine. The tractor slid to a halt in front of Charlie. Ben stayed framed in the barn doorway. Lorraine let the engine of the tractor idle and Charlie thought that was strange. She'd been careful to save gasoline by letting the machine roll in neutral and yet she didn't bother to shut off the engine. It was as if she were somewhere betwixt and between decision. Lorraine shifted a little on the hard plate of the tractor seat and her eyes moved over the rifle scabbards on both ponies and then fastened again on Charlie. She was still looking at him when she spoke to Ben.

"Thought you were gonna take the horns off my calf."

"I mean to," said Ben.

"When?"

"Yeah, I'm gonna do it," Ben repeated.

"They're just little bitty things now."

"Uh huh."

"Be a good time for it."

"Yeah."

Charlie didn't quite understand why, but as he listened to his father and Lorraine, he thought of the chess games he used to watch between Ben and Pete. Father and son would study the board and each would make his opening moves so slowly that Charlie would want to cry out, get on with it, get on with the game, but he never did cry out because he knew that those slow moves *were* the game. Charlie wished that Lorraine would stop staring at him, would look over at his father, so that whatever they were playing would pick up a little speed. But her eyes never wavered from the boy as she spoke again.

"He's awful young, Ben," she said.

Ben looked at the ground in front of him. His booted toe moved barely an inch as he turned over a small stone. Then he lifted his head and looked at the sky. He seemed to study the high clouds which were drifting in a pleasing pattern, but Charlie noticed an unusual opaqueness to Ben's eyes and so he wasn't surprised when his father looked away and, without a word or a nod or even the hint of a gesture, walked back into the barn.

It was then that Lorraine finally shut off the tractor's engine and looked away from Charlie. She followed Ben into the barn.

Ben was loading a point-two-seventy Weatherby Magnum. His back was to Lorraine but she could see the slant of his face and she could see the cartridge he was pushing into the chamber of the rifle. For a moment, she thought about Tom. He had gone each year to the high mountains for his buck, and the night before each of those hunts he would sit up with Lorraine and discuss his choice of weapons. His face animated with the thought of the coming chase, he would tell her about velocity and trajectory and grain load and foot pound of energy and muzzle thrust. He had been an efficient killer. But not, she thought, as efficient as the enemy soldier who had gunned him down.

"That load," she said, looking at the cartridges, "that load'll sure blow a moose apart."

"Hundred and thirty grains," Ben muttered.

"Regular giant killer."

"Uh huh."

She looked around the barn and saw the empty stalls where the Appaloosa and the Pinto usually stood and switched the flies away. She saw the straw bedding in the stalls and she wished the day were damp and dank so that the fragrance of the straw would rise pungently to her nostrils and wash away the acrid smell of gunpowder she knew she was only imagining and yet could really smell. And the click of cartridges could not drown out the sound of Charlie's silence.

"Ben," she said, "I'd like to take his place."

There was a long silence before Ben answered.

"Can't anybody take anybody's place. Not ever. You oughta know that as well as me."

Click. Click. The sound of cartridges reminded Lorraine of Jim Dandy's toenails on the plain pine floor.

"Town thinks you're made of ice and rock," she said.

"That what you think?"

"Was it Sarah's dyin' that closed you up?"

Ben stiffened and slammed home the final shell.

"You through?" he asked.

"I'm through."

Slowly, Ben turned and faced her.

"Then I've got work to do," he said.

"Well," she said, "that's one way of livin'." And she walked out of the barn.

Side by side, Ben and Charlie rode to the slaughter ground. The Hereford herd milled about in the huge enclosure. Morgan, and the ranch hand who had laughed at Ben in the feed store, stood in front of the wooden gate. Ben and Charlie reined up next to them. The Appaloosa tossed his head restlessly. Ben clucked to him quietly and soothed him down. Charlie's Pinto was as still as a coin.

"Morgan," Ben said, "first couple of shots, these cows are going to spook. You'll need to ride 'em down."

"You an' your boy," Morgan said, "you're gonna be alone an' ass-high in blood."

"It's going to be a long day," Ben said.

He glanced at Charlie. The boy was staring through the wire enclosure. Ben followed Charlie's gaze. A cow was giving suck to her calf. The calf had a perfect white star on its forehead. It was the calf Ben and Pete had birthed in Morgan's barn.

Sweet Jesus, Ben thought, and he closed his eyes for a moment.

He opened his eyes and edged the Appaloosa closer to the fence. He leaned down and unlatched the gate. Morgan ripped him from the saddle.

Ben sprawled in the dust at the feet of the cattle inside the pen. Morgan dived at him. Frightened at the sudden flurry of motion, the Appaloosa reared, his front hooves beating the air. The ranch hand grabbed his bridle and pulled the horse's head down and then shoved the horse backwards, away from the gate, away from the two fighting men. Charlie's Pinto shied but Charlie kept him on a tight rein and the horse was still. Charlie half stood in his stirrups so that he could see over the wire fence into the enclosure.

The two men were locked together as they rolled in the dust. The dangerous hooves of the milling cattle stomped close to their heads. Ben and Morgan pulled loose from each other and scrambled to their feet. They threw fast, hard punches, banging each other into the flanks of the moving herd. The cattle began to bellow and steers tried to turn away from the furious men but the animals were pressed close together and they had no room to wheel free and their sharp horns raked each other's flanks. Surrounded by the cattle, neither Ben nor Morgan had room to swing freely. They jabbed and hooked in short, vicious punches, driving their weight behind each blow. Ben stumbled and threw his arm up to avoid the slashing horns of a terrified steer. Morgan's huge fist hammered down against Ben's neck and Ben banged across the back of the steer. Morgan thrust his fingers into Ben's hair, lifted his head, and tried to slam it down onto the wicked point of the steer's horn. Both men were bent over the back of the bucking steer as they strained against each other and then Ben arched upward and drove his knee into Morgan's belly and the older man gasped and let go of Ben's head. They fell away from the animal who spun around and ran. There was a sudden space between the men. Ben crouched, drove a left hand and then a right hand into Morgan's belly and Morgan's head dropped from the pain. Ben anchored his heels hard into the bloodied ground and smashed Morgan high on the head and Morgan's eyes rolled white and he dropped.

Together, the ranch hand and Ben dragged Morgan out of the enclosure. They carried him to the pickup and laid him flat onto the truck bed and then the vehicle sped off.

Ben's hands were still slightly cocked in front of him, his fingers twitching just a little as if, on their own, they were searching for something to hold or tear at. The fight had brought a sudden return to recklessness and Ben's body tingled. He spat blood into the dust and he knew he was ready.

Ben and Charlie rode through the gate and into the enclosure. Ben leaned down from his saddle and pulled the Savage ninety-nine from its scabbard. He looked at Charlie. The boy hesitated. Then he slid the Winchester free. His eyes on Charlie, Ben levered a shell into his rifle. After a long moment, Charlie did the same. Ben's voice was gentle.

"Knew a man once. Nice feller. Jim Ringtail was his name. Part Cherokee. Told me the Indians swear the world shines after a buffalo hunt. Know why?"

Charlie just shook his head. There were tears in his eyes.

"Cause the souls of the buffalo rise up and wash the sky clean," Ben said. And then he took a deep breath. "All right, Charlie, let's do it."

Someone has to. Someone always has to, Pete said.

Ben raised his rifle and he knew he would shoot the white-starred calf first because after that the world would spin into sound and deafen the cry of death.

He squeezed the trigger.

In the nights to come, when he would awaken sweat-drenched and trembling, he would not be able to reconstruct the sequence of events. He knew only that certain things happened.

The calf dropped instantly, blood gushing from its heart.

The cattle spooked and ran blindly into the wired fence.

Charlie Remington Custer shrieked in anguish and dug his spurs into the Pinto and the horse leaped high over the barbed wire and boy and horse raced wildly across the prairie away from the killing.

And he, Ben, rode into the stampeding herd and swung his rifle from left to right and then left again and pumped bullet after bullet into the rampaging cattle and he did not stop until the carnage was complete. As an early moon rose in the western sky turning the land into a sea of silver, Ben Custer, Doctor of Veterinary Medicine, previously pledged to the well-being of stock, thought that he was floating outside himself and that his soul had fled. But when he felt the pain of his burning hands and smelled the drift of dust he knew he was forever locked in the vise of an awful and bloody reality.

Finally, there was only the sigh of wind and the soft bray of a single steer. Ben walked through the corpses until he found the steer which still lived. Sweat ran down his face. He blinked it out of his eyes. He raised the Weatherby to his shoulder and aimed at the sweet place between ear and eye and squeezed off the final kill and it was then that the trembling began. It started in his hands and then ran up his arms and into his shoulders until his whole body shook uncontrollably and he moved in a spastic stumble to the banks of the creek where he fell forward, his face crushing the last of the purple flowers. He slept.

And while his father slept, Charlie sat among the withered heads of lettuce in the victory garden, tears running down his face, the unfired Winchester cradled in his lap, and talked to the scarecrow.

"He did it so easy," he said, "just shot 'em away, just banged them dead, and he didn't care, he didn't care at all. Oh, God, he's so deaf, he's so goddamned deaf!"

Charlie Custer was convinced that his father did not hear the awful cries of pain from the slaughtered cattle. In his mind, pain was the bridge to death. It was a path of sound which led inextricably to that silent place where his guilt was known. It was the sound, he felt, which mutually defined his own birth and his mother's death, and, regardless of consequence, he was determined to avoid it.

His inability to accept the irreversible violences of life had created a sorrowful distance between him and Ben. But it was a distance Charlie longed to close. So it was with resignation that when the moon reached the exact center of the sky, he raised his rifle and blew the scarecrow's head apart.

It was, of course, one more act of pretense. It was a simulated death with no pain.

16

Tom Tower was coming home.

The citizens of Crowley Flats, standing silently alongside of the railroad tracks, waited to pay their respects. They were careful not to crowd the center of the depot platform. They left space for those most desolate, Lorraine and Dippsy. The woman and her boy stood where they had been told the boxcar would slide to a stop. There were no surreptitious glances toward the bereaved. There were no whispers. There was just a quiet sharing. The world was at war and men died and that, as Sam Hanks had said, was the sweet and sour of it.

Morgan Crowley pushed Lottie forward from the edge of the crowd and rolled her wheelchair toward Lorraine. And if an eye flicked quickly at his bruised face, no voice was raised. The men and women of this town knew what must have happened. Knew what was happening now. They had only to raise their eyes to the sky where the black plume of smoke bisected the wide horizon.

The morning birdsong was interrupted by the distant whistle of the train. Straining against her own pain, fretful that it would engulf her, Lottie placed her hands on the wheels of her chair and rotated them forward until she could reach out her hand and take Dippsy's in her own.

"You all right, boy?" she asked.

Dippsy nodded, his eyes seeking to curve around the blind turn of track where the train would first be seen.

"Where's old Jim Dandy?" Lottie asked.

"He musta know'd Papa was comin' home," the boy replied. "He run away."

"Yeah, they know," Lottie nodded. "They know."

The whistle sounded again and the train was so close that a cloud of steam floated over the round-house and then rose like a puffed smoke ring around the old water tank. The locomotive rounded the bend and chugged slowly toward the depot. As the engine rolled past the center of the platform, the engineer saw Lorraine and he touched his cap. She nodded. The great wheels of the locomotive slowed in their clanging circles. The engineer looked out his window and to the rear and when he saw that the boxcar was sliding up to the center of the platform he pulled harder on the brake and, with a sigh of steam, the train stopped.

Directly in front of Lorraine and Dippsy, the large wooden doors of the boxcar opened. Two soldiers of the United States Army, both attired in their dress uniforms, stood on either side of the open door. Between them was a wooden coffin. It was draped in the stars and stripes of America.

Together with the two soldiers, Morgan and Caleb lifted the casket down to the platform. The wind turned one corner of the flag and Lorraine could see that the pine box was the color of wheat and she was pleased that Tom would sleep like a prairie man who had paused forever in his fields.

She heard a man's stifled sobs and she looked up and away from the casket, but not before she saw that the flag had fluttered back to place, and she saw Virgil Foster standing alone under the faded depot sign which swung slightly in the wind, announcing to

all who traveled the prairie that this weathered Kansas
town had a name.

Lorraine heard a slow, deep peal. She turned toward it. The engineer was ringing his bell. The clapper
bounced rhythmically against the sides of its bronze
cap and the sound of mourning covered the chug of
wheels and spit of steam as the locomotive and the
now empty boxcar moved slowly up the steel rails
and away from the depot and out of Crowley Flats
and westward toward the Pacific where other men
lay in their clean pine boxes.

As the train rounded its farewell bend, the engineer
saw a solitary figure crouched in the shadows underneath the water tank. It was a man staring at the
water which leaked slowly through the rotten boards.
His head bobbed up and down to the cadence of the
drops and his mouth opened and closed in a similar
rhythm. He seemed hypnotized by the falling stream
and, just before he lost sight of the crouched figure,
the engineer thought how strange it was that the man's
mouth moved like the jaws of a snapping dog.

The train had disappeared by the time Sophie left
the depot and walked alone in the road bed along
the tracks. She knew where to find Ernst. She had
found him there before. Last night and the night before that and the night before that night. Three times
she had felt the unweighting of the brass bed. Three
times, through her narrowly slitted eyes, she had
watched Ernst pad across their bedroom floor which
was thinly carpeted with their only remnant from
Berlin and she had seen him push aside the white
cotton curtains and stare into the night, blinking at
the moon. Three times she had heard the awful
whimper that seemed to bubble at his lips. Each night,
Ernst had left the diner and Sophie had followed,
always keeping her distance as she walked through
shadow. Hidden in the surrounding bushes, she had
watched him hunch down under the tower and, still

whimpering, count the silent drops of water. Looking at him, she had been reminded of when she was a little girl at school, before Germany shook under the heels of the Chancelor, and she had listened in rapt wonder as her teacher read from the works of an English playwright. Her favorite passage had been spoken by a weary prince who had asked his soldiers to sit on the ground and tell sad stories of the death of kings. For three nights Ernst had appeared to be waiting for the death of kings and there had been something in his demeanor which had precluded interruption, had denied an invasion of his privacy. Sophie had been disturbed but not surprised at his quixotic behavior. Ever since the night he had been wounded by the rock, Ernst had moved steadily toward withdrawal. He refused to report the attack to any authorities. He refused to see a doctor. Perhaps most indicative of his state of mind was his refusal to tend his war map. The armies of little tacks marched no longer.

Now, the echo of the engine bell still floating on the morning air, Sophie stepped gingerly over the steel rails and moved into the shadows under the water tank where Ernst squatted, immobile except for the movement of his head as he followed each downward drop of water; and except for his jaws, which separated and closed and separated and closed, as if he were working loose a chicken bone which had pierced his throat.

"Ernst," she whispered.

The jaws moved up and down. Silently. He didn't turn.

"Ernst."

Nothing.

Sophie reached down and took his hand in hers. Gently, she pulled him around to face her. She helped him rise to his feet. He was sweating profusely and she took a handkerchief from his pocket and wiped his face. He is like a little boy, she thought, a little boy waiting patiently. But for what? He was looking at her with the eyes of a bewildered stranger and then, very softly, with infinite courtesy, he spoke.

"*Einen Augenblick, bitte. Wie lange halt der Zug hier?*"

My God, she asked herself, where does he think he is? And she knew the answer. She remembered the journey from Vienna to Salzburg. When they had been very young, they had trained through the Tyrol and each wayward stop had revealed new Alpine wonders. Just before they had reached their destination, the train had halted at some tiny mountain village. Ernst had looked out of the window and up into the snowy hills and, delight bursting on his face, had exclaimed to her:

"*Hinüber! Die Edelweiss!*"

The flowers' woolly white leaves had blended perfectly into the fresh fields of snow but their yellow petals had revealed their hiding place. Ernst had leaped from his seat and turned to a fellow passenger, a bold-looking man who might have been a Burgermeister of Munich, and it was then Ernst had asked:

Einen Augenblick, bitte. Wie lange halt der Zug hier?

He had not waited for an answer. He had run from the train, thrashed his way thigh-deep through the snow, picked a cluster of golden disks, and swung aboard the train just as it had huffed hotly forward.

Somewhere in the diner's attic, the leaves of edelweiss lay flat between the pages of a book, a memory without fragrance.

"Ernst?" she asked gently, "do you know me?"

He looked at her very gravely and she saw that he owned his own eyes again.

"You are Sophie," he said, "you are my darling."

"*Ja*," she said, "I am your darling."

They were still holding hands as they moved out of the shadows beneath the water tower and walked the long ditches of the railroad tracks toward the graveyard where a soldier was to be lowered into the ground.

It was not until she heard the first toll of church bells that Sophie Jurgen remembered the words of the bold Burgermeister of Munich. He had stared out the window watching Ernst scramble through the snow and then he had turned to her.

"There are some," he had said to Sophie, "there are some who believe that those who seek the edelweiss seek their own death."

God is our refuge and strength, a very present help in trouble. Therefore will not we fear, though the earth be removed, and though the mountains be carried into the midst of the sea. There is a river the streams whereof shall make glad the city of God. The heathen raged, the kingdoms were moved: he uttered his voice, the earth melted. Come, behold the works of the Lord, what desolations he hath made in the earth. He maketh wars to cease unto the end of the earth: he breaketh the bow and cutteth the spear in sunder; he burneth the chariot in the fire. Be still and know that I am God: I will be exalted among the heathen, I will be exalted in the earth.

The farmers and the ranchers and the storekeepers and the widows and the brothers and the children, all heard the minister, all but one. Tom Tower who rested in the wheat-colored pine. Nor, in his long and unwelcome silence, did he hear the congregation intone the Twenty-third Psalm. Neither did his cup runneth over.

He was dead.

The mourners left the church and followed the coffin to the burying place. Among the pallbearers were Morgan and his ranch hand and Virgil and Sam Hanks and one of the soldiers who had escorted the body home. Ahead of them were Lorraine and Dippsy and the minister. Next to them was the other soldier from the train. He carried a bugle. At the rear of grieving friends and neighbors were Ernst and Sophie. As the

funeral procession wound its way through scattered
box elders and across the flat and lonely land, the
church bells were ringing. The sound was resonant
with grief.

The mourners ringed the open gravesite and
watched the lowering of the flag-draped casket.

*Earth to earth, ashes to ashes, dust to dust. In sure
and certain hope of the Resurrection unto eternal life.*

The pallbearer soldier neatly folded the flag of
America and when its corners were triangulated
square he stepped forward and held out the flag to
Lorraine. She looked at it for a long moment and
then, with an almost imperceptible nod, indicated to
the soldier that she wished him to present the flag to
Dippsy. The soldier did so. When she was certain that
Dippsy was holding the flag securely in his hands,
Lorraine closed her eyes. Dippsy did the same. Lorraine took one small step sideways so that her body
could make contact with Dippsy, so that her flesh
could be warmed by Tom's son. Silent in their private
prayers they ignored the sound of an engine.

Lottie was the first to look up and then the eyes of
the other mourners joined her gaze. Some distance
away, on a rise of land, Ben stood in front of his
pickup truck and, behind him, on the far horizon, a
thin plume of black smoke penciled the sky. Some of
the mourners noted that Ben's face was a mask of
dust, others saw that his clothes were blood-stained,
many thought he stood as stiff as a scarecrow, but all
of them understood that he had come from the dead
cattle he had set on fire and so they turned their backs
toward him.

Ben wheeled around and returned to his truck.

He drove swiftly, not bothering to brake at the
curves, down-shifting so hard that the gears almost
stripped, sliding away from the ditches. He saw another truck in front of him but he didn't slow down.
He leaned on the horn and then punched it with his

fist, over and over, so that it blared in harsh, quick bursts and when he overtook the truck he swerved around in too tight an arc and almost sideswiped it and when he rushed past it he could see the frightened face of the old man who drove it. Then the face disappeared in the dust.

But not the stink. He thought maybe the stink would never disappear. He was covered with it. The odor of blood and intestines and burning flesh enveloped him. And the sound of the funereal bugle still hummed in his ears.

When he reached the road to the barn he whipped the wheel over hard and he grunted against the pain in his shoulder. He knew the flesh there was raw and swollen and discolored from the constant slam of recoil.

His foot smacked down on the brake and the truck skidded to a stop in front of the barn. He jumped out and started for the house, already feeling the hot needlepoints of the shower which would scald away the slaughter.

He saw the headless scarecrow.

Now what, he thought, *now what has Charlie done?*

He marched across the porch and into the house. He took the stairs to his bedroom two at a time. He threw open the door. He stopped. He stood in the doorway. His voice was ugly.

"Why?" he asked. "Jesus Christ, Charlie, tell me why?"

Charlie's back was to the door. He stood in the middle of the room and faced one wall. He was staring at the picture, at the woman who leaned and listened. He didn't turn at the sound of Ben's voice and when he spoke, his tone was gently quizzical.

"Did she know, Pa? Did Ma know she was going away?"

"I . . . needed . . . you!" The words popped like pellets from Ben's mouth.

"Did the doctor tell her? Or you, did you tell her?"

"I said I needed you. Why did you run away? Why did you run like that?"

Slowly, the boy turned to his father and Ben was startled to see that Charlie's face looked as if he were dreaming.

"Is it done?" Charlie asked, as casually as if he were inquiring about the weather. "Are they dead?"

"Yes. Yes, they are dead."

"Then you didn't need me," Charlie said politely.

Ben felt a pain in his hand and when he looked down he saw that he was gripping the doorknob so tightly that in a moment he might twist it off. He forced himself to unclench his fingers. They were trembling. He took a long breath and let it out slowly and then he did it again.

"I don't know where to begin," he said. "I don't know where to begin with you. I can't find you, Charlie, I don't know where to look."

"It's okay," Charlie shrugged indifferently, "you don't have to."

"Yes. I have to." Ben wished his shoulder didn't hurt so much and that his clothes were not so encrusted with blood. He crossed the room and sank down on the edge of the bed. He shut his eyes for a moment and when he opened them again he saw that Charlie had turned once more and was looking at the picture on the wall.

"Sit down, Charlie, sit down here with me." The boy didn't move. "Okay. Okay, you stand there. But you listen. I want you to listen."

Charlie cocked his head but Ben wasn't sure whether he now had his son's attention or whether Charlie was just imitating the pose of the woman in the picture.

"The night before Pete left," Ben began, "I told him something. I told him that killing something, killing anything, is lousy. It's rotten. It stinks. But there are . . ."

"Oh, I know that," Charlie said, his head nodding in a kind of disinterested logic. "I know that already."

"Goddamn it, will you listen! Turn around and look at me."

Charlie turned around and looked at him. He moved as mechanically as if he were a puppet on a string. And with the same detachment.

"There are times," Ben continued, trying not to be infuriated at Charlie's remoteness, "there are times you have to do things you don't like, things you hate, things that are no good. But you *have* to do them, Charlie. You can't walk around them or jump over them or shut your eyes and pretend they're not there. They don't go away, Charlie. They never go away. Can you understand that?"

"That's interesting," Charlie said remotely, "that's really interesting."

Ben wanted to hit him.

Charlie's gaze shifted to the window.

"It's getting dark." Charlie was indifferent. "I think I'll go to bed now."

"Yeah," Ben said softly. "Yeah, you do that."

Lorraine sat on the old porch glider. On a table next to her was a bottle of whiskey, a bowl of ice, and some random glasses. The porch window behind her was open so that she could hear the softly playing radio. The only other sound in the night was the creak of rusty springs as she rocked back and forth, back and forth, on the glider. Her eyes closed, she sipped from the whiskey glass in her hand and listened to the radio song.

I'll walk alone because to tell you the truth I'll be lonely. It was number one on the Hit Parade.

"Figured it's about time to take that horn off."

Lorraine opened her eyes. She hadn't heard Ben arrive. She saw that his truck was parked by the barn and that he had moved across the hard-packed earth to the porch. Ben had one foot on the first low step and he wore a clean shirt which was carefully ironed, and a pair of boots which had never smelled of dung and Lorraine knew that the slender stick of caustic potash he held in his hand had little to do with this night's visit. She picked up the bottle of whiskey and turned it slowly in the moonlight so Dr. Ben Custer could see what she was up to.

"Last of Tom's sour mash," she said.

"Wasn't much of a drinking man."

"Nope. Saved it for . . ."

"Frostbite and collywobbles." They finished it together.

They both smiled at the shared memory and in the following silence Ben climbed the rest of the steps and crossed the porch and accepted the bottle of whiskey, placing the stick of potash next to the bowl of ice. He gestured toward it as he poured himself a drink.

"This stick, this potash stick, she's easy to use."

"That so?"

"Yep. Just don't spread it around too thick as she can burn some. Calf won't feel much pain. What there is, why, it'll go quick. Always does."

"Not always," she said softly.

"Tom," Ben said, "he used to build a pinchgate that'd stop those critters from turning when he'd root-lift the horn. But this stick, well, she's just as quick. Maybe quicker."

"Well, we won't tell him, will we, Ben?" she said.

"No, we won't tell him. Anything. At all. Any more."

Ben leaned against the railing of the porch and drank some of the sour mash.

"Knew a man once," he said, "nice feller, he . . ."

"Beats me how every man you knew was a nice feller."

". . . he had this problem. Called it his Thursday problem."

"Thursday."

"Uh huh. Every Thursday he'd put flowers on his wife's grave and, of a sudden, why, he'd be hit with feeling sorry for himself. 'Fore he knew it, Thursday'd stretch to Sunday and just like that he'd lost half a damn week. Bad thing, a Thursday problem."

Lorraine realized that in attempting to strip her of her own self-pity, Ben had himself become partially naked. That's a beginning, she thought, that's a beginning for any two people. She wondered if Ben had ever exposed his vulnerability to his son, Charlie. She thought of the boy who had stood so still in the barnyard sunlight, his eyes narrowed against the glint of rifle, his head cocked as he listened to a sound only he heard. So much like Sarah, Lorraine remembered, so exactly like Sarah. Ah, Ben, she wanted to say, don't punish him because he is the reminder of your loss.

She reached up and let the tips of her fingers brush against Ben's wrist and in that way guided him to the glider. He sat next to Lorraine and his weight added to the creaking of the springs.

"House is an awful quiet place without a woman," he said. "Funny thing. She used to leave a kind of clatter behind her. Soft. Like a hen pecking corn. A kind of sweet clatter."

They rocked together. The cicadas were not singing. The moon had lost its face.

"Jesus," Lorraine whispered, "I miss the weight of him, Ben. The heft of him. The way he'd make this old swing creak. The way he touched . . ."

She stopped.

"What? The way he touched what?"

"Just touched, that's all. The way he touched."

Behind them, in the house, the radio was playing "Blue Champagne."

Lorraine began to sing softly to herself.

"*Blue champagne . . . purple shadows . . . and blue champagne.* Ben, did you ever see blue champagne? I mean really blue?"

"Uh uh."

"Me neither."

"Maybe," he said, "maybe one day I can find us some. Maybe."

"That'd be nice," she said, "real nice."

After a while, Lorraine leaned back against him, and they both watched the night die.

PART THREE

17

Dear Pa,

    Well, I did it. I made my first combat jump. It
was on September xx at XXX. The censor guy will
probably cut that out but what the hell they can't shoot
me for trying. But they sure tried to that night. It was
a son of a bitch. I mean they don't really tell you what
it's going to be like but I guess they can't. Maybe if
they told you, nobody would join up with this outfit.
You can tell Charlie it's not like the movies. Ha ha.
It was kind of crazy because even when all the shit
was coming at you, you know, the flak and the tracers
and everything, it was sort of pretty. I know that
sounds dumb but it was true. There was no moon and
so the only light in the sky was from the tracers. It
was like thin red lines curving up at you and then
sort of crisscrossing away and it reminded me a little
of the sparks from our campfire when we go fishing
at night. Only this time, we were the fish. There's this
guy I met. A Jewish kid from New York. Bobby Horowitz. He's a tough little bastard and I guess he's about
my best buddy. Was, I mean. He was here a lot longer
than me and had already made maybe seven or eight
jumps but he didn't act like King Shit if you know
what I mean. He knew I was scared to death and so he
kind of hooked up with me and made me laugh a lot
and told me that if I stuck with him nothing could
happen and that he would keep a giggle in my belly

and my dingle-dangle warm. Honest to God, that's how he talked. Anyway, he worked it out pretty good so that he was hooked up on the jump line just in front of me. All the time we were flying over xxxxxx Bobby kept reciting these cuckoo poems. You want to hear one? It goes like this. "As she opened her kimona, she shouted happy roshashonna!" And there was another one. "Don't you dare touch that zipper. Don't you know it's Yom Kippur!" Bobby said they were special holidays but that the poems would keep your dingle-dangle warm. He was really crazy. He was making the guys laugh when we reached the jump zone and got the orders to go. They open the hatch door and you snap on to the static line and then they tap you when it's your turn and you jump. I mean it's simple. You just jump. But I'll tell you something, Pa. It's a long way down. They get you low over the target so the guys won't be in the air too long but it's still a long way down cause you're just hanging there in the shrouds, floating like, and the goddamn Jerrys are zinging all their shit at you. Well, the guys were doing pretty good. Going out fast, you know? And then Bobby, he was standing right in front of me, he got the tap and out he goes and I'm in the hatchway looking down and I guess it was the flak that did it. That caught Bobby, I mean. See, when the shells explode you can see these puffs of black and they're all around you, everywhere you look. But like Bobby said, if you can see 'em, fuck 'em. The only thing I figure, he didn't see the one that hit him. I didn't either. All I know for sure is that he stepped out of the plane and then he was gone. I mean his parachute was still there, floating down nice and easy, but there wasn't anything at the end of it. It was like the flak blew him into dust. Well, the word just came down the line that we got to saddle up so I have to stop now. Take care of yourself and tell Charlie to keep my mitt oiled good. Oh, and would you do me a favor if you can? Bobby told me that his father's name was

*Saul and that they lived in a place called Washington
Heights. I think it was Audabon Avenue. Could you
maybe call Mr. Horowitz and tell him that the whole
outfit thought Bobby was a swell guy. I miss him. I
miss you and Charlie, too. Our platoon leader is a
big mother and he's yelling something at us so I guess
I'd better shag ass now.*

Pete

*P.S. After we jumped, we got into a hell of a fire-fight
and I did something, so now, if you look real close,
you can see two stripes. But you gotta look real, real
close cause most of the time the stripes are covered
with mud. Boy, could I use some Kansas sun!*

Ben looked at the sun. It was a circle of red lowering in the western sky. It lacked heat. It was the color
of blood. It was not the kind of sun about which Pete
dreamed.

Ben sat in the dark shadows of the cottonwood
trees which bordered the alfalfa field. His double-
barreled twenty-gauge shotgun, its breech open to reveal the unloaded smooth-bored barrels, rested against
his knees. Pete's letter was in his hands. The paper
was stained slightly from gun oil and in the stain Ben
recognized the partial ridges of his own fingerprints.
He studied them. They resembled the contours of a
topographical map, a map such as a soldier might use
as he surveyed the terrain over which he would do
battle. Ben thought that the imprimatur of his fingerprints was appropriate to his son's letter. Ben was glad
that he had taught Pete the geography of a hunt. He
knew that stalking men would be wholly different
from stalking animals but there would be common de-
nominators to the killing ground. There would be wild
brush and the gentle contours of sloping hills and
valley dips and tree tangles and the ever-shifting wind,
which would reveal the sound of approach and the
scent of danger.

He shifted his position and felt the spikey stalks of

alfalfa trying to puncture his dungarees; he heard the
click of the loose shells in the pocket of his canvas
hunting jacket. The cartridges were loaded with number seven-and-one-half buckshot. The rubberized
game pocket in the back of Ben's jacket was empty,
unstained by the blood of a pheasant. You're a damn
fool, Ben told himself, a goddamn fool. If you really
wanted the birds, you'd have taken the twelve-gauge
and loaded her up with number-six shot. He knew
what he was carrying was better suited to the gunning
of grouse or dove or woodcock. But then he mocked
himself because he knew it would not have made any
difference. Not once during the two hours he had
searched for the ring-necked birds had he fired his
rifle. There had been no reason. He had not loaded the
gun.

He had flushed one bird. The red-faced pheasant
with its necklace of white feathers and head of iridescent green had exploded over the stalks and winged
westward, its red rust body losing itself in the sun,
camouflaged by God's flame. It was at that moment
that Ben, half-heartedly, had fumbled in his pocket
for a cartridge, knowing all the while that he would
not use it, knowing that on this windblown day when
he had received Pete's letter, he could not kill. He had
lost his taste for prey.

He sat under the cottonwoods and thought about
his son's postscript. *We got into a hell of a fire-fight
and I did something.* What? What had he done to earn
corporal stripes? Pete had been able to write about
a boy who had been blown into a puff of smoke but
had not seen fit to talk about his own action. Was it
modesty that precluded an account? Or was the thing
he had done of such awful nature that by eliminating
its detail the boy could hide it from his heart? Ah,
Pete, Ben whispered to himself, you are a young,
young man but even in your youth you have been introduced to the truth. No one of us, Ben said aloud to
the dying sun, no one of us can hide. Not ever.

I did something.

And I, too, thought Ben and looked toward the narrowing horizon where dusk joined the sky and the earth and where only a few days ago the black smoke of burning flesh had left its smudge.

For the tenth time, Ben reread his son's letter and he mused about the irony of violence. *By participating in some undefined brutality, Pete had been welcomed into the company of men.* Ben had been isolated. He thought about his trip to Crowley Flats that morning. He and Charlie had driven in to make the week's purchase of supplies. The fact that men still drowned in the Coral Sea and crumpled behind German trees did not alter the simple needs of those at home. There was milk to buy and flour and beans and chicory-flavored coffee and a sack of Bull Durham and the newspaper with the bitter humor of Mauldin's Willie and Joe. These simple excursions had been, in the past, a sharing of the common pretense that an unmanageable world was manageable. Simple, everyday tasks relieved all of the citizens of Crowley Flats of the painful monotony of waiting to discover which distant man would live or die, would return whole or maimed. But on this morning as Ben and Charlie had idled from store to store there had been little social exchange. It was as if the storekeepers of the town had formed a secret society, hoarding words instead of gold. Ben was irritated by the constant greeting of silence but he refused to acknowledge the quarantine. Purposely, he had chatted amicably with the men and women who wrapped his packages and measured his sugar and, in short, sharp strokes of anger, had torn the stamps from his coupon books. They answered him in economical grunts and their eyes had never met his. Man or woman, each had riveted his glance on Ben's chest or shoulder or on some mesmerizing hole in the air just above Ben's head. What the people of the town did not know was that Ben had become quite familiar with that certain but ephemeral spot above his head because that was where Charlie's eyes had focused, too, ever since the killing of the herd. And from the look in the boy's eyes, Ben knew that his younger son was not searching for some suspected halo about to descend over his father's head.

The combination of grunted silence and wavering eyes had made Ben seek the comfortable solitude of a pheasant hunt in the prairie dusk.

There was another reason. He wanted to taste the wind in his throat and hear the whir of a bird's flight and feel the warmth of an October sun on his skin. He wanted to walk alone in a Kansas field and let his senses ebb and flow with nature's rhythmic pleasures. Perhaps then, he thought, I will know what to say at five o'clock. It was at that hour that he would talk with Mr. Saul Horowitz of Audabon Avenue, Washington Heights, New York City. Earlier, Ben had placed the call and then picked up his gun and walked into the field of alfalfa.

Hunched under the cottonwoods, Ben studied the awful phrase in his son's letter. *It was like the flak blew him into dust.* He folded the letter carefully and returned it to his pocket where it rested alongside of the unused cartridges. He looked at his watch. It was a few minutes before five o'clock. He rose. He started home.

Ben turned on one lamp in the bedroom. The lamp was on a chest of drawers, placed directly under the unframed Grant Wood print, "Dinner for Threshers," so that the lamplight spread upwards and over the painted figure of the woman in the farm kitchen.

He sat on the bed and waited for the telephone to ring. He let it ring twice before he picked up the receiver. In between the first and second ring he thought he saw the woman in the picture turn slightly but he knew it was only his imagination and that he, not the woman who looked like Sarah, would have to take the call.

"Hello."

"Dr. Custer?"

"Yes, this is Dr. Custer."

"This is Horowitz. Saul Horowitz."

"Thank you for calling, Mr. Horowitz."

"Tell me, do I know you, sir?"

The man's voice sounded tired and too old to be the father of a boy who had been blown into dust.

"No, no, you don't know me, Mr. Horowitz. My son knows ... knew ... your son."

"Ah."

"He wrote and asked me to call you. He wanted you to know that Bobby was a very fine soldier."

"Yes."

"The boys in his outfit ..."

"Men, sir, the men in his outfit."

"Yes. The men in his outfit had great respect for him."

"Yes."

"My son, Pete, he will miss him very much."

"I, too, miss him."

"Of course."

There was a long silence while the wire hummed softly between two strangers. Ben heard Saul Horowitz clear his throat.

"I am grateful for your call, sir," the old man said. "I will tell Bobby's father of your kindness."

"His father?"

"I am his grandfather, sir. My son and his wife do not wish to take calls at this time. Please understand, there is no rudeness intended."

"I understand."

"Your son, Dr. Custer, he is all right?"

"Yes."

"Good. Let it be so always." There was another pause and then the old man spoke again and Ben thought he detected a kind of thin tentativeness to the tone. "Perhaps you have a moment?"

"Of course."

"Was your son, by chance, with Bobby for some time?"

"I don't know."

"Ah."

"Is there some reason you ask? Something special?"

"Special? Yes, special. Please, I do not wish to burden you."

"Mr. Horowitz, Bobby meant a great deal to Pete. If there is anything I can answer ..."

"I have been making a supposition."

"A supposition?"

"In our calendar, September is the seventh month of the year, and it is written in Leviticus that in the seventh month, in the first day of the month, there will be a sabbath, a memorial of blowing of trumpets. Now it is further implied that he who does not hear the blowing of the ram's horn has not fulfilled his obligation to God and will be cut off from his people. Are you following me, Dr. Custer?"

"Yes, sir."

"On that day I, of course, blew the ram's horn but as I did so, I thought to myself that it was much like blowing a trumpet in a barrel in so far as my grandson was concerned because, is it not a fact, that where he was he could only have heard the echo, the echo of the ram's horn?"

The old man's voice stopped. Ben was not sure whether he was expected to answer the question or, indeed, how to answer the question, and so he remained silent. Saul Horowitz spoke again.

"Are you still there, doctor?"

"Yes."

"Do you understand my concern?"

"I'm not sure, sir. I think you are telling me that if Bobby heard only the *echo* of the ram's horn, he would not, in your terms, have fulfilled his obligation to God."

"And do you see what follows in terms of theological fate? I repeat, from Leviticus, he who does not hear the horn will be cut off from his people. Naturally, I speak not of the flesh but of the spirit. Now for my supposition. What if, listen carefully now, doctor, what if God were a robber?"

Ben blinked.

"I beg your pardon?"

"Why?"

"Why what?"

"Why do you beg my pardon?"

"Well, sir, I'm not sure I heard you correctly."

"Please, doctor, pay attention. I asked you what if God were a robber? *What if He stole the sound from the horn?* Given such a circumstance, would it not be accurate to say that there would be nothing to hear? No man, not even Bobby Horowitz, could be expected to hear that which is not there. So far, so good. Yes?"

"Yes. I think so." Ben spoke carefully.

"Well, then. If Bobby Horowitz could not be expected to hear the ram's horn, if such an expectation was only smoke, so to say, then Bobby would not, I repeat, would not have failed in his obligation to God and so, my dear doctor, his spirit would not now be cut off from his people. A dybbuk he would not be. And, please believe this, the family of Saul Horowitz has no need for a dybbuk."

The old man paused and cleared his throat and then continued.

"You can see, of course," he said, "that this supposition rests on whether God is, in fact, a robber. I would appreciate your feelings on this matter."

Ben looked across the room and thought that the serene face of the woman in the picture, too, was waiting for his answer.

"I think," he said, "I think God is a robber."

"Ah," the old man sighed, "thank you, sir. Such knowledge makes me feel a little bit better. Not good, you understand, but better. These things are complicated."

"Yes," Ben said.

"*Zie gesundt*," said the old man.

"Sure," said Ben.

He heard the click on the other end of the wire and then he, too, replaced the receiver in its cradle. He rose, walked across the room, and turned off the lamp.

He stood in the darkness for a long time.

18

"Daaaaandy! Jiiiiiiim Daaaaandy! Goddamn you to
hell, where are you? C'mon, Dandy, c'mon!"

Lorraine looked out the kitchen window. Dippsy
was standing on the back porch, his hands cupped to
his mouth, as he called for his dog. But there was no
sound of running footpads, nor was there the anticipated deep welcoming bark of the dog. Each evening
since Dandy had run off, on that long gray day of Tom
Tower's return, Dippsy had placed a bowl of scraps
on the back porch and had tried to summon the German shepherd. The boy had whistled special tunes
that only he and Dandy knew, he had raised his high,
thin voice in cluckings of love, he had threatened,
cajoled, stomped and sworn but the dog had not appeared and so each evening Dippsy had returned to
the kitchen, scraped out the bowl, rinsed it clean,
rubbed it dry until it glistened, placed it carefully
under the kitchen sink and then retreated to his room,
his young eyes filled with puzzlement as he pondered
the treachery of canine love. Lorraine had not tried
to ease the boy's feelings by promising that, one day,
Dandy would return. She was equally puzzled by the
dog's disappearance but had concluded that Dandy's
instincts informed him about the death of Tom. Somehow, the dog must know that he will never again feel
the hard fingers of the man he loved. Lorraine understood that all too well and so could not find real fault

215

in Dandy's running. She missed him and, she admitted to herself, she envied his freedom. She pictured herself, much the way she had been as a little girl, running against the wind across the prairie fields and into the hills, shoeless and sun-fed, as light as the windblown chaff. She had, during those moments as a little girl, resolved never to grow up and join the company of adults where she would be burdened with responsibility. She would remain, forever, shoeless in the wind.

Now, standing at the kitchen sink, a paring knife in one hand, a bush bean in the other, Lorraine looked down at her shoes. They were an old pair of riding boots, the heels worn and rounded at the edges, the leather soles thin and unevenly ridged from endless repair. The sole of her right boot curled away from its last where the threads had finally just sighed and died. Lorraine smiled to herself, thinking that it would not be long before her feet would come right through the boots and then she would, once again, feel her toes in the dust.

"You're a no good shitheel, Jim Dandy, and I don't give a tinker's fart. I just don't care. I don't care at all."

Lorraine looked out the window again and shook her head. He was too old to have his mouth washed out in soap and, besides, she understood that he emulated the men in the fields and the soldiers who passed through town, thinking that each curse was another signpost on the road to maturity. She would, she supposed, have to take him in hand. The naked bulb of the kitchen-porch light glowed over the boy's head, gave him a crown of cornsilk and made him look like a boy king surveying his troops on the night before battle. He looked vulnerable in the golden light. She was pleased that he didn't try to hide this vulnerability, that he was willing to show his disappointments as well as his delights. There was no distance between them. They would, she thought, remain forever accessible to each other.

She thought of Ben, and how, over the years since Sarah's death, he had edged away from sharing either the pain or the pleasure of *his* life. Unable to move out of the dark circumference of memory, he had trapped himself in a web of steely self-protection. The young man whose hard flesh had so sweetly filled her as she lay in the root cellar had become a stranger who had turned his passion out to pasture. And yet. There was an unquiet about him. A fumbling restlessness. She had known, that night at the windmill, that he wanted her, but he had refrained from any yearning move. And then again, on the porch, he had offered her the casual comfort of his strength but had retreated from any overt act that might lead toward commitment. Strictured by the subtle sense of his withdrawal, Lorraine had been unable to act boldly. She had wanted to shake him, to shout: Look at me! Look at me! I am in need. Let us touch, flesh on flesh, and grind our sorrows into the dust. She had wanted to tell him that there would be no obligation in the touching, there would be only a splendid sharing of their dark night. But she had said nothing, and, finally, her senses dulled by sour mash and the echo of cicadas and the perfume of dying honeysuckle, she had closed her eyes and slept. She had been awakened at dawn by the bleating of her calf. Stiff and chilled by the morning dew, she had risen from the porch glider, its creak of rusty springs a harsh sound under the birth of sunlight, had winced at the sight of two empty glasses, and had taken note of Ben's absence. The calf had bleated again and she had turned toward the sound.

With some irony, she had seen that Ben's physical energy had not been wasted. He had, during her sourmash slumber, dehorned the calf. He had done more. He had removed the large, heavy barred cage from the rear of his pickup and placed it near the barn. The calf was in it, lying comfortably on a bed of straw. Lorraine had remembered Ben's warning not to let the calf run free through the clover until the scar on the butt end of the horn had healed. She had placed a small pail of milk in the cage and when she stroked the feeding calf's head she had been careful not to touch the scar where the stick of caustic potash had burned off the beginning of horns. When she had touched the warm flesh of the young animal, she had thought again of Ben's hands and how much she desired them on her skin and she had known with absolute clarity that she would have to initiate such a touching. Perhaps, she thought, perhaps if ever he reveals his own vulnerability to pain, I will believe again in his willingness to share.

She sliced the bean in two. She tossed both parts into the pot on the stove where other bush beans were parboiling in preparation for canning. Not canning, exactly. Jarring. Lorraine and the other prairie women put up their preserves in Mason jars. They peeled, trimmed and blanched beans and carrots and beets and apples and peaches and hermetically sealed them in glass jars. They bathed the glass jars in pans of steaming water until the heat destroyed any microorganisms which might be lurking within. They cooled the jars. They labeled them. They stored them. And on that day when they went to the cellar and returned to the kitchen with a jar of preserves, each woman dared hope that the hand which would pluck a peach from its sweet syrup would belong to a man returned from war. Such a possibility no longer existed for Lorraine. From habit, she continued to preserve her garden.

And from habit, Lorraine glanced at the window again, unconsciously checking on her son, but steam from the pan of water had coated the glass pane and she could see only the smudge of yellow light from the porch lamp. She hoped Dippsy had remembered to saddle their horses. They would have to leave soon for the roundhouse. Her gas-rationing coupons were almost depleted and what was left would have to be saved for the tractor. They would ride to town where they would spend the evening helping to rip the old locomotive into scrap.

Behind her, she heard the screen door open and she automatically tensed, waiting for the child slam of door. In that fraction of silence, she wondered about the conspiracy of children. Surely, boys and girls from all parts of the world had exchanged secret instructions on the technique of opening and closing screen doors, a technique guaranteed to torment adult sensibilities. She heard the slow rasp of springs as Dippsy pulled open the door. She actually heard the silence as the door remained cocked. She shut her eyes for an instant and prayed, hopelessly, for a soft easing of the door. Her shoulder muscles bunched as she waited. *Crack!* The screen door slammed against its frame and bounced once inside its own echo. Lorraine cut herself on the paring knife.

"You ready, Mama?"

"Uh huh." Lorraine opened her eyes and sucked on the small cut on her finger. She turned off the stove and looked at Dippsy. He stood inside the doorway, leaning nonchalantly against the jamb, a straw Stetson tipped low over his eyes, a piece of grass drooping from a corner of his mouth.

"Hooie!" she said. "Don't you look a dandy."

"Randy," he said.

"Huh."

"I'm randy."

Lorraine just stared at him. Now where in hell's damnation had he learned that? Well, enough was enough.

"Now, you listen, boy," she started.

"Randy Scott," he said. "And I'm aridin' against the Purple Gang."

"Oh," she said. "Oh, yeah. Randolph Scott. Well, that's nice. That's real nice, Dips."

"Randy."

"Yeah. Randy."

"Charlie's gonna meet us at the roundhouse. He's gonna be Duke."

"Duke?"

"Duke Wayne. Don't you know nuthin', Mama? Him and me, we're gonna have it out tonight."

"That's nice."

Dippsy looked at her strangely, and there was a kind of puzzle in his voice.

"Ain't you a bit scairt?"

"Should I be?"

"How'd you know he ain't a faster draw than me?"

"Oh," she said, "nobody's faster than Randy."

He thought about that for a moment and then nodded, still chewing on the blade of grass in his mouth.

"You bet your ass," he said.

"Now, Randy, you stop that!"

"Yes'm."

He turned and started out of the screen door. Lorraine caught it before it could slam. She saw that Jim Dandy's bowl was still on the porch.

"You just gonna leave it tonight?"

Dippsy looked down at the bowl. And so swiftly did the face of a Western killer disappear that Lorraine wanted to cry. The boy's voice trembled.

"Could be he'll come back if there's nobody here. I mean, he knows he's been bad, runnin' off like that, and he might be thinkin' we was gonna punish him. We ain't gonna do that, are we, Mama?"

"No."

"You think then maybe ol' Jim'll come back? Maybe?"

"Maybe," she said, and put her arm around the boy's shoulders as they moved to the saddled horses outside the barn.

*　*　*

The dull clump of horses' hooves awakened Jim Dandy. Lying in the weeds under the windmill by the waterhole, he stretched and his ears pointed toward the sound. He was belly-flat in the grass. He didn't want to move. He didn't want to leave the cool comfort of the grass. A fire burned in his body, that heat which made his muscles contract and spasm. The sound of moving horses came closer and the dog's great white head jerked convulsively as if he had been touched with an electric prod. His muzzle slid along the grass and was moistened by the night dew. It terrified him. His throat constricted immediately as he protected himself from swallowing any of the offending moisture which he knew would strangle him. Viciously, he snapped at the grass, trying to destroy it. He slithered through the weeds toward the roadside. Hidden in the cottonwood clump, he watched the horses pass. He heard the voices of a woman and a boy and, stirred by some blurred memory, his tail twitched, slapped once against the ground, and then was still. The muscles rippled along his croup and he started forward but the boy's horse shied for just an instant and a horseshoe iron snapped against a stone. A crimson spark flashed from the road. The dog quivered with fright and pivoted back into the cottonwoods.

Dandy waited until he could no longer hear the sound of the horses and then he edged out of the trees and across the roadside ditch. He stood in the road, his massive head angled down as his jaws opened and closed, opened and closed, forcing forward the thick yellow saliva which was choking him and which, finally, dripped into the dust. Then, a gleaming ghost in the moonlight, he ran toward the farm.

And as the citizens of Crowley Flats, innocent of impending crisis, sledged the steel sides of an ancient engine, and as the roundhouse resonated with the

clang of community, a shadow of fury sprang toward
the steel cage and the dehorned calf within it.

The pounding of a locomotive into scrap was not
a casual effort. The fugue of sledge and hammer was
music to the men and women and children in the
roundhouse. They listened to the rasp of hacksaw and
the rip of metal and they were pleased by their own
sound. They knew that at this moment their husbands
and brothers and sons were shuddering under shell attacks, were crawling under stuttering guns, were being
assaulted by explosions. The deafening noise in the
roundhouse gave them a sense of participation in the
distant violence.

They were not demonstrative people and yet they
did a curious thing. Each time a man or woman
crossed the floor of the roundhouse to pick up a hammer or borrow a crowbar or carry his or her small
bundle of scrap to the growing heap, he or she would
find a way to brush against his neighbor. Sometimes a
knee would slip, inadvertently of course, against another's knee. Sometimes, a hand would touch a hand.
No one acknowledged the glancing contact. No one
voiced the fleeting pleasure of such physicality but
each was secretly gladdened and felt more fully drawn
into this circle of toil.

There were exceptions. Working alone in one corner
of the roundhouse, Ben and Charlie were prying loose
a section of roof on the locomotive's cab. No one bor-
rowed a tool from them. No one bent knee to knee.
The memory of black smoke in the sky hung like a
veil between the Custers and their neighbors. In the
minds of most, Ben's act of slaughter had been pre-
cipitous. He had not been forgiven. Only Lorraine
and Dippsy had acknowledged his presence. When
they had entered the roundhouse, Lorraine had smiled
across the littered floor and nodded at Ben and then
turned to the task assigned her by Morgan Crowley.

Dippsy and Charlie had exchanged a fierce and narrow look and each had moved his right hand toward
his hip, lightly touching their mythical holsters, giving
fair warning of the dreadful shootout to come.

Cora Zink's eyes were closed as she circled the jukebox, dancing cheek to cheek with some pretended
partner, and moaned the words of the song.

*You're as pleasant as the morning and refreshing as
the rain. Isn't it a pity that you're such a scatterbrain?*

Caleb Dodd and Virgil Foster watched her as they
hacksawed a piston rod.

"Wisht I were younger," Caleb whispered.

"Chet Beam," Virgil giggled, "he declared she was
sure somethin' to get holt of."

"Shit, he never."

"Said he did. Said she peckered him out. Said she
was like a flyin' fuck in a rollin' doughnut."

"Goddamn," Caleb said and he leaned down sur-
reptitiously and shifted the weight in his crotch.

The platter in the jukebox fell onto the stack of
previously played records and another one slipped
into place. Caleb stopped sawing for a moment so
that he could hear what song was about to be played.
He hoped it would be that good old country boy, Elton
Britt, wailing about the Star-spangled Banner waving
o'er the land of heroes brave and true. But it wasn't.
It was some goddamn furriner clickin' his teeth over
rum and Coca-Cola. Caleb started to get angry but
then he thought about how maybe one day he would
slip some of that Spanish fly into a great big ol' glass
of rum and Cola-Cola and give it to Cora Zink to
suck on. That and somethin' else, too. The thought of
it was almost more than he could bear and a sigh
shuddered through him.

"You gettin' tired?" Virgil asked.

"Shit," said Caleb.

Sam Hanks and Willie Mae pulled hard on a sheet
of boiler plate they'd chiseled loose. They winced at

the shriek of steel and let the rusted metal clatter to
the floor. They stepped back to admire their handi-
work and wipe sweat from their faces. Willie Mae
spat out her matchstick and reached for a fresh one.

"David, that's my cousin Neeley's son," she said,
"landed on Thursday and, by gum, he were right in
the thick of it the followin' Sabbath. Didn't have no
time to pray, neither."

"Well," Sam sighed, trying to blink away the black
letters of the telegrams which, he felt, were perma-
nently painted on his eyes, "we're sure givin' 'em what
for to fight with."

Morgan Crowley sledged loose a spoke from a great
iron wheel and carefully arranged Ben Custer's face
under each hammer blow. It seemed so long ago that
he had promised Lottie that they would sashhay up
Wichita way and that he would wrap her in a yard of
yellow ribbon. After the slaughter, he'd ridden his
land and examined the remainder of his herd, the
cattle that had never grazed by the creek, but the
animals had not been ready for the feedlots. There was
no longer reason to take his wife to Wichita and bind
her in gold.

"Well," she'd said, "oh, well."

He lifted his sledge and drove it down on the iron
spoke and saw the shattering of Ben's face.

Ernst stood at the bottom of a ladder. The ladder
had been placed in front of a huge boiler wall which
had been hoisted in the air. He lit the acetylene torch
in his hands. Flame erupted out of the nozzle. He
pushed a pair of goggles down from his forehead and
covered his eyes. He climbed the ladder. With his
torch, he began to cut through the boiler plate. The
flame seared into rusted metal and sparks bounced
off the steel. Ernst stared through the goggles at the
sparks and wondered why he was standing in the sky,
why God had chosen at this moment to explode the
stars. His mouth fell open. Saliva oozed across his
lips. It was thick and yellow. He jerked the goggles

from his eyes and swiveled his head from right to left and then back again. He looked down.

He saw the eighth circle of hell. He saw the writhing figures of penitent sinners, their arms and legs flailing through steam as they sought to crawl from purgatory. He heard the clang and clatter of condemned and he heard the awful shriek of dying angels and he heard the bells of a burgomeister calling him home. His jaws snapping like a vicious animal, he cried to Gabriel.

Was . . . ist . . . mein . . . Name?

And all the boom and blast, the clack and rattle, the hiss and whomp, the blare of jukebox and shriek of shredding steel, could not cover the sound of Ernst's anguish.

Every man and woman and child in the roundhouse froze at that awful cry. Their heads turned and looked up as they sought the source of horror.

Ernst Jurgen stood at the top of his ladder. His eyes rolled wildly in his head and his face was scarlet-streaked from where he was tearing at his flesh with his fingernails. His tongue, thick with pus-like saliva, hung loosely out of his mouth. His clothes were soaked with sweat and tears and urine and his body writhed in pain. He was sucking in great gasps of breath and then hawking up his phlegm, and yellow spittle flew out of his mouth, fanned in tiny drops as it fell to the floor below where men and women ran screaming from its path. And then the terror increased because those below the ladder saw Ernst's hands swing down from his face and claw at his genitals. They saw him rip the clothes away from his body and reveal himself. He clutched his testicles and semen spurted from his rigid penis as he ejaculated over and over again.

Sophie screamed.

And in the valley of his mind, Ernst saw her eyes, dark circles of surprise, and, in final agony, his hands flew to his mouth and he tried to rip the tongue from his mouth.

He howled like a wolf.

He hurtled off the ladder and a piston rod impaled him through the exact center of his chest and as the echo of the burgomeister's bells died in his head, he whispered.

Kommen Sie . . . kommen Sie . . . my darlings!

19

Dr. Douglas Root had driven most of the night. It was almost dawn when he turned into Ben Custer's barnyard. A light burned in the clinic. Root parked the Department of Public Health van near the open barn door. He got out, yawned. He stretched and scratched himself. He started for the barn. He paused outside the window. He looked in. Ben was hunched over a table littered with pamphlets and open books. Root rubbed his eyes, grainy from the long drive. His back ached. There was acid in his belly. He belched softly. He was, he told himself, too old for this kind of work. He was responsible for too many miles and too many mules. For the tenth time that night a musical refrain floated through his mind. *When the boys come marching home.* Being a man of scrupulous self-honesty, he admitted to himself that the musical phrase had not been provoked by any patriotic fervor; rather, it was a selfish reminder that one day the boys *would* come marching home and, among them, surely there would be one who would take his place. He dreamed of that day. And of a future without fungus or parasite, without death or disease. He dreamed of eating waffles. He belched again, and as he turned away from the window and entered the barn, he wiped away the dream and tried to remember all he had read about rabies.

When Root walked into the clinic Ben didn't look up

from the pamphlet in his hands. He just waved a hand
toward a cluttered shelf.

"Coffee's on," he said.

"Thanks."

"You bring it?"

"Much as I had."

"Enough?"

"Hell, Ben, how do I know? How many animals you
gonna shoot?"

"Inoculate."

"You plan to fuss about words?"

"I plan to fuss about everything."

"You're sure riled up, doctor."

"Wouldn't you be, doctor?"

"Yeah. Yeah, I guess I would. Tell me where you're
at with this thing."

Ben closed the pamphlet. His fingers slid along the
words printed on the cover. It was a pamphlet issued
by the Department of Public Health. It contained a
description of rabies and it instructed the reader on the
ways and means for combating a possible epizootic
of that dreaded disease. Ben picked it up. He folded
it into a paper airplane. He floated it across the room.
It arced in a gentle parabola and landed at Root's
feet. He picked it up.

"You don't approve?" Root asked.

"Oh, sure. It's got all the rules, the ABC's. The history, the symptoms, how it spreads, period of incubation, how to control by vaccination, everything. Almost
everything."

"What'd we miss?"

"How to find the carrier."

"Begin with what you see, Ben, that's all any of us
can do."

"I don't see very goddamn much."

"That German feller tonight, he like to hunt?"

"No."

"Fish or ride?"

"Uh uh."

"Well then, it's a safe bet he wasn't in contact with any wild animals. That limits it some."

"I already figured that."

"How so?"

"You speak German?"

"Can name you some beers."

"Funny. Very funny."

Root took a sip of coffee and thought how its acid would probably burn another hole in his stomach. He put down the cup. He spoke carefully.

"You're drawn tighter'n a cinched saddle, Ben. I know what you face. I've been there. From what you told me on the phone, most of this town saw a man die tonight and the way he died isn't ever gonna leave them. They're gonna ponder that, Ben, and they're gonna start wonderin' what did it to him and where that 'what' is. At first, they're gonna tell themselves it was a stray coyote or a mad dog or some strange animal what just passed through town. But the face of that German is gonna be tattooed behind their eyes and pretty soon they're gonna figure out the odds. And the odds are that that poor feller was sent to the glory road by some plain, decent, sweet, ordinary little pussycat or house mutt that every goddamn citizen of this town touches, pets, fondles and feeds seventeen times a day. And then they're gonna panic. They're gonna lock the doors. They're gonna shoot at shadows. The streets are gonna be empty, Ben, and there's only one sound you're gonna hear on the prairie."

"What's that?"

"Your name. You told these people about rabies, about what it could be, an' why you had to shoot those steers, and there wasn't one damn fool lifted a finger for you and now they've seen it, they've stared right into it and they feel guilty and that's no good, Ben. Because when a man feels guilt he turns it around and blames the feller what give it to him and pretty soon he hates that feller. Oh, yeah, you're gonna hear your name and the sound's gonna be sour. And so I suggest,

Ben, that you better unwind just a little bit and let the good Lord touch you with lightness. Amen. I'm done. Now what about the German?"

Ben grinned. "You sure call a spade a spade, don't you, Doug?"

"Only way to play poker."

"I guess."

"I know."

"Ernst," Ben began, "he loved animals. I mean really loved them. Took care of them. Fed them. I guess every stray in this town knew when to show up at the diner. He'd carry out a bowl of scraps and he'd call to them. '*Kommen Sie,*' he'd call out, '*kommen Sie,* my darlings.' And that's what he was saying when he died. Damn it, Doug, that piston rod stuck right through him and he had this funny smile on his face as he called to all those strays he loved."

"So you figure it was any one of those animals he used to feed, is that about it?"

"It's an educated guess, but it's the best I can do."

"The people cutting up that train," Root asked, "they hear what the German said?"

"They heard."

"They understand what it means? That it could be any one of their pets?"

"What they might of missed was made real clear by Morgan. Son of a bitch couldn't wait."

"And they spooked, am I right?"

"You are right. They backed away from Ernst like he had cholera."

With his finger, Root stirred the cold coffee in his cup. He put the cup on a makeshift hotplate which had been placed over a Bunsen burner. He turned up the flame of the burner. He whistled softly to himself but there was no tune to it, there was just a thin wheeze of breath slipping out between his teeth.

"Ben," he said, "you're in trouble."

"I'm going on the streets tomorrow morning. First thing. I've rigged a loudspeaker on the pickup. I'll set

up the Grange Hall and tell 'em to bring in their animals for vaccination. That's why I asked you to bring
the serum. I don't know how much I'll need. More'n
likely, most of the animals have already had their
shots but there'll be some people who've overlooked
it, just let it slip their minds."

"There always are."

"Till we trace it down, they'll have to keep their
pets leashed and muzzled." Ben was silent for a moment. The muscle on one side of his face jumped, and
when he continued his voice was hardly audible. "I
guess I'll have to do the other thing, too."

"You don't have any choice," Root said. "You'll have
to shoot any stray on sight."

"Yeah."

Root saw thin spirals of steam rising from his coffee.
He turned off the burner. He lifted the cup to his lips.
The coffee scalded his tongue. He sucked in air to
cool the burned spot and to give him time to decide
whether or not to just plain level with Ben, to lay the
truth on him, hard and clean. And, of course, he knew
he would.

"It won't work, Ben."

"What? What won't work?"

"They won't come to the Grange. Oh, they'll start
to. They'll check the tags on their dogs and they'll
throw their minds back trying to remember the last
time the animal was inoculated and some of 'em will
see real fast that they'd best get it done lickety split
and so they'll leash the dog and open their doors and
look down the road to the Grange. But when they look
down the road, their minds'll start working and their
eyes'll see funny things. They'll see shadows crouched
and ready to leap and they'll convince themselves that
one of those shadows is the real killer, the mad dog
foaming at the mouth, the one who's going to tear
out their throat. And so, nice and easy, they'll close
their doors again and sit in the dark and hold their
pet real close to them and tell the little feller that it

ain't him, no sir, it ain't him that's bad. No, Ben, they won't come to the Grange."

"I don't know, Doug, these are good people. They face up."

"Oh, sure. Just like when you slaughtered that herd." Silence.

"Shit," Ben said.

"Can't blame 'em much, Ben. God made men, not angels, and some of us let fear get hold, turn us inside out. And some don't."

"Then I'll have to go to them," Ben said to Root.

"That's about the size of it."

"You still short of men?"

"I'm short of everything but bile."

"Too much coffee."

"I suppose."

"You're welcome to stay for the night."

"Night's gone."

And it was. Both men moved to the open door and looked at the eastern sky.

"Pretty," Root said.

"Best time of day," Ben said.

Together, they unloaded Root's van. They stored the small bottles of anti-rabies serum in the giant refrigerator Ben kept in the barn clinic. When they were finished, Root had a last cup of coffee, ignoring the rumblings from his belly, walked outside, sniffed the air, slid behind the wheel of his car and drove away. Just before the car disappeared down the road, Ben saw Root's arm poke stiffly out of the window, his fingers V'd in a victory salute, and he heard the elderly doctor's faint voice.

"Good luck."

"Yeah," said Ben.

He stood in the doorway of the barn and watched the sky turn salmon. The sky was a delicate embroidery. A lacy filigree of color. Coral and cinnamon and burnt rose ribboned the horizon and plumed into a peacock bloom of feathers which spread into a lifting lattice of lemon yellow and then finally shadowed into salmon.

Ben marveled at the swirl of shapes.

Behind him, the telephone rang. He backed into the barn, not wanting to take his eyes from the pastel wonder above him.

"Ben?" Lorraine's voice was tight.

"Uh huh," Ben answered as he watched the salmon shade into a darker apricot.

"There's something awful," she said. "There's something awful here."

20

The calf was dead.

There was not a mark on him.

There were other things. The steel rods of the cage were twisted and bent and pushed inward. Many of them were scarred with teeth marks. And blood. A few strands of animal hair clung to one of the twisted bars. The hairs were white.

Inside the cage, the calf lay on its side. It had died from fright.

"Was it Dandy?" Lorraine asked. "Was it Jim Dandy?"

"I don't know." Ben hunkered down on his heels. He looked through the bars, which he carefully avoided touching, at the dead calf. Christ, he wondered, what must it have been like? What kind of fury could have caused that small animal's heart to just stop? He examined the teeth marks on the bars and the blood and the matted hair.

"Listen," he said to Lorraine, "it could have been anything. Another coyote, maybe. If it was a dog, we can't be sure it was Dandy. Those white hairs don't mean anything. They could belong to a hundred animals on the prairie."

"But you don't think so. You don't really think so."

Ben didn't answer. He moved to his truck. He removed a pair of clean white coveralls and a heavy pair of gloves and he put them on. He pulled out the

steel cable from the winch and hooked it to the cage.
He winched the cage up and onto the bed of the truck
and as he did so the dead calf slid against the bent
bars and made a soft plopping sound. Ben removed
the coveralls and gloves and bundled them into a
corner of the truck. Lorraine hadn't moved from where
she stood. Her eyes never left Ben's as she waited for
an answer.

It had been a long night. She was tired and she was
frightened. Sheriff George Carter had removed Ernst's
body from the roundhouse and immediately driven
to the county coroner's. Lorraine had accompanied
Sophie to the diner. She had wrapped Dippsy in a
blanket and he had curled up in one of the diner's
booths. She and Sophie had gone to the back room
where the German woman lay down in the dark, saying nothing, asking nothing, not weeping. Lorraine
had not tried to comfort the other woman. She knew
there was no way to do that. She knew that all she
could offer was to share the silence.

*A house is so silent without the clump of a man's
boots. The silence is so long.*

Sophie had not spoken until just before dawn. And
then she had said:

"It is time."

"Time?" Lorraine had asked, startled by the night's
interruption, "time for what?"

"Ernst's radio."

She had risen from her bed, smoothed her rumpled
dress, and walked through the swinging doors into the
diner. Lorraine had followed. She had watched as
Sophie had turned on the counter radio and then
moved to stand in front of the wall map of Europe,
one hand poised over the little thumbtack armies.

The newscaster's voice on the radio had awakened
Dippsy and, his eyes still filled with sleep, he had
shucked the blanket from his shoulders and, together
with the two women, had listened to the daily news
report. The first words they had heard had been a

comment on President Franklin Delano Roosevelt's cutting words about the Republican attack on his dog. The newscaster quoted the President.

"The Republican leaders have not been content with attacks on me or my wife or my sons. No, they now include my little dog, Fala. Well, of course, I don't resent attacks, and my family doesn't resent attacks, but Fala does resent them. His Scotch soul was furious."

Sophie had laughed softly.

"*Er schmeckt*," she'd said.

"I don't understand," Lorraine had said.

"*Er schmeckt*. It tastes bitter."

And then, in an act of absolute dismissal, she had turned her back on Lorraine and Dippsy and, as she listened to the newscaster describe the ebb and flow of battle three thousand miles away, punched the red, blue and black thumbtacks into the bacon-smeared map of death.

Quietly, Lorraine and Dippsy had returned to the farm and to the dead calf.

Now, her eyes still on Ben, she waited for an answer and she was still confused because she was not quite certain what question she had asked. Had it been about the death of the calf or the death of Ernst?

"How long's it been since Dandy got his shots?" Ben kept his voice as casual as he could. He saw how tired Lorraine looked and he didn't want to add panic to weariness.

"I don't know. I don't remember."

"Tom was a careful man. He must have kept a record."

"I don't know. He took care of it. He just always took care of it."

"Whereabouts would he keep such a record?"

"I don't know. Christ, I don't know."

"Okay. Okay."

Ben studied Lorraine. He saw that her eyes were fastened on the white hairs which matted one of the rods of the cage. He pulled the sack of Bull Durham from his pocket and carefully rolled a cigarette.

"I'd like a favor," he said. She didn't answer. She just nodded and kept her eyes on the white hairs. He continued. "Be best all around if we kept this thing between ourselves."

"It was Dandy, wasn't it?"

"I'll have to report it, of course, but it'd help if I can get folks to bring in their animals before they get wind of this. They're sitting on the edge now and it's not going to take much to push them over. Maybe you could get that across to Dippsy, too."

"If it was. If it was Dandy." She stopped.

With some surprise, Ben saw that the cigarette he rolled was almost perfect. Then why, he asked himself, am I going to throw it away? He tossed it to the ground and pulverized it under his heel. He pulled himself up onto the bed of the truck. He unfolded a large canvas tarpaulin and covered the cage with it. He leaped off the truck, moved to the cab door, and slid behind the wheel. He turned the ignition key. The engine throbbed. He double-clutched into gear.

"If it was Dandy?" she said.

"Then we'll have to find him," he said. "And kill him."

He drove away and, through the side-view mirror of his truck, he saw Lorraine standing in the cloud of dust and then he saw her double over and clap a hand to her mouth and, in this bent position, she stumbled toward her house. As he pulled away, the image in the mirror widened and he saw Dippsy watching from an upstairs window.

He wished the boy would wave.

He didn't.

During the long morning vigil in the Grange Hall, the door opened only once. Richie Grover brought his bloodhound to Ben. The hound's ears drooped

forlornly and his eyes were almost as sad as Sam
Hanks' eyes. But not quite.

"Woulda had the shots. Only thing is, I jus' didn't
get around to it. That's the only thing." It was a long
speech for the man with pale eyes.

The bloodhound didn't utter a sound when Ben
vaccinated him. Richie lifted him off the table and
led him out by his leash. All the way across the floor
the old man's eyes were on the leash in his hand,
staring at it with distaste. At the doorway, he turned
back to Ben.

"Bad," he said, "bad for a hound dog not to run
free." And he closed the door behind him.

Ben looked out the window at the long main street
of Crowley Flats. It was almost deserted. He saw the
door to the grocery store open and a little girl stepped
out and just as quickly a woman's arm darted through
the open door and the woman's hand clawed at the
girl's dress, ripping the fabric as the girl was yanked
sharply back into the store. Chet Beam's convertible
rolled down the street and pulled into Virgil's gas station. Virgil was nowhere to be seen. Chet honked his
horn. The door to the gas station office didn't open.
Chet honked again. He kept his hand on the horn. The
sound assaulted the morning. Virgil stepped out. A
massive .45 Colt revolver was strapped around his
waist. Virgil kept his hand on the butt of the gun as
he peered nervously toward the gas pumps.

Virgil's hand remained on the butt of the .45 as he
fed the convertible from the gas pump.

The door to the Western Union opened and Sam
Hanks stepped out. He held an orange-striped cat
in his arms. He began walking toward the Grange.

Bessie, manager, major domo, ticket taker, popcorn
maker of the picture show, swept her lobby.

Outside his feed store, Caleb Dodd hoisted a burlap
sack of seed onto his shoulder, hawked, and spit
phlegm into the dust.

A truck appeared at the far end of the street.

Ben started to turn from the window and then stopped, his eyes frozen on the truck.

Bessie paused in her sweeping. Caleb, his shoulders hunched under the weight of the seed sack, looked up the street. Virgil failed to take the final step into his office. Sam Hanks halted before he reached the Grange, the orange cat mewing softly in his arms. They all stared at the truck.

It was Emmett Flack's truck and it was out of control.

Behind the wheel, Emmett was desperately sucking in air, trying to clear the terrible constriction of his throat. He shook his head violently, needing to avoid the shaft of sunlight which was turning into a golden river in which his eyes were drowning. The bones of his fingers were alive. They were tiny little rats gnawing at his flesh. He yanked his hands from the wheel and pounded them against the windshield. The glass broke and Emmett cried with ecstasy as the little rat fingers were ripped from his hand.

The truck swerved wildly and paint cans toppled from its bed. Rivers of white and green and red gushed down the street and all those watching heard the squeal of brakes and saw the truck skid into a three hundred and sixty-degree circle. It bounced over the curb of the gas station and Virgil dived behind a gas pump. The truck slid past it and banged into a mound of discarded tires and then ricocheted back into the street and ran up the opposite sidewalk and crashed through the plate glass window of the grocery store.

Emmett's shriek filled the air. It mingled with the scream of the cat which leaped out of Sam Hanks' arms and raced down an alley. Bessie rammed her fists against her ears to shut out the awful noise and she prayed for Sunday when she could again receive the sacrament of the Lord's last supper. Caleb dropped his sack of seeds and stared at the street which was stained by the streams of white paint and he thought how much they looked like salt licks melting in the mountain sun. Sam Hanks and Ben Custer ran toward the demolished truck. Virgil closed his eyes.

The front of the truck was rammed up over the counter, its wheels still spinning, when Ben reached the grocery store. Bags and boxes and bottles were scattered everywhere. A slab of uncut bacon lay soaking in a puddle of bleach. A bag of salt slowly drained into a barrel of dried beans. Torn leaves of lettuce were covered with coffee beans. A mixture of sugar and blood ran down the walls.

And in a haphazard circle of glass and cornflakes lay Emmett Flack's severed head.

On that same night, Virgil Foster heard a strange scratching sound behind one of his oil drums and so he drew his .45 and blew the head off an orange-striped cat. When he saw what he had done he wept. He could not stop weeping. He hunched over his tool counter and sucked on a bottle of Chet Beam's potato dew until his tears drained onto the road maps of the prairie.

Men and women were gathered in the back room of Caleb's feed store. Chet Beam pulled a large black stone from the pocket of his white linen suit. Everyone stared at the stone. The yellow cast of kerosene lanterns gave it a sheen like hardened pus.

"This here," whispered Chet, "is a madstone. Comes from sunbaked deer guts. It's a sure cure for the bite. Put it on the wound and it sucks out all the poison. Just two dollars and your flesh'll be Jesus-baby sweet!"

Caleb was the first to reach for his money.

Some miles away from the winking madstone, Lottie sat in her wheelchair and watched Morgan at the window. He was peeling away the torn and dried points of his son's gold star.

"Wind done it," she said.

"Done what?"

"Dried it out." She shifted just a little bit and saw

the fragile image of herself in the mirror. "Dried all of us out."

"It's not the wind," Morgan said.

"Then what?"

"Things."

"What things?"

Morgan didn't answer. The blade of his jackknife squeaked against the window pane. The dried glue on the glass crumbled in his fingers. He brushed it off his hand and onto the open pages of an old seed catalogue he'd placed under the window to catch scraps of the star. Underneath the bits of paste he could see the catalogue pictures of sweet peas and phlox and climbing roses. And Lottie's favorite flower. Yellow jonquils.

"Could be," she lied, "could be this spring I'll plant a garden."

"Could be," he lied.

And he wasn't sure whether he was lying about her ability to move again or whether he was lying about another spring coming. Lottie's wrong, he thought, it ain't the wind laid rot on us. It's fear.

In the beginning, the mutilation of their sons had been a distant thing but the gradual return of bodies had made death drift closer. Now Morgan had seen the sporadic swift blankness which curtained the eyes of his neighbors. He had seen men take one step off the curb as they started across the Flats' main street, and then pause, the second step never taken. It was as if these men had seen something sliding along the horizon which had stripped them of action, had stolen purpose from them. The sight of tentative men disturbed Morgan. It was Morgan who had read first of the ancient 4-4-0 locomotive standing frozen in its field of ice and it was he who had activated the scheme to turn her into scrap. He had known that the community of Crowley Flats needed focus, needed a return to purpose.

But now what, he wondered. Now that death was no longer distant, no longer defined by the return of a pine box on the westbound train, now what? His eyes lifted from the last remnants of his son's gold star and he looked out the window and he knew that it was not moonlight which lay over the land. It was fear in a handful of dust. And it had locked the doors of the town. The roundhouse would be empty of men.

"You and me," he said to Lottie, "you and me, we'll do it."

"Yes," she said, not knowing or caring what he wanted to do but staring at the window pane which was now smudged with the shadow of her son, "you and me. That's all that's left."

There were no flowers in front of Lorraine. She was in the pantry of her house. It was just a small room off the kitchen. A huge oak roll-topped desk overwhelmed the space. One wall was lined with cardboard filing cabinets. A gun rack hung on the opposite wall. It held a Winchester repeating rifle and a twelve-gauge shotgun and a target twenty-two. One corner of the room was piled high with old catalogues from Sears and Roebuck and Montgomery Ward and J. C. Penney. A number of pages were dog-leafed. A wide strip of cork board had been nailed into the wall over the desk. Thumbtacked to it was an eclectic collection. Advertisements from farm journals and newspaper clippings and bulletins from the Department of Agriculture and a faded blue ribbon from a 4-H Club fair and photographs. Snapshots mostly. Casual mostly. Out of focus often. Showing no professional flair. But it was an amateur's record of love, for within each snapshot there was an image of Tom or Lorraine or Dippsy or Jim Dandy. One of the photographs had been posed. It was a picture of all three Towers and their dog. They were standing in front of their tractor, squinting into the sun, grinning. Even Dandy was grinning. Lorraine and Dippsy were dressed in Sunday best. Tom was in his uniform. Willie Mae had snapped the picture on the day Tom had left for war. There was only one later picture of Tom and it, too, was tacked to the wall. It showed Tom and two other soldiers standing in front of a tank. The tank did not look like the tractor but Tom was still grinning. At least it looked as if he were grinning. It was hard to tell. The wet sands of Omaha Beach plastered the faces of the men and blurred their features. Lorraine didn't like the picture but she kept it tacked to the wall because she thought that maybe, just maybe, that was the tank in which Tom had died.

There was, also, a calendar on the wall. It was very large and rather ornate. Each month had a separate page to be flipped over and behind when the days had run out. On the top of each page was a glossy photograph depicting some view of the prairie. There were wheat fields and grazing lands and a stone quarry and the Smoky Hill River and a silo. There was a printed legend at the bottom of each of those pictures reminding the viewer that these glimpses of landscape were offered as a courtesy of the Wichita National Bank. Each date on each page was outlined by a black box. There was space within the box to allow the calendar user to jot down his or her schedule of daily chores.

The calendar on the wall was for the year 1944. The little black boxes were crammed with Lorraine's notes and reminders.

Another calendar lay on the desk. It was for the year 1941. Lorraine stared at one of the black boxes on a page, looking at Tom's neat printing, red-inked within an early December box. There were notations about mortgage payments on the farm and a due bill on the tractor and a square dance at the Grange. There was a reminder to purchase lumber to repair a box stall in the barn. There were telephone numbers. Two of them she didn't recognize. One of them she did. It was Ben Custer's number. Next to it was a red circle. Within the circle was a name. Dandy.

Had he taken the dog to Ben? She didn't remember.

She stared at the number on the page. She swiveled in her chair and reached for the telephone. She saw the clock on the wall. It was long past midnight. Tomorrow, she would call tomorrow. She leaned back in the chair. She saw the gun rack on the wall.

Then we will have to find him. And kill him, Ben said.

She closed her eyes.

Charlie wished he could close his. The orange which rested on the laboratory table was brighter than the light which shined on it. But not as bright as the hypodermic needle which protruded from the syringe in his father's hand. With a quick snap of his wrist, Ben plunged the needle into the orange. The action was so deft and swift that no sound accompanied it but, in his mind, Charlie heard the squeal of an animal. He winced. Ben pulled the needle free, and when he handed it to Charlie his voice was sharp.

"Go on," he said.

The boy handled the needle gingerly. Slowly, he raised his arm and aimed the needle at the orange. He deliberately took his time, hoping that the face of the animal would disappear from the round curve of fruit. It didn't.

"Damn it," Ben said, "just try."

Charlie struck half-heartedly at the orange. The needle grazed the fruit.

"Again." Ben tried to check the impatience in his voice. He tried not to think about how many dogs, how many cats he and Charlie would find behind the closed doors of the town.

Again Charlie's hand lifted and the silver needle glittered under the single light in the barn. This time the boy closed his eyes as he stabbed downwards and the needle rammed against the metal of the table.

"Jesus," Ben sighed.

A small towel was folded next to the orange. Ben

lifted it and placed the orange in it. He pulled the cloth tight around the fruit.

"Same as an animal's skin," he told Charlie. "Now don't think about it. Just do it!"

The silver spike lanced toward the orange but the towel deflected it and the glass syringe shattered on the table and the orange rolled to the floor. Ben's voice was a cutting edge.

"Wonderful, doctor," he said, "you've just cut my dog's throat."

"It's an orange!" Charlie leaped up from the table. "A lousy dumb orange! And I'm not a doctor. I don't want to be a doctor. I hate doctors!"

He spun away and started out of the barn. Ben grabbed him and his fingers dug into the boy's thin shoulders.

"Listen to me!" His voice whipped the boy. "Pete was eight years old when he learned that. Eight years old, Charlie! Christ, he stabbed that orange faster'n spit fries on a griddle. Pete has hands, oh Jesus, he has hands . . . My God, he broke his first bronc when he was your age. That skinny ass of his slapping the saddle till I thought he'd break in two. But he held on. Those hands of his held on and he whooped and hollered and dug those little spurs of his into that damn fool mare and, by God, she knew! She had a man up there. She had a rawhide man who was going to whip her ass. Oh, Pete, he has hands!"

And for the first time since the death of Sarah and the birth of his younger son, Ben heard the anvil ring.

"*Goddamn you!*" Charles Remington Custer said. "*Goddamn you. My name is Charlie!*"

21

"Fuck you," said the parrot.

Sheriff George Carter blushed. He stood in front of the open door and stared over Cora Zink's shoulder into the room of the house. It was a back room with a separate entrance which led to a vegetable garden and which allowed its tenant to come and go as he or she wished without disturbing the rightful owner of the house. It afforded privacy for loneliness or lust, neither of which in Cora's case canceled the other. Carter could see that the walls were entirely obliterated by huge posters of Hollywood's reigning actors. Robert Taylor and Clark Gable and Tyrone Power leered from the walls and all the posters had been hung in such a way that the eyes of the paper actors were trained on the huge brass bed in the center of the room. The bed was unmade. The sheets were wrinkled and musty and across the top one was a path of tiny tracks. The tracks led to the pillows and disappeared. Carter raised his eyes. A parrot clawed to the brass headboard. Its mottled green feathers looked as wrinkled as the sheets. Its blunt yellow beak snapped open.

"Fuck you," it repeated. "And your brother."

George didn't know what to do. He was embarrassed to look directly at Cora as he had when she opened the door to his early morning knock. He'd already seen too much of her. She had come to the door in her nightie. It was a short nightie and very sheer. The sunlight from the window behind her had outlined every curve and mound and fissure of her body. It had made him quite faint. But he was afraid that if he kept his eyes on the parrot the bird would continue talking and Jesus alone knew what words would drop from that beak. He shifted his gaze to Cora, making damn sure that his eyes stayed on her eyes and didn't stray below. He handed her the holstered .38 Police Special.

"Here," he said.

She blinked at it and then licked her lips. Damn Kansas wind, she thought, dries out a body. She'd be old before her time, she didn't find some soldier boy to fly her away from the prairie. Some lootenant with shiny bars who'd dance her to St. Loo or Chicago or maybe even New York. Standing in the doorway, staring at the .38 Special, the sunlight heating her ass, she got quite teary.

"Take it," Carter said, "it ain't gonna bite."

"I don't do it for nuthin' like that," she said.

"Morgan," Carter said, dutifully ignoring Cora's implications, "he burned up the wires last night. Called just about every Mama and Papa west of Big Muddy and guaranteed, I mean he personally guaranteed, that all them little tykes on your school bus was gonna be safe and sound. Then he got hold of me and told me to give you this iron. So you take it, hear?"

"I don't know. These things make me itchy."

"You got an itch, girl, I'd be obliged to scratch it." The words just slipped out. He hadn't meant to make so bold but when he saw that Cora was grinning insolently at him, he rushed on. "And I'm the feller could do it. You better believe it."

"Fuck you," said the parrot. "And your sister."

"God damn," said Carter. "He sure got a way with words, don't he?"

"A sailor boy gimme him. Come all the way from Panama."

"What'd you give the sailor boy?"

"Wouldn't you like to know?"

"I *know*."

For a moment Cora contemplated letting George enter her room but then she thought how if they did do it he'd sure God get himself messed up with the guilties and then he'd probably run her out of town which would let the purity back into his blood and would, at the same time, point her toward destinations unknown. Therefore, when his foot edged forward, she closed the door on it.

"Hey, now," he grunted as he pulled his foot away.

"Hay's for horses," she giggled, "an' that's the only thing you're gonna ride."

She closed the door all the way. Well, Carter thought, I give her the gun an' I give her sumthin' to think on an' one of these fine days, I'll give her the rest. I *mean*, he said to himself, I am gonna make that parrot *sing*.

As he walked away through the vegetable garden he kicked off the top of a carrot green.

Cora dressed in the tightest blue jeans she could find to emphasize the roundness of her hips and then strapped on the .38. She examined herself in the mirror. She liked what she saw. She looked like Annie Oakley or Veronica Lake on Bataan. She wished she could chew wooden matches like Willie Mae so that she'd look really fierce but every time she'd tried she'd gagged on the splinters and had been forced to spit. She didn't think spitting was ladylike so she'd given up the matches.

"I love you, darlin'," she said to the parrot as she left the room.

"Fuck you," said the parrot.

As she eased the school bus through town, Cora glanced at the roundhouse. Scattered parts of the locomotive littered the outside area. The red and white and blue bunting left from the earlier ceremony had started to shred. No sound came from the building.

No one was working. The place looked forlorn and it made Cora sad. She was glad to drive past it and onto the stretch of road which led to the rural lands where the schoolchildren would be waiting. The idea of anyone waiting for her made her less lonely and the fact that the kids, *her* kids, wanted nothing, demanded nothing of her, gave freshness to each of her mornings.

In the evenings, she sat with her parrot and waited for a knock on her door.

The road curved across the prairie, bisecting wheat fields and grazing lands. The bus slowed and stopped at every farm road where there was a congregation of children. Usually, it took considerable time for Cora to complete her route. This morning the journey was made swiftly. Regardless of Morgan's promise, only a handful of children greeted the bus.

Three boys and two girls sat silently in the bus. They did not joke, nor did they whisper. Their eyes searched the flat fields they passed. Occasionally, one of the boys would turn away from a window and stare at the hostered pistol on Cora's hip and he would shift nervously in his seat and speculate on whether or not a girl knew how to use such a weapon. He would decide that she didn't and then his eyes would return to the window and to the view of the fields.

And to the possibility of a raging animal.

Cora saw the huge Burr oak in the distance and pumped her brake gently so that the bus would slide to a stop exactly in the center of the road which ran between Custer's alfalfa field and Lorraine Tower's wheat land. She had played a game with herself all along the morning's route. She had slowed down when she approached the roads where she figured children might be waiting, children whose parents would not dare buck Morgan Crowley's admonition; and she had sped by those houses where she guessed fear would override even Morgan's words. She kept score of this game, giving herself one point when she had guessed correctly, and subtracting one point when she had been wrong. To her surprise, she was losing the game. Fear was the winner. It made her uneasy. She drove with one hand. Her other hand rested on the leather holster.

When she saw that both Charlie and Dippsy were waiting for her, she gave herself no points, neither did she deduct any. She played fairly. She knew that neither Ben Custer nor Lorraine Tower would allow terror to disturb ritual. Their actions would not have been dictated by Morgan. Looking out the window at Charlie's pinched face, she wondered about the fairness of it all. Shoot, she thought, that little ol' boy wants to hide himself. She waved to him.

"Climb aboard, tiger," she said cheerily, "the Chattanooga Choo-Choo gonna smoke the road."

Charlie tried a grin. It was not successful. Dippsy winked at her. She winked back and wondered how it was that such a young boy could look like a lecherous owl. She resisted the temptation to pinch his ass as he and Charlie made their way to the rear of the bus. Dippsy's swagger made her think of the windmill nights and the swimming hole and how warm the water was when she and Pete had swum bare-ass and she was glad that the bus route took her by that place.

Dippsy and Charlie sat together on the long rear seat of the bus. Unlike the other children, they were not looking out the windows. Their eyes were focused on the round perfection of Cora's chest. Their faces were very serious and when they whispered to each other, it was out of the corners of their mouths.

"Wait'll we hit a bump," Charlie said, "you'll see."

"Who told you?" asked Dippsy.

"My brother."

The bus bounced across a rut and veered sharply toward a roadside ditch but Cora twisted the wheel and the bus resumed its straight path. Underneath Cora's sweater, all remained firm.

"What'd I tell ya?" Charlie asked soberly. "They don't jiggle. They're rubber."

Dippsy's eyes narrowed.

"Shit," he said, "I owe ya a dime."

"Cap'n," Charlie said.

"Oh, yeah," said Dippsy. "Cap'n."

There was a sudden boom and hiss and the bus swerved sharply and then there was a squeal of brakes and both boys grabbed for the seat in front of them so they wouldn't fall and the bus zigzagged down the road and finally came to a screeching stop. Looking out the rear window, the boys could see the black tracks of burned rubber and they could hear the final flat fizz from a blown-out tire.

As Cora jammed the tire jack under the rear bumper of the bus, Dippsy inserted a steel pry bar between the hubcap and the wheel which held the torn tire. He was too small and lacked the strength to ram the bar home. Charlie stood next to him, watching. He recognized the problem. He moved to the roadside ditch and located a large rock. The faces of the other children in the bus peered through the windows as Charlie began to pound the rock against the tire bar.

The white dog turned toward the ring of stone on steel.

The hubcap fell to the road. Swiftly, expertly, Cora spun loose the wheel lugs. She jacked up the rear of the bus. Together with Dippsy and Charlie, she tugged off the wheel. It was heavy and it flip-flopped out of their hands and teetered into the ditch. They left it there and removed the spare tire from underneath the bus, wrestling it into place. Cora lowered the rear end of the bus until the new wheel rested solidly on the road. She replaced the lugs and began to spin them tight with a tire wrench.

Dippsy and Charlie crossed to the ditch and strained at the discarded wheel. They jockeyed it out of the ditch and started to bulldoze it toward the bus. But the weight of the tire made it unwieldy and cumbersome. It slipped away from under the boys' hands and began to roll down the road, swiftly gathering momentum. Dippsy and Charlie raced after it and Cora started to laugh at the sight of two little boys playing grab-ass with a bouncing rubber wheel. She tightened the last lug, banged on the hubcap, and backed up to the door of the bus as she watched the unequal race. She was still laughing, joined now by the children in the bus, as she slid into her seat behind the wheel. She stuck her head out of the window and, two fingers to her lips, pierced the air with a derisive whistle.

The tire sped down the road, tiny shreds of blown-out rubber snapping against its sides. It hit a rock and bounced high into the air and sailed over the road ditch and fell finally into the tall grass.

Cora whistled again and she could see the sheepish grins on the boys' faces as they turned at the sound. They stood in the middle of the road, panting from the run. Then they moved toward the tire.

Jim Dandy moved out from behind the windmill, one hundred feet away.

The boys stopped.

"Well, I'll be sumbitch." Dippsy sucked in his breath at the surprise of seeing the runaway dog. And then he shrilled in pretended anger. "Goddamnittohell, where you been, Jim Dandy? C'mon, boy, c'mon!"

He started toward the dog. He took three steps and then Charlie grabbed him.

"Don't, Dippsy! Don't move!"

Dandy's teeth were bared and yellow saliva dripped from his jaws which were snapping convulsively. An awful rasping growl came from his throat. His head lowered, ears flat on his skull, and he took one small step toward the boys. Slowly, they retreated a few inches but when the dog lifted his head and howled and raced toward them, the boys whirled around and sped back toward the bus. The faces of the children in the bus were pressed against the rear window. Cora leaned out of the driver's window, frantically waving the boys on, and then she remembered the .38. She fumbled with the holster, tearing at the leather strap which secured the pistol, her eyes still on the dog raging toward the boys. She clawed at the gun but she couldn't free it and when she heard the children in the bus begin to shriek and cry, she slapped at the key in the ignition and the engine sputtered and then died. She kicked at the accelerator and the engine coughed and backfired and died again. Oh, Jesus, she shouted. Jesus jesus jesus! She darted a glance in the mirror and saw that the boys were tearing up the road, their eyes filled with terror as the huge white dog gained on them. The engine fluttered and caught and she slammed in the clutch and the bus began to roll just as the boys lunged through the open doors. Cora seized the door lever and yanked it toward her and the double glass doors swung shut as Jim Dandy hurtled toward them. His body crashed against the glass and all the children screamed and Cora rammed the accelerator to the floor and the bus jerked forward spilling the children and their books and papers and lunch boxes into the aisle. Cora's head cracked into the windshield and blood ran from her nose and her foot slipped off the gas pedal. Outside the bus, Jim Dandy leaped high into the air and his body banged against a window and then dropped to the road and he scrambled up, snarling, and charged again but the bus was moving now, the wheels spinning and then catching on the asphalt, and the dog's body just glanced against a fender. Cora whipped the wheel over and swerved away from Dandy as she fed gas to the engine and the bus sped up the road, swaying dangerously as it caroomed around a curve and, finally, Cora saw that the mirror no longer held the image of terror.

But she could taste the blood in her throat and knew she would dream forever of a foam-flecked fury.

By acclamation, the citizens of Crowley Flats closed the school.

the school.

22

The carrier was identified.

He would be killed.

The four horses moved slowly across the grassland. The afternoon sun burnished the leather of saddle and scabbard. The riders were silent, their eyes intent on the distant hills toward which they rode. As they listened to the occasional soft neigh of a pony and the creek of stirrup, each wondered which one of them would be chosen to make the kill. The decision would come at the quarry.

The Wichita National Bank calendar had given them the clue to their destination. After Dandy's attack on the school bus, the boys had rushed home to Lorraine. Ben and Lorraine were sitting in the pantry office, a red-inked calendar on the desk between them. The story of Dandy's fury had burst from the boys and when their explosive recitation ended, so, too, did the time of guessing. And Ben was no longer puzzled that his office records failed to reveal a visit by Tom Tower and his dog.

Ben drove to the windmill, his thirty-ought-six loaded and resting on the seat beside him, but there was no sign of the dog. He returned home, saddled the Appaloosa and the Pinto and rode to Lorraine's. There Charlie, his eyes glued to the floor, his voice low and hesitant, asked why they had to kill Jim Dandy. You said yourself, he reminded his father, that if a dog goes savage, why then, he's only got a handful of days left to him. Maybe we could just let it be, he implored Ben in a thin little voice, just let it be.

"He's roving now, Charlie," Ben said, "and that's when he's most dangerous. We'll go after him and we'll find him and we'll kill him and *that's* how it has to be."

After that, Charlie didn't speak again. Until he made a small choking sound when Dippsy broke the silence.

"There," Dippsy had said, pointing at the calendar on the wall. "Ol' Jim, he'll be there."

On the top of the dated page was a picture of a stone quarry. Although it was in an unidentified section of the state, it reminded Dippsy of where Jim Dandy liked to roam. And it reminded Charlie of the same thing.

The abandoned stone quarry.

The place where the dead Pawnee chiefs were burned back into breathing by the rising sun. In Charlie's mind, a place which had to remain free from violence.

The horses moved into a field of thorny bush soon to be stripped of foliage by the early autumn chill. Ben drew in sharply on the Appaloosa's reins and held up his hand signaling the other riders to halt. He pointed at a bush. A tuft of white hair was caught in the thorns. Ben leaned back in his saddle and withdrew his Winchester from its scabbard. He withdrew one boot from a stirrup and curled his leg around the horn of the saddle, assuming a casual purchase on the horse. He raised the rifle. It was fitted with a powerful Weaver scope which he placed to his eye. Slowly, he scanned the landscape. He lowered the rifle, replaced it in its scabbard and he shook his head. He had seen nothing. He spurred his horse forward. The others followed.

A narrow stone ledge ran around the single thrust-
ing wall of the quarry. Jim Dandy slithered out of
the surrounding grass. He inched onto the ledge. He
stared down the sloping land at the distant riders. His
jaws slashed a rock and a tooth broke away from his
bleeding gums.

In single file, they rode up the slippery shale path
toward the quarry. Suddenly, a small rock was dis-
lodged above them and it came clattering down. Ben
grabbed the Winchester and rose in his stirrups and
wheeled toward the sound. All of them looked up at
the ledge. It was empty. Ben motioned the other
riders upward toward the rise. Lightly, they touched
their heels to the horses' flanks. The horseshoe irons
rang against stone and shale.

A white blur exploded in front of them.

The horses shied and reared on their hind legs and
snorted in fright, their nostrils quivering with the
scent of Dandy. As the riders fought to settle their
ponies, the dog streaked through the tall grass above
them and then was gone.

Ben dug his spurs into the Appaloosa and charged
into the grass. The other riders raced after him. They
were swallowed up by the tall bluestem and had to
shout above the pounding hooves in order to keep
track of each others' ride. They reached the far edge
of the long plateau and they pulled up the snorting
horses. Not one of them had seen Jim Dandy.

For just a moment, Charlie thought he saw an Indian slide along the quarry wall.

Then he heard his father's voice and the shape disappeared.

"He's in there," Ben said. "He's in the goddamn
grass. We'll have to fire him out."

As the others watched, Ben dismounted. He flipped
open his saddlebag and removed a wire-cutting pliers.

"You, Dippsy, and Lorraine," he said, "give me
your rifles."

They did. Ben broke open the chambers and began to pump out the unfired cartridges, letting them scatter on the ground in front of him. He untied the bandana from around his neck and spread it flat next to the cartridges. He picked up the pliers and inserted the blunt, rim-fire end of one of the cartridges into the teeth of the tool. He gripped the handles of the pliers in both of his own hands and strained against the metal. He scissored the shell in two. He discarded the lead slug and then, carefully, poured the explosive gunpowder from the open end of the cartridge into the square of bandana. As he proceeded to cut the other cartridges in the same fashion, and to pour their powder load into the bandana, he explained his plan to the others.

"Indians use to call it a 'great surround.' They'd make a circle of hunters and drive the buffalo up toward the cliffs and then they'd fire the grass. Buffalo'd be boxed in, afraid of the fire, and they had only one place to run. Over the cliff. It wasn't pretty but it sure as hell fed the Indians."

Dippsy was puzzled. "But they're ain't no cliffs here."

"There's a quarry," Ben said. "And that's where Dandy's gonna run. Charlie and me," Ben glanced quickly at the boy and then looked away from his dark face, "we'll be waiting for him."

He instructed Lorraine and Dippsy to divide the mound of gunpowder between them and to scatter it in a circling path around the perimeter of plateau. On his signal of a single shot, they were to light the powder. Their bodies bent in a low crouch below the tall waving grasses, he and Charlie ran to the far end of the wide field and hunched down on the narrow ledge of rock that rimmed the quarry's edge.

"You ready?" Ben asked his son, but he didn't wait for an answer because he was too busy levering shells into the chamber of his rifle. Ben surveyed the quarry, his eyes skimming the dark water below them and then over the broken ledges along the rock sides. He was surprised to see a narrow passage through the rimrock on the other side of the quarry.

"He's got to come this way, Charlie, or try that passage across from us. You stay here."

He hesitated. He squeezed the boy's shoulder and he was instantly aware of the slight withdrawal of flesh from under his fingers. He looked at the boy and saw that Charlie was studying the walls of the quarry intently. Good, Ben thought, he's paying attention. He's going to be all right. Yes, sir, he's going to be all right.

Ben scrambled down the rock face which would lead to the opposite passage. When he was in place, he lifted his rifle high. He squeezed off a shot. Its echo bounced off the walls of the quarry.

Charlie held his breath. He was panicking at the thought of violating the peace of Indian chiefs.

Lorraine and Dippsy leaned close to the path of gray gunpowder and put matches to it. There was an instant spurt of flame. Fire circled the plateau quickly and began to eat inward across the tall grass. Lorraine and Dippsy leaped back into their saddles and stood high in their stirrups and looked across the burning field.

"There he goes!" Dippsy yelled at his mother.

Just before flame and smoke blinded Lorraine's view, she saw a streak of white rushing through the bluestem. It was headed toward the quarry.

"I see him, Ben! I see him!" she shouted.

Smoke billowed across the stone passage and flames snapped above Ben's head where the grass reached the edge of rock. His eyes burned and watered and he began to cough so hard that it was difficult to steady the rifle at his shoulder. Quickly, he glanced across the quarry but the smoke was a screen between him and Charlie and he couldn't see his son. The smoke was roiling over him, a thick gray mat. An avalanche of stones and pebbles splashed onto his head and shoulders. He looked up.

Jim Dandy sprang through the cloud of smoke.

"He's coming, Charlie!" Ben yelled. "He's coming!"

Ben scrambled out of the passageway and, slipping and sliding on the loose rock, clawed up toward where Charlie was waiting.

Crouched on the ledge, the smoke swirling around him, Charlie was desperately trying to see. He heard a quick drop of stones into the water below him.

Jim Dandy leaped out of the flames.

The dog's momentum carried him onto the ledge. His body skidded across the damp shale, then slammed into the rocky wall. He was stunned and he lay flat on his belly. Charlie saw that the dog's white coat had been blackened from smoke and he could smell the burning hair.

Charlie jumped to his feet. He leveled the rifle. His finger tightened on the trigger. The dog's jaws opened and Charlie heard a piercing wail of pain. He did not know if it came from Jim Dandy or Ernst Jurgen or the Indian shadows on the wall or maybe even from the far-off killing ground over which Pete walked but he knew it was the sound of those journeying toward *the silent place.*

He could not pull the trigger.

The dog staggered up from the ledge and, in a final bunch of muscle, leaped high over the rock face and out of the quarry. Into the freedom of the sloping land.

Slowly, Charlie lowered his rifle. He started to climb through the drifting smoke but when he looked up he could no longer move because he saw his father's face. What he saw was worse than anger. Ben stood on the rim of the quarry, the rifle dangling loosely in his hand, his eyes filled with a dark and final disappointment. He said nothing as he turned away.

It was dusk when they returned to the barn. The silence remained between father and son as they un-cinched saddles and sponged them clean of horse sweat. Side by side, they brushed down their horses. As the stiff bristles slid through the Pinto's flanks, Charlie sneaked glances at his father but he saw nothing in Ben's face to which he could relate. It was as if his father had moved inside himself and taken refuge in some secret place. Out of the corners of his eyes, Charlie watched Ben curry the Appaloosa. Ben's brush moved in a slow and gentle arc across the horse's withers. Occasionally, he would pause and rest one open hand on the mane of the animal and he would play idly with the long, silken hair. Ben's fingers seemed to be seeking something, reaching out for something, searching, trying to close on some elusive thing. The fingers hypnotized Charlie and so he was startled when Ben finally spoke.

"Charlie," Ben said, his voice softer than the falling dusk, "get in the truck."

They drove to the roundhouse. They entered it. They stood in the center of the rubble. A single work light hung from the ceiling, its naked bulb casting huge shadows over the scraps of rusted steel. Ben's eyes moved over the torn pieces of locomotive. He spoke as quietly as he had in the barn.

"If we can't send this old lady to war," he said, "then just what the hell are we?"

He put his hand lightly on Charlie's head and turned the boy toward him and, as he continued, Charlie wondered at the sound of wind in his father's voice, wondered if Ben would have enough breath to finish what he wanted to say.

"You let fear get a lock on you," Ben continued, "and the calendar stops. You just stand still. Before you know it, you forget to plant next year's crop and then you blame the good Lord for being hungry. There's no end to it."

He leaned down and picked up a bent piston rod and turned it in his hands and when Charlie looked at his father's hands he thought it was just possible that Ben's fingers had found what they had been seeking, had ended their quest, had touched and closed on that which was no longer elusive, but even as he thought this the boy knew it had little to do with the piston rod itself.

"If we stop trying, Charlie," his father's voice went on, "if we stop trying, we're going to end up like this old lady. We're going to be all rusted out. We're going to be nothing. We're going to be dead."

Charlie's voice was terribly quiet.

"Like Ma, you mean," he said, "dead like Ma."

Ben looked down at his son and he saw that Charlie's head was once more tilted in that strange simulation of Sarah's stance. He spoke very carefully.

"No. No, it wouldn't be like your ma. People who stop trying die because there's nothing left of them. They're hollow. They're made of air. Your ma, your ma, Charlie, died because she took a chance. She wanted something. She wanted something very much."

"What?"

"You."

Ben tossed the rod back into the scrap heap and it clanged in the hollow silence.

"Come on, boy, we've got work to do."

Outside, twin headlights stabbed at them and then blinked off. Morgan swung down from his truck and moved to the rear of the vehicle. He didn't acknowledge either Ben or Charlie who stood framed in the door of the roundhouse. His legs wide-spread and braced hard, his body leaning forward, arms outthrust, Morgan prepared to lift Lottie and her wheelchair from the bed of the truck. His huge hands closed on the wheels. Charlie took a small step forward but Ben's hand restrained him. Morgan grunted softly as he heaved against the weight and his foot slipped in the soft ground. The chair tipped to one side and then righted itself.

"Oh," Lottie said.

For a moment Morgan stood very still and then he turned toward the square of light in the roundhouse door.

"Be obliged," he said.

Ben nodded. He walked to the rear of the truck. He took hold of one side of the wheelchair. Morgan held the other. Their eyes met. Morgan's head dipped a fraction. Together, they lifted Lottie and the chair to the ground. The wheelchair rested in the edge of light and Ben saw there was an unfinished piece of needlework across Lottie's lap. The cloth had been stitched into a garden of yellow jonquils. A silver needle punctured one of the petals. Ben knew that Lottie's crippled fingers were incapable of plying that needle and he wondered why she was carrying the cloth. When he looked up, he saw that Morgan's eyes were on him and those eyes held a plea. Silently, Morgan was asking him not to destroy the illusion of Lottie's future.

"Her and me," Morgan said, "we're gonna pass us some time."

Ben's eyes returned to the needlework.

"Pretty," he said, "that's real pretty."

"Gonna be," Lottie said, "when I'm done. Yes, sir. When I'm done. Gonna hang her on the wall. You come see, hear?"

"I look forward," Ben said.

"Do you?" Lottie whispered, her eyes bewildered. "Do you?"

Morgan stepped behind the chair and rolled it across the night-dewed grass and into the roundhouse and Ben thought how the tracks left by the wheels looked exactly like those of early prairie schooners. He wasn't surprised because he knew it had been men like Morgan who had settled the Kansas land. Looking through the doorway, Ben saw Morgan glance up at the tarnished brass bell which he had proclaimed would ring with victory when the town had finished its task. Morgan locked the wheels of the chair and Lottie smiled as she watched the huge rancher spit into his hands and lift a sledge and pound a wheel apart.

Charlie waited until the truck turned into the barn road before he began to listen to the tires. The road was roughly graveled and the rhythmic thump of the spinning rubber over rock and stone and rut always produced a special sound. He and Pete used to play a game based on that sound. In rhythm with the bouncing wheels, they would each call out the name of a baseball player and whichever boy missed the beat would loose the game.

Mickey Cochrane.

Dizzy Trout.

Bill Dickey.

Bucky Harris.

But on this drive, Charlie heard something else. It was almost as if the wheels were singing.

She wanted you she wanted you she wanted you she wanted you she wanted you!

Perhaps it was this song that impelled Charlie to help his father without waiting to be asked. Perhaps it was the image of his father's sad face at the round-house.

Or perhaps it was that he was frightened that his father might never ask again. Not ever.

They made preparations for the coming dawn. At the first light of day they would cruise the streets of Crowley Flats and knock on every door. They would inoculate the animals of the town. They'd battle against the rage of a roving dog. Charlie dreaded it. He felt quite sure that he would be incapable of stabbing live flesh, of inflicting pain on a warm and unsuspecting creature.

And wherever he looked, he saw the foam-flecked jaws of Dandy. He could not blank it from his mind. It terrified him. Secretly, he prayed that his long night's efforts would bring their own reward; that when the sun rose, Ben would turn to him and maybe touch him lightly on the neck, the way he touched Pete, and say, all right, Charlie, all right, and tell him that he'd done enough and done it well and there was no need to come to town. And, perhaps, that was the real reason, unasked, he helped his father.

Ben and Charlie moved in and out of the barn with the last of what they would need. The back of the pickup was crammed with fresh white coveralls, two hogsticks whose rawhide loops would be slipped over the heads of reluctant animals and hold them steady and keep infectious jaws from reaching, heavy gloves, boxes of syringes and hypodermic needles, chests of ice in which the tubes of vaccine rested, leather muzzles for those animals without, and a shotgun zippered in its case. If necessary, it would be used on unleashed strays.

Or on Jim Dandy.

Between them, they carried the last ice chest to the truck. They placed it on the bed and then unfolded the tarpaulin nearby. At the same time, they both saw the distant light moving across the dark horizon. They watched it. It changed course.

It moved toward them.

It was round and bright and close when they saw what it was. The headlight of a bicycle. Sam Hanks' bicycle. It rolled to a stop in front of the barn. The little man with the sad eyes dismounted. He leaned the bike against the barn wall. He moved slowly to Ben and Charlie. He stood in front of them. He wet his lips. He cleared his throat.

Ben stopped breathing.

"Might best be," Sam said softly to Charlie, "might best be, you go inside."

Charlie didn't budge.

Ben reached into his pocket and withdrew the sack of Bull Durham and the wafer-thin rolling papers and held them out to Sam.

"Smoke?"

"Got store-bought," Sam said, and pulled a package of Camels from his shirt. "I'd take it kindly if you'd have one."

"No thanks. Trying to get the hang of these."

"Tricky devils."

"It's all in the fingers."

"Yeah. And how much spit you use. Tobacco gets wet, she don't pull good."

"No, she doesn't. That's a fact."

"It ain't easy."

"No, sir, it is certainly not easy."

"Then, nuthin' much is. Not these days."

"No," Ben said.

"No," Sam said.

Both men took long drags on their cigarettes. The smoke curled between them and across Charlie's face. The boy thought he'd never heard such a terrible silence.

"When I was a boy, used to slop the hogs," Sam said.

"I remember," said Ben.

"Thought it was the worst job a man could have." The old man sighed. "It ain't. I got a worser one."

Slowly, Ben pinched out the glowing ember of his cigarette. He felt no heat.

"Expect you'd better do it then, Sam," he said.

The old man's hand looked like the wounded wing of a bird as it fluttered in the air and picked off the hard black bowler and fumbled inside it and, finally, withdrew the telegram.

Sam cleared his throat again.

"Law says I got to read it," he said.

"I know," said Ben.

Sam Hanks twisted a pair of metal framed glasses onto the bridge of his nose and, when he started to read, his voice sounded like a tired and angry schoolchild who was forced to repeat aloud the lesson he had learned over and over and over again.

"I regret to inform you that your son Corporal Peter Custer has been officially listed as missing in action. His unit engaged the enemy in . . ."

Ben turned and walked back into the house.

23

Throughout the last hours of the night, Charlie sat in the truck and waited for his father to come out of the house. He waited in vain. The door never opened. Charlie fell asleep. He dreamed of a hognose snake which could roll over and just play dead and the snake's head shimmered into Pete's face. He dreamed of an oiled baseball mitt being held by a shadowy hand but when a horsehide ball slammed into the cracked pocket of the mitt it echoed to the boom of cannon and it split the leather into a thousand tiny floating fragments which, at first, appeared to be dark slivers of bone and then turned into the charred hairs of a dog.

At last he opened his eyes to the red sky of morning. He thought the sky was bleeding. He heard a dripping sound but when, fearfully, he turned toward it, he saw only the melt of ice. Water dripped from the chests. It had spilled over the white coveralls and soaked them. The heavy protective gloves floated in a pool of water in one corner of the truck bed, their wet fingers curled in a sad salute. It was as if a disembodied hand were waving farewell.

He looked toward the house. He saw no movement. He climbed out of the truck. He stood there, not knowing what to do. Knowing he had to do something. He retreated to the comfort of objects. He pulled the tarpaulin from the ice chests. He lifted their lids.

Vials of vaccine floated among the last shreds of ice. Straining against the weight, he tipped the chests and let the water run free. He removed the coveralls and the gloves from the truck bed and draped them over the vehicle's hood so that they might dry under the rising sun. He wiped off a hogstick on his jeans, drying the handle, and then ran his fingers around the loop of rawhide and watched the moisture slide away.

He looked back at the house.

Slowly, he walked to it and opened the door and climbed the steps to his father's room. He stood outside and listened. He heard nothing. He knocked and waited and heard nothing. He tried the doorknob. It turned in his hand. Gently, he pushed open the door.

Ben was lying on the bed. He had not removed the clothes of last night, not even the boots. The white cotton spread was muddy. His father's eyes were wide open and staring at the picture on the wall. Not a sound came from him.

"Pa?"

There was no answer.

"Pa?"

Ben did not even blink. He did nothing. He could have been dead. Charlie backed out of the room and closed the door. When he reached the kitchen, he thought maybe a month had passed, so slow and silently had he moved downstairs. He felt light-headed and dizzy and then remembered that he had forgotten to breath. He forced himself to take long pulls of air into his lungs. It made him dizzier and he sat down. He wished there were something familiar that he had to do but he could think of nothing. He picked at the wooden table top. Green paint flecked under his fingernails. He looked at the stove. An enameled coffee pot stood on the front burner. He wondered if he should make coffee but even as he thought of it he knew he could not take it to his father. He could not enter that room again.

The telephone rang. He started across the kitchen to

where it hung on the wall. He paused. He looked up. He pictured his father reaching for the phone. It rang again. His eyes still on the ceiling, Charlie tried to will his father to answer it. It rang again. Reluctantly, Charlie lifted the receiver from its hook. His voice was flat and old before its time.

"Yeah?"

"Charlie?" It was Lorraine.

"Yeah. Yes, ma'am."

"Oh, Charlie," she said, "I'm so goddamn sorry."

It didn't surprise him that she had heard about Pete. He knew that by now the word had spread across the prairie town. In his imagining, he could see the early gathering of neighbors, the respectful dip of heads. He could hear their low murmurings and chicken clucks of sympathy. And, suddenly, he hated his own vision. It stifled him, moved in on him, left him no space.

"Mrs. Tower?"

"Yeah? Yeah, Charlie?" She heard the thin desperation in the boy's voice and she waited for him to continue. But he didn't. There was only the sound of his breathing. "Charlie, what? What is it?"

"Pa," he said. "Pa."

"Yes, Charlie?"

"Pa," he said. And he hung up.

He crossed the barnyard and stopped in front of one of the open ice chests which he had placed at the rear of the truck. He reached into the chest and removed a glass vial of vaccine. He entered the barn and walked into the laboratory clinic. He opened a large medicine chest. He compared the vial in his hand with others on the shelf. They were similar. He examined them carefully because he wanted to be positive. He decided to use these rather than the ones which had soaked in ice water throughout the night, afraid that the latter might have been harmed in some way. He removed the vials from the shelves of the

chest and stuffed them into various pockets of his
jacket and trousers. He looked around the clinic. He
saw what he wanted. A small ice chest which was not
too wide, nor too long, to fit into the wire basket on
his bicycle. He moved to the old-fashioned giant ice-
box. Using a steel pick, he chiseled at the huge block
of ice which he found and filled the ice chest with
the broken-off pieces of ice. He unloaded his pockets
and shoved the vials into the chest, packing them on
all sides with the shaved ice. He lifted the chest and
carried it outside. He put it into the handlebar basket
of his bicycle, moved to the truck, leaned through the
open door and reached over the steering wheel to the
dashboard. He picked up a small leather case which
held a hypodermic syringe and needles. On his way
back to his bicycle, he circled the front of the truck
and whisked a hogstick off the hood. He looked at the
gloves. They were still drenched and stiff from their
soaking, their leather fingers curled in contempt at
the sun. He left them. He strapped the hogstick onto
the handlebars of his bike. He shoved the leather case
of syringe and needles into his jacket. He mounted the
bike. And in a matter of seconds, he was a small,
lonely figure pedaling toward town.

She pushed the button on the tractor. The starter
hummed but there was no cough of engine. She pulled
out the choke and tried again. The starter motor
whined but the engine failed to turn over. Lorraine
cursed herself for not having covered the tractor. Her
concentration had focused on the search for calendar
clues and on the ensuing hunt for Jim Dandy. She had
left the tractor parked alongside the barn and now its
sparkplugs had been rendered useless by the dew of
a prairie dawn. She thought about removing them
and wiping them clean and dry with a gas-dipped
cloth but she knew that even then they might not
sputter to life. Frustrated, she climbed down from the

tractor seat and kicked sharply at a tire, succeeding only in bruising a toe. Dumb, she said to herself, you are grade-A-head-of-the-class-number-one dumb.

She saddled her horse and started across the alfalfa field toward Ben Custer's house. She wanted to dig her boot heels into the flanks of the animal but she knew the field was made hazardous by black-tailed prairie-dog burrows. She let the horse pick his own path through the stubble. The horse shied at a sudden explosion of wings and she saw a bird rise from the stump of an ironwood tree. For a moment, she thought it was a hawk but then recognized the small head and black-gray wings of a Western turkey vulture. The bird flattened against the sky and continued its cruise for carrion. Lorraine talked softly to her horse and gentled him down and the animal circled the stump of ironwood in small, mincing steps, snorting once and letting his own hot steam cloud the morning. Lightly, Lorraine touched him with her heels and the horse returned to his path across the field.

Lorraine glanced backwards at the ironwood. It had been the last tree timbered by her father before his final journey westward. The wood was as hard as its name and her father had used it to make all the handles for his tools, and during the long, bitter nights of the old man's last Kansas winter they had huddled in front of the fireplace grate and burned the ironwood scraps. It had the heat of coal. It was cheaper. During that same ice-brittle winter, she had learned to scout for soapweed which grew along the edge of fields and she had turned the roots into soap, and its leaves into brooms. It had been a time of survival; a time when she had changed from a girl, shoeless in the wind, to a prairie woman. The loss of innocence had been completed in the following summer.

In the root cellar.

She rode toward the man who took her there.

She saw the parked truck and its open door and its hood layered with damp coveralls and curled gloves.

Her horse picked his way past open ice chests and she reined up in front of the house. She dismounted and tied the reins to a porch railing. She studied the house. No lights burned within. Outside the kitchen, the lilac bush was budless and stripped of blossom. It gave no fragrance to the morning air. Without knocking, she entered the kitchen.

"Hello?" she called softly.

No one answered. She touched the coffee pot on the stove. The enamel was cold. She started toward the living room and then stopped, suddenly afraid that if she walked into that room she would see all the furniture covered in shrouds. She shrugged off the feeling and entered the room. There were no shrouds, only antimacassars of yellow-faded lace covering the arms of horsehair sofas and easy chairs. In front of an eastern window, a brass lamp gleamed dully in the entering sun. The dark oak floors were dustless. A chessboard rested on a walnut table, its ranks and files peopled by wooden players. A captured Bishop lay on its side, half hidden behind an array of pawns. It looked beheaded. She shivered and returned to the kitchen. She filled the enamel pot with cold water, letting the water just trickle in, not wanting to disturb the dark silence. She found a kitchen match and scratched its sulphurous head against a burner ring and winced at the tiny abrasive sound. She spooned coffee into the tin percolator basket, then set the pot on the burner. She sat at the kitchen table. Idly, her fingers played with the fresh flakes of green paint and she wondered who had scratched them there.

She tried to delay her move to the stairwell which rose to Ben's room. She knew he was there. She sensed his presence. She was frightened. When I open his door, she thought, I will strip him of privacy as surely as the wind strips an oak, and he will know that I have seen him grieve. And after I have witnessed his vulnerability, he will do what?

He will turn away.

"Don't," she said aloud, "please, please don't."

The coffee perked and bubbled. She placed an asbestos mat between the burner and the pot and turned the flame low. She stood for a long time in the center of the kitchen and then, taking one long, deep breath, walked through the living room and slowly climbed the stairs. She knocked once at his door. There was no welcoming word. She had not expected it. She pushed open the door.

On the bed, Ben lay as rigid as a pine plank. The knuckles of his hands were blue white from the force with which he clenched his fists. His eyes were hard slits staring at the ceiling and the muscles of his jaws bunched and twitched. His whole body tremored with the effort of not weeping.

"Ah, Ben!" she cried.

Not turning, his tone low and harsh and ugly, he ground out the words.

"I never told him," he said. "I never told Pete that I loved him."

She said nothing. She closed the door behind her and crossed the room and lay down on the bed. They were side by side, thigh touching thigh. She did not reach for him. She waited. He felt the warmth of her body and her stillness and he caught the fragrance of weather and field. Slowly, the trembling of his body ceased. His gaze slid from the ceiling to the picture on the wall and he spoke silently to the lovely, leaning, listening dark-haired woman.

Sweet Jesus, Sarah, he said, *life is so much shorter than death.*

Without haste, tears running silently down his leathered face, he turned to Lorraine. Their bodies pressed together, disarmed by anguish, made eager by memory. They moved toward the center of hunger and toward the sweet cracking of each other's soul.

24

As he pedaled down the prairie road toward town, Charlie was aware of the morning sounds. He listened to the rustle of weeds where field mice scurried through the flanking ditches and to the sudden snap of wings when a crow burst from a cottonwood clump. He listened to these things but all he heard were the words of his father.

If we stop trying, we're gonna be all rusted out.

Only once did he interrupt his journey. He stopped pedaling when he reached the windmill. His toes scratching the dust, he straddled his bike and held it steady and he stared up at the turning wooden blades. The sun had climbed higher now and it gave glitter to the rusted jackknife. Charlie longed to feel the heft of the knife, to turn it casually in his hand and then, perhaps yawning a little so as to paint the act with boredom, scrape his initials into the mill while all the boys below cheered and whistled and stomped and shouted yeah, Charlie, oh yeah.

But he saw the tall grass bend in front of him and the picture of Dandy's jaws sprang to mind and he slammed his feet back onto the pedals and pumped furiously until he had left the windmill and the jackknife and the dream far behind.

When he entered Crowley Flats he tried to cloak himself in the image of his heroes. His bicycle became a stallion and the leather hypodermic case a holstered

.45 slung low on his hip, ready for a lightning draw.
The whoosh of his rubber wheels was erased by the
sound of prancing hooves. He was a slit-eyed, mean
and ornery cowboy riding toward the badlands, one
hand clawing close to his shooting iron. He had the
sneer of Bogie, the quick hands of Scott, the drawl of
Cooper, the muscle slab of Wayne. He rode to glory
along the empty street of town.

Until a tomcat sauntered out of an alley.

Charlie jammed his heels to the pavement, stopping
the bicycle and jolting loose the fantasies of his mind.
He was again a young boy, hollow-bellied and fearful.

He stared at the entrance to the alley which ran
alongside of Sophie's diner. The cat looked at Charlie
and then stretched in a path of sunlight. There was no
collar around the animal's neck. His tiny pink tongue
flicked his whiskers. He arched his back and the
muscles rippled under his black and white chain-
gang coat. Slowly, Charlie unstrapped the hogstick
from his handlebars. Keeping his eyes always on the
cat, Charlie dismounted and rolled his bike toward
the diner. He leaned it against the latticework of the
garbage bins. Holding the hogstick high, its rawhide
loop dangling in front of him, he took a step toward
the cat. He took another step. He was afraid that he
would drop the stick, his hands were so damp with
sweat. He took one more step and then began to twirl
the rawhide. The cat hissed and whirled back into
the alley. Charlie raced after it. As Charlie plunged
into the alley he saw that its far end was boarded up
by a high wooden fence. In front of him, the tomcat
hurtled over crates, caterwauling as it fled, and then
it leaped high and its claws dug into the board fence
and chewed it into pulp. The cat screeched its way up
and over the fence as Charlie crashed headlong into
the boards. The hogstick flew into the air, smacking
against the sidewall of the diner, and the handle split
in two. His forehead welted from the slam against the
boards, Charlie spread-eagled his weight against the

fence and then slowly slid down the boards and sat in the dust of the alley. He saw the broken hogstick and he kicked it away from him. The angle of the alley prevented the sun from reaching the lower portion of the fence and Charlie shivered in the shadows. He wished Dippsy were with him because he knew what the boy would say at this moment.

"Fuck 'em," he would say. "I mean you tried, Charlie, so just fuck 'em."

But he saw his father's face staring at the wall in that awful silent room and so he rose from the cold shadows and walked out of the alley, leaving the hogstick behind. He jerked the bicycle away from the garbage-bin doors, mounted it, and pedaled toward a side street of the town, toward the series of closed doors on which he would knock. Thinking of what might lie behind them made him queasy and he could feel the tiny trembling of his leg muscles. He started to loose his balance so he skidded the bike sharply to avoid tipping over and the squeal of rubber tires covered the sound behind him. The sound of bone on rock. The sound of animal claws.

The dog's dark eyes gleamed behind the latticework and his jaws snapped at the scorched flesh on his paws.

Looking up the street, Charlie felt better. It looked as safe as a Norman Rockwell sketch. On either side of the elm-lined street were neat white-clapboard houses. In front of each was a square of green lawn and each was boxed by a low picket fence and each fence was centered by a gate clasped to its post with black wrought-iron hinges. The only differences among the house exteriors were the varied spots of color which accented individual gardens.

Charlie was undecided on which door to knock first until he saw that something special stood in a garden halfway down the block. It was a row of black dahlias. They looked like brooding sentinels standing watch at the door. It was, strangely, their ominous quality which attracted Charlie. He felt that if he could march by them and enter the house which they guarded, he would find ease in the remainder of the day.

He left his bike on the sidewalk, carefully positioning it against a telephone pole. He opened the leather case and removed the syringe and a needle. He fitted the needle into the syringe. He dipped a wad of cotton into a small bottle of alcohol packed in the ice chest alongside the vials of vaccine. He wiped the needle with the cotton, inserted the needle into the cork top of a vial and, pulling up the plunger of the syringe, he filled it with vaccine.

Making sure that the needle could not come into contact with anything that would contaminate it, he held the syringe in one hand, and with his other hand he unlatched the gate and walked toward the neat white house, his eyes squinting sternly at the row of black dahlias which he passed.

Above him, behind a second-floor window, a white window shade lowered into place. He could see the hand of a woman on the shade as she completed the action. It was an old hand. The skin was wrinkled and browned with liver spots and the fingers curled stiffly as if, like the gloves he had left behind, they, too, were waiting to warm in the sun. The hand disappeared.

He knocked on the door. He heard a tiny clicking of heels descending stairs and a soft rustling of cloth. Then there was a rattling noise as a chain disengaged behind the door. The door inched open.

Charlie saw the eyes of a witch. The irises were coal black and the surrounding corneas were criss-crossed with crimson lines as if a rooster had scratched them red. The woman stared at him and then nodded knowingly and her voice was a dry, conspiratorial whisper.

"He ain't here," she said.

"What? What?" Charlie was bewildered.

"The man you're lookin' fer, he ain't here."

"Ma'am. I just gotta know if you have a dog in there."

"A what?"

"A dog."

"What's his name?"

"Whose name?"

"The dog."

"I don't know."

"You're a dumb one, ain't ya?"

She slammed the door.

"Oh, boy," Charlie said.

They dared not waste the sweetness of discovery.

Finger tracing each other's body, they revealed scars and blemishes, moles and freckles, and they marveled at each other's imperfections. In this small, hushed room, everything was significant. The curve of breast. The weight of leg. The touch of tongues. Mutually unfolding their appetites, they joined in sexual sorcery. And when muscle and bone and skin ceased to vibrate, when the urgency was spent, they lay in a silken stream of sunlight and they whispered vivid words and then returned to a new and exquisite harmony.

The world was this room.

They betrayed time.

Charlie's expectations of brave acts dissipated as the sun rose higher in the sky. Doug Root had spoken the truth. It was not that the citizens of Crowley Flats were mean-spirited. They had not collected grievances and turned them toward the boy. There was no planned vendetta. There was no act of vengeance.

There was, simply, no act at all.

What Charlie saw as he pedaled through the streets was a fabric of small motions, and what he heard were the scratchings of fear. A curtain moved behind a window and then dropped back in place. A window shade was raised. Lowered. A door slid shut. A chain rattled. Slippers shuffled toward the rear of rooms.

There were muffled coughs. A sneeze suppressed. Faint
hums and whirs and ripples. Pinfalls of smothered
sound.

An occasional door opened. A gentle man with
bright, bright eyes held up his dog for Charlie to see
and pointed out the vaccination tag on the animal's
collar. A woman, her freshly shampooed hair wound
tightly in a purple towel, advised Charlie to come
back when he was grow'd. A fat man growled at him
that what Charlie wished to do was a man's work and
that if his father was a man, he'd a'showed. Charlie
turned away from that door before it closed behind
him. A pretty little girl from school invited Charlie
in but when he entered, his hand trembling just a bit
as he held the syringe up high, he discovered that the
house was petless.

The ice melted in the basket.

And with it, Charlie's resolve.

*Dressed now, chilled still from their hours of naked-
ness, they took their coffee to the witness tree. They
sat under the druid limbs and talked as if they had
newly invented words. The words tumbled out like
beans from a broken bag as they reviewed the small
splendors of an earlier sharing. Everything reminded
them of something else. The chicory coffee smelled
like the row of bushes they had set aflame so many
years ago. The acorn bed on which they sat had a
hardness similar to frozen turnips and the thought of
the root cellar made them yearn again but they made
no move toward each other because there was no
rush now and because suspending their desire gave
it a fierce intensity. They talked of such important
things. Things like the speed of a riverboat's wake
and the taste of green wheat and the smell of thunder
and the sound of cricket wings. Such important things.*

*When at last they rose, their bed of acorns was in
shadow. The sun dipped in the western sky. They*

touched each other lightly and then turned away and walked their fields toward home. Tomorrow they would talk of Pete and Sarah and Tom. Tomorrow.

Life is so much shorter than death.

The house was on the outskirts of town. Paint peeled from the clapboard siding. The window panes had been replaced with squares of cardboard and sheets of corrugated tin. Charlie wondered how anyone inside could breath. He wasn't sure he cared. His day had been blighted as surely as black frost kills the grain. He was tired and discouraged and not once had he used the needle. He was, he supposed to himself as he shuffled up to the warped door, secretly glad of that. He wasn't sure. He wasn't sure of anything.

He knocked on the door. It was just a cursory gesture, one that demanded no response, and, with an equal negligence, he turned away and started back down the weedy path to where he'd left his bike.

"He'p ya?" a man said.

Charlie looked back. A square of cardboard had been removed from a window which flanked the door. What looked like a gnome's head rested on the sash. At first Charlie thought the man must be a dwarf but then he realized that the man was bent double in his effort to see out of the lower portion of the window. The man's face was creased dry from too much sun and his bald skull was an angry red. A thin trickle of tobacco juice stained the gray stubble of his jaw. His eyes were rheumy. He spat and a stream of tobacco arced out of the window and into the weeds at Charlie's feet. The man winked. There was no humor to it.

"He'p ya?" he asked again.

His voice was grating and Charlie could hear the hidden impatience behind it.

"I guess you don't have a dog or a cat or anything, do you?" Charlie asked and then quickly added, "sir?"

The man stared at him for a long time, the bulge working in his cheek.

"Ain't got *anything*," he said, "but I got a dog."

"Uh . . . you sure?" Charlie's heart sank.

"Looks like one," the man said.

"Oh."

"Got two ears."

"Uh huh."

"Tail."

"Yeah. Well."

"Lifts his leg when the urge comes."

"I guess he's a dog," Charlie said.

"You could check him out, it be your pleasure."

Charlie started to tremble. He had been holding the syringe behind his back but now he wanted the man to see it. He wanted to show the glint of steel and the awful point so that the man would tell him to get the hell away with that thing, to just get the hell away. Slowly, deliberately, he brought the hypodermic out from behind his back and he held it high in front of him. He remembered seeing his father pull back just a little bit on the plunger and then press it forward a fraction so that the vaccine would spurt and there would be no injection of air. The man's eyes were on him, the tobacco working steadily in his cheek. Charlie depressed the plunger. The vaccine sprayed out of the needle and for just a moment it looked as if crystals hung in the air, a watery curtain between the man and Charlie. And then the curtain was gone and Charlie's eyes challenged the man.

"Purty, ain't she?" the man said. "Set yerself front of the sun, like be you could make you a rainbow." He spat again and then continued. "Door ain't locked. Jus' push her in."

His head disappeared from above the sash and he jammed the cardboard square back into the window.

Charlie edged the door open with his foot. The room he entered was piled high with stacks of old newspapers and empty cartons. Broken bric-a-brac littered

the floor and a table made of old plyboard and saw-
horses. Torn magazines and bindless books leaned at
crazy angles on a dozen wall shelves. Used tea bags
were scattered throughout the room, their split sacks
dripping dried leaves and staining everything they
touched. The furniture was an indiscriminate mixture
of prairie tag sales and town-dump treasures. The
bald-headed man sat in a rusty tractor seat, its descending iron column screwed directly into the floor.
A battered cuspidor was at his feet. The floor around
it was dark with chaw. The man's eyes were on the
needle in Charlie's hand.

"Had much practice with them things?"

"Oh, sure," said Charlie, "been doin' it since I was
a kid."

"Long time," the man said.

"Yep."

"Well, then," he spat and missed the cuspidor, "you
won't be scairt none of Hannibal."

Charlie froze.

"Hannibal?"

The man pointed to a far corner of the room.

"Behind the saltines," he said. "Look out now, here
he comes!"

There was a large carton in the corner. Shreds of
brightly colored paper curled away from its sides but
Charlie could still make out the ripped letters which
identified the past contents of the carton as saltine
biscuits. The carton moved. It was being pushed from
behind. Charlie wished to God that he were out of this
jumble-shop room so that he would not have to see
what was edging the carton forward. It moved again.
Charlie backed up a step. He heard a soft whine and
then Hannibal crawled out from behind the carton.

"One day, ol' Hannibal," said the man gleefully,
"he's a'gonna crack a pig's knuckle right in two. I mean
to say, he is ornery!"

From the tip of his nose to the tip of his tail, Hannibal measured ten inches. On a good day. When he

stretched. He was a furry, bouncing, tail-wagging
puppy. Charlie thought he had never seen such soft
eyes.

"He's a pisser, ain't he?" The man's face was radiant.

"He's a pisser, all right," said Charlie.

"Named him for them critters what crossed the Alps.
Course he ain't got no heft to him now, no heft a'tall,
can't weigh but a bitty pound, but you give him time,
boy, an' he is surely gonna chomp them pig knuckles."

Gently, Charlie picked up the puppy and perched
him on top of the empty saltine carton. The dog's
eyes were full of trust and he turned his head and
licked Charlie's hand. The thought of stabbing that
small bundle of fur was unbearable.

"Sweeter'n a belly button on a two-bit whore, ain't
he? Beggin' yer pardon, boy."

"Nuthin' wrong with belly buttons," Charlie said,
stalling for time. " 'Less, of course, they're Colorado
belly buttons."

The dog's soft tongue was working over Charlie's
fingers and the boy prayed that he and the man could
just keep on talking all day and that he would not
have to use that goddamn needle.

The tractor seat squeaked and the man worked his
chaw of tobacco around to the other side of his mouth
and he was chewing furiously now and bending back
and forth on the seat and shuffling his feet a little,
moving the cuspidor around, as he pondered what
Charlie had just said. He spat and this time the stream
of juice pinged into the cuspidor and made it ring.

"What in tarnation's wrong with a Colorado belly
button?" the man demanded.

"Knew a man once," Charlie said, trying desperately
to deepen his voice. "Nice feller, and he told me that
it freezes so cold in Colorado, you unscrew a man's
belly button, why, his ass falls off. And that's a fact."

"Sumbitch," said the man.

For a moment, Charlie thought he would just turn

around and walk out of the room and leave the man with the wonder of it all but then the man spoke again.

"You sure you know how to use that thing," he asked, referring to the needle that Charlie still grasped, "I wouldn't want ol' Hannibal to get scratched up bad or nuthin'."

The dog squirmed a little under Charlie's hand and the puppy teeth bit playfully into the boy's palm. They tickled. Hannibal's tail beat a soft tattoo on the carton and Charlie could see that the dog was truly smiling. And the man's voice was a wasp in Charlie's ear.

"Well," he said, "you gonna do it or ain't you?"

Charlie wanted to bat the voice away. He clenched his teeth. He raised the hypodermic needle. The dog looked at it. His tail stopped wagging.

"Shoot," the man said, "oughta go through him like a knife through butter."

Charlie hurled the hypodermic across the room and when it crashed against a wall, the glass syringe shattered. The boy whirled around.

"Fuck 'em," he shouted at the man, "fuck 'em! I tried!"

25

It had not been difficult to figure out. He had seen
that the shelves of the medicine chests were empty
of vials and that an ice chest was missing and a hogstick and he had heard no sound of a boy, and when
he had climbed behind the wheel of the pickup, he
had been acutely conscious that the leather needle
case was missing.

He sat in the pickup and rolled a cigarette. When,
as he knew it would, the cigarette shredded in his
fingers, he tried again. This time, he was as deliberate
as a jeweler cutting diamonds. He made a perfect "u"
of the thin paper and poured the exact amount of Bull
Durham into it and delicately licked the gummed
edge and pressed it tight to the other edge of paper
and gently twisted one end. He struck a match. The
brightness of flame against the dusk startled him. It
emphasized the lateness of the hour. It made him
keenly aware of the passage of time and of how he
had spent that time. He was not fool enough to blame
himself for the risks Charlie might have taken. Or
might now be taking. He did not now falter from his
own belief that without risk there is nothing. The
spontaneity with Lorraine had been a risk. Unspoken.
Undefined. But there.

Sharing was a risk. And he had, at long last, per-
mitted it.

He dragged deeply from the cigarette, pleasured by

the nicotine burn in his lungs. He tossed the butt out the window, snapped on the ignition, eased into gear and started the search for his son.

The pickup rolled down Main Street. The grocery-store window was still taped and boarded from Emmett's crash. Virgil's gas station was dark. Blinds were lowered across the windows of the diner but there was a light burning within. Slowly, the shadow moved back and forth behind the blinds. Sophie was pacing. A harsher light illuminated the Western Union office and in its brightness, Ben saw Sam Hanks. He was sitting behind his desk, his head bowed so far forward as he slept that it seemed impossible that his black bowler could retain its precarious balance. But it did. Bessie sat in the glass cage of her cashier's booth staring at the empty street in front of the picture-show lobby. The lobby was empty. An entrance door between the lobby and the theater itself was wide open and as Ben's truck passed by, he could see through the theater door to the flickering light of a running film. Perhaps, Ben thought, the half-glimpsed projected images would seduce strangers from the street. But there were no strangers. The streets were quiet and empty except for one vehicle. Morgan Crowley's truck was parked outside of the theater. There was no chair on the truck bed but Ben saw the leather straps bolted to the steel floor of the truck bed and he hoped that in the darkness of the theater Lottie was still dreaming of her future. At the edge of town, Ben saw the naked work light suspended behind the cobwebbed windows of the roundhouse. No sound came from behind the walls. There was no sledge of hammer, no rip of steel.

He turned the corner and cruised down the safe street of elms and clapboard homes. He looked for the bicycle which would signal Charlie's whereabouts. He saw nothing but neat gardens and small lights glowing behind blinds. It was too dark to see the black dahlias.

In his mind he made the geographical grid of

Crowley Flats into a chessboard and he drove up and down the ranks and files of that board, his eyes moving ever more restlessly over the night's landscape. Familiar forms assumed alien shapes, and when, in the passing edge of light from his headlights, for one startled moment he mistook a hedgerow for a beast, Ben realized that he was sharing with Charlie the potential terrors of the night. By the time he had crisscrossed the prairie town and reached its far end, he was no longer sanguine about the earlier satisfactions of his flesh. He was susceptible to guilt. That guilt had little to do with the day's lust. He had not rutted like a bull. Rather, in that sweet connection, he had confessed to wounds and made self-evident the partnership of strangers. He had accepted his own fragility and that of Lorraine. Together, they had unmasked. What he recognized now, what chilled him, was that he had not offered the same privilege to his son.

He saw him. On his final sweep through Crowley Flats, he reached the town dump. The headlights picked up Charlie, sitting on a torn and sweat-stained mattress which had been tossed toward the edge of burned rubble. He was hunched over, his head bowed between his knees. Next to him, his bicycle lay on its side. The wire basket had been twisted off the handlebars and it was empty. The ice chest had been hurled into a heap of rubbish, its only value now as a cave for rats.

Ben slowed, and when the truck rolled in front of Charlie, he turned off the engine. He leaned across the seat and opened the cab door. Charlie didn't move. Now, Ben thought, now. Say it.

"It must have been hard, Charlie. It must have been awful hard."

The boy didn't look up and his voice was muffled.

"No," he said, his tone a strained bravado, "no, it wasn't so awful hard. I just took that ol' needle and . . ."

"It's all right, Charlie," Ben said, "just tell me the truth. No magic, okay?"

Behind the boy, unseen, a rat scuttled across the rubbish but Charlie didn't hear the scratch of claws because, in his head, he was weighing another sound. The tone, the timbre, the fiber of his father's voice. It was so gentle it took his breath away. He looked up. He swallowed against the dryness of his throat and then, like a Kansas hail, the words exploded.

"I never knew this dumb ol' town had so many doors Pa most of 'em just kept locked they wouldn't answer or anything and there was this guy said you had to do it and a lady in a towel and Hannibal he was nuthin' but fur but I tried to make believe he was an orange and his heart sounded like a train and I took the needle but that old heart was and his eyes and Pa I couldn't I just couldn't but I tried I tried I swear I tried."

The storm passed and in the silence neither father nor son moved.

"Your mama," Ben said finally, "your mama would have liked you, Charlie. She'd have liked the hell outa you."

And Ben thought that it might be a hundred years or more before he ever again saw a smile such as the one on Charlie's face. But he was wrong because after the boy climbed into the truck and slid across the seat so that he was close to his father, Ben touched him lightly on the back of his neck.

And he saw the smile again.

Ben slipped the clutch into gear and made a U-turn in front of the dump and headed back into town.

"Hey," Charlie said, "aren't we goin' home?"

"Well, now," Ben said, "there's something special we got to do."

"We?"

"We," Ben said.

As they drove away they heard a clatter behind

them. Charlie swiveled on the truck seat and turned toward the sound but his father's voice was reassuring.

"Rat," Ben said, "just a poor old rat."

And for the second time that night, Ben was wrong. It was not a rat.

It was a white dog.

26

They parked the truck outside the theater and when
Charlie looked up at the marquee he knew what special thing they were going to do. Even though unlighted, he could see the tarnished letters under the
drift of moon.

The Phantom Lady.

"Hot dawg," he said.

Bessie slid open the window in the cashier's booth.
She took Ben's money and gave him two tickets.

"How's business, Bessie?" Ben asked.

"You kiddin'? With that dog loose? They say that
beast's the devil come to claim his own."

"He's sick, Bess," Charlie said. "He doesn't *mean*
any harm."

"Vengeance is mine, saith the Lord!" Bessie said.
"Ben, you lay an eye on that hound, you gotta blow
his heart out!"

Charlie hoped to God that he would not be around
to see any animal get his heart blown out.

"C'mon, Pa," he said. "Gonna be late."

"Already late," Bessie said with some satisfaction,
"picture's half done."

"Don't make a damn, Bessie," Ben smiled, "we'll sit
through it twice. Three times, maybe."

"Hot dawg," Charlie said.

In the dim beam of light angling down from the

projecting booth above the balcony, Charlie and Ben could see the dark silhouettes of a few customers scattered throughout the theater. They stood at the head of an aisle and waited for their eyes to grow accustomed to the darkness so that they could find seats. On the screen in front of them a smokey-eyed Ella Raines was denying any complicity to a crime. Her voice was low and throaty and Charlie couldn't decide whether she was telling the truth or not and he wished he knew the facts of the case. He thought that maybe if he could just sit down and study her, see if her lips twitched suspiciously as she talked, see if her hand trembled when she lit a cigarette, he would be able to determine her guilt or innocence. Although he still couldn't see clearly, he took a step forward. His shin cracked into something.

"Oh," a voice said.

"Darn," said Charlie and when he squinted against the pain he found that he could also see more clearly. Directly in front of him, in the aisle, Lottie sat in her wheelchair. "Gee, Mrs. Crowley, I'm sorry. I'm awful sorry."

"It's all right, boy," she whispered, "this is a good 'un. Now set."

As they skirted the wheelchair, Ben saw that Morgan was in the aisle seat next to Lottie and he thought the rancher nodded at him. Ben nodded back and then he and Charlie moved down the aisle and took seats in the center of the theater.

Ella Raines was crying.

Jim Dandy brushed against the refuse cans outside of Virgil's gas station and when he heard the rattle of tin he spun around and tried to sink his jaws into the metal but the force of his move knocked over the can and it rolled away from him and thumped against a gas pump. His brain so ravaged by virus now, he thought the thing an animal and an enemy and he watched to see if it would move again. When it didn't, he turned away from it and moved through the shadows of the street.

Charlie leaned forward in his seat. He knew trouble was coming. It always did when Elisha Cook, Junior, leered at you. And there he was. On the screen, the scene had shifted from the merciless grilling of an innocent Ella (Charlie had quickly determined that she was the heroine and heroines were intrinsically good) to a small nightclub. The club was murky with cigarette and cigar smoke; each of the tiny tables was covered with whiskey glasses and ashtrays and the ham hands of mobsters and bejeweled fingers of disreputable women. All the hands were beating the table to the syncopated rhythm of a jazz combo. The drummer of the combo was Elisha Cook. A cigarette dangled from the corner of his mouth and the smoke curled into one eye, stinging it, making it water, but the drummer never blinked. His eyes grew wider and wilder as the sticks flew in his fingers. Charlie knew those fingers well. They had wrapped around twin .45's when ol' Elisha Junior had been Wilmer the gunsel in *The Maltese Falcon* and had gone up against Bogie. Bogie had just laughed and slapped the guns away. Charlie saw the door of the nightclub open and for one crazy moment he thought Bogie had come back. But he hadn't.

Ella stepped into the club. His hands high over his head, like eagle claws ready to rip, the drummer paused. And the look between him and Ella burned through the smoke.

Oh, boy, Charlie thought, it's comin', all right. It's comin'!

The eagle claws descended and nearly ripped the skin off the drum. The sticks beat a furious tattoo. They flailed a rat-a-tat-tat.

Boppedy-bop-bop-bop! Brrrrrrraaaaat! Brrrrrraaat! Boppedy-bop!

The dog's head arched back until the cords of his throat almost snapped and when he howled it was made more awful because there was hardly any sound to it. There was just a thin wail of anguish, and blood and spittle flew into the air. Tiny yellow gobs of it splattered against the door in the alley. The door was open. It led to the stage of the theater. Jim Dandy walked through it.

Dandy inched across the bare backstage and then stopped and stared at the barrier before him. It was a large screen onto which the movie was projected. The dog's head twitched as he watched the strange silhouetted shapes flicker across the screen and when he heard the staccato snap and tap of drum and the high wild scream of the sax, his legs began to quiver and shake and his belly spasmed and his urine ran freely to the floor.

Bopbopbopbopbopbopbop! Briddellyoo-bop! Dedumdum! Dum! Brrrrraaaaat!

The flailing sticks whipped and pounded the drum and the hard slap of a bass thumped into the rhythm, drove it forward until, not unlike the dog's thin cry, the trumpet wailed in alarm and was joined by the crushing chords of a piano.

And as the jazz combo frenzied toward its percussion peak, the white dog hurtled through the screen, ripping it to shreds.

His jaws dripping, Dandy stood on the edge of the stage. The torn images of actors flapped behind him, but the drum rolled on. Lottie screamed. The dog snapped his head toward the sound and leaped off the stage. He smashed into a seat in the front row and a harsh brawl of pain escaped from him and his rear leg dragged at a strange angle as he raced up the aisle. Ben shoved Charlie down behind a seat and then he hurdled the row in front of him, and as he sped after the dog, he tore his jacket off and he was trying desperately to wrap it around one arm when the dog charged the wheelchair. Morgan saw it coming and he dove out of his seat and his wild yells almost drowned the terrified screams of his crippled wife. Morgan's body smashed into the chair and his great weight toppled it. His body covered Lottie, and then, together, they were rolling down the aisle which pitched sharply toward the stage. He could hear the wracking sobs underneath him, and just as he was struck with the terror of cracking her bones, he felt the dog's sharp claws dig into his back and he heard the slashing teeth close to his throat. He threw up his arm to protect himself and turned to see Ben's cloth-wrapped fist lash across Dandy's skull. With a stran-gled whine, the dog whirled away and rocketed to-ward the lobby.

Ben grabbed Charlie's hand and almost lifted the boy off his feet as they ran to the truck. He yanked the door open and scrambled onto the front seat. He reached up and pulled one of the two rifles from the gun rack. He broke it open. He saw that it was loaded. He slapped the bolt home and Charlie heard the click of a shell as it entered the chamber.

"Listen to me," Ben spoke swiftly, "I want you in this truck. Door locked. Don't move. Just stay here. You understand me?"

"Pa, I can . . ."

He stopped when he saw his father's eyes. He knew Ben was thinking about the slaughter of the herd and the unfired gun at the quarry.

"No, Charlie," Ben said. His voice was deliberate but not unkind. "It's better you stay. I'm going to kill that dog."

Ben slid off the truck seat and down onto the street. He looked quickly toward both ends of the street, and then, making his decision, flicked the rifle's safety switch to its off position and started walking west-ward toward the dump. He was swiftly lost in the darkened street.

The footsteps faded away. Charlie looked back toward the theater. The cashier's booth was empty. Bessie must have gone to Morgan's aid. The door between the lobby and the theater was still open but no images projected their flickering lights. No sound came from within. The drummer had been silenced. Charlie stared up the street, a long tunnel of darkness. There was no end to its mystery. There was no longer a light in the diner. There was no burning bulb behind the window of the Western Union. Charlie put one foot on the running board of the pickup and started to climb into the cab. He saw the remaining rifle in its rack. The wind moved a cloud and moonlight flecked the cab and gave a dull glow to the rifle.

For a moment, Charlie thought his body had left its skin. He saw a boy reach up and remove the rifle and check its load and slide its bolt into firing position. He saw the boy, rifle at his hip, move toward the eastern reaches of the street but when he heard the hollow boom of boots, he recognized the boy.

It was Charles Remington Custer.

Step by step, softly, Ben eased toward the darkened doorway of the barbershop. It was deeply recessed and he couldn't see into its shadows. His finger tightened on the rifle trigger and he held the gun straight in front of him. He paused and looked at the night sky. The wind was gusting, sporadically pushing the clouds across the moon and covering the town under an opaque curtain. He waited for the slow slide of cloud and when the moon once again revealed an edge he moved swiftly, lunging into the doorway, his rifle pointed at whatever he would find. He found nothing. He wiped beads of sweat from his face and stepped out of the doorway, moving westerly again. There was a sudden rustling sound above him. His head jerked up toward it. The sound stopped.

The barbershop was housed in a long, low building. Attached to one side of the building was a rickety wooden staircase leading to the roof. It was an easy

climb for a man. Or a dog. Ben started up. The ancient
boards creaked under his weight. Above him, the
rustling resumed. It stopped. When Ben stepped onto
the roof, he heard nothing. The moon was quartered
now and under its sheen Ben saw a weathered tarpaulin in the center of the roof, its heavy folds bulging
over some object. When the sounds of rustle and flap
started again, he was certain that the tarpaulin trembled. One finger remaining on the trigger, he crouched
down and scooped up a handful of loose pebbles. He
tossed them at the tarpaulin. Underneath the canvas,
there was a swift drumming. Ben inched toward the
covered mound. He eased the muzzle of his rifle under
one corner of the canvas and, in an almost simultane-
ous motion, jerked it up and sprang back, the rifle at
his shoulder.

Softly, the caged pigeons cooed.

Charlie stared into the alley. At the far end he saw
the board fence. Knowing that the only way in or out
of the alley was the opening in which he stood, he
debated about entering. If Jim Dandy were crouched
low, ready to spring, there would be no way for
Charlie to evade the charge. Charlie glanced down at
the rifle in his hand and wondered how fast he could
fire. And then a worse thought made him weak.

He wondered if he could fire at all.

He turned away from the alley. Behind him, something clattered. He spun around. The rifle butt
smacked against a wall and he almost lost his grip.
His fingers clutched the rifle breech and he brought
the rifle sharply to his shoulder as his gaze darted over
the refuse cans and broken boxes in the alley. He
heard an animal scratching. His finger trembled on the
trigger. The moon was brighter now and he saw an
uncovered waste barrel standing halfway down the
alley. The barrel was stuffed, overflowing, with vegetable scraps. Crowned with a wad of discarded
butcher's paper, its greased sides were stained dark

with blood. The paper moved and for a dreadful instant, Charlie thought the blood was fresh and running.

A tomcat's head poked out of the barrel and his eyes gleamed at the boy.

Charlie backed out of the alley.

Along the street of elms it was difficult to identify sounds. The wind whipped the trees and dead twigs snapped loose from their limbs as if they had been scissored by a bullwhip. Underneath Ben's boots, brown leaves crackled and crunched in tiny dry raspings. Each falling twig or scuffed leaf or the whine of a bending bough goaded Ben, mocked him, challenged him to isolate the sound of scraping claws or the snap of jaws. Under the wedge of moonlight which the wind inconstantly defined, his eyes searched the dark gardens. He prodded bushes with the tip of his rifle and poked into hedgerows and, warily, circled a huge planting of hydrangea. The picture of Dandy smashing into the seats of the theater was in his mind. He could see the dog racing toward the wheelchair, his injured leg angled from his body. Working his way up the street and through the gardens and across the autumn lawns, Ben explored every sheltering patch which might harbor a wounded animal.

He stopped when he saw a moving shadow on the lip of moonlight. He crept forward. His finger slipped through the trigger guard and curled around the trigger. Cautiously, he leveled his rifle. And then lowered it. The shadow came from the wind-bobbing head of a black dahlia.

Ben reached the end of the street. He turned north toward the depot.

The open sheds of Caleb's feed store were piled high with burlap bags of grain. Spilled seed was scattered along the sagging floor boards. Charlie tried to shuffle softly across the blanket of grain but he could hear the tiny pop as an occasional seed split its skin. He thought of a dog's sensitive hearing and he wondered if Dandy, too, were listening to the pops. Filled with apprehension, he edged between the bulging burlap. There was just a narrow file between the bags and as Charlie walked it he could feel the rough material scrape the skin of his hands which held the rifle. A cobweb brushed his face and he clawed at the silken thread, pulling it away from his eyes, rubbing it off his lips. He was breathing in short, nervous gasps and the cobweb entered his mouth and he thought for a terrible moment that a spider was crawling down his throat. He spat desperately, over and over again, until he was sure that nothing alive was in his mouth. Trembling, he leaned against a bag of grain. Something dark and evil-smelling scuttled across his shoulder and he heard the tiny click of teeth. He leaped back in fear and as he sprawled onto the floor, the rifle flew from his hands and its hard-edged muzzle tore through a burlap sack, half burying the weapon and choking its barrel with seed.

He looked up. Sitting on the torn grain sack, a rat stared at him, its beady eyes malevolent and greedy. The rifle butt protruded a few inches below the rat. Staying on his belly, Charlie inched forward and stretched his arms toward the rifle. The rat's tail twitched and his small, fierce teeth clittered. Quickly, Charlie withdrew his arm. He slid away from the sack until he felt his back against a wall of the shed. Keeping his eyes on the rat he rose, and when he felt something press against his shoulder blade he turned to the wall. Harness equipment hung from nails on the wall. He removed a leather bridle. It was a fancy bridle with small silver bells. He faced the rat. He whirled the bridle over his head, the silver bells tinkling sweetly, and then hurled it at the rodent. It hit squarely and the rat squealed and leaped off the sack and ran into the darkness. Charlie lunged forward and yanked the rifle from the sack and darted out of the shed.

He fled north toward the depot.

There was a momentary lull to the wind and, once again, the moon was covered with cloud. In the darkness and the silence, Ben straddled the center track of the roadbed. He shifted a little and he heard the crunch of gravel under his boots. He squinted into the night, trying to see any moving shape or form. He could barely make out the outline of the water tower which was west of the depot and adjacent to the roundhouse. He shut his eyes. He listened for any movement but all he heard was the distant plink of water dripping from the tank. He wanted a cigarette but the thought of busying his hands with anything but a gun filled him with caution. He opened his eyes and peered both east and west. He needed to choose one path to follow.

Behind him, something banged. He spun around. Above the depot platform, a wooden sign identifying Crowley Flats hung from rusted strands of wire and swayed in the rising wind and banged against its post. Ben realized that the wind had stiffened and that the moon was clean. In the growing light, the post cast a shadow toward the east. Ben turned in the same direction and started down the tracks.

Charlie heard the crunch of gravel. He crouched on the other side of the depot. He was in a pool of shadow, in the lee of moonlight. He couldn't see. He couldn't remember in what position the safety on his rifle was locked. He fumbled at it trying to recall whether clicking it to right or left would free the pull of trigger. Oh God, he thought, which way? Which way? He heard a shuffle of stone. He thumbed the safety to the right and prayed. A pebble cracked against a rail. Charlie rose from his crouch and, hugging the depot wall, started toward the tracks. The rifle felt terribly heavy as he slid the stock against his cheek. He reached the corner of the depot. His finger curled across the trigger.

And then he froze. He remembered how the rifle

had been buried in the sack of grain. What if, he asked himself in rising panic, what if the barrel is jammed? If that were true and he pulled the trigger, the weapon would explode in his face. He eased the rifle down and, in the darkness, poked one finger into the gun's muzzle. The barrel was choked with seed. Swiftly, Charlie stepped away from the corner and back behind the protective wall. Face forward, he rested against the wall, rubbing his forehead against the cool clapboards and letting the rifle dangle uselessly in one hand. He waited there until he could no longer hear any sound of rolling pebbles. He knew that if he were going to continue the hunt, he would have to unclog the rifle barrel. He needed light. He needed a round strip of steel, a rod which could slide through the barrel. He knew where to find both rod and light.

He ran to the roundhouse.

The dismantled pieces of locomotive loomed like midnight statues scattered among the weeds. Charlie threaded his way through them and entered the roundhouse. The suspended worklight glowed naked and dim but the bulb was bright enough for Charlie to accomplish what he had to do. He searched for what he needed. He pushed aside arresting chimneys and marker lights and valves and gears and pipes and brackets, and he climbed over the split cab roof and driving wheels and cylinder saddles, avoiding the wicked cutting edges as best he could, and tried not to think of every shadowed mound of scrap as a hiding place for Dandy.

At one end of the roundhouse, opposite the open door, was a huge, hanging sheet of boiler plate. The top of it was blackened from the acetylene torch once held by Ernst. His ladder still stood nearby. Underneath it was a thin, round strip of twisted steel. Charlie saw it. Too swiftly, he crossed the floor. His boot slid across an oil spill and he tripped and tumbled into a pile of scrap. The roundhouse reverberated to the clang of steel on steel.

Dandy's teeth bit into his own flesh, gnawing at the animal of pain which crawled inside his wounded leg. His white coat was matted with soot and blood and yellow spittle. His body shook so violently that his shadow seemed to dance under the water tank. He head the crash of metal. His head snapped up from his leg and he stared toward the roundhouse. His muscles bunched and spasmed and he pushed himself out of the brush and then, half walking, half crawling, moved forward.

When Charlie untangled himself from the last loose coil of wire, his hand was bleeding from a gash. He sucked on it as he picked up the steel rod and carried it and the clogged rifle behind the sheet of boiler plate. He pulled the ladder behind the iron sheet and sat on a lower step, resting the gun upright between his knees. He tested one end of the rod in the rifle's muzzle and saw that it would fit if it were straightened. Using both hands, he slowly unkinked the steel.

The dog bellied through the doorway, pus dropping from his jaws.

The rod was untwisted. Charlie slipped one end of it into the rifle muzzle and carefully reamed it toward the breech. He grunted a little, surprised at how thickly packed the seeds were. He worked the rod around in little circles, steadily pushing it forward.

There was a foot of space between the lower edge of the boiler sheet and the floor. The dog saw the bottom of the ladder and the boy's boots and the butt of the rifle. The stock was made from the walnut tree and it was grainy, and as Charlie worked the rod back and forth it slipped from one side to another and the dog saw the streaks of walnut grain come alive, take shape, shimmer and coil. He saw them roll off the wood and slide toward him, hissing. His hackles stood straight up and his loins quivered as he tightened sinew and bone toward his leap.

The rod bit deeply into the seeds and with one hard thrust from Charlie the barrel was free, the seeds spraying swiftly to the oiled floor. Charlie tossed the rod away and leaned back against the boiler plate.

The twang of the rod cracked against the dog's ears and when he saw the huge rusted sheet sway toward him, he leaped to attack. The dog sprang high into the air and banged against the boiler plate. On the opposite side, Charlie fell from the ladder. His face slammed into the floor, and underneath the hanging sheet he saw the dog. Dandy had fallen back from his crash and a harsh whine seemed to rip from his bowels. He shook himself, trying to throw off the stunning impact, and then he saw the boy.

Dandy howled like a dying wolf.

Charlie leaped up, scooping the rifle with him. He scrambled up the ladder just as Dandy rounded the corner of the hanging sheet of steel. The dog bounded up, his hind legs clearing the floor, his jaws snapping toward Charlie. But the boy was too high to reach. The dog backed up and charged the ladder. It shook under Charlie. The dog lunged again, his body smashing into the legs of the ladder. It tipped and the dog heaved against it and the ladder toppled.

The rifle in his hands, Charlie jumped. He plummeted into a mound of tangled wire and broken gears and wicked shards of steel. He was almost buried under a mass of metal and, near him, the rifle lay trapped in debris. The boy's clothes and skin were torn and blood streaked his face and ran freely from the gash on his hand. Dandy smelled the blood, was frenzied by it, and ran in wild circles around the heap of scrap, his howl a harsh and rising rasp. The metal which trapped Charlie acted as a barrier but the dog plunged into it over and over again, his jaws ripping at wire and steel.

Dazed, Charlie struggled in the snare but he couldn't pull free. He saw the rifle. He tried to ease it out of its entrapping coil of wire but it was caught too tightly. The muzzle pointed up, but the best Charlie could do was rock the rifle back and forth in a small arc. There was no way for him to level it at the charging dog. With horror, he saw that Dandy was pulling at the surrounding rods and pipes and that the dog's jaws were getting closer. He saw the saliva spill near his hand. Near the open wound.

And he saw something else.

Ben walked along the eastbound tracks. He was accustomed to the darkness now and even when the night was dimmed by cloud cover he could accurately determine the shape and form of things. He was no longer fooled by a bending bush or a speared tree or the concave hollows in a gravel bank and when, once, something rushed in front of him, he saw it was a jack rabbit speeding toward its lair and when he heard a shivered sound he knew it was only the cry of an owl.

His fingers ached from the pressure with which he held the rifle. He was tired and he was alarmed by the strange absence of any signs of the dog. The picture of Dandy's leg kept flitting before his eyes and he was certain that the dog could not have escaped into the wide stretches of the prairie. He cursed the dog and he felt a slow panic rising within him and he decided he would, goddamn it, have a smoke. He fumbled with the makings, hugging the rifle under his arm, keeping his hands free. And when he looked at his hands, he thought of Pete and he remembered the quick wonder of the boy's hands as he had helped at the birthing of the calf. *I did something*, the boy had written. *And you will do more*, Ben whispered aloud, *I promise that. I promise it.* Missing, he thought to himself, missing. But not lost. Never lost.

He lifted the rolled cigarette to his lips. But he never lit it. As he reached for a match, the night shattered into sound. The iron clangor of a bell crashed against the sides of its brass hood, and then beat back and forth inside of its own echo. The brassy peals rocked the air and exploded over the prairie. The whole of Kansas seemed to vibrate.

Ben wheeled toward the source of that metallic

din, and when he sprinted up the tracks toward the roundhouse he could see the pop of distant lights in the houses of the town.

When he charged through the roundhouse door he heard the splat of a bullet against the bell. He saw Charlie, pale and bloodied, squeeze off another shot and he saw the dog whirl away from a tangle of wire and then the dog was racing toward him, his eyes filled with rage, his jaws wide as he howled. Ben slammed to a stop. He had no time to sight his weapon. He slapped the rifle against his hip and snapped off a shot. The firing pin clicked against a shell. The weapon misfired. He swung the rifle around and grabbed the barrel in both hands and raised it high over his head to club down on the dog when he leaped.

Dandy left his feet in a long, lifting thrust, his jaws snapping toward Ben's throat. Ben heard the crack of a single shot. The dog dropped. His heart was blown apart.

Neither Ben nor Charlie moved. They didn't speak. They stared at each other across the body of the dead dog. Charlie had torn loose from the mound of scrap and he lay prone on the coil of wire, the rifle still held to his shoulder.

Outside, there was a squeal of brakes and then a man's shout which was overlapped by the shrill voice of a woman. The beam of a flashlight sprayed through the doorway and then Sam Hanks rode his bicycle right into the roundhouse. He was followed by Sophie, her nightdress clutched around her. More people pushed in, their voices high and quick with excitement until they saw the dead dog and then they were silent. Caleb Dodd and Virgil Foster ran in, Virgil holding up his unbelted pants with both hands, Caleb clenching a pair of aces in his hand, a pasteboard reminder of his interrupted game. And then Morgan Crowley pushed through and the crowd separated to let him closer. When he stood in front of the dog, the others, unaware of what they were doing, formed a circle around the dead animal as if they were stepping toward a long forgotten ceremony of slaughter.

They watched Morgan, waited for him to speak, each of them hoping that perhaps Morgan would find the right words for this bloody moment. He looked at Charlie who still rested on the wire, the gun to his shoulder but his eyes closed now. Morgan shifted his gaze to the brass bell which no longer rang and all those in the roundhouse remembered that the big rancher had promised that the ancient engine bell would sound a song of victory when they had finished ripping the locomotive into scrap. Morgan stared at it for a long time and then he looked back at the dead dog at his feet.

"Well," he said. "Well, then. You done good, boy. You done real good."

Ben moved across the floor to the coil of wire. He lifted Charlie in his arms. The boy's rifle lay on the wire. Charlie looked at it and then at his father. The boy sighed. It was, Ben thought, the sound of a very old man. Charlie leaned down from his father's arms and he picked up the rifle.

When Ben started toward the door, the crowd moved aside, opening a path, and Ben heard the beginning of their murmurs but he said nothing. He acknowledged nobody.

They gathered at the door and watched him carry his son across the littered ground and past the water tower and down the weedy path which led to town. They watched until he disappeared into the dark, dark night.

27

Sam tossed a chunk of wood into the pot-bellied stove. It was a piece of soft white pine and it caught instantly, the flames leaping along its length. He clanged the iron door shut and warmed his hands over the stove. He heard the whistle of the eastbound train and he crossed his office and looked out of the window. He stood so close that his breath frosted the glass. Idly, he scratched his fingernail across the frosted pane and drew a diagram of tic-tac-toe, but before he could begin the game he heard the chatter of tele-type keys. He returned to the machine and bent over it, listening to the quiet clickings. He pulled out a strip of yellow paper and read the message.

He smiled. If a stranger had happened by, had casu-ally glanced through the Western Union window, he would never have known that the man who reached for his black bowler hat had the saddest eyes in Kansas.

It had rained hard the night before and the street was puddled. The surface of the puddles shimmered under layers of bright ice crystals. November lay on the land. Sam had neglected to put on a coat or gloves and he hugged himself and blew into his hands as he crossed the street to the diner.

Sam opened the storm door and entered the diner. He sniffed deeply, savoring the fragrance of fresh coffee and hot baked buns. The radio was playing softly and Sam recognized the tune of a familiar waltz, and knowing what was stuck inside his hat he thought about reaching across the counter and taking Sophie's hand and asking her to dance but his toes were cold and, besides, he was impatient to share his news.

"Mornin', Sophie." He sat down at the counter.

"Sam," she said. Without asking, she drew a cup of coffee from the urn and placed it in front of Sam. She saw that he was smiling and that his eyes were on the map of Europe. "No sugar, *ja?*"

"Well, now," he said and the smile was even wider, "I'm just gonna have myself a lump this mornin'. There's a real sweetness to the day, Sophie, yes, sir, a real sweetness."

With an unexpected flourish, he removed his bowler and picked out the strip of yellow paper. He handed it to Sophie and then stirred a single lump of sugar into his coffee. She read the teletyped message. When she raised her head and looked at Sam, she, too, was smiling, and she made a little clucking sound of pleasure.

"The Siegfried line, *ja?*"

"Yep," Sam said, "it's all broke through."

Sophie crossed to the map and began to remove a row of tacks. Sam leaned across the counter and turned up the volume on the radio. The diner filled with the hum of cellos and Sam thought that he would, by gum, finish his coffee and slide her into a waltz.

Outside, the train whistle blew.

Buttoned up in sheepskin jackets, their breaths white in the air, Morgan and his range hand sat easily in their saddles and whistled softly at the herd of cattle they were driving through the creek. The cattle were small and young. It was a fresh herd. The men watched the animals drink.

"Gonna be a spell 'fore they get real weight on 'em," the ranch hand said.

"Well," Morgan said, his leathered face creased

in quiet contentment, "I ain't goin' nowheres, Mr. Hawkins. I ain't goin' nowheres at all."

He dismounted and crouched at the creek bank and cupped his hands into the water. He was drinking from the cold stream when both men heard the distant, lonely whistle of the train.

"Listen to her," the ranch hand said, "gives a man itchy feet, don't it?"

"Mr. Hawkins, there ain't nuthin' out there that can beat the prairie. Nuthin'."

Morgan looked at the yearlings in the creek and he thought about how many yards of yellow ribbon he would buy in Wichita.

When they heard the whistle, they were kneeling at Tom's grave. Dippsy turned toward the sound of the train.

"Where you think they're takin' the train, Mama?"

"Lordy, Dips," Lorraine said, "how'd I know? Big factory, I 'spect."

"Virgil says whole town's gonna get a prize."

"A prize? We don't need a prize, Dippsy, only did what we pledged."

"Well, that's somethin', ain't it?"

"Yeah," she said quietly, "yeah, that's a whole big somethin'."

They rose and climbed the rise of the cemetery hill to where Ben and Charlie stood by the pickup.

"Thanks, Ben," she said, "appreciate the ride."

He nodded. She joined Ben on the front seat of the truck and Charlie and Dippsy climbed onto the truck bed behind. On the drive back to the Tower's place, the wind whipped hard across the boys' faces, burning their cheeks and making it difficult to talk, but when they passed the windmill Dippsy pointed up to the turning blades and to the jackknife below and he shouted loudly into the wind so that Charlie could hear.

"Come spring," he yelled, "you gonna do it, Charlie? You gonna take that fucker?"

"Yeah," Charlie shouted back, "yeah!"

And he knew he would.

When they reached the farm, the boys turned around and looked through the rear window of the truck and they saw that just before Lorraine climbed down from the seat, she and Ben touched each other lightly. Their fingers met, lingered, and then slowly drew apart. The boys looked at each other and rolled their eyes and giggled, but by the time Lorraine was standing on the ground they had set their faces straight.

Lorraine looked through the cab window at Ben.

"I'll see you," she said.

"Yeah," he said. "Oh, yeah."

As Lorraine and Dippsy strolled together toward the farmhouse, Charlie scrambled up onto the seat next to his father.

"Now?" he asked.

"Now," Ben said.

The truck bounced and swerved over field ruts as it sped across the prairie. They rushed by fields of winter wheat where the short green stalks speared through the November ground and as they drove due east the sound of the train whistle grew louder. At the far end of Morgan Crowley's spread there was a pasture lying fallow. The pasture land curved up to a bluff. The truck beelined up the land and when they reached the bluff, Ben slammed on the brakes. He and Charlie jumped out and ran to the edge of bluff. They looked down.

Below them, a train clacked by. It was a rolling stock of freight. A hundred boxcars traveling east. At the end of it was a boxcar whose roof had been removed and even the great, rolling clouds of engine smoke could not hide its contents. Its wooden seams looked as if they would split from the pressure of its load.

It was the last journey of an ancient engine stripped to scrap.

Ben and Charlie sat on the edge of the bluff, their legs dangling free as they watched the train curve slowly around a distant bend. Both of them were quiet. Ben pulled his Bull Durham and papers and started to roll a cigarette. The tobacco spilled between his fingers. Without looking at his father, Charlie reached over and took the makings and, expertly, rolled a perfect smoke.

"Knew a man once," he said, "nice feller. Had the clumsiest hands west of Big Muddy."

On the seat of his pants, he scratched a match alive and lit the cigarette and took one long, deep drag and then, his eyes still on the clacking train, he handed the smoke to Ben.

They sat there for a long time, saying nothing, just passing the smoke between them, two small figures on the landscape of the prairie.

At last, the long, long train disappeared.

A hawk spiraled in the sky.

There was no sound.

Slowly, Charlie raised his arms as if he were sighting an imaginary rifle.

"Pow. Pow," he said softly, a strange, small smile on his face.

And, surprised at his own swift grief, Ben Custer welcomed his son into the company of men.

ABOUT THE AUTHOR

WILLIAM DARRID has been an actor, teacher, Broadway producer, film company executive and screenwriter. *The Blooding* is his first novel. He is currently completing his second.

A Special Preview
of the opening pages of
the #1 Canadian bestseller

ACT OF GOD

The super-thriller novel by

Charles Templeton

"Superb. I was spellbound. I do not recall when
I last read a book so totally satisfying in every
way."

—Arthur Hailey

Prologue

The box had been three days in the belly of the Pan Am 707 cargo aircraft, having been shipped from Amman, Jordan to John F. Kennedy airport but being delayed in Amsterdam by reason of the need to replace an engine in the aircraft. In the freight warehouse, a cargo-handler picked it up and dumped it onto a long steel-sheathed table.

"Goddammit!" the supervisor snarled, "It's marked fragile. Can't you read?"

"I can read."

"Then read, for Christ's sake."

The box, three feet long and a foot wide, was made of unpainted half-inch pine. It had been securely nailed and was bound with metal strapping. A bill of lading, glued to the rough surface of the wood, yielded the information that the box had cleared customs at Amman and weighed 11.4 kilograms. A rectangular piece of paper, also glued to the wood, read:

SHIP TO: Dr Herman Unger
Curator, Department of Anthropology
HOLD FOR: Dr Harris G. Gordon
Museum of Natural History
Central Park West at 79th St
New York City, 10024, USA

Carefully hand-lettered in red ink on the wood itself were the words: FRAGILE! HANDLE WITH CARE, and beneath them the neatly printed injunction: *Contents archaeological artifacts. Not to be opened except in presence of addressee. Avoid extreme cold, heat or humidity.*

The cargo-handler pivoted the box on the table, picked it up and placed it on a wooden pallet. A forklift truck thrust its tines beneath, wheeled and trundled away. On a long aisle of open-shelved racks the driver spied a space. He stopped, raised the lift, dismounted and slid the box onto a shelf alongside a carton containing a computer keyboard, a box of pharmaceutical supplies, a crate of Jensen automatic rifles and a metal container for motion picture film bearing the label, *Sex Practices in Sodom.*

The cargo-handler made a note of the coded digits on the shelf, mounted his machine and drove off.

Chapter One

That late afternoon In Rome the setting sun was gilding towers, cupolas and crosses, and impatient traffic contended in the streets as a small black Fiat bearing the distinctive SCV license plates of the Vatican State separated from the flow at the lower end of the Via Venetto and turned in at the entrance to the United States embassy. An enormous flag over three wrought-iron gates waved an indolent welcome and two marines in dress-blues drew themselves taut to snap and sustain a salute as the car moved the length of the building, made a 180-degree turn and drew up before the bulletproof glass doors within the security of the inner courtyard. The driver leaped from the car to open the door, and the Most Reverend Michael Cardinal Maloney, Bishop of the Archdiocese of New York, his fame less suited to Fiats than to limousines, emerged. As he approached the doorway, the ambassador strode swiftly down the broad sweep of the marble staircase, hand outstretched.

"Good afternoon, Your Eminence," he said, his voice sepulchral in the vaulted vestibule. "Right on time, but then you always are. Good to see you."

"And you, Mr. Ambassador."

The ambassador was a very tall man, taller by inches than Cardinal Maloney's six feet two, and lean to the point of gauntness. He had a narrow, bald head and lank hair hanging in spikes down the back of a long neck. Not wanting to intimidate by his height, he compensated by thrusting his head forward.

Michael never saw him without recalling the great blue herons that stilted solemnly about in the stony shallows near The Cottage in summer.

"You had a good flight from New York?" the ambassador asked, pumping Michael's arm as though trying to draw water.

"Couldn't have been better."

"The Holy Father, he's well?"

"I'll tell him you were asking."

The ambassador flicked a glance at his wristwatch. "I think perhaps I'd better get you to the telephone. It's going on five and Mr. Lieberman . . ." He left the sentence dangling, and cupping Michael's elbow lightly, disdained the tiny elevator and turned him toward the staircase. "I've put you in the conference room," he said, "There's a scrambler on one of the phones there. . ."

What would be on Josh Lieberman's mind to cause him to take the most extraordinary measure of having him come to the embassy? There was only one likely explanation: Lieberman had heard about the Holy Father's illness. But why the embassy; could he not talk more easily and as safely—and certainly, more appropriately—at the Vatican? Perhaps, for all the recently intensified security measures, the telephone system there was not invulnerable.

On the telephone a light flashed. He picked up the receiver and said, "Hello."

"The Secretary of State calling from Washington, Your Eminence. Will you hold please?" There was a sustained buzz, a series of automated beeps and the line cleared.

"Are you there, Eminence?"

"Yes, I am," Michael said, his voice cordial. He held a particular affection for Joshua Lieberman. They had met often and had spoken on the telephone daily during the period just before and after the Communist party took power in Italy.

"Good to hear your voice," Lieberman said, the hint of a chuckle in his tone. "I won't ask how you are because virtue must reward its possessor with a serene mind and a—"

Michael feigned a groan: "Beginning like that you must want an enormous favor . . ."

"Sorry to have brought you to the embassy," he said.

"Am I to take it that our switchboard leaks?"

"The way things are I wouldn't be surprised. But if you have bugs they're not ours." He laughed. "At least not that I know of. It's just that I feel more confident on this line."

"I understand."

The Secretary's manner changed. "Three things on my mind: Number one, I hear the Holy Father is ill."

Michael's hesitation was so brief as to be undetectable. In that microsecond he balanced the wisdom of admitting the truth against the risk involved and knew that the secret would be secure. "You have good sources," he said.

"How serious is it?"

"He's had a stroke."

"I'm sorry to hear that. A bad one?"

"He's been in a coma off and on for days."

"I *am* sorry." He paused a moment. "My second question is a somewhat indelicate one but I think you'll understand. If the Holy Father should pass away . . ."

"Who will succeed him?"

"Yes."

"It's not a matter about which there can be any certainty. We like to believe that God takes a hand in the choosing."

"Let me put it another way: there must be certain men who are more likely to be selected than others."

"There will be perhaps five candidates."

"Would you be among that five?"

"It would mean a radical break with tradition, but to answer your question, yes."

"Good."

"Why?"

"Because it'll make things a hell of a lot simpler at this end." He was silent for a moment and Michael could hear his wheezing over extraneous sounds in the background. "Sorry to leave you hanging but I wanted to put my hands on a report here. The reason for my chasing you down—beyond my concern for the Holy Father, of course—is that I've just learned that the Italian government is about to take steps that may seriously affect your church and I thought I'd better get the information to you while you're over there in Rome. Our people over there, after a bit of kite-flying to test the wind, Premier Gordini has plans to . . ."

When, ten minutes later, Michael put down the telephone, his face was grave.

The summons to Rome had come in an early morning telephone call from Paolo Cardinal Rinsonelli, Dean of the Sacred College of Cardinals and one-time visiting Professor of New Testament at the North American College in Rome with whom Michael had done graduate work after his conversion to Roman Catholicism. At eighty, straight as a pillar and with the vitality of a man half his years, Rinsonelli was the terror of the Vatican bureaucracy. He suffered fools not at all, was intemperate with temporizers, impatient with mediocrity and disdainful of subtlety. He was a man of patrician tastes and often earthy language, whose seamed and craggy face, beneath a mane of purest white hair, suggested a relief map. A Sicilian, he delighted in intrigue, and when he had occasion to telephone Michael long distance— seeking his counsel or relaying messages from the Holy Father —often used the name Giovanni, employing an elaborate code and speaking exquisite Italian in what he fondly believed was a perfect simulation of underworld argot. He was indifferent to the six-hour difference in time between Rome and New York City and as a consequence often broke Michael's rest. On this morning, when the private telephone beside the bed jangled him from his deep sleep, Michael had glanced at the illuminated face of the clock beside his bed, noted that it was just past four, and on hearing Rinsonelli's organ tones identifying himself as Giovanni (double fortissimo because it was long distance), muttered a sleepy, "Damn."

He was soon fully alert. Rinsonelli spoke of "your pal Tony in Genoa"—his code name for the Holy Father—and despite the convoluted ambiguity of his sentences, it quickly became clear that the pope was seriously ill and that Michael was to come immediately. . . .

There was no reason to discuss the arrangements to be made should he die: they had been established by long tradition and specifically in the Apostolic Constitution of 1945. Those cardinals resident in Rome—the Curia Romana—would meet in "preparatory congregation" on the day of his death to choose a *cardinal camerlengo*, a chamberlain. He would immediately decree that the papal apartment be sealed, take charge of the properties of the Holy See, require that the Fisherman's Ring and all other papal seals be brought before the Curia and the seals defaced in its presence, set in motion the complex preparations for the burial and name a date for the beginning of the conclave to elect a new pope.

Gregory, his body having been prepared for public viewing by the embalmers, dressed in full pontificals, a mitre on his head, would be borne to the Sistine Chapel to lie between gigantic white candles beneath Michelangelo's fresco of *The Last Judgment*. With the Holy City draped in black and Rome itself solemnized by the tolling of bells from every tower, they

would mourn him with nine funeral Masses, give him nine ab-
solutions and, his face covered with a purple veil and his body
with an ermine blanket dyed blood-red, bury him on the third
day in the sacred grotto beneath the Basilica close to the tomb
of Peter: bury him in three coffins, one of cypress within one
of lead and both within one of elm, to make him in death kin
to the humblest of men borne to their graves in a plain wooden
box.

Chapter Two

Despite a difference of nearly twenty years in their ages and centuries in the worlds from which they'd sprung, the two men had become each other's best friend. They were walking idly now across the spongy turf, shoes gleaming with dew and with the musk of night in their nostrils. Michael had just finished recounting the burden of his conversation with the Secretary of State: specifically that the Italian government was about to withdraw all tax exemptions and privileges granted the Vatican State, not only in Rome but from all Catholic churches, schools and monasteries throughout the country, and after testing the wind, would so announce.

"In effect, tear up the Lateran Treaty," Rinsonelli rumbled.

"Lieberman says the economy is in worse shape than outsiders dream. Their balance of payments is way out of line and the probability is they'll have to devalue the lira again. Probably raise taxes."

"So much for election promises."

"So much for the workers' paradise."

They need a scapegoat, and who better than the church?" Michael imitated the intonations of a public speaker: "No longer should a wealthy church get a free ride on the backs of the workers. *Their* rhetoric."

"The rhetoric of all our enemies," Rinsonelli gloomed. "Little do they know."

"Let's face it, Paolo, it's an argument they can sell."

"Our wealth!" Rinsonelli snorted. "In real property we are as Croesus; in cash-flow we approach beggary." . . .

Rinsonelli was fuming: "I wonder what those tongue clacking critics of our wealth would have had us do? Would they have had Michelangelo and Leonardo use their gifts only for emperors and princes? Would they have had Bernini render unto Caesar that which is God's?"

"That's hardly the point, Paolo—"

But Rinsonelli wasn't listening. He pressed on, tugging at the dewlap beneath his chin with brown spatulate fingers. "Where would they have placed the *Pieta,* these critics? In the parliament which now has an atheist majority? Should Michelangelo have painted the *Creation* on the ceiling of an army barracks?"

"I agree, I agree," Michael said. "But will you not in turn agree that that same conspicuous wealth in a world in which millions have hunger as their daily companion is to many a reproach? I almost said a scandal."

Rinsonelli shrugged and turned up his palms. "The trouble with you, Michael, is that you're an American. Not enough centuries flow in your veins. The poor you have with you always; are they advantaged if the church also is in rags?"

They walked on in silence for a moment. "I keep remembering that summer in Ethiopia," Michael said softly. "Thousands of people literally starving to death; old and young, mothers with babies like bundles of sticks at their dry breasts, children without the energy to cry." His voice thickened in the memory. "I saw a skeleton draw his last breath before an altar plated with gold."

Rinsonelli stepped in front of him, tilted his massive head and peered at him over his half-spectacles. "But suppose," he said pianissimo, "suppose, as some would have it, that that altar had been taken to the smelters and sold to buy bread. There would only be more poor tomorrow, and in the meantime something of infinite value lost. That supplicant of yours came to die at the altar because it was the one place he encountered God. Swords into plowshares, perhaps, but altars into bread . . . ? Your man would have been fed but empty." . . .

Michael had not seen the doctor when he entered; he had been seated in the shadow beside the door. Now he approached and stood with Michael by the bed: a swarthy man of fifty with a hound's face, stooped and cadaverous but with an inappropriate paunch. "I'm Dr. Sabatinni," he said in a whisper. "You're Cardinal Maloney?"

Michael had to clear his throat. "Yes."

"I'm glad you're here. The Holy Father was asking for you again this morning, but I don't know . . ." He sounded dispirited. "He hasn't moved now for three hours."

Michael looked down at the waxen face, blotched with liver spots. "Perhaps it would be better if I didn't stay," he said.

He had seen death often, but a primeval fear was on him, a dread that the man on the bed would convulse and die before his eyes, that he would be there when the wrench from earth to heaven happened. He thrust the thought away with a flash of anger at himself, but it remained.

"No," Dr. Sabatinni said, "he wants to see you. I told him it was unwise, that he must save his strength, but he looked at me in that way he has . . ." Sabatinni spread his hands in a gesture of impotence. "Who am I to instruct the Holy Father?"

"Is he sleeping?" Michael asked.

"Sleeping . . . ? In a coma . . . ? Who can tell much of the time?"

"Will he recover?"

Again the noncommittal shrug. "The first forty-eight hours we were sure he would never come back to us. Some of us stayed with him right through, expecting the end. But now he seems stable."

"I'll stay awhile and pray," Michael said.

As he put a hand on the bed to lower himself to his knees, the frail figure stirred. As they watched, it seemed he summoned his spirit from far off and brought it to the room. There was a quiver, a sudden shuddering intake of breath, a slight flushing of the skin and the eyes opened slowly. It was a moment before they were drawn into focus. They rested first on the doctor and then moved to Michael's face. The voice when it came was not much more than a breathy whisper. "Michael . . ."

Michael forbade the tears that blurred his eyes. "Holy Father," he said.

This was the man, this fragile figure in the great bed, who had loved him, had seen the possibilities in him, had encouraged him. This was the man who, when he was himself a cardinal, had singled him out and set his feet on the ecclesiastical ladder, who had intervened with Paul VI to have him made a prince of the church and who had helped him with his vestments before the Consistory in which he had received his cardinal's biretta. This was the man who, when he became pope, had taken him into his counsel, with whom he used to meet privately and correspond and speak to at length on the transatlantic telephone, explaining the attitudes of presidents, the vagaries of Congress, the mood of the American people. This was the man who had set his faith in the papacy to soaring after the difficult years of Paul VI. Antonio Giulio d'Annunzio, son of a Genoese pharmacist, trained as a lawyer, member of the Society of Jesus, specialist in foreign affairs, papal nuncio to France, named a cardinal by John XXIII and elected Pope Gregory XVII on the first ballot. And this man was his friend.

The fingers of a hand fluttered like a broken butterfly. "Come closer," the voice whispered. Michael knelt by the bed. Gregory's eyes turned toward Sabatinni. "Leave us alone," he said.

Dr. Sabatinni hesitated. "Your Holiness . . ."

"Enrico," the pope said. "I shall leave this world when *I* decide to."

The doctor went off quietly, drawing the door closed behind him. The slightest smile touched Gregory's lips. "Doctors," he said. "They understand the body; they know little of the spirit."

Though some of his words were blurred, he seemed to be gaining strength and Michael's hopes began to rise only to plummet with the next words: "Michael, come closer. This may be the last time we'll speak . . ." Michael began to remonstrate but Gregory shook his head slowly. "We must all die," he said. "My time is not far off. Don't fret, it doesn't trouble me." The breath suddenly caught in his throat and he was racked by coughing. It was a minute before he could continue.

Michael asked, "Are you all right?"

It was as though Gregory hadn't heard. He ran the tip of a dry tongue over his lips and swallowed hard. "Michael," he said, "Our Lord may call you to succeed me . . ."

"Holy Father . . . please."

"No, no. Hear me out." Again he paused to gather his resources. "It will be you or Benedetti or Della Chiesa, and I want a last word with you. There are difficult times. They'll be worse. You must be strong." There was a pause, a frown, and a wandering of the eyes as though the thought was a bird that would not alight. "Yes. . . . Be strong, but be wise. Try to avoid confrontation. . . . God can use you with your countrymen. Perhaps he has raised you up for such a time as this." His breathing grew shallow and pain drew the corners of his mouth into a grimace. "No time . . ." he said, "No time."

Now the tears would not be forbidden. They inundated Michael's eyes and fell unnoticed to the floor. He lowered his head. "Bless me, Holy Father," he said.

Gregory began to raise a hand but it faltered and fell back. He opened his mouth; the lips worked, trying to form words, but the only sound was a dry exhalation. The concentration that earlier had enabled him to summon his strength ran out as sand in an hourglass and he slipped again into a coma. Michael remained on his knees, his mind numb. He thought he should pray but couldn't; he was empty. There were no words in him. He struggled erect but didn't look again at the motionless figure on the bed.

When he opened the door, Dr. Sabatinni looked past him. "Good morning, Eminence," he said, and went into the room. Michael closed the door.

At Rinsonelli's quarters there was a note. Michael tore open the envelope. In a script as precise as hieroglyphic were the words:

Madame Ovary has lost her Bee—or does the memory-bank of a cardinal retain such trivia? Spotted you at the airport but you were gone when I got through customs. I'm at the Hotel Lombardia. Can we have dinner? It was signed, *Harris Gordon.*

Harris!—the name exploded in his head and each fragment was a memory. Harris! The irrepressible, the zany! Best friend of his undergraduate years at Princeton, roommate in his senior year, fellow member of the track team, fellow graduate *magna cum laude,* he in philosophy and Harris in archaeology. After the ceremony in the chapel there had been pledges, soon forgotten, to keep in touch. Later, as Michael had gleaned from newspapers and periodicals, there was celebrity: Harris Gordon, discoverer of the lost city of Horan, Dr. Gordon with the Leakeys at Olduvai Gorge, Dr. Gordon with Yigdal Allon in Israel. . . . A half dozen times Michael had made a mental note to be in touch and each time had procrastinated. And now here was Harris in Rome.

He rang the hotel and gave the operator his name. There was nothing familiar about the voice that came on except the note of banter.

"Mike Maloney, I presume," the voice said, "or do I call you father, Father?"

"Harris! How marvelous to hear from you."

"So you *do* remember Madame Ovary."

The film, *Madame Bovary,* had played the Princeton Playhouse and the ribald comments of the undergraduates at each line of dialogue had kept the theater in an uproar. Afterward, Michael had boosted Harris onto his shoulders and he had removed the letter *B* from the title. For the remainder of the run the marquee read, MADAME OVARY. They had mounted the battered metal trophy in a place of honor on the wall of their rooms in the dorm beside a STOP sign in French and English smuggled from Canada.

"I remember *all* the crazy things we did," Michael said.

"Even that blind date at Mingles?"

A slow smile moved on Michael's face. "I refuse to answer on the usual grounds," he said.

"You're one hell of a correspondent," Harris grouched. "You were going to send me your address. We were going to get together at least once a year."

"I presumed you were too busy digging up somebody's mummy."

"Or you, kissing somebody's ring."

"Believe it or not, I've followed most of your adventures through the newspapers, even the honorary doctorate at Oxford. Then you dropped out of sight."

"Been in Israel the past four years," Harris said. "On digs with Freeling and Allon. Spent about six months at Hazor Tell. I was getting ready to head home at the end of my sabbatical when I got . . ." a slight tension entered his voice even as it continued lighthearted, ". . . how shall I put it?—waylaid by history."

Michael wasn't sure how to respond so he said, "Uh, huh."

"I was planning to come see you about it back home, and here you are. What are the chances of our getting together?"

Michael was apologetic. "I'd love to," he said, "but it's impossible. But why not in New York? I stop off in London on the way back but—"

"Could we have dinner in London?" Harris asked. "I'll be there from tomorrow."

"Perfect."

They refined the arrangements and chatted on tangentially for another five minutes, each relishing the resurrection of the past, both discovering that nothing of their old camaraderie had altered.

"Question," Harris said.

"Ask away."

"I thought your old man was a Presbyterian."

"He was."

"A preacher."

"Right."

"So how come you're a mick? Nobody was about to nominate you altar boy of the year when I knew you."

Michael laughed. Harris's irreverence pleased him. He was so accustomed to sycophancy and formality that his old friend's impudence gave delight. "Happened during the war," he said lightly.

"I even hear talk you may make pope. Mike Maloney, pope! Boggles the mind."

"I wouldn't hold my breath."

"No, I'm impressed. I really am. In my line of work you don't get to meet many of the Almighty's Mafia. When I finally buy it, can I use you as a reference?"

There was more of the same, and when Michael put down the phone he was warmed, smiling. It was a few minutes before the memory flooded back of that frail pale figure on the great bed upstairs . . .

Dr. Harris G. Gordon, Chairman of the Department of Oriental Studies (Emeritus) in the Faculty of Archaeology at Albright University, Philadelphia, Pennsylvania, was taking inventory. Shouldn't take but a few seconds, he thought with a wry grin. There on the glass stains on a grubby hotel room table were most of his worldly possessions: in cash, $442.78, two American Express travelers' checks for $100 each, and a one-way plane ticket Rome-JFK. In the closet, two suits, a pair of slacks and two sweaters. On the luggage rack, two scruffy suitcases stuffed with a mix of mismatched and threadbare haberdashery and assorted toilet articles. Aboard a ship en route to New York City, a steamer trunk filled with those oddments commonly described as "personal effects." As well, in the care of Manhattan Storage, perhaps two dozen cartons of books and papers, concerning which a professional bill-collecting agency had been hurling intemperate *Last Warning!* thunderbolts at him for months now. There were also—if one might list them in an inventory—three wives: one lost somehow, one divorced and one deserted. And seven children by wives Two and Three, although the children, he thought, had always been more of an expense than an asset. Granted a few inadvertent omissions, that was about everything he owned in the world . . .

It was not that Harris Gordon was feeling sorry for himself. He had never been an accumulator of things and never thought of himself as rich or poor—they were categories into which it would never occur to him to place himself. What was important at the moment was the fact that his scarcity of tangible assets was damned inconvenient. The airline had charged him $46.75 to insure and ship home his precious box, and that, as the saying has it, had made a small dent in his bankroll. The box would by this time be safely ensconced in the atmosphere-controlled storage room at the museum in New York and probably better housed than he would be. Which, he decided, was not inappropriate.

The immediate problem was: where was he to live when he'd finished his research and was back stateside? He grimaced; last thing in the world he'd do would be to go crawling to the university. "Bastards," he said aloud. How did the letter go? *I regret exceedingly, my dear Harris, having to inform you that it has become necessary to terminate your employment here at Albright. Your sabbatical has already been extended twice, and the Board of Trustees etc. etc. etc. . . . Permit me to say, Harris, that your obduracy in refusing to disclose the nature of your discovery or the location of the dig has left us with no option but to etc. etc. etc. You upbraid us, it seems to me, unfairly.*

So be it, but they would dance to another tune shortly. By God, wouldn't they though!

His thoughts returned to the telephone call. It had been good to talk to Mike. He'd sounded a bit stuffy, but only a bit, and that was to be expected. Perhaps he was the man to talk to about his find. He'd had the secret bottled up within him so long that it was becoming unhealthy. What he needed more than anything else at the moment, more even than money, was someone he could take into his confidence and from whom he could get counsel. Mike would, of course, be shocked when he broke his news—it would be fascinating to watch his reaction—but he was a sophisticated and worldly man and would soon adjust. And who better to tell? *Cardinal* Maloney, no less! He grinned: after all, if you can't trust a priest, who can you trust?